THE WAYWARD ONE

DANELLE HARMON

Published by Oliver-Heber Books & Gnarly Wool Publishing

0 9 8 7 6 5 4 3 2 1

Connected Series

The DeMontforte Series

"The bluest of blood; the boldest of hearts;

the de Montforte brothers will take your breath away."

The Wild One

The Beloved One

The Defiant One

The Wicked One

The Wayward One

The Admiral's Heart

The Fox & the Angel

My First Noel

The Heroes of the Sea

Love the characters in the DeMontforte Series? Continue on with the Heroes of the Sea to revisit shared characters.

Master of My Dreams

Captain of My Heart

My Lady Pirate

Taken by Storm

Wicked at Heart

Lord of the Sea

Heir to the Sea

Never Too Late for Love

Scandal at Christmas

My Saving Grace

Prologue

AUGUST, 1779—SOMEWHERE OFF THE COAST OF NEW HAMPSHIRE

"Make some eight sail off to the westward, sir, bearing east nor'east."

Lieutenant John Morgan of the American Continental Navy brig *Tigershark* tried to contain his nerves as his captain, hastily summoned from his cabin, joined him at the larboard rail.

"Well, now. 'Tisn't exactly a fine sight this evenin', is it, Mr. Morgan?"

"No, sir." He offered the telescope to his commander. "They're British."

It was summer, but this far out to sea and this late in the day, the wind had a bite to it. Tucking the glass between elbow and hip, the captain pushed the last two buttons of his fine white waistcoat through their embroidered gold slits. The methodical nature of the action was deliberate, Morgan knew. Meant to show he was not overly concerned about what could be a very real and dangerous threat, meant to instill confidence in a fifty-man crew that had yet to know if this commander, so new to them all, was deserving of their trust, their obedience, their as-yet untested faith in him.

Morgan caught the questioning glance of the sailing master. He looked away and clasped his hands behind his back.

Waiting.

Beside him, the captain finally raised the glass to his eye. Long ocean swells broke in hissing spray against the brig's quarter, becoming airborne and spattering his fine white waistcoat. He was an enigma, this man. Unruly black hair pulled back from a hard, angular face and queued beneath his tricorne. A mouth that seldom smiled. His eyes, long-lashed, deceptively roguish and concealing a temper that Morgan had found to be razor-sharp, squinted against the setting sun.

"Probably Admiral Collier's squadron, headin' to Penobscot," the captain observed, the heavy glass steady in his hand. "Bastards."

"The American fleet is in Penobscot. They'll be sitting ducks up there if we don't warn them."

"Warnin' them is neither our mission nor part of our orders, Mr. Morgan."

"Aye, sir."

Young Midshipman Andrew Cranton stood nearby, nervously biting his lip. Morgan knew what he was thinking, what they were all thinking: A new ship, a crew who'd only had a week to get to know each other, a mission that none of them knew much about and understood even less, and a captain whose leadership was unproven, whose loathing for the British and reputation as Boston's hero back in '75 were the only real things any of them had to hang their hats on. And now this. A line of enemy ships between themselves and the safety of the distant coastline, any number of which could, should they be inclined, take advantage of the weather gauge and swoop down on them like a sledgehammer on a trunnel.

All eyes on deck, in the rigging, and high in the tops were on the captain.

"The wind, Mr. Tackett?"

"Veering a bit, sir," said the sailing master.

"Our heading?"

"Unchanged, sir."

The captain was still studying the distant squadron, its sails orange in the fading evening light as it continued on a northeasterly course parallel to their own. No one said a word, and only the sea dared to speak as it pushed against the brig's quarter as though trying to hurry her along.

And now, movement. Signal flags rising and breaking to the wind aboard the admiral's flagship. A frigate bringing up the squadron's rear sending up a signal flag of her own. Moments later, she was turning her prow toward them.

"They've seen us, Captain."

A rumble of nervous excitement pulsed through the men assembling at the rail.

The captain, still peering intently through the glass, motioned for the young midshipman with an impatient wag of his forefinger. "Light the stern lantern, Mr. Cranton. I want those shite-stains to continue to see us."

"Uh ... yes, sir." The youngster, only fifteen years old, hurried off to do his bidding, wondering, as did they all, if the captain had a death wish. *Wanted* the enemy to see them?

"Fancy a brawl, Mr. Morgan?"

"A brawl maybe, sir. But not annihilation."

"Of like mind, we are." He lowered the glass and shut it with a decisive snap. "However, we've somewhere to be. No time for brawlin'."

"Might have to make time, sir. They'll be on us by nightfall."

"Not if I have anythin' to say about it." He handed the glass back to Monroe, wiped salt spray from a cheek that was dark with stubble and leaned against a nearby gun, crossing his arms as he studied the frigate with the naked eye. There was a gleam in that eye, a hard smile around the mouth, a certain hunger for both trouble and action—like that of a tavern brawler spoiling for a fight. O' Devir was Irish, and tall and imposing in both physique and temper. Personable, when he wasn't staring moodily off over the sea, his eyes veiling some private and indescribable pain that nobody actually gave voice to but everyone whispered about.

They say he never used to be like this ... that something changed him.

That he's done bad things.

Terrible things....

So the man had his demons, Morgan figured, as every man did—but right now his confidence was reassuring because the wind was in the frigate's favor and that frigate was a hell of a lot bigger, faster, and stronger than they were—and manned by sailors from the most powerful Navy in the world.

"She's setting her royals, sir. Might get that brawl after all."

"She'll have to catch us, first. 'Tis blowin' too hard to fly the stuns'ls, but we've got a fast keel under us and a good crew. Get the t'gallants on her and let her fall off a few points until we've got the wind right up our arse. That English scrote out there may catch us yet, but we'll lead her a merry chase all the same."

"Aye, sir." Morgan turned to bellow orders through his speaking trumpet. Men ran to the braces and scrambled up the shrouds. At the tiller, Tackett put the helm up until *Tigershark* turned nimbly on her heel and the wind, dead astern now, swelled her sails. Beneath them, the motion of the sea quieted as the brig ran before both wind and wave, and the sound of the water became a rolling, desperate hush.

Above, topmen moved out along the yards. Moments later, great clouds of canvas spilled down with a noise like thunder and were sheeted home; beneath their feet, the brig seemed to dig into the cold Atlantic as she found more speed.

But not enough.

"Frigate's gaining, sir," Morgan said ominously.

Far off behind her and to the west, the great squadron from which the enemy ship had detached herself was hull down on the horizon and a few lights, winking like fireflies in the distance, appeared as lanterns were hung in the rigging of the individual ships against the incoming night.

Astern, the British frigate was steadily growing larger.

Large enough to see the bone in her teeth, curling back from her stem, seemingly growing larger by the moment.

The first metallic taste of fear burned on Morgan's tongue. His stomach, never dependable, always nervous, gave an uncertain quiver and he quietly reached into his pocket for a piece of the dried ginger that he always kept on his person. He welcomed its sharp bite, chewing it clandestinely and not wanting to call attention to himself. O' Devir hadn't moved. O' Devir, a fellow he hardly knew, a man who had a coiled, savage edge about him that even the smart new uniform could neither soften nor disguise. Morgan swallowed, feeling the ginger slide down his throat and relief coming with it. You could put a ribbon around the neck of a wounded wolf but it was still a wounded wolf no matter how pretty the ribbon happened to be.

He looked again at the oncoming frigate, her lights growing brighter as darkness descended.

And it was never wise to corner a wounded wolf.

A fast ship. A good crew. The Continental Navy's main champion, John Adams, had selected *this* captain and *this* ship—newly launched, still smelling of varnish and tar—for this mission, one that called for raw courage and utmost secrecy, one which might well be the most dangerous—and important—one of the war. A mission that meant they had to get to England at all costs, where the risks would become even greater, the dangers even more pronounced, once they found themselves under the noses of the Admiralty and the reach of the mighty Duke of Blackheath. They could not afford to be delayed. They could not afford to engage a British frigate, and they certainly could not afford to be captured or sunk by her or anyone else. There was no time to lose.

Adams was depending on them.

The sun had sunk below the horizon. The ocean had gone from blue to indigo and now, as the light faded by the moment, was turning to pewter. The air grew colder and the captain plucked his blue undress coat from the quarterdeck railing where, during the earlier heat of the day, he'd tossed it. He shrugged into it, pulling his shirt cuffs down so they wouldn't bunch beneath the sleeves of his coat, his actions, like they'd been earlier, deliberately methodical.

The frigate was closing in, two miles off now.

Boom! Smoke and flame coughed from one of her bow chasers a second before the report of the big gun rolled toward them from across the water. The enemy ship was still out of range, but the demand to heave to was there all the same.

At the stern, the approaching night made the lantern seem to glow brighter and brighter.

"Think they'll chase us once it's fully dark?" Morgan asked, wishing he felt as calm inside as the captain appeared to be.

"As long as it's only our stern lantern they're chasin', I hope so."

Another *boom!* came from the frigate, and this time the ball splashed a half-mile off their quarter.

Morgan glanced at his commander. There was a

crafty fierceness in that hard face, an eager, savage glee, and suddenly Morgan understood.

"You're planning on using the stern lantern as a decoy, aren't you?"

The captain's smile was tight. "Let's hope our pursuer out there doesn't figure out what we're up to as fast as you have, Mr. Morgan." He motioned to the returning midshipman. "Mr. Cranton, look lively."

"Sir?"

"Take the smaller of our two boats and prepare to lower it from the sta'b'd side. Attach a towline to its bow. A fierce long towline. In a few moments we'll be changing course and taking the wind across the larboard beam once more, and 'tis quick ye must be if we're to make our escape."

"Yes, Captain."

Boom!

"He's getting impatient to have that brawl, sir."

The captain took off his hat to rub at his forehead, a few tendrils of his wildly curling black hair escaping his queue to snake around his face in the falling darkness. "He'll be firin' on 'is own imagination, if all goes as I intend it will."

The western sky was just a dimming glow now, fading by the moment. The lights of the squadron were well beneath the horizon and they were all alone out here now, just the pursuing frigate and themselves. To the east, the night had turned black.

Cranton returned. "Boat's all ready, sir."

"Good. Ready a second lantern, but keep it below the gunwale so those butt-buggers out there won't see it. We'll be making a switch, shortly." He strode to the tiller. "Bring her up three points, Mr. Tackett, and steer north, if ye please."

"Aye, sir."

Hesitantly, the American brig turned back towards the wind and once again the seas started to buffet her quarter ... her beam. She began to roll with motion now that they had lost the following seas, and astern their relentless pursuer also changed course, running now a mile away and beam-on to them, her lights cutting through the gathering gloom.

The captain's teeth flashed white in the darkness. "Got that lantern ready, Mr. Cranton?"

"Aye, sir."

"Put it in the boat and secure it well. If it goes out, we're done for. When I give the word, lower the boat over the sta'b'd side so that ball of shite back there won't see it, and prepare to extinguish our stern lantern at the exact same time. Do ye understand?"

"Aye, sir. I understand."

It was a trick, but it would have to work. A bright tongue of orange flame and another angry, demanding *boom* came from the frigate, crashing across the water like a bolt of thunder. This time it wasn't one of her small bow chasers, but one of her big guns.

Morgan watched as the captain crossed to the starboard side and oversaw the men beginning to lower the ship's smallest boat. If he was at all anxious, he didn't show it. As the boat descended, young and agile Midshipman Andy Cranton shimmied down one of the lines, lit the lantern someone passed down to him, secured it to a thwart and then scampered back up the rope as eager hands worked in the darkness to get the boat lowered before the next salvo from the frigate could find them and do what could be crippling damage.

Immediately, the boat hit the water and began to fall back, and as it emerged from behind the brig's protective, concealing hull, the captain hurriedly motioned for their own stern light to be doused.

It was a clever ruse. With any luck, the pursuing frigate would mistake the small boat for its real target in the darkness and pursue it instead, allowing them to slip away into the night.

The towline paid out, farther and farther still, until the lantern that marked the little boat was only a pinpoint of light in the darkness well astern of them.

Boom! And again: *Boom!* No iron screamed overhead, and Morgan quietly put his fingers behind his back and crossed them, hoping that the frigate was aiming at that tiny, bobbing point of light falling farther and farther astern, hoping that it would hit it and extinguish it long after they had gotten neatly away.

The captain was speaking again. "Loose the towline and let 'er go. Put the helm up once more, Mr. Tackett, and let's get the divil out of here."

Far behind them now, there was another *boom* and the light that marked the decoy boat went out. In moments, the frigate would come up on nothing but the smashed remains of the little boat, and her English captain would realize he'd been cleverly tricked.

Tigershark fell back off and once again settled as the wind, strengthening a bit, filled her sails and sped her into the inky blackness to the east.

Her captain put his hands on the rail and raised his face toward the open Atlantic, the salt wind damp in his unruly dark hair and his spirit as alive as it ever could be these days. Kind of like old times, he thought. The lights of the frigate were growing smaller and smaller, and he smiled as the wind whistled past him, the ship moving up and down, up and down, through the long Atlantic swells beneath a canopy of stars spread like a blanket in the skies overhead.

Ahead of him lay three thousand miles of open ocean.

Beyond that, England.

Where Lord Andrew de Montforte—a man whom the Continental Navy wanted at all costs, a man whom the captain of *Tigershark* would spare nothing and no one to obtain—was blissfully unaware that they were coming for him.

England.

Where the most important mission of the war awaited them.

Chapter One

LONDON, FOUR WEEKS LATER

"You really didn't have to accompany me, Nerissa, but I'm terribly glad that you did."

They were in the ballroom of an elegant London townhouse which had been filled with chairs for the guests who were arriving by the boatload through the big doors at the back of the room. Lady Nerissa de Montforte, resplendent in pearls and aquamarine silk, the light from the chandelier above gleaming on her pale ivory hair, took a seat beside her brother Lord Andrew. She touched his hand, noting his nervousness and trying to put him at ease. He did not like getting up and speaking in front of the public and surely, was wishing that his dear wife Celsie was here with him instead of his younger sister. But Celsie was once again in the family way and when the Royal Navy had issued this invitation to Andrew, Nerissa could not bear to let him face the top brass of Admiralty all alone.

"Well, it's not like I have any great parties or other events to attend," she said wryly. "The Season hasn't yet started and life is pretty boring up in the country, especially with Lucien and Eva wrapped up in each other and nothing with which to amuse myself."

The truth, though, was significantly more concerning. Yes, her brother Lucien, the Duke of Blackheath, was wrapped up with his beautiful duchess, but not so wrapped up that he wasn't starting to cast about for a husband for the one unmarried sibling who had yet to find marital bliss.

Herself.

Best to get away from him so her presence wasn't a constant reminder of the fact that she was unmarried—and fair game for Lucien to manipulate into an unwanted union.

But by the look of his pale face, Andrew wasn't thinking about Lucien and his devious matchmaking, though he himself had also "benefited" from it. Instead, he was looking more and more nervous as several naval officers, resplendent in blue and white and gold, came in, many glancing at him with curious speculation before taking seats nearby. The low buzz of conversation was getting louder as the room began to fill. Laughter ... snippets of conversation ... chairs creaking ... someone coughing.

She forgot about Lucien, for the moment.

"Are you quite well, Andrew?" she asked, eyeing him with concern.

"I just want to say my piece, give my demonstration, and get the devil out of here."

"Oh, do stop. This is your moment! You've worked hard to gain recognition and respect as a scientist and an inventor. This new explosive of yours might well be your legacy. It could change the outcome of this war. Of *course* the Royal Navy is going to be interested in it, and you should care enough to want to go up there, talk about your invention, and be proud of it."

"What if I have an attack?"

"You won't. You haven't had one in ages."

"What if something goes wrong?"

"Don't think that way. Everything is going to be fine."

Beside her Andrew tightened his lips, impatient as

ever. This explosive, which was supposed to have more thrust and energy than mere gunpowder, had been the only reason their host, Captain Christian Lord, had been able to get his warship safely away from a French fort and warships in time to save not only their brothers Charles, Gareth and Lucien and his duchess Eva, but also Nerissa's betrothed, Perry, Lord Brookhampton.

Though in the months that had ensued since that rescue, Nerissa wondered bitterly if Perry had, indeed, been saved.

A shadow darkened her pale blue eyes and she looked down, fingering the elegant painted fan that lay in her lap.

"I'm sorry, Nerissa," Andrew said. "I know you're only trying to help."

She nodded, suddenly unable to speak. Let him think that. Let him think that her sadness was because she was impatient with his inability to embrace his own genius, the brilliant mind with which God had blessed him. Let him think that and maybe if she tried hard enough, she could think it too.

It hurt far less than thinking about Perry.

But Andrew was more perceptive than she gave him credit for being.

"You need to put him behind you," he said gently, so that people filing loudly into the chairs behind them would not hear. "It's time to move on, Nerissa."

She stared down at the fan, trying to anchor herself against the emotion that the very mention of Perry's name evoked. "I can't."

"You have to. It's over, Nerissa."

"It's not over as long as I still love him."

Andrew's face softened, and he reached out to cover her hand with his own. "He does not love you. Not anymore." His eyes darkened with sympathy. "And I'm not convinced, dear sister, that he ever really did."

Nerissa looked away, blinking back the sudden tears. This was Andrew's night, and she would not spoil it for him with her own troubles. "Well, at least we all know his true colors now. Or maybe I knew them all along and just didn't want to see it."

"Well, you see them now. We all do. And Nerissa, there *are* other men out there." He smiled. "Plenty of them here tonight, in fact. I must say, though nobody will ever be good enough for my little sister, it pains me to see you so unhappy."

She forced a smile and looked directly into his worried eyes. "I am not unhappy. See?"

He shook his head, sighed, and nodded in acknowledgement as another group of naval officers filed in. One of them came over, his hand extended in greeting.

"Good evening, Lord Andrew."

Her brother rose, exchanging pleasantries with their host; it was Captain Lord, fair-haired and handsome, his gray eyes crinkling in a smile and his beautiful wife, Deirdre, on his arm. Nerissa had taken an instant liking to them both when she and Andrew had arrived earlier this evening: the taciturn Royal Navy officer who had saved her brothers' lives and his Irish wife, who wore her dark, curly hair unpowdered and whose genuine warmth and country charm had helped to put the increasingly nervous Andrew at ease. Captain Lord seated her beside Nerissa, leaned down to kiss her cheek and then moved on toward the stage at the front of the room where an easel had been set up along with a podium; there, he was joined by his older brother, Rear Admiral Sir Elliott Lord.

"I suppose this infernal affair is about to commence," Andrew muttered darkly.

"You'll be fine."

"And if the explosive doesn't work?"

"It will."

"I wish I could get out of here, and fast. I'm having second thoughts about this whole thing as it is."

"Relax. Just get up there, talk about how you created the explosive, give your demonstration outside when it's all done and after a bit of mingling we go back to our own townhouse. Tomorrow you can head home to Celsie and baby Laura, and all this will be behind you. It's as simple as that."

"You make it sound easy, Nerissa."

"It *is* easy. And I'm here to help you in case you feel ill or indisposed."

Andrew watched glumly as Captain Lord called for silence. Nerissa noticed that her brother's hands had tightened around the arms of his chair, the knuckles whitening. He looked ready to bolt. "Ladies and gentlemen," the captain said in a voice that Nerissa imagined had been honed on a quarterdeck and which had no trouble carrying the length of the room. "Tonight is a very special evening in that we have an esteemed guest as our monthly speaker. It was his timely intervention and genius application of a new explosive that saved his family, not to mention my own ship and crew, from certain disaster off the coast of France earlier this year. It is my highest honor and deepest pleasure to welcome and introduce to you, the scientist and inventor, Lord Andrew De Montforte...."

Applause swelled the room.

Andrew hesitated, paling.

"Go on," Nerissa whispered.

He pushed his chair back, tall and resplendent in olive velvet that set off his auburn hair, and joined Captain Lord and his brother, Sir Elliott, at the podium. Only Nerissa could see the signs of his discomfort—the stiffness in his stance, a smile that was too quick to come and go as he formally greeted his host and the admiral. Only his breeding and upbringing enabled him to maintain an air of casual authority and confidence as he thanked his hosts and assembled guests, and began to describe how he had created the explosive that had, as Nerissa understood it, far more "blowing-up power" than ordinary gunpowder could ever have.

But Andrew, for all his genius, was not at ease in front of a group, and he soon retreated into the arena where he was most comfortable: talk of formulas, alchemy and mathematics, and Nerissa, who did not consider herself to be much of a genius at all, found her mind drifting to other things as she nevertheless kept a protective eye on her brother in case he needed her support.

Perry. She wondered what he was doing right now. If he was back in the country, or here in London. If he ever thought of her, as she did him. If he missed her, as she did him. If he had ever loved her....

As she had him.

He could never be hers and probably, in the truest sense of the word, never had been. But there were no others for her. Even in this room full of smartly dressed officers and the highest ranking men in the Navy there was nobody to catch her eye and she realized, with a bitter, sinking truth, that she was probably going to die an old maid.

"...So therefore, I took the best properties of sulfur and saltpeter, added a chemical that would boost the accelerant, and began testing the mixture on the grounds of Rosebriar Park, my residence...."

Yes, Andrew was doing just fine, as she knew he would be.

But Nerissa was not.

She cast a surreptitious glance over at Mrs. Lord, who was listening with fascination to her brother's words. How lucky the woman was to have found someone with whom she could share her life, who worshipped the ground she walked on, who had given her a strong and handsome child with more, surely, to come.

Wasn't it what every woman wanted? Someone who loved them without end?

"…. The first attempts were unstable and to be frank, quite dangerous. But then, that is the natural course for any experiment of this nature…."

The minutes crept by, and Andrew made some notations on the easel behind him, turned it so that the audience could see, and began to take questions. Nerissa realized she'd had little idea what he'd even said, but that didn't matter—he had not had an attack, he looked confident and secure, and he was well on his way to selling his innovative explosive to a very interested and eager Royal Navy.

Suddenly, applause shook Nerissa from her reverie, and she realized Captain Lord was back at the podium and Andrew had stepped aside.

"And now, let us all file outside into the garden for a demonstration of this new explosive," announced Captain Lord and around them, chairs began to scrape, the buzz of conversation grew loud, and a sea of starched and powdered naval officers moved eagerly towards the back door of the room.

"Well, tha' 'twas most interesting!" said Deirdre Lord, rising from her chair as her husband rejoined them. "I can't wait t' see it in action!"

"London will never know what hit it," Nerissa returned, smiling as she watched Andrew, happy and finally at ease, delaying his own departure as he took questions from two admirals who had trapped him back on the stage.

"'Tis what I'm afraid of. We have neighbors who retire early … I hope this doesn't startle them out of a sound sleep! I'd better go get my little Colin so the sound of the explosion doesn't frighten him."

She hurried off. Captain Lord gallantly offered Nerissa his arm. They all moved toward the door and suddenly Nerissa's gaze, as though drawn by an invisible magnet, went to a man who was leaning negligently, arms crossed, against a spinet near the exit. Tall and lean, he was a good inch or so over six feet and while the simple lace at his throat was clean and presentable, his bottle-green velvet coat was a bit worn at the elbows and straining at the seams to contain his broad, powerful shoulders. Glossy black hair, thick and heavy with curl, was drawn back from a face of hard angles and planes and caught in an unruly queue at his nape; he had a bold nose, black and arching brows, a gleam in his eye and a mouth that was both ruthless and smiling. Not classically handsome, but there was something intensely attractive about him, something that demanded one's attention and kept the eyes on him. She stood frozen, unable to move, unable to look away.

He was the most virile man Nerissa had ever seen. And he was staring insolently, brazenly, straight at her.

She felt Captain Lord's arm stiffen beneath her fingers.

"I thought you were going out for the evening," the captain said tightly.

The man lifted a brow. "New explosive, eh?" His voice was deep and melodic. Irish. And, judging by the fumes issuing from him, he was quite soused. "'Twill make Guy Fawkes Day all the more interestin', I wager. Boom!" He hiccupped and laughed and looked pointedly at Nerissa through absurdly long, jet-black lashes, until she felt roses blooming on her cheeks and her heart did a funny little skip somewhere beneath her breastbone. "And who's this lovely lass on yer arm, eh, Christian?"

"This is a private *military* gathering. You need to leave. *Now.*"

"I'd really rather not. Besides, as yer houseguest and brother-in-law 'tis rude to deny me curiosity, it is." He was not looking at Captain Lord, but at Nerissa in a way that made her want to blush—or slap him soundly on the cheek for daring to stare so at her, a lady. And staring, he was. He cocked his head, one corner of his mouth lifted in a smile as he studied her face, the pale column of her neck, the gentle swell of her bosom before Deirdre, just returning with a tow-headed toddler in her arms, intervened.

"Roddy, ye heard Christian—ye can't be here. This is a—"

"I don't go by 'Roddy' anymore, *mo deirfiúr daor*. 'Tis a boy's name and I've left boyhood far behind me, I have. My real name, please. Ruaidri."

"Whatever ye're calling y'rself these days, ye've got to leave. Now."

"Come now, Sis." He pushed back from the spinet, swayed drunkenly, and grabbed desperately at the door to hold himself upright. "What harm am I to whatever big secret was unveiled here tonight? I'm just a lonely landlubber now." *Hic.* "I've got the old cottage back home. I raise sheep and eke out a meager livin' from a cheap and stingy land owned by a cheap and stingy English landlord, I do. I've no mind t' leave. Not yet. Besides—" he was still looking down at Nerissa and swaying a bit, his eyes twinkling roguishly as he noted her discomfort and saw that he was the reason for it. "I'm still waitin' for an introduction."

"It'll be a donkey's age before you get one," Captain Lord bit out through gritted teeth. "You are drunk and embarrassing yourself, Roddy—"

"*Ruaidri.*"

"—and this is your last warning."

The Irishman was still perusing Nerissa, his lips twitching with merriment as he gazed pointedly at her lips. "With that mouth I'm bettin' ye're a good kisser, aren't ye, lass?"

Nerissa gasped and this time Captain Lord, his gray eyes going frosty, relinquished both women into the care of Andrew who, flushed with success over the reception his explosive had received, was just joining them.

"Outside," Captain Lord snapped.

"What, fisticuffs in the garden?" the Irishman asked, raising one brow and flashing an amused grin at Nerissa. "Saints above, Christian, 'tis beneath ye, don't ye think?"

Sir Elliott, who'd lingered at the stage looking at Andrew's notes, was frowning as he joined them. "What is this?"

"My brother was just leaving," Deirdre said hurriedly, seizing the tall stranger's arm. "Aren't you, Ro—I mean, Ruaidri?"

"Actually, I was rather lookin' forward to watchin' things go boom in the night."

"What?" the admiral demanded.

"Fireworks." He cocked his head and again, Nerissa felt the heat of his bold gaze as it moved over her lips, her throat, the swell of her breasts, and a strange and not unpleasant sensation centered itself between her legs and spread upwards into her belly, outwards into her blood. "With the pretty lass here, of course."

Andrew came alive. "Now see here! How dare you speak to my sister like—"

"Enough! All of you!" Deirdre was losing her patience. "Ruaidri, you told us ye were goin' out for the evenin' and 'tis time ye left. Christian and Elliott, ye're drawin' the attention of our guests and I won't let this evenin' be spoiled by such nonsense. Lord Andrew, I have this situation well under control. Go on out to the garden with our guests and we'll join ye shortly." She transferred the sleepy toddler to her other hip. "Lady Nerissa, I apologize for me brother—he's a rogue and at the moment, a drunken fool. Don't take him seriously."

The man straightened up, adding another inch or two to his already commanding height, and letting his gaze rake over Nerissa's bosom in a blatantly carnal way, reeled drunkenly towards the door and yanked it open. He staggered off into the night, his form melting into the darkness.

It was all she could do not to flick open her fan and drive cool air into her suddenly hot face. Dear Lord, he might've been foxed, but there'd been a gleam in his eye, something compelling and sharp that didn't look at all drunk, and the paradox left her unnerved. Thrown off balance.

Confused.

And that hot, raking gaze....

Roo-ah-ree? Roor-rie? Rurr-ee? Nerissa's tongue struggled to make the sound of the strange name.

It wasn't until after he had gone that she realized he never did get his introduction.

Chapter Two

"What an odious man!" Nerissa whispered to Andrew as she slid her gloved fingers into the crook of his elbow and allowed him to escort her out of the room. Her hand was trembling, and she was glad of her brother's anchoring strength because her knees had gone suddenly quite weak. He had rattled her, that brash and ill-bred drunk, and her heart was still banging a bit too hard in her chest for comfort. "For a moment there, I thought Captain Lord was going to challenge him to a duel at dawn."

"If he didn't, I was about to. Maybe I still will."

The evening was warm, with a light breeze blowing through the chestnut trees overhead. A string of lanterns had been set up in the back garden, and gentle light glowed against the faces of the two dozen or so naval officers who had gathered to watch what was sure to be an entertaining, if not exciting spectacle.

"Lord Andrew?" It was Sir Elliott, resplendent in his blue and white gold-laced uniform. "If you're ready, I think we're all eager to see the demonstration."

Andrew frowned as he looked at the people all gathered around in a circle. "They will have to stand back. Much farther back than that."

Sir Elliott nodded. "Gentlemen, if you could retreat

a few more feet, just to be on the safe side, it would be to your benefit."

Andrew watched the group murmuring, exchanging jokes and glances, and laughing as they widened the circle a few more feet. He shook his head, concerned.

"This won't do."

"Just use less of the explosive," Nerissa said. "It will make a smaller impact, will it not?"

Andrew though, being what Nerissa knew was a typical male, was not interested in making a smaller impact. He shook his head. "This garden is not big enough to keep everyone safe. Perhaps we should ask people to remove to the house." He voiced his concerns to Sir Elliott and Captain Lord, but upon making that suggestion to the guests who all stood around waiting to see what promised to be a hole blown into the ground all the way to Australia, only laughter and bravado greeted his remark.

"We're naval officers, and most of us are used to ship-to-ship action at close quarters. I'll be damned if I'm going inside!"

"Aye, you won't catch me hiding behind brick walls!"

Laughter rang out and Andrew's mouth grew mulish with impatience.

Nerissa touched his arm. "Really, Andrew, it can't be *that* potent."

He just slanted her a look that told her it very well was.

"Maybe *you* should go into the house," he said, his concern growing. "It will be loud. It could be dangerous."

"I am not going into the house. You may need me."

"What I *need* is for you to go into the house. It will be safer there."

She took a deep, steadying breath and felt the ire building. When she had been younger, much younger, her brothers' over-protectiveness had made her feel safe and secure. Eventually, it had become amusing. Now, as a woman who'd recently turned one and twenty, it was no longer amusing. It was restrictive.

Stifling.

And increasingly infuriating.

"And now you are coddling me, Andrew. Just like Lucien and Charles and to a smaller extent, Gareth ... I may be the baby sister, but I can assure you that I am not fragile. I get tired of the coddling, Andrew. I am not an egg."

He just looked at her. "Egg?"

"Coddled? Egg?"

He stared at her blankly, too distracted by the impending demonstration to match wits with her. "Oh, never mind," she said with a frustrated sigh. "I'll go inside and watch from an upstairs window if that will make you feel better."

"It would make me feel a lot better."

She turned and headed back toward the door that they had all just exited, hating herself for giving up so easily—but it was Andrew's night, and she would not spoil it for him. Still. All her life, her four brothers had sheltered her. Protected her. Guarded her so zealously there had been times she'd felt as though she couldn't breathe. She wondered if she would ever be treated as anything other than a fine bit of china by those who loved her most. A porcelain doll. Would Captain Lord ask that his wife also watch from the "safety" of the house?

Unbidden, an image of Mrs. Lord's rude and loutish brother flashed into her mind, and she credited her shortness with Andrew to her own troubling response to him. Odious man, indeed. She was glad that he had gone.

Why on earth am I thinking of him?

The door shut behind her. The house was empty and still, only the distant sound of a clock breaking the silence. She heard a carriage passing on the street outside. Sir Elliott out in the garden, calling for everyone's attention.

She tightened her mouth and began to climb the stairs, one hand on the balustrade, the other holding up her heavy skirts. They rustled softly with every step she ascended.

I ought to go right back out there. Andrew seeks to protect me, but I am here to protect him *in case he needs support or has an attack. What am I doing inside?*

Vexed with herself, with her brother, with the situation, with everything, she reached the second level of the house. She turned right, heading for the rooms that looked out onto the back garden, hurrying now so she would not be too late to watch her brother either blow himself to Kingdom Come or emerge as Britain's next hero. She needed to get her ire under control, to cool down, before facing everyone once again.

There, that room, to the right—it would do.

Nerissa swept through the doorway—and froze.

"We meet again."

She gasped, her hand flying to her mouth. It was him. *Him.* Mrs. Lord's brother, he with the hard, angular face so at odds with those striking long-lashed eyes, he with the unruly black hair and wicked, smiling mouth and, judging from his antagonistic attitude toward Captain Lord and her brother, a wish for an early death. He was leaning against the window embrasure, arms folded, looking over his shoulder and down at the garden below.

Nerissa stood unmoving, her heart suddenly banging in her chest. "Oh! I'm so sorry, I didn't know you were here, I thought you'd left."

He didn't look up. "I only wanted people to *think* I'd left."

"What are you doing here?"

"Watchin' the demonstration. I might ask the same of you."

"I feel no need to explain myself to you, of all people."

"Fine, then. Don't."

His blithe dismissal of her only stoked the resentment she already felt at being sent away from the action out in the garden like a child. He was back to looking down over his shoulder again, and had dismissed her as easily and quickly as everyone else had, her brother included. What was she, invisible?

"Fine then, I will. You wish to know why I'm here and not out in the garden with everyone else? It's because my brother thinks I'm made out of glass, that I might crack if I stay out there and watch him demonstrate his explosive, that something might happen to me. I'm sick to death of my brothers' over-protectiveness. Some days I feel as though I can barely breathe. God forbid I end up in any danger! God forbid I ever have any sort of adventure! They treat me like a child, like a fragile doll, and I'm tired of it!"

He had finally looked up and met her gaze, one black eyebrow raised in either amusement or surprise that she'd confess so much to him, a perfect stranger. "Well," he said, eyeing her, "why not make the most of the situation? Ye're here, I'm here, and we've got the best seat in the house. Come watch with me."

"No, I'm going back outside. I came here to support my brother and I'm going right back out there whether he likes it or not. Besides, it's not proper for me to be up here with—"

"It's only *im*proper if anyone but us knows ye're up here," he added, pointedly. There was something languid and predatory about him, something dangerous, and Nerissa tensed, wondering how long it would take her to get to the door. "So come and watch with me.

We'll both have the last laugh. Unless ye're afraid, of course."

"Afraid?"

"Ye're still standin' over there. Come over here. Ye'll be able to see better."

"I can't do that!"

"Why not?"

"Because—because *you're* there!"

He was looking back down again at the garden below. "Aye, don't tell anyone. I'm supposed to be gone, remember?"

"I must leave, it was foolish of me to stay as long as—"

"So your brother down there designed some sort of new firecracker?"

She backed toward the door. "Not a firecracker, an explosive."

"What kind of explosive?"

He looked up again and the intensity of his gaze, the raw virility of him as a man—and a very tall, powerful, and attractive one at that—caused her heart to do a little tripping flutter. She clapped a hand to her chest. Oh, this was all wrong. Wrong, wrong, wrong!

"What kind of explosive?" he persisted.

"Oh, I don't know." She took another step back toward the safety of the door. "A loud one. A powerful one. I don't know much about Andrew's inventions, he's far smarter than the rest of us and I'm sorry but I must go—"

"We were never introduced, ye know. I'm Mrs. Lord's brother. You can call me Ruaidri."

"I'm not calling you anything, I'm leaving."

"And what is your name, Sunshine? Ye're his sister, aren't ye?"

"Yes, I'm his sister, and there is no need for you to know my name, no need for you to be asking me all these questions and trying to detain me, no need for me to stay here when I must go."

He grinned, wickedly. "I won't tell if you won't."

"Tell what?"

"Yer brother, if you let me steal a kiss."

She gasped, coloring hotly. "You—you are a rogue and a scoundrel to even suggest such a thing!"

"I may indeed be a rogue and a scoundrel but if I am, it's not for wantin' a kiss from a pretty lass." He straightened up from the window, his strong, perfect teeth very white in the glint of moonlight. "Oblige me?"

"No!"

"I'm bettin' it'll be far more *explosive* than what's about to transpire down there in the garden. Come here, Sunshine. I've a mind to see if those lips of yers were made for kissin'."

Nerissa's mouth fell open. Her face went white, then flooded with color, and she was so shocked she could not even take another step backward.

Seeing it, the Irishman laughed and made a little dismissive gesture with his hand. "Ah, don't mind me, lass. I'm just messin' about with ye. I'd never hurt ye, not in a million years. I'm perfectly harmless."

"You—you don't look harmless."

"No?" He arched a brow, his gaze dropping pointedly to her bosom, the nip of her waist and the flare of her hips with undisguised interest. "How do I look?"

Dangerous. Virile. Predatory. Fascinating. "I can't answer that."

"Not scared of me now, are ye?"

"After what you just said to me? No, I am not *scared*. What I am, sir, is offended. Outraged."

"I paid ye a complement and ye're offended? Outraged? Saint's alive, what would your reaction be if I paid ye an insult?"

"I can't believe I'm standing here having this absurd conversation with you. You are rude and obnoxious and drunk, and I have already given you far more time and attention than you deserve. Good evening, sir."

He went back to looking down at the garden below, his gaze far more keen and watchful than his drunken state should allow. "'Twould be a better one if ye came over here and let me give ye that kiss."

"Ohhh!" Incensed, she turned on her heel and hurried for the stairs, hearing his laughter ringing out behind her. Her slippered foot had just reached the first of the steps leading down to the ground floor when an earth-shattering explosion all but shook the house off its foundations. Startled, she missed her footing ... grabbed wildly for the balustrade ... and suddenly the stairs were coming up to meet her, ceiling, balustrade, walls and stairs all whirling past her eyes as she tumbled and fell.

Her scream was lost to the wild applause outside.

❧

Ruaidri had only pretended to exit the townhouse earlier, just as he'd pretended to be drunk so that nobody took him seriously—but he'd never had any intention of leaving, and had slipped quietly back into the house after everyone else had filed outside. He had not expected to be disturbed, and certainly not by the ivory-haired beauty who had swept so forcefully into his room. He had no love for the English—not after what they had done to him as a young lad, not after the years he'd spent pressed into the Royal Navy, not after the innate scorn with which most of them treated him and anyone else who happened to be Irish. In fact, truth be told, he hated the English. It amused him to have outsmarted them all into thinking he was nothing but Deirdre's foolish brother, a tenant farmer who drank too much and was only a few steps above an idiot, obligingly leaving the house when told. It also amused him to rattle the imperious ice princess when she'd come flying into the room. Poor little canary. He could have stayed all night talking to her, as he'd sensed she was not just a spoiled aristocrat but a young woman of depth, passion and feeling, but there were times for the pursuit of a skirt and there were times for the pursuit of duty.

Tonight belonged to duty.

And so, he'd deliberately frightened her to get her to leave. He hadn't moved from his place at the window as she'd stormed off, and he had fully intended to go back to watching the much-anticipated demonstration of this "new explosive" unobserved and unnoticed up here in the upstairs window of his darkened room, when a horrendous *boom* at close range had nearly blown the glass out of that very window; he heard her shriek and then the terrible, thudding sounds of a body falling down a flight of stairs.

The explosive forgotten, he charged from the room and to the head of the stairs. There at the bottom she lay, a beautiful broken doll with one outflung arm, her hair down from its elaborate coiffure and now in helpless disarray over her face and her skirts, the blue-green color of Galway shallows under a bright sun, twisted around her legs.

He took the stairs in three bounds.

"Yer ladyship!" He knelt and took her gloved hand, alarmingly limp within his own. "Answer me!"

She stirred, moaned, and fell motionless once more.

From outside came the sounds of applause, excited voices, congratulations to the clever inventor. Ruaidri picked up one of the dainty white wrists, examined first one arm and then the other for broken bones. She appeared to be intact even if she were unconscious, and Captain Ruaidri O' Devir of the American Continental brig *Tigershark* suddenly realized that Fate had just delivered the perfect opportunity to obtain what John Adams had sent him three thousand miles to get.

The explosive.

He was nothing if not innovative. Without another thought, he slid his hands beneath the blonde beauty, lifted her in his arms, and before the first guests began to return from the back garden, ran out the front door and to the street beyond.

The night wasted no time in swallowing him.

Chapter Three

"By Jove, that was quite spectacular, Lord Andrew!"

"Amazing! Simply amazing! I've never seen the like, have you, Captain Danvers?"

"Never, not in a quarter century of being at sea." Excited faces all around, laughter, blue-and-white-clad officers clapping him on the shoulder, pumping his hand, toasting him with their glasses until Andrew felt like his head was swimming.

This was what he'd been waiting for. Recognition. A purpose in life. Something that would leave his mark upon history....

The small crowd all but carried him back into the house, and he frowned when his sister didn't immediately come to greet him. He had expected her to be at the door. Rushing out to the garden to support him. She must be indisposed, doing whatever females did to tidy their hair or fix their clothing or—

"I do believe your invention is a hit," Captain Lord said, smiling. "If you'll pardon the pun."

They went back into the converted ballroom where brandy, gin and rum began to flow in an amount to float any one of these officers' warships.

Andrew pulled out his watch.

Still no Nerissa.

The excited questions and congratulations from the guests began to fade, and alarm began to prickle at the base of his spine.

"Excuse me, gentlemen," he said, and went in search of his host's wife. He found Deirdre Lord in a corner of the ballroom holding the blond-haired little boy whose eyes were wide with wonder as he stared at the sea of officers in their handsome blue-and-white uniforms.

"M' poor Colin—the explosion woke up the wee mite and now I can't get him t' go back to sleep," she said, holding the child to her heart and kissing his bright hair. "There, there, nothin' t' fear, m' little love."

Little Colin Lord looked anything but fearful.

"Mrs. Lord, I think I need your assistance."

Her face immediately registered concern. "Ye look worried. Are ye well?"

"My sister," he murmured, trying to quell his sense of alarm. "Have you seen her?"

"Not since she went back inside."

"I can't find her. I don't know where she could be, and it wouldn't be like her to leave me all alone."

The beautiful Irishwoman nodded and handed the baby to her husband, who was just approaching. "Let me see if she's upstairs—maybe the excitement of the evening got t' her and she's lyin' down."

Nerissa was a de Montforte, Andrew thought. She was not likely to be affected by anything of the sort. If anything, she was in a snit at being sent back inside and off sulking somewhere. Or so he told himself, even though that wouldn't be like her, either. He took a deep and steadying breath as he watched Mrs. Lord head for the stairs. The hour was late. Maybe Nerissa *was* just lying down.

After *that* explosion?

The little prickle of fear at the base of his spine, unreasonable as it was, began to creep upward. He heard himself answering a question from a lieutenant with ruddy cheeks and a missing front tooth, making the polite response, fielding the inevitable questions, and then Mrs. Lord was hurrying back downstairs, frowning.

She hurried over to Andrew. "She's not upstairs. I searched every room."

"Where the devil could she be?"

"Christian!" she motioned urgently to her husband, who quickly left the gathering of naval officers with whom he'd been deep in conversation, his young son in his arms. "We can't find Lady Nerissa. I checked upstairs. She's nowhere to be found."

"Any chance she wandered into the kitchen? Retired to a drawing room?"

"I checked. So did Lord Andrew."

"Maybe she just went outside to get some fresh air and is sitting in your coach. Stay here and double-check every room. I'll go out and have a look."

Returning the toddler to his wife, Captain Lord strode past a group of guests on his way out, many of them well into their cups and oblivious to the quiet drama that was playing out right under their noses. Andrew rushed to the kitchens and found them empty save for a pair of weary servants sitting at a table playing cards and awaiting any further requests from their employers. No, they had not seen a tall, pale-haired young lady wearing pearls and blue-green silk.

Andrew hurried out of the kitchen in time to see Captain Lord coming back in, his face grave. He met his wife and Andrew near the door.

"She's not in the coach," he said, and Andrew felt the prickle of fear in the base of his spine become downright terror.

❧

Her arm hurt. Her shoulder hurt.

But above all, her head hurt.

It was the pain that finally prodded her awake.

Nerissa opened her eyes and lay there in the dimly lit darkness for a long moment, wondering where she was. Her confusion over her whereabouts only increased when her surroundings proved to be most unfamiliar. This was not her bedroom at De Montforte House in London. It was not the bedroom of the London townhouse where she and Andrew had gone to demonstrate his new explosive. In fact, it was not a room at all, though it was indeed a room—of sorts.

Most rooms did not move. This one did, slightly; she could feel her body swaying gently from side to side on the small bed-of-sorts on which she lay, and she remembered, then, the terrifying fall down the stairs.

I must be dreaming. Or hallucinating.

She moved her arm—the one that did not hurt—and pinched herself. *Ouch.*

This was no dream.

Gingerly, she pushed herself up on her good arm, pressed two fingers to her aching forehead and saw, by the glow of a lantern that made his features sharp and distinct, Mrs. Lord's rude, odious, unmannerly, uncouth, and thoroughly awful Irish brother standing a few feet away, leaning a hip against a small table and watching her.

Her mouth opened, but no sound came out.

"Sleeping Beauty awakes," he murmured, and a coiled tenseness went out of him, as though on a great breath of relief. He lifted a tin mug to his lips.

She was decently covered, still clad in her teal silk gown but even so, she snatched at a folded blanket from the foot of the bed and pulled it up over herself as she recoiled in horror and confusion. What had happened? Where was Andrew? Where was Captain Lord, Sir Elliott, everyone else? Where was *she*? And why was this man gazing at her from over the top of his mug with a gleam in his eye, a thoughtful watchfulness that prickled her skin and made her want to get up and flee?

As if reading her mind, he lowered the mug and said, "Ye fell down the stairs earlier this evenin', lass. So I brought ye here."

"Here?" She frowned. "Where is 'here?'"

"About three miles east of Margate." At her blank look he added, "We're at sea."

"What?" This made no sense at all, though it certainly explained the swaying of her surroundings, the sounds of wood creaking, easing and straining, and the heady scent of salt that filled the air. At sea. Which meant she was on a ship. *A ship?* "I don't understand ... my brother Andrew would never have allowed this ... What have you done with him? Why am I here?"

He toasted her with the mug. "Ah, well, I'm an enterprisin' sort. Saw a chance and took it, I did."

"A chance for what?"

"A chance to obtain something I've come a long ways to get."

"It didn't occur to you that I might need a doctor?"

"Surgeon's come and gone."

"What?"

"Several times, in fact."

She stared at him, wondering if she was in the middle of a dream. Or a novel in which she was a mere character, infused with thoughts and visuals written by someone else. This was not real. It couldn't be. Confusion tangled with alarm, and then indignation.

She swung her legs out of bed—and he was suddenly beside her, one hand firmly gripping her arm.

His hand.

His strong, masculine, hand.

On her person.

How dare you.

She glared at him, then pointedly at his hand before meeting his calm, slightly amused gaze once more.

"Remove your hand from my person this instant."

"Promise to stay put?"

"I'm not promising anything until you give me some answers."

He removed the offending fingers from her arm but with a certain mocking reluctance, a faint brush of her sleeve that infuriated her, and pulled up a stout ladder-backed chair. "Answers, eh? Right. Well then, first things first. Ye're on the Continental brig *Tigershark* out of Boston."

"Continental brig?"

"American Navy."

"America doesn't have a navy."

"Aye, it does, and I'm part of it. Ever hear of John Adams? Sent me here himself, he did. Oh, we have a navy all right."

"What you have is men in ships who are pirates. Men who are committing treason against their king. You are British, and as such any 'navy' you think you belong to should be the Royal one."

"No, ma'm. I'm *Irish*." The teasing light had gone out of his eyes and his voice hardened, aligning with the ruthless, dangerous part of him she had sensed but so far in her limited interactions with him, had not yet seen. He leaned close, close enough to see that his eyes, which she'd thought were blue, were actually a striking shade of amethyst beneath their heavy black fringe of lashes. "Don't *ever* make the mistake of calling me British."

She glared at him, hating him. The uncouth, ill-bred, savage lout. *Oh, when my brothers catch up to you....*

He pinned her with that cold stare. "Are we clear on that?"

"Trust me, I would *never* make *that* mistake."

It was an insult, aristocratically delivered. It was an

insult letting him know that no Irishman could ever measure up to an Englishman in class, quality, and manners, and he wasn't so dull that he didn't register it immediately. Getting to his feet, he planted his hands on either side of her body and leaned down and close, right up into her face. "You, Sunshine, are a hostage on my ship. Do as ye're told and your stay here will be short, much to the benefit and relief of us both."

That close, she could smell him. Salt water. Fresh wind. The lye soap that his shirt had been laundered in.

His point made, he straightened up, shot her a dark glare over his shoulder, and reached for a bottle with which to refill his mug.

Nerissa swung her legs out of the bed. "I am leaving."

"And going where?" He nodded toward the windows behind him, one of which was open to admit a heady balm of salty night air. "There's a whole ocean out there. Unless you can walk on water, Sunshine, you aren't goin' anywhere."

"How dare you speak to me that way! I am Lady Nerissa de—"

"I don't give a tinker's damn who you are. Now, get up and move around if ye've a mind to, but we're at sea and unless you plan to throw yourself overboard with all the drama of a Shakespearean heroine, ye're stuck here as a guest of America in general and myself in particular. Get used to it."

Nerissa stared at him, mouth agape, too shocked, too flabbergasted, to even muster a response. Nobody had ever spoken to her in such a way or treated her—the daughter and sister of a duke—with such a staggering level of rudeness and disrespect. She felt as though he had slapped her across the face. Gone was the teasing, roguish, outrageously flirtatious and rather foolish drunk he'd been—or pretended to be—at the naval gathering back in London. This man had a sharp intelligence about him, an edge like a freshly-honed knife. That hard mouth was unsmiling, almost cruel. Those glittering eyes were cold beneath their thick black lashes. Those shoulders were wide and powerful, the legs long and well-shaped in their white breeches, and there was an almost untamed savagery about him that dwelt, she sensed, just beneath the surface.

Well of course there was. He was, after all, Irish.

And she was alone with him.

Fear gripped her heart and she forced herself to remain composed, telling herself that she had nothing to worry about, that Lucien, that all of her brothers would be turning the world upside down to get her back and punish this—this *savage* for his audacity.

There was a knock on the door.

"What is it?"

"Wind's backed a point, sir. First lieutenant sends his respects and wants to know if you want to change tack."

"Aye, 'tis as good a time as any. I'll be on deck shortly."

The footsteps retreated and her tormenter stuck the mug, now empty, onto a hook that protruded from the painted planking that would pass, in any other space, for a wall. He picked up what looked to be a smart blue and white uniform coat from the back of a chair and began to shrug into it, already dismissing her.

"Sir?"

Blue uniform?

Answers. She wanted answers.

"You can't just abduct me and hold me for hostage! And hostage for what? Who do you think you are? My brother is one of the most powerful men in England! When he catches up to you, he'll slit your belly and strangle you with your own entrails! Do you know what you've *done?*"

The Irishman just shrugged, unconcerned, and shoved his other arm into his coat sleeve.

"Does your sister Mrs. Lord know that I'm here? Does your brother-in-law, Captain Lord? The admiral, Sir Elliott?"

"Don't be stupid, of course not."

"Does anyone know?"

"Not yet."

"Who are you? In actuality?"

"Ruaidri O' Devir, ma'm, just as ye thought." He picked up a tricorne hat and headed for the door.

"I wish to know why I am here!"

He stopped then, his patience exhausted, and looked her straight in the eye. "Your brother developed an explosive which he's about to sell to your country. *My* country needs it so we can win this miserable struggle with yours. Since I doubt England or your brother are going to just hand it over to us, ye're my payment for it. A ransom, if ye will. Understand?"

"What do you mean your country? Ireland is not at war with England ... you are mad."

"No, Sunshine. I'm not mad. I'm a commissioned captain in America's Continental Navy if ye must know, and because John Adams decided there's nobody in the Navy as audacious, reckless or downright foolish as I am, he chose me to come and get that explosive. Ye're my ransom. If yer family wants ye back, they'll hand it over as well as the formula on how t' create it. Now are ye finished? I've a ship to see to."

She stared at him, aghast. "Your sister is married to a captain in the Royal Navy ... her brother-in-law is a famous admiral ... you would dare do this right under all their noses?"

He smiled then, his long lashes throwing shadow against his cheekbones in the dim orange glow of the lantern and in that moment, he looked almost handsome. Almost. "Indeed, I would." The smile spread. "Indeed, I have."

And with that he shoved open the door and without a backwards glance, left.

❧

On deck, a cool breeze was blowing out of the south and a slice of moon glinted against the breaking crests of dark, nearby seas.

Ruaidri was glad to be out of his cabin. That woman back there—she stirred things in his bones, put unwelcome thoughts in his head, caused his cock to stiffen in his breeches in a way it had no business doing. She was a bloody Englishwoman, for the love of Christ. He'd told himself he'd only stayed with her to ensure she was fine after that terrible fall down the stairs several hours before—after all, what good was a hostage that one had taken for ransom if that hostage were dead?

He received the salute of Lieutenant Morgan, who had the deck.

"How is the lady, sir?"

"Quite recovered, and just like the rest of her kind, thinks I'm nothin' but a bug under her damned shoe. We'll be well rid of her once we get that explosive." He looked at Morgan. The lines of strain around his mouth and the smell of ginger did not escape him. He knew all about his lieutenant's queasy stomach. His voice gentled. "Go below and get some rest, John. I'll take over from here."

"Aye, sir."

Morgan gave his salute and melted off into the darkness, leaving him alone with his thoughts.

Imagine. He, a captain in the Continental Navy now, enjoying a status that once, a long time ago, he would never have even dared to dream about. But that had been before his brother-in-law Christian, had outsmarted him back in '75 and taught him a thing or two about humility.

Before the duel.

Before Josiah.

Before Dolores Ann.

The brig moved easily beneath him as though sharing his thoughts, his memories, and far off in the night he could imagine he saw the distant coast of Ireland.

"Delight."

There. He'd said it. Her name.

And there was nothing but the sound of the waves to repeat it back to him.

He turned from the rail.

Some memories were better left alone.

Chapter Four

B*lackheath Castle, Berkshire, England*
Late the following morning...

Many miles away, in one of the most majestic and important homes in England, the sixth duke of Blackheath had just sat down to breakfast with his duchess, Eva, when a footman approached the table with a message for His Grace:

My dear brother,

I have urgent and distressing news. Tonight, while entertaining the Royal Navy with a display of my explosive (as you had advised), Nerissa went missing from Captain Lord's townhouse. I am turning London upside down in my attempts to locate her and have enlisted the assistance of everyone I can find, but at this point I am at a loss as to what has happened to her or where she could be. Needless to say, I fear the worst. Please come to the City immediately.

—Andrew

Lucien felt the blood drain from his face.

Eva was instantly alert and on her feet, already coming to his side. "What is it, Lucien?"

He waved the footman away and passed the message to his duchess, already throwing his napkin down and pushing back his plate. "I must go to London. Immediately."

Eva hastily scanned the short message, then hurried after him as he stalked purposely from the room, already calling for his valet.

"I'll go with you."

"No, please. I would rather you stayed here with little Augustus. He'll need his mother, and I won't subject him to travel or the hot stinking pit that is London in the summertime any more than Andrew wished to subject Celsie or little Laura to it," he said, referring to Andrew's baby daughter. "I know you mean well, Eva, and at any other time I'd want you with me, but not this one."

She followed him down the corridor. Phelps, his valet, was already there, not blinking an eye as his master ordered traveling clothes laid out, luggage packed and the ducal coach to be readied. "Please, Lucien, try not to worry. We both know she's not been the same after ... after Perry. She still grieves him. Maybe she ran off to try and call on him. Maybe she had a disagreement with Andrew. It could be any number of things. You'll find her."

Lucien said nothing. His wife was only trying to assuage his sudden fear, as all loved ones do when bad news hits. She was making excuses, offering rational explanations for Nerissa's disappearance when really, there were none.

Was it possible that she had, indeed, taken it into her head to make a last gallant effort to win back the heart of the man she'd loved?

Had he missed something? Was his sister that desperate?

Lucien felt sick. It was his fault that Perry had broken off the engagement and his fault that his little sister's heart had been broken. If he'd not sent Perry on that ill-fated trip to Spain–

No, he could not think of that, not now when regrets and recriminations would only cloud his thinking and get in the way of finding his little sister. Cold dread clawed at the base of his spine and as Phelps returned, Lucien knew he could not wait for his earlier orders to be carried out. There was no time to lose. The coach could catch up to him later.

He embraced his duchess, said a hurried goodbye to his nine-month-old son and heir and then strode purposely to the library, already calling for his fierce black stallion and yanking open the case where his deadliest, most accurate set of pistols waited.

My little sister. If she has met with foul play, I will kill *the person responsible.*

❧

Nerissa opened her eyes. Beyond the brig's stern windows, she saw thick banks of slate-colored cloud that seemed to press down upon a heavy gray sea streaked and laced with foam.

She must have slept, as she had no recollection of time having passed after that wretched Irishman had left. The day, however, was obviously well underway. Her stomach growled, and she put a hand over her belly, trying to ignore it as she took in her surroundings. The details that had been lost to the darkness when she'd woken earlier had now taken shape. A seat beneath the stern windows, covered with a canvas cushion. Two cannon, one on each side of the cabin, trussed down and poking their long muzzles out of open gun ports that let in a warm sea-breeze from outside. A chair pushed up to a small pine table bolted to the deck flooring, atop which stood an inkwell and a quill in a square tray, brass dividers holding down a water-stained chart, a battered tin coffeepot and a book that she supposed was the ship's log. Near one gun, a washstand with a bowl and pitcher and a small mirror above it. Near the other, a sea chest with a lap-sized writing desk. An exquisite little model of a ship carved of bone or driftwood, strung with rigging and hung with miniature sails. There was a small, primitive painting of green hills, steep, rocky cliffs and a turquoise blue sea on one wall, and while Nerissa knew there were no walls on ships, she also knew she lacked nautical vernacular and decided that that was what the heavy, lateral planking that framed this cabin and held out the sea beyond, would be called during her—hopefully very short—stay here.

Even now, Lucien would be on his way to rescue her. No force in the world could stop her brother.

None.

The certainty brought her comfort. A sense of constancy when, for the first time in her life, there was nothing expected, predictable, or usual about the time or place in which she currently found herself. Being abducted and held for ransom was a far cry from the usual pattern of her life—an endless round of teas, visits, balls, soirees, Seasons, hunts, and being managed by her brothers. Or at least, fiercely guarded by them. Sheltered, even. No, this situation was altogether different, and there was nobody to guard her. Shelter her. Protect her, even, unless she reached down deep inside and did it herself.

Nobody.

A shiver of fear went through her and she took a deep and steadying breath. *If he's holding me for ransom, surely he doesn't mean to harm me. That would defeat the purpose, wouldn't it?*

I am safe.

I am. Another deep, calming breath. *Safe.*

But there were no guarantees, were there? She was quite alone. Alarmingly so, really. She glanced around the cabin, wondering what she might use as a weapon should the need arise. Not a pistol in sight. Not even a dress sword. Nothing but the dividers with their needle-nosed points which, she supposed, were better than nothing. Probably ineffective against a large, strong man like her captor, but they would give her confidence, if nothing else. Show him that she wouldn't go down without a fight if he decided to try and compromise her. She had her pride, after all, and she was no shrinking ninny. Until Lucien or the full force of the Royal Navy arrived to pluck her from danger back to safety, she had a choice. She could allow herself to become a victim, or she could do something about it.

She was a de Montforte.

She would do something about it.

She sat up and found her feet. The deck beneath her rolled with a life of its own, and she grabbed the table to keep her balance as she crossed the small cabin. As expected, the door to the world outside was shut, enforcing her status as both prisoner and hostage. She picked up the dividers, testing their weight. What would one of her brothers do in this situation?

She pushed a hand through her disheveled hair, trying to think, and found what felt like a goose egg just above her ear. It was sore to the touch, though it wasn't the only part of her that hurt—she could feel bruising in her elbow, and her ribs protested when she moved a certain way. However, if there were small blessings for which to be thankful, it was that she appeared not to be prone to seasickness.

Her stomach growled, and still holding the dividers, she considered what to do.

That ... that ill-bred Irish lout out there. Did he intend to starve her while he awaited the ransom money?

At the thought of him, her head began to hurt and she despised him all over again. Oh, how dare he put his hands upon her, take her away from her family, make demands of them that were just the other side of outrageous.

Resolve.

I am a de Montforte and I will not let him rattle me.

Footsteps sounded just outside. The latch bumped upward and the door swung open.

It was him, the scoundrel. He paused for a moment, silhouetted by bright morning light flooding the deck behind him before he stalked into the cabin. If she'd had any lingering hopes that their conversation last night had been a dream, his sudden appearance was a bucket of ice water. No, she had not imagined the proud bearing, the air of command. She had not even imagined the uniform. In fact, the tatty coat he'd worn in London and the careless, slouching laissez-faire he'd adopted then seemed to be the dream, for this man, virile and strong, bore little resemblance to that drunken, bumbling fool at all.

Hiding the dividers in a fold of her skirts, she let her gaze rake contemptuously over the white waistcoat buttoned over a fine lawn shirt, the open blue coat that emphasized the width of his powerful shoulders, the snug white breeches. The hilt of a sword peeked above a scabbard at his side, and his shoes were hazed with dried salt.

This was not the down-on-his-luck poor relation he'd pretended to be back in London.

No, this was a man of business. Of intent.

Of danger.

He doffed his tricorne and tossed it to the window seat.

"Top o' the mornin' to ye, Sunshine," he said, piling on that awful Irish accent in a manner that felt intentional. Mocking. As though he wanted her to know that he'd turned the tables, Irish over English, for once. "Or rather, afternoon."

"My name," she retorted coldly, drawing herself up and fixing him with what she hoped was her iciest, most haughty glare, "is not Sunshine."

"Ehm, well, probably an ill-chosen moniker at that, as I've yet to see ye smile."

"You, sir, have not exactly given me anything to smile about."

"Come now, lass." He picked up the dented coffee pot, retrieved his mug, and splashed a pitiful trickle of black liquid into it with a casual, careless flip of his wrist. "How have I harmed ye?"

"You took me from my family and brought me to this ship. You've caused them what has to be unbearable worry and grief. The scandal will be beyond imagining and my reputation will be ruined because of this. Because of *you*." She glared at him. "And you ask how you've harmed me? When my brother Lucien catches up to you, you will wish you had never, *ever* laid eyes on me."

His lips twitched. "Oooh, 'tis frightened, I am."

"Stop smirking, you ought to be!"

He laughed. "I'm not afraid of some pompous, mincing, English tosser bloated by his own sense of importance. And I'll *never* be sorry for layin' eyes on you. I like women. I like pretty women. I like spirited women, and you, Sunshine—"

"Stop calling me that!"

"—happen to be all three. Aye, a fine bit of stuff, you are. 'Tis a pity, though, that ye're English."

Anger blazed in her cheeks. "You are the most insufferable man I have ever met."

"Aye, well, ye're not exactly sugar and sweets, yerself. Ye've got the demeanor of a shrew and ye're a damned snob, as well. But never mind that. Breakfast'll be here soon. Hungry?"

"No."

But at that moment her stomach growled like a caged lion. Mortified, she clamped a hand over her belly as though to hold in the sound, her face flaming red.

He laughed again, and pushed the door shut behind him so they were both alone.

Nerissa's hand, damp now with sweat, tightened around the hidden dividers.

"I do not find this amusing at all," she snapped, moving away and putting the table between them.

"Aye, by the look of ye, I doubt ye find much at all that's amusing. You should try smilin' once in a while, Sunshine. 'Tis good for the spirit as well as the face."

She'd be damned before she gave him the satisfaction of a smile. Incensed, she turned away and stumbled toward the open stern windows. Beyond, the ship's wake left a faint line through the sea behind them.

"I'll bet ye're pretty when ye smile," he said from behind her. She wished she could step forward, away from him, but there was nowhere to go unless she fancied a dive out those windows and a swim. "And why don't ye? Missin' a tooth or two?"

She stiffened, refusing to turn around.

"Or maybe ye're afraid that smilin' will give ye wrinkles before yer time."

She clenched her fist around the dividers, solid and reassuring beneath the fabric of her skirts.

"On the other hand, maybe ye've just got too much stubborn pride. Given that ye're English and all."

She turned then. "Are you quite finish—"

—And gasped, as he had come right up behind her, as silent as a cat.

He had been in the process of reaching up toward her hair, and she froze at his brazen audacity. He did not pull back, did not pretend he wasn't about to touch her, and did not step away to give her space.

"Are ye afraid of me, lass?"

She could not answer. Could do nothing but stare at that hand while her own tightened against her makeshift weapon, still hidden in her skirts.

"I'm the last person ye should ever be afraid of," he said soberly. "I'd swallow boilin' oil before I ever lifted a hand to harm ye."

"You—you were about to touch me," she managed.

"Ye've a beautiful head of hair. It's like a paintin', backlit by the light from outside. Aye, I wanted to touch it, just to see if it was real."

And he did. Touched it. Let his rough, calloused fingers drag down a length of it that fell haphazardly over her shoulder, while Nerissa, trapped between him and the window seat behind her, froze. Her heartbeat quickened and her hand tightened harder around the dividers.

And just like that, he reached down and grasped the hand hidden in her skirts. Found the dividers. Smiled indulgently, knowingly, and took them away from her as he might've forced a trinket from the hand of a child. He had known all along that she'd had them, Nerissa thought in alarm, and as he put them on the table behind him she realized all over again that he was far bigger than her, far stronger, and far, far more observant than he let on.

Dear God.

He said nothing, just stood there looking down at her with a speculative and faintly admiring gleam in his eye that began to unnerve her even more.

She glared at him, determined not to show fear. "I wish you would leave."

"I wish I could."

"You have two feet. Why don't you use them."

"Because I also have two eyes that can't help but drink in yer beauty, Sunshine. Two ears that enjoy the sound of yer voice. Two hands that itch to touch ye just to see if ye're real or a vision. Two lips that ache to—"

"Enough!"

He stepped closer. And pushed his hand—his very strong, scarred and calloused hand—past her jaw and into the fall of thick, pale hair that had long since come loose from its pins, and with his thumb, tilted her chin up so she was forced to meet his eyes.

She could feel the heat of his large, powerful body, could smell the sea on his clothing, on his skin. The blood froze in her veins. Sometime between last night and now, he'd loosened his hair from its queue and now it hung in disarray to his broad and capable shoulders, unruly, untamed, a fall of thick, riotous black curls that made him look like a pirate. She felt her body responding to him, her mouth going dry, and a fluttery sensation beneath her breastbone. She fought to breathe. He had no business making her feel this way. No business talking to her like this. None at all.

And then, with his thumb, he pulled down on her lip like a buyer might examine a horse, exposing her pretty white teeth and letting his finger rub wickedly over the sensitive skin of her bottom lip before releasing her.

Recovery was instantaneous. Nerissa's hand flashed up to slap his face, the full force of her rage for this latest insult behind her swing. But he had anticipated her reaction and easily caught her wrist.

Once again, she was reminded how much bigger and stronger he was than she.

Once again, she had underestimated him.

Caught helplessly in his unyielding grip, she glared up at him.

"Stop it," he said softly, his voice no longer cajoling but full of menace, and she saw the hard crystalline glitter that had come into his eyes and it frightened her. The sheer strength of his fingers dwarfing her wrist frightened her, as he could break the bones there with one savage twist if the fancy took him. The nearness of his mouth frightened her, a mouth that was playful one moment and cynical, hard, and dangerous the next.

Everything about him frightened her.

She jerked free of him and backed away, chafing her wrist as though she could rub away the offensiveness of his touch. Her lower lip still tingled where he'd touched it, and she realized all over again how perilous her situation was, trapped here in this small cabin with a man who hated the English, who appeared to hate her, who could ravish and destroy her without a single soul on earth to stop him.

I will get through this. I will survive. Even now, my brothers will be turning London upside down to find me. He won't get away with this. My brothers will make him pay. They will kill him, if I don't find a way to do so myself, first....

There was a knock on the door.

"Come on in," her captor muttered.

A young man with light ginger hair clubbed at his nape entered. He was dressed in some sort of a blue uniform and carried a wooden tray. On it were two bowls of something gray and ugly and steaming. Another dented coffee pot, two tin mugs and a pair of pewter spoons completed this sad and very un-elegant ensemble.

Nerissa's nose wrinkled.

"Thank ye, Mr. Cranton," said her captor. "'Twill be all."

The young man nodded and quietly left.

"Sit down and eat," the Irishman said, pulling out the single chair for her.

"I am not hungry." She gave the contents of the tray a baleful look and turned away, her gaze directed on the horizon beyond the stern windows.

He eyed her for a moment, then sat down in the chair she'd refused. "Suit yerself. But starvin' yerself won't change yer situation. Might as well make the best of it."

She said nothing. Out of the corner of her eye, she could see him reaching for one of the bowls of gruel and plunging a spoon into it. He ate rapidly, not savoring the food but shoveling it down with the same finesse that one might find in a hungry horse.

Ill-bred cretin.

"You have the manners of a trough animal," she said scathingly.

"Aye, well, at least I won't be as hungry as one when I've finished both my portion and yers. Good stuff, this. Are ye certain you don't want any?"

"It looks disgusting."

"Oatmeal and peas. Navy food. Puts hair on yer chest."

"I don't want ... hair on my chest. I want to go home."

"Worth much to yer brothers?"

"That is a stupid question. But considering its source, I'm not surprised."

"Because if you are, then this business will be over and done with before ye even have time to starve yerself. I dispatched a ransom note before we put to sea. You in exchange for the explosive and the formula on how to make it. I'm glad ye're a close family. 'Twill be nice to have them hand over that formula with no trouble and no questions asked." He looked up, smiling and all but batting those ridiculous long lashes of his, and wiped his mouth with a linen napkin. "To think, the mighty Duke of Blackheath doin' me bidding. Now there's a thought!"

At this, Nerissa actually laughed, for the idea of Lucien doing anyone's bidding was about as ludicrous as that of a mermaid popping up in their wake and waving hello.

"Ah!" said the scoundrel beside her. "So ye do smile, after all. Laugh, even. Should do it more often. Makes ye even prettier, it does."

She immediately sobered and glared at him. "My amusement comes from imagining what is going to happen when that *mighty duke* catches up to you."

"Ye think he can best me in a fight?"

Nerissa laughed again, harder this time.

And now even her captor's lips were twitching and the hard, intimidating edge to him had softened, his eyes sparkling with merriment. "Ye mustn't love yer brother much, lass, if the idea of his demise brings ye such delight! Saints alive, Sunshine, if he doesn't love you either, we might be stuck with each other longer than we both thought."

"That is *not* why I'm laughing."

He dug his spoon into his bowl and shoveled another glob of oatmeal into his mouth. His eyes were mischievous again, happy, bright. "Oh?"

"I'm laughing because it brings me delight to imagine your heart speared on the end of his sword."

"Got a lot of faith in this brother of yers, do ye?"

"Captain O' Devir, I think you have a death wish."

"Aye, maybe I do," he said, scraping the bowl with his spoon, "but at least I won't die hungry."

Chapter Five

Ruaidri left her with the untouched bowl and, hoping she'd eat something by the time he returned, picked up his hat and left the cabin.

He shut the door behind him, donned his tricorne and let out a deep breath.

God almighty, involve a female and a situation was never simple. Involve a rich, spoiled, aristocratic English one who felt she was above everyone else on God's green earth and it made things even more complicated.

And amusing.

He enjoyed baiting her. Making her angry. Thawing the ice in her lovely blue eyes and watching her try to maintain her composure, probably thinking he didn't notice when he couldn't *help* but notice every damned thing about her. Like her pretty pink mouth that he ached to kiss—and almost had. The willowy elegance of her body that he longed to mold with his hands. The curve of her cheek and the shade of her hair, like wheat bleached by the late summer sun or the sand on a Connemara beach. What he did not like, though, was that bruise on her elbow—and the fear that had come into her eyes when he had come purposely up behind her.

That bothered him fierce, it did. He might have been an absent son and brother. He might be a rogue and an ex-smuggler and yes, even a murderer. But he would never, not as long as God's sweet air filled his lungs, *ever* force himself upon a woman.

The morning sun was cracking through massed clouds above as he moved to the weather side of the quarterdeck.

"Wind's come 'round to the east, sir," said Morgan, who greeted him with a salute.

"Grand. We'll stay on this tack for another hour, then."

"The lady, sir. Has she recovered?"

"Aye."

"What is the plan?"

Improvise as we go. "We'll stay near the French coast in case we need to duck in, and hope the lady's worth enough to her family that they'll give us the explosive and its formula in exchange for her."

"Don't like how the wind's blowing, sir. It'll make it hard to beat back to safety if the Royal Navy comes after us."

"The Royal Navy isn't goin' to come after us. Have faith, Mr. Morgan."

"So what next?"

Ruaidri buttoned his coat as the sun went back behind the clouds once more, bringing a chill to the air. "We wait for a response to our ransom note."

Or I go back to London. Continue to play the fool so my little sister's heart won't be broken when she finds out what I've done. Far better to let her go on thinking I'm tending the cottage back in Connemara. And far safer to let her husband think it, too. Not one I want to tangle with in a sea fight ever again if he comes looking for us.

"Sounds rather dangerous, sir. These waters are crawling with Royal Navy ships."

Ruaidri make a sound that was half scorn, half laughter. "Well then, instead of exercising the guns with no real target as we've been doing every day for the last month, maybe we'll find something to actually shoot at—"

He halted in mid-sentence as a sudden tension fell over the ship. The entire company had turned their attention aft. Not toward him. But beyond him.

He followed their gazes and the breath caught in his throat.

It was her, of course. He'd known it would be, the moment every man in his crew had stopped what he was doing and turned. She looked strangely out of place here on a naval ship full of rough tars, her fine clothes and proud bearing reminding him that he had plucked her from a world he had never known, would never know, a world that was as different from anything he had ever inhabited—even when he was the Irish Pirate and celebrated, feted and entertained by some of the most influential leaders of patriot Boston—as ice was from flame.

She was English quality. High-born and haughty, her father and now her brother, only one step down from a prince.

Whereas he was just a poor Irishman trying to make a fresh start in a new and emerging country.

She was, in short, unreachable.

Untouchable.

Unobtainable.

No matter how heavily she invaded his thoughts, no matter how much he enjoyed needling her, no matter how hard his damned cock pushed against his breeches at the very sight of her.

Unreachable.

The memory of another blonde beauty rose up in his mind, buxom, common, bawdy and warm ... his kind of lass, chalk and cheese from this aloof and elegant aristocrat whose veins ran with ice water.

Someone coughed, bringing him back to the present and his duties as a sea officer. He went up to her, bowed, and made as gallant a leg as he knew how to execute.

"Lady Nerissa," he said, replacing his hat.

She looked flatly at him, one pale brow raised in slight disdain, cool and composed despite the fact that every officer and seaman on the deck had stopped what he was doing to stare at her.

"Get back to yer duties, ye pack of laggards," Ruaidri snapped.

The men didn't argue. One or two cast a last longing glance at the vision in their midst, then returned to their work.

"So," she said, for his ears alone. "Is this the garb of your so-called Continental Navy?" Her haughty gaze swept the tars in their hats, neckerchiefs and red waistcoats, the officers in blue and white. "Looks remarkably similar to ours. Do you copy our English uniforms as well as our songs and the colors in our flag?"

Ruaidri moved toward her, offering both his elbow and most blinding smile. "I was hopin' ye'd say we wear it better, but tha' 'twould be stretching me expectations, eh?"

"I am delighted, Captain, that you do. *Think*, that is. Because so far I have seen little evidence of that claim."

He grinned, because he was indeed thinking. Thinking of how soft and silky her skin looked and how he ached to run the back of his knuckles along the little hollow beneath her cheekbone. Thinking of what it would be like to push his fingers up through her hair and claim that disdainful mouth in a kiss. Thinking of how her lips would—

"I cannot eat that gruel," she said.

"What's wrong with it? Find a weevil?"

"The spoon is dirty."

At this, young Cranton, standing several feet away near the helmsman, let out a guffaw.

"Quiet," Ruaidri said, unwilling to let the lady suffer

humiliation at the hands of his crew. Again, they were turning to stare at her, some of them grinning like love-struck schoolboys. "Get back to work, all of ye. And the first one of you slackers who casts more than a fleetin' glance at our guest goes without his grog tonight."

A few elbow-jabs to ribs, one or two veiled smirks, but the men did what they were told.

He turned back to his hostage, one brow raised in amusement. "So here you are again. Can't get enough of me, eh?"

"Do you know, Captain, I think you take a great and perverse delight in irritating me."

"Aye, I might indeed."

"And so, because I have an equal desire to irritate you, I am not going to respond to your baiting."

"'Tis a pity, that. I rather like it when ye're irritated. The way yer eyes flash. The way yer mouth makes a tight line and the roses bloom in yer cheeks."

"All the more reason not to let your odious presence affect me."

"You accuse me of not thinkin', Lady Nerissa. But I can't help it. Thinkin', that is. Thinkin' that if ye found me so objectionable, ye'd have stayed in the cabin and not sought me out here on deck, eh?"

"Yes, well, I am bored."

"'Tis a pity, that. I have no balls, soirees, fancy dinners or silken sheets to offer ye. Ye'll have to make do until ye get back to yer fancy lifestyle."

"And how am I supposed to 'make do'? I have no maid. I have no change of clothing. I am a prisoner."

"Life's what ye make of it. Ever been on a ship before, Sunshine?"

She snorted in contempt. "Of course not."

"Why not?"

"What reason would I have to be on a ship? I live out in the country. I do not go anywhere, except to

London once in a while or for the Season. I have no need to go anywhere."

"That's yer life?"

"It is a very good life," she said defensively.

"Ah, well, then. I can see why ye're bored, I can."

She did not deign to answer him, merely turning away to gaze with unwilling curiosity at her surroundings. Her nose was small and pert, her skin as white as milk, and her blue eyes were fringed with long, pale lashes and down-turned at the outer corners. A proper English rose, she was, ripe for the plucking but guarded by the thorns of class, culture and breeding. He wished he had a hat for her—five minutes of the sun, when it came out, would burn her like toast. So caught up was he in simply gazing at the perfection of her profile, wondering where he could find one, that it was a moment before he realized she had spoken.

"I said, Captain O' Devir, what does that sail do?"

She was standing there, her head tilted back as she looked up at the huge mainsail and the topsail above it, a bulging rectangle against the clouds.

"What all sails do, Lady Nerissa. Powers the ship. That one just happens to be the biggest one."

"What is it called?"

"Lucy."

Her proud head turned to look at him. "That is absurd."

"I name them all in me mind. Lucy ... Megan ... Little Susan. But if ye wish to know its proper name, that's the mainsail. Or main course."

"And where is dessert?"

"What?"

"If that is the main course, which one is the dessert?"

He laughed. He couldn't help it. The sound was out of his mouth before he could stop it—not that he would have, even if he could.

"Are you quite mad, Captain O' Devir?"

"Enchanted," he admitted. And then, before her brows drew close in confusion and the brief moment of sparkling civility between them began to fade, he impulsively offered his elbow.

"What are you doing?" she asked, staring at it the way she might the tail of a scorpion.

"Offerin' me arm. Would ye like a tour o' the deck before ye go back to that boring life ye lead?"

She stared at his elbow for a long moment as though debating whether she could tolerate the idea of touching him. Then her mouth curved the tiniest bit at one corner, a reluctant smile that was gone as quickly as it appeared. "Only if you promise not to irritate me."

"Oh, lass, 'tis beyond me to make a promise like that," he returned with mock seriousness. "On the other hand, while I rather *like* to irritate ye, I'd rather save my real fighting for the Royal Navy if and when the occasion arises."

She was still staring at his offered elbow. Perhaps she was thinking the same thing he was: That she would not be here long. That soon enough, he would have the explosive and be on his way back to Boston and he would be a distant memory for her, as she would be for him.

"Might be the only chance ye ever get to tour the deck of a warship," he prompted.

She nodded, once. Then, raising her chin and refusing to look at him, she reached out her small gloved hand and slid it into the crook of his elbow.

Chapter Six

At about the same time his sister consented to a tour of the American Continental brig *Tigershark*, the Duke of Blackheath arrived at De Montforte House.

He was in a mood of sheer violence.

He had traveled hard throughout the day, and his temper was foul as he strode swiftly up the steps of the townhouse, handed his hat and gloves to the silent footman, and stalked menacingly toward the parlor where he found his brother Andrew, pale and gaunt, his russet eyes haunted as he stared down into a cup of steaming brew.

"What the devil are you doing here drinking coffee when you should be out looking for her?" he roared.

"Good afternoon to you too, brother."

"Has she been found? Where was she last seen? Why are you sitting here doing nothing?"

"I've been out looking for her since she went missing early last night," Andrew said hollowly. "So has Captain Lord and the admiral and every authority I can think to contact. She's disappeared into thin air."

"Not even dust just disappears into thin air. She has to be somewhere." Lucien's black eyes were savage in his harsh and commanding face, and the very walls seemed to shrink from his anger. "Has anyone been to inquire of Brookhampton?"

"Twice. He denies knowledge of her and told me to leave in no uncertain terms."

"So where the hell is she?"

Andrew raised tormented eyes that were red from lack of sleep. The suffering on his face mirrored that of his eldest brother's. "If I knew where she was, I wouldn't be sitting here."

Lucien took a deep and controlled breath. Panic clawed at his heart and he forced himself to take control of his temper, his emotions, his fear. He turned away so that Andrew would not see how close he was to losing his composure.

"Tell me exactly what happened."

Andrew tipped the back of his head against the sofa and looked up at the ornately plastered ceiling. "It was a fine evening," he began, telling Lucien about their arrival at Captain Lord's townhouse, Nerissa's supportive words and her moment of missing Perry, the planned exhibition out in the garden for which he'd asked her to watch from the safety of the house. "She went back inside. I demonstrated the explosive, came back into the house, and she was gone."

"That makes no sense whatsoever."

"Tell me something I don't already know."

"Was she angry with you? About anything?"

"A bit peeved that I was trying to protect her by sending her back inside, but not enough to desert me and run away."

"And this moment of missing Perry. You don't think she went to him to try and win him back, to change his mind about her?"

"Lucien, I've been there twice. He said he hasn't seen her."

"Did he even offer to help find her?"

Andrew looked down, his face tragic. "No. He did not."

The duke began to pace back and forth on the heavy Aubusson carpet. "Nothing happened to upset her, then. No reason for her to leave the house. There has got to be more to this than what is on the face of it."

Andrew, exhausted, just shook his head in defeat.

Lucien was persistent. "Who else was there at this demonstration? I presume it was a gathering of naval officers."

"Yes."

"And were they all accounted for? Did any of them remain in the house when you all went outside?"

"No, not a one."

"All servants and staff accounted for?"

"Yes."

Lucien swore under his breath and continued to pace.

"Wait," Andrew said, frowning. He looked up at his brother. "There *was* a fellow there who was a guest of Captain Lord and his wife. An Irishman. Mrs. Lord's brother, if I remember correctly. Captain Lord wasn't happy when he turned up, probably because I was demonstrating something that was supposed to be quite secret. There seemed to be a bit of a history between them. But he was a drunken idiot, a fool, and he left before the demonstration began. I can't imagine that—"

"Did he return?" Lucien asked sharply.

"No, but we were all frantic and out searching by then. Maybe he did come back while we were all out combing the streets and knocking on doors. I don't know. Honestly, Lucien, I don't think he's anyone to be concerned about. Didn't seem very bright, to be honest."

But Lucien's face had hardened like that of a marble bust. "I'll be the judge of that. Stay here in case anyone delivers any news. I'm going to Captain Lord's to pay him and his wife a visit."

❧

"And this," Captain O' Devir said, as genial a host as any officer in their own navy might be, "is a gun."

"It looks like a cannon to me."

"And so it is, lass. On land. But aboard ship, we call it a gun."

Nerissa, despite her resentment toward this man who had plucked her from her safe if not altogether happy life and brought her here, was quite glad of the support of his strong, unyielding arm beneath her hand though it would be a sunny day in December before she'd ever admit it. As they moved about the quarterdeck—well, that's what he said this part of the ship was called—she could feel the immense power of the sea beneath them, and every so often the brig rose on a particularly large swell rolling in from the west and she'd sink her fingers into that arm to keep her balance.

She felt less fearful of him, out here in the open. He had introduced her to his officers. He was polite and smiling, and surely he wouldn't dare accost her in front of his crew. The sunlight that filtered down through the clouds gave her a sense of security. Broad daylight. He was behaving like a gentleman. But oh, dear God, what would the night bring?

Hopefully a Royal Navy ship to rescue me before I have to find out.

The ship smashed through another deep swell. Nerissa clutched at Captain O' Devir's arm, but he seemed to suffer no such trouble keeping his footing. Neither did the many men she saw on deck, all going about tasks that were, for the most part, alien to her. Seamen, their hair long and caught in oiled pigtails, were busy scrubbing the deck with buckets of seawater, mops, and what looked like large round stones on the ends of poles; others were coiling lines, a young midshipman was supervising a small work crew around one of the guns, and tilting her head back she saw a few men high aloft, clinging like monkeys a hundred or so feet above her head as they stood on footropes and brought in a sail that seemed to scrape the clouds above. The sight made her dizzy, and her fingers tightened on her escort's arm. She wondered if her balance would become natural in such an unsteady setting should she remain here at length; but of course, she would not be here at length. Even now, she took comfort—and satisfaction—in the knowledge that Lucien would be turning the world upside down to rescue her.

Lucien.

But not Perry, who wouldn't care. Who probably wouldn't give a second thought to her disappearance.

"Are ye well, lass?"

She snapped herself back to the moment. "Well enough, considering I've fallen down a flight of stairs, been abducted by a madman, and find myself in primitive conditions while my reputation goes the way of a heavy rock thrown into a particularly shallow pond."

"Ah. Ye looked faraway there, for a moment."

"I'm fine."

"Bollocks."

She set her jaw and looked out over the endless waves parading toward them from off to her right. Starboard, her captor called it. "You have no respect for the fact that you're in the presence of a lady, do you?"

"Given I've got no practice in being in a lady's presence, no." He shrugged. "Got plenty of practice being in the presence of other kinds of females, though. But I'm sure ye don't care to hear about that."

"You're entirely correct. I do not."

"So why the sad look in those pretty blue eyes?"

"I just told you."

"And I don't believe ye."

"I don't care if you believe me or not. My business is my own and I don't care to share it with you."

He shrugged again and let it go. Dropped it the way he might discard a dirty plate and with no visible evidence that her rebuff bothered him in the least. But Nerissa wanted him to care. She wanted him to persist if only for the chance to deny him and withhold from him something he wanted. It was the only power she felt she had left.

She let go of his arm and moved to the side. He moved dutifully beside her, either because he figured it was the gentlemanly thing to do or because he was afraid she'd fling herself overboard. What did it matter? She wrapped her gloved hands around the rail. It was wet with spray that quickly soaked through the gloves, and looking ruefully down at them she realized that they were ruined. That they served no further purpose.

And that she really wanted to feel the cold seawater against her fingertips, the feel of the wind and sun against the bare skin of her hands, the smooth, varnished wood of the rail beneath her palms. She stripped off the gloves and threw them into the sea, and immediately felt less burdened.

Free.

The wind tore at her hair and the sea flung cold, hissing spray in her face. And in that moment Nerissa realized she felt more alive than she had in months, and certainly since well before Perry had broken off their engagement and told her he never wanted to see her or anyone in her family ever again.

Free.

Alive.

Captain O' Devir still stood beside her, scanning the horizon beneath a hand to shade his unfairly gorgeous eyes. She sneaked a furtive glance at him. He caught her eye and grinned.

"So who ye pinin' for, lass?"

She turned away and stared resolutely over the endless swells, loving the feel of the ship beneath her. It was almost like riding a spirited mare. Heady. Faintly dangerous. It gave her a sense of freedom.

"You are irritatingly persistent."

"Aye, that I am. 'Tis why I was sent here."

"I thought it was because you were the most audacious, foolish, and downright reckless captain in your so-called Navy."

He simply shrugged and raised a brow, still wearing that faint little smile. He was ignoring her barb and refusing to give it a response. Waiting. Patient in his persistence.

Damn him.

She sighed, her gaze on the distant horizon. "I was just thinking about someone I miss," she said, her pride losing out to the fact that she wanted his attention back after she'd so recently thrown it away. That she wanted him to care. Or that maybe she just needed to talk, to share a bit of her still-healing heart with someone who had pretended to care. Because of course, he didn't care. He didn't even know her.

He leaned down and rested his elbows atop the rail beside her, his hands dangling over the bow-wake as the brig pushed through the seas. He stood closer than she would have liked, but to step away would give him the satisfaction of knowing he was rattling her. She would not give him that.

He glanced over at her. "Did ye love him?"

"For a long time." She smeared her fingers, her delightfully bare fingers, through the fresh droplets of seawater dotting the varnished rail, quelling the urge to touch them to her mouth just to taste the salt. "But what does it matter, now? In the end, some people are not worth the time and heartache we put into even thinking about them, are they, Captain O' Devir?"

He remained looking out over the sea. "Indeed not."

"I don't even know why I'm telling you this. I vowed not to speak to you, and here we are conversing like old friends. I am determined to dislike you, no matter how charming you endeavor to be. You abducted me, for heaven's sake."

"If it's any consolation, it wasn't in my original plans."

"No?"

"I was actually plannin' to abduct yer brother. The inventor one who made this innovative new explosive. But I tend to think on me feet and when ye fell, well ... I figured ye were the far more advantageous hostage."

"You are very naive if you think that."

"And you are very naive if ye think otherwise. If yer family loves ye as much as ye claim, yer brother will give me the explosive with no questions asked if only to get ye back safe and sound. If he were here instead, he'd have no reason to. He could hold out as long as he felt like it. But rest assured, Sunshine, I'll have ye back t' yer family just as soon as my demands are met. The sooner I get what I crossed an ocean for, the sooner we both can get on with our lives."

"Your life won't be worth living once my brother the duke catches up to you." She relished the idea of that sweet eventuality. Or told herself she did. "That is, if there's anything left of you."

"Ehm, right." His lips were twitching. "The one who's going to strangle me with me own entrails."

"I can't believe you're not taking me seriously."

"Is he a sailor, this fearsome brother of yours, with a ship able to catch this one?"

"You think it's funny, do you?"

"Hilarious, actually."

"You won't be laughing when you're facing him from the sharp end of a sword. Lucien does not tolerate—"

There was a sudden cry from above. Turning and looking up, Nerissa sank her fingers into Captain O' Devir's arm in horror. One of the men working so high aloft had lost his footing and was now tumbling, down, down, down toward the sea, screaming as he fell.

"Man overboard!" cried the lookout, high above.

Before the sailor even landed with a splash in the cresting blue swells, Captain O' Devir was running to the side. "All men to stations! *Hard down!*" he roared.

The floundering man, helpless, quickly fell astern. The captain grabbed a hammock lashed under the rail and flung it overboard, obviously intending it to float down on the drowning man.

Chaos erupted as the crew rushed aft, anxious to help the man in the water.

Captain O' Devir's voice pierced the confusion. "*Silence fore and aft!*"

Lieutenant Morgan was gesturing wildly, grabbing a speaking trumpet to make his voice heard. "Ready about and stations for stays! Clear away the boat. Prepare to heave to!"

And then it hit her. That man out there struggling in the heavy seas, crying out for help as he went under, reappeared, went under again, was going to die. He was going to die right here with her watching, with all of them watching, and there wasn't a thing she could do but stand in helpless horror along with everyone else as the dark head that marked him fell further and further astern.

Captain O' Devir's voice roared through her horror. "*Square the mainyard and lower the boat!*"

Men ran to various lines. Orders were bawled. The brig was turning, coming around onto the other tack, retracing her course and closing the distance to the man in the water. He was now well off their larboard bow.

Even Nerissa could see that there was no way the boat could be lowered in time, no way that it would reach the drowning man before it was too late.

It was obvious the poor soul could not swim.

Captain O' Devir had long since reached the same conclusion. He had kicked off his boots, torn off his coat and waistcoat, and as the brig came up on the man, still well to windward of him, he climbed up on the rail and threw himself out into the sea.

Nerissa stood frozen. She did not want to see the man who had fallen, drown. She did not want to see Captain O' Devir fail in his attempt to save the poor fellow or, as much as she loathed him, succumb to the seas, himself. She did not like the fact that she cared about the fate of any of these American—and Irish—mariners who had had the audacity to take her from her family, right out from under her brother's nose and the presence of the top echelons of the Royal Navy.

But she did.

She *did* care.

Her heart in her throat, she watched as the captain swam with strong, steady strokes toward the man floundering in the water. The sailor was tiring, his desperate cries for help already fading as he tried futilely to reach the hammock, tossed up and down by the seas, some ten or fifteen feet away from him. But Captain O' Devir had the hammock now and he was pushing it toward the drowning man as he swam, calling encouragement to him in a strong, authoritative voice that brooked no argument.

"Hold tight, there, McGuire, ye clumsy gobshite. I've almost got ye."

As she stood frozen, she felt the motion of the brig changing. The ship nosed back into the wind and slowed, the great sails above thundering in protest; more shouted commands, men around her hauling on thick lines while she tried to stand out of the way, the hush of water beneath them stilling until there was only the lonely sound of the wind whistling through lines and flapping sails and a low murmur from the crew, watching anxiously from their stations.

"We'll let the wind carry us down on them," said someone beside her, and tearing her gaze from the drama in the water ahead and off to larboard, Nerissa saw young Mr. Cranton. "He'll be all right. Captain O' Devir's not going to let a man drown, I can tell you that."

Nerissa nodded, her lower lip caught between her teeth as she watched the drama unfold. The captain had reached the stricken man and hooking an arm across the hammock to anchor himself, was now pulling him up and over it, holding him there across it so he would not slip back into the seas that undulated like a live thing all around them. She marveled at his strength. His courage. His selfless devotion to a subordinate.

The brig continued to drift helplessly down on the pair, moving up and down, up and down on a vast expanse of hard blue water while her captain, one arm still locked around the motionless sailor on the hammock, kicked his way toward his waiting command.

It was all done with orderly neatness; lines were thrown down to the men in the water, and first the sailor was hauled up, a dozen hands reaching for his lifeless body as he was quickly brought aboard and laid on the deck. A stooped, gaunt man came rushing up from below; she heard Cranton say he was the surgeon. He got on his knees beside McGuire, rolled him onto his stomach, and began to work on him until he coughed, vomited seawater, and weakly began to move. A great cheer went up from his shipmates and immediately, they picked the poor fellow up and carried him below, the doctor at his side.

A few moments later, Captain O' Devir was back aboard the ship with the aid of a rope thrown down for him to scale, his inky black hair streaming water down his broad back, the shirt plastered wetly to the skin beneath, his angular features and prominent cheekbones defined all the more with his hair soaked and flattened to his skull. Someone pressed a towel into his hand, and he scrubbed vigorously at his face and hair for a moment before looking up; at that moment, his intense, purple-violet gaze met Nerissa's through those absurdly long black lashes and something tingled in her belly. Lodged itself in her heart. He had said nothing, and yet with that look, he had said everything.

He winked roguishly at her. She flushed and dropped her gaze.

"Back the tops'ls, bring her about and continue on our previous course," he said to Lieutenant Morgan, and tossing the towel over the quarterdeck railing, turned and walked away.

And Nerissa found herself staring after him, looking at his broad, tapered back through the drenched transparency of his shirt, the line of his powerful thighs and calves through the soaked white breeches, as he strode to the hatch and, following the procession bearing the hapless sailor, went below.

Chapter Seven

Captain Christian Lord was just returning from an appointment at the Admiralty when, upon entering the ornate London townhouse he'd rented while awaiting his next command, he was given the news by a servant that the Duke of Blackheath was waiting for him in the parlor.

He didn't blink an eye. He knew, of course, why the duke was here.

He had first met Lucien de Montforte many months before when he'd been selected by Admiralty to carry out a dangerous rescue mission to get the duke's brother Charles, and family friend Lord Brookhampton, out of France. The mission had ended in success, a life-threatening injury to His Grace, and Christian's vow that he would never again allow a member of the aristocracy aboard his command.

Oh, yes, he knew what this was about.

He gave his fancy gold laced hat to the servant and grim-faced, went to meet the duke.

Lucien de Montforte, however, was already coming out of the parlor to meet him.

"Captain Lord."

"Your Grace."

"You know why I'm here."

"I'd be a fool if I didn't."

The two men returned to the parlor. Christian poured a glass of brandy for the duke, and another for himself. He was going to need it.

Blackheath, his face lined with tension, wasted no time in getting straight to the point.

"Tell me everything you know about your brother-in-law."

Christian sat down, wondering where to begin. Roddy. Brazen, reckless, proud, foolish, Roddy. Never in a million years would he think his wife's older brother would have reason for or interest in harming Lady Nerissa. But Roddy was gone. Lady Nerissa was gone. And that brought him to only one conclusion, one that pained him to even think about because of the hurt it would bring to his wife. It couldn't be Roddy. There was no rhyme or reason for it. But what other conclusion could any sane person reach? He had exhausted all possibilities and leads. He felt numb from trying to make sense of the senseless. It was easier to just answer the question than to keep letting his mind go round and round in an empty pursuit, to try and figure out why Lady Nerissa had disappeared from his own house—a mystery that he, Elliott and those to whom he was closest had been trying to solve since she'd gone missing after the demonstration last night.

He took a long, bracing swallow of his drink.

"Roddy O' Devir," he began, staring down into his glass. "Press-ganged by the Royal Navy back in '62 from his native home in Connacht." Christian pursed his lips. Did it matter that he himself had been the young lieutenant who'd led that press gang? "Disappeared in the Service for thirteen years, but managed to jump ship sometime before things got hot in Boston and set himself up as a successful smuggler calling himself the Irish Pirate. Got in tight with Adams, Warren and Hancock, and they had him smuggling arms into the Boston area.

He was a local hero. A dangerous complication. I was sent to apprehend him by my brother Elliott, and did so under the command of Sir Geoffrey Lloyd."

The duke leveled his inscrutable black stare on him. "So there is good reason to believe he hates the Royal Navy, if not the English."

"He was press-ganged. His father was long dead, and that left his sister and mother to fend for themselves. Yes, he most certainly harbored a good deal of resentment toward us and that's putting it mildly."

The duke gave a barely imperceptible nod, his hooded gaze intent. Hard. Penetrating. Christian noticed that he had not touched his drink.

"He was a thorn in our side. The last thing General Gage in Boston needed was an armed populace, and O' Devir was supplying them with not only arms, but food, supplies, everything that couldn't be brought in through the closed port of Boston. He was making a laughingstock out of the Royal Navy. Someone figured I could get the job done."

"And did you?"

"Yes." *But not without cost.* "I did."

"Why wasn't he hanged?"

Christian swirled his drink. He would not disclose the truth, even to the duke. "He escaped. Went back to Ireland with his sister and that was the last I saw of him until he showed up here last week."

"Why was he not apprehended then?"

Christian leveled his own gaze on the duke. "He *is* my wife's brother. And I deemed him quite harmless."

"He's still a traitor to his king."

Christian just took another sip of his brandy.

The duke was persistent. "What was he doing in Ireland all this time? And was he even *in* Ireland?"

"Damned if I know. He had a cottage near the sea. A small farm. I assume he was tending to it, trying to eke a living out of it. His father was a fisherman. Perhaps he was doing that. Once I went back and claimed Deirdre, I didn't really know or care what happened to him."

"And you haven't heard from him since?"

"Not until he showed up here last week saying he wanted to met my son. Colin is his nephew. I didn't think it all that unusual." Christian shook his head. "Roddy O' Devir is many things, Your Grace, but he's not someone who would ever harm a woman, and I can't think of a single reason why he'd have an interest in your sister. There's no motive for him to abduct her. And yet...."

Blackheath's penetrating black stare was on him. "What?"

"I sent him off before your brother demonstrated the explosive. He had no business being there—the explosive was secret, something that the fewer people outside the Navy knew about, the better. Besides, there was a chance, albeit slim, that one of the officers in attendance that night might've recognized him and dragged him right back into the Navy or worse, managed to get him hanged. He was a deserter. For his own good and the continuing happiness of my wife, he was best not being there. I asked him to leave, and he did."

"And where was my sister during this time?"

"Lord Andrew was concerned for her well-being in case the explosive proved unstable or fiercer than he expected it to be, so he sent her back into the house."

"And O' Devir was gone by then?"

"I saw him leave."

"And is there anyone here in London whom he might know, anyone with whom he might be staying?"

Christian shook his head. "He's Irish. There's nothing and nobody here for him, except for us."

"And yet he has not come back. Neither has my sister. That tells you something, doesn't it, Lord?"

"It tells me that two people are missing and not just

one." He drained the last of his drink and set the glass wearily down. "And before you ask, yes, I've scoured London for him. He's disappeared without a trace."

Blackheath pursed his lips, thinking. He had barely touched his brandy. He looked directly at Christian. "Are you're sure he stayed in Ireland?"

"At the moment, I'm not sure of anything."

"Because I'm wondering if he went right back to America and picked up where he left off."

"Well, even if he did, it doesn't explain why Lady Nerissa is missing or what he could possibly want with her." Christian sighed and kneaded his brow. "In any case, it hasn't even been twenty-four hours since they both disappeared. He probably went out on the town and spent the day lying drunk in a gutter somewhere. It wouldn't surprise me if he shows up for tea in another hour or so and has no idea that any of this is going on."

Blackheath steepled his fingers and leaned his brow against them. He said nothing, just thinking. After a long moment he picked up his glass and drained it. He put the vessel down, rubbed at his noble forehead with one elegant finger, and stood up. His eyes were fierce. As black and cold as a winter night.

"Thank you, Captain Lord. It seems I have work to do. I will be staying at de Montforte House here in Town. Send word immediately to me should this brother-in-law of yours show up for tea or show up at all. I have a hunch that he will not."

Christian got up and walked him to the door. "I still don't think he did it."

"You are too close to the family to be objective in your judgment. Time and perseverance will tell whether or not you are wrong. And if he did do it, I can promise you this." The duke's black eyes were chilling as he looked over his shoulder on the way out the door. "He's a dead man."

❧

Lucien went directly to Perry's townhouse himself, though his every instinct told him that he was on the wrong scent. That Nerissa's disappearance had nothing to do with her former betrothed and everything to do with Captain Lord's rebel brother-in-law who, whether or not he was responsible for Nerissa's absence, should have had his neck stretched back in Boston the minute he'd been apprehended as this so-called Irish Pirate.

Perry received him coldly. He was deep in his cups, sullen, and clearly annoyed at what he said, in no uncertain terms, was harassment when he'd already told Andrew all he knew—which was nothing. Disgusted by both his attitude and his lack of concern for the woman he had once purported to love, Lucien went to the Admiralty and spent the rest of the waning day poring over naval records and dispatches from the spring of 1775, trying to learn all he could about Roddy O' Devir and any clues or insights he could glean as to the man's character. There was a flurry of information about him from the time, but in the years since, nothing.

It was hard not to conclude that he really had gone back to—and stayed in—Ireland. If he was anything like Captain Lord had described him—a braggart, a man who loved attention—surely he would have resumed his identity as the Irish Pirate.

But there was nothing more here.

Nothing.

It was dark by the time Lucien finished poring over old log books, dispatches, naval orders. He left the Admiralty and made his way home, feeling more frustrated, powerless, and increasingly afraid, than he had ever been in his life.

Andrew met him at the door. He was as eager for news from Lucien as Lucien was eager to hear that Nerissa had come safely home. Andrew's face fell when his infallible, seemingly omniscient brother returned empty-handed. Lucien seeing it, turned wordlessly away and headed upstairs. He was failing his sister. He was failing his family. He needed time alone.

To think.

He went to bed with nothing in his stomach but black coffee, tossed and turned and stared up into the darkness until he finally fell asleep sometime in the wee hours, and was up at first light, ready to pound on doors and call in favors. He strode into the dining room and found Andrew already there, his face haggard as he watched a footman pour tea into his cup and put a plate before him.

The footman began to set a plate down in front of Lucien. He put up a hand and gave a barely perceptible shake of his head. The footman took it away.

And the butler entered.

"This just came for you, Lord Andrew."

The butler offered a silver tray to his brother, on which lay a folded piece of vellum. Andrew's gaze met Lucien's as he took it and slit the seal. Lucien was already on his feet and coming around the table, looking over his brother's shoulder as Andrew opened the letter and both began to read:

To Lord Andrew de Montforte,

By now, all of London must know of the disappearance of your sister. While you're all turning the city inside out in your search for her, I thought I'd make things a little easier for you. The lady is with me, and in return for the explosive that you invented—as well as the formula on how to make it—you can have her back, unharmed.

I will expect these demands to be met at the port of Saint-Malo in France, where my agents will be waiting to make the trade at noon this coming Saturday at Le Cheval de la Mer tavern. You will know them as they will greet you with the code word, "America." They will know you as you will be wearing black coats and red waistcoats and there will be no more than two of you. Do not come armed, as my men will be stationed in places that defy your knowledge. Do not attempt to trick me, or you'll never see your sister again.

Further details will be forthcoming.

Failure to comply with my request will, of course, merit the lady's future unpredictable.

My regards to both yourself and the Duke.

—Captain Ruaidri O' Devir, of the American Continental Navy

Rage burned behind Lucien's eyes. His hunch had been right. This wretched bucket of Irish scum had *his little sister*, thought he was calling the shots, and was about to find that his days, indeed, his hours, were sharply numbered.

They said that death didn't hurt.

Lucien would make sure, very sure, that it did.

His eyes savage, he shoved the missive into his pocket and called for his horse.

❧

Two hours later, a black coach drawn by two grey cobs stopped within the courtyard of an esteemed brick building facing Whitehall and discharged its occupant just outside the great portico and the four tall columns that supported it. The man hurried purposely up the stairs between the two innermost ones and into the Admiralty.

It was a building he knew well. Three stories of brick built in the shape of a horse-shoe, it was the seat of Britain's naval power.

Hat under his arm, he strode down the corridors of

that hallowed institution. Another might have taken time to admire the beautiful architecture, the gilt-framed paintings of naval battles and heroes, but not him. Beeswax and polished floors. Elaborate plaster-work, high ceilings, men in uniform bustling past, some grim-faced, some wearing an expression of harried impatience. Admiralty's stately tradition and formality suited Captain Lawrence Hadley the Fourth quite well. He was a naval man, as his father and grandfathers had been before him, and the awe he'd felt when first visiting the Admiralty as a youngster had long since faded into one of perpetual but well-disguised dread as he wondered what its fate would have in store for him this day. Resplendent in a gold-laced uniform so starched and carefully pressed that it appeared he'd been poured into it, he was shown by a young lieutenant into an office lit with dingy London sun struggling to get through the grime and soot on the opposite side of the window.

"Larry," said the portly gentleman who looked up at him from behind a massive desk. "Do sit down."

"I'd prefer to stand, sir."

"Sit down, damn your eyes, and make haste about it."

Rear-Admiral Lawrence Hadley the Third was in his mid-sixties and the effects of drink—florid cheeks, heavy jowls, a nose gone bulbous and red over a mouth stretched tight with pain—were showing. This morning he had an overall jaundiced look about him beneath his carefully powdered and curled wig which meant, quite likely, that whatever reason he'd summoned his son wasn't a particularly good one.

The older man shuffled through some papers while Hadley dragged up a chair. He knew that his esteemed sire wasn't demanding him to take a seat just to put him at ease. Oh, no. the miserable old bugger had injured his neck in a fall aboard his flagship five years past, and the rheumatism was setting in. It pained him to look up at anyone standing, and the drink he sought to dull the constant ache in his neck and shoulders was doing him no favors, though his mind was as sharp and bilious as ever.

Lawrence the younger took a seat, feeling his starched waistcoat all but cracking as he did.

"Hello, Father."

"No time for formalities, Larry, no time." The old man shoved a sheet of vellum across the desk at him. "We have a problem."

"A problem?"

"His Grace the Duke of Blackheath brought this to us earlier. It's a note his family received this morning. Read it, please."

The younger man's eyes, steady and showing no emotion, flicked up once to his father's before he reached out and took the paper. As he read it, his cheeks flushed in outrage.

"What utter *rubbish* is this?" he howled, his cultured polish momentarily forgotten as he lunged to his feet. "Continental *Navy*? What navy? Damn their eyes! America remains part of Britain, and any 'navy' they proclaim to have is nothing but a pack of treasonous rebels with necks just itching for the noose." He shoved the vellum back across the desk. "I'll give them the damned noose, starting with *this* rogue!"

"Sit down, Larry. When you have composed yourself, we will talk."

Larry sat, eyes blazing.

"This is not only an embarrassment, it is a matter of international importance," his father continued. "Obviously, an explosive such as the one Lord Andrew de Montforte has developed cannot end up in the wrong hands, and it certainly cannot end up in the hands of the Americans or God help us, the French. We need this traitor found and brought to heel. *Immediately.*" He lowered his head, looking up at his son in a way that was meant to convey the gravity of the situation. "The military repercussions aside, I trust you understand the other *sensitivity* of the matter ... ladies, especially the sisters of dukes, have reputations and all that."

Reputations that would be blown as sky-high as anything her brother's explosive could destroy should anyone find out she was being held captive by some American pirate who would have wasted no time debauching her, Hadley thought sourly. He didn't even know the lady but he had sisters, and the idea of something like this happening to them made him see red.

"First John Paul Jones, and now this one. Is there any end to the audacity of these rebels?"

"Apparently not."

"Someone needs to put an end to this."

"*You* will put an end to it, Larry. You manage to bring Lady Nerissa home safe and sound and exterminate this vermin in the bargain, 'twill all but guarantee you both promotion and the word "Sir" in front of your name. His Grace is close to the King. You save his sister, George will knight you."

....And maybe the duke will give me his sister's hand as a token of his own appreciation, Larry mused, always one to open the door when opportunity came knocking.

His father was shaking his head. "Of all people in England to abduct, this arrogant rascal had to choose the Duke of Blackheath's sister. The Duke of *Blackheath*? My God! There's not a man in England I'd be less inclined to want as an enemy. Lord Sandwich himself came to me with this letter, and I don't often see him, the First Lord of the Admiralty, looking nervous, but he was as white as the hair of my wig, and y'know why, Larry? Because he's thinking he doesn't want Blackheath as an enemy, either." He reached under his desk, opened a drawer, and slammed a half-consumed bottle of gin onto the desk, then went back to rooting for a glass. "I am assigning you the frigate *Happenstance*.

She's here in London, already fitted out for another mission which isn't one iota as important as this one, and fully manned. You'll need a swift, well-armed ship that'll be more than a match for anything the Frogs might send against you in case they decide to shelter or protect this scoundrel. Bring the explosive and make the exchange. And bring back not only the lady, but the rascal who abducted her as well, preferably with his head on the end of a pike." The thin mouth tightened as he looked up through the knobs of flesh that supported his graying eyebrows, pinning his son with a look of intent. "Is that understood?"

Larry got to his feet and snapped off a salute. "Consider it done," he said, thinking how nice "Sir Lawrence" sounded, and turning on his heel, swiftly exited the office.

There was not a moment to lose.

❧

Nerissa's fears about where Captain O' Devir would spend the night had been unfounded.

After the poor seaman had fallen from the rigging yesterday and been brought below, she had felt overwhelmed by both her situation, the lingering effects of her fall, and the near-horror of what she had just witnessed. Though the protection of Captain O' Devir was dubious, that of his crew was even more so and when, after a quarter hour had passed and he still hadn't returned, she had retreated to the cabin and spent the rest of the afternoon napping in his cot. Night had fallen. A boy had come in to light a lantern and bring her a tray with something on it that might have been food, and she had been left alone once more.

And now it was morning. Her second one here.

Maybe, just maybe, that Irish rogue was just a little bit honorable, after all. He could have come into the cabin and had his way with her last night. But he had not.

She had spent the night alone.

She felt an unwelcome softening toward him. Far better to loathe him. To consider him the monster she wanted to believe him to be, even though reason and the soothing glow of daylight told her that no monster would have risked his life to save a drowning seaman, and no monster would have left her untouched while she was alone and vulnerable in his cabin.

But one couldn't stay in a cabin forever.

And she was hungry.

Her stomach growling, Nerissa tried the door to the cabin and found it unlocked. It opened onto the deck and hesitantly, she stepped out into the sunshine.

Salt-laced wind, the plunging up-and-down of the ship, the hiss of spray against the bows, the taste of it in the air. It was a glorious morning and she felt good, very good, to be alive. She saw a group of rough-looking, pig-tailed seamen leaning backwards on a line that led aloft, bracing a sail under the watchful eye of Lieutenant Morgan. A few others sat in the shadow of the foremast some distance away, mending a sail. They grinned and elbowed each other at her appearance, making no secret of the fact that they found her presence here amusing at best and an imposition at worst. Captain O' Devir was nowhere to be seen, and she wasn't sure if that was a blessing or not.

She looked around her, wondering what to do with herself. She could watch the crew go about their various collective and individual duties, but she did not want to get in the way of the running of the ship; it would be best to just watch from a distance. But where? She made her way to some shade created by one of the great square sails above and looked about for a place to sit, her balance unsteady as the ship rose and fell in great rolling motions beneath her. Someone was approaching; it was the young, ginger-haired midshipman, bobbing like a schoolboy and reddening beneath a sea of freckles and a tan that was more burn than brown. He had an earnest, smiling face made slightly comical by the slight crookedness of an upper front tooth, and was garbed in a scaled-down version of Captain O' Devir's blue-and-white uniform, its sleeves too short and the seams stretched at the shoulders; obviously, the youngster had already outgrown it since someone, presumably far across the blue, blue Atlantic, had made it for him.

"Midshipman Cranton, my lady." He attempted a bow, probably the clumsiest she had ever received, but endearing in its sincerity. She returned his attempt at gallantry with a smile. "The captain asked me to see if you needed anything. Come with me, and I'll find you something to sit on."

"Thank you," she said simply, and accepted his elbow. As they began to walk, she was aware of the crew pausing in their tasks and staring, one or two elbowing each other and smirking. Were women that scarce aboard ships that her very presence attracted such attention?

"Pay them no mind, Your Ladyship," the young officer said beside her. "Most of these tars have never seen a real lady before, let alone one as—I beg your pardon—as pretty as you."

Now her escort was blushing. He was just a boy pretending to be a man, trying to live up to the uniform he wore with such pride. She knew that pretense, she knew that pride; after all, she had four brothers. As for the crew, she didn't know whether to give them a haughty glare above a loftily carried chin, avoid their stares, or smile to acknowledge their interest in the hopes they'd then find something else to look at. She had little experience with such rough, common folk in general and sailors in particular.

Another thing from which her brothers had sheltered her all of her life—rubbing elbows with the great unwashed, the teeming multitudes that made this dirty, chaotic, rough-and-tumble world beyond the pristine walls that contained and protected her own existence, run.

Midshipman Cranton escorted her to a nearby deckhouse. "Sorry, my lady. Being a warship and all, we don't exactly have chairs on deck, but if you sit here, and hold onto this here rope if you feel a bit unsteady, you'll be safe, secure, and in the shade."

"Thank you."

"Would you like me to fetch you a hat? We don't have anything fancy, but I'm sure I can find something to keep the sun off your face."

"You are very kind, Mr. Cranton."

Having seated her he retreated a step, smiling and clutching his hands behind his back, obviously uncomfortable but blushing a bit beneath the praise. "I was raised right, my lady. My ma taught me manners and just because I'm on a ship doesn't mean I've forgotten them. I know you probably think we Americans are a low and awful sort, but we're not."

She smiled, despite herself. "Actually, my more uncharitable thoughts are directed toward a certain Irishman aboard this ship, not the Americans." She looked ruefully down at her skirts, the expensive blue-green silk now wrinkled and stained by the spray of foam and seawater, her fine shoes wet and ruined. "Three of my sisters-in-law are American."

"And my ma, she was English. Devonshire lass, she was. Worked for a high lady there before she married a sailor and off they went to Philadelphia." He shrugged, not knowing what else to say. "I guess we're all in this together, aren't we?"

She smiled, for he was trying his best to put her at ease and it would be nice to have a friend here even if her stay was likely to be a short one.

"Some, not by their own choosing," she allowed, with a sigh.

"I'll fetch you that hat now, my lady," he said, and strode hurriedly off, leaving her alone once more.

Ignoring the curious stares of the men around her, she looked past the stout, varnished wood of the mainmast and off over the starboard bows. She had never been aboard a ship before, and the experience was actually proving to be quite novel, even rather exciting, now that she was increasingly confident that her captor meant her no harm. The twin rows of guns on either side of the vessel only emphasized the fact that Captain O' Devir wasn't playing at being in a navy, and punctuated the reality that he would do what he must to accomplish his objectives. She bit her lip. Best not to think about how he would bring them about.

An image of him walking away after rescuing the sailor yesterday rose in her mind, of how his wet, dripping clothes had emphasized the hard lines and muscles of his back, his thighs. Of how he had looked up as though he knew just what she was thinking, and winked at her.

She blushed. Best not to think about Captain O' Devir, either....

Instead, she gazed off across the dark blue water, ruffled by foam and whitecaps like the lace on a lady's gown and saw, far off in the distance, a coastline that looked almost purple in the haze. France, she imagined. Soon enough, a Royal Navy vessel would fill the horizon and blast Ruaidri O' Devir and his ship of misguided Yankees to Kingdom Come. Soon enough, she would be returned to her family, and Lucien would hastily marry her off to not only save her reputation from the damage this shocking event will have caused but because, in his mind, enough would be enough.

Lucien.

Marriage.

And to someone of his choosing, not hers. Someone who could never be Perry. Someone to whom she would dutifully provide an heir to preserve a bloodline as old or noble as her own, someone to share—if she was fortunate, as most aristocratic matches were ones of lonely separateness once the heir was produced—a life of constant parties, fashion, *ton* gossip, and cultured domesticity. She was a female. Her dowry would be huge, and though she knew Lucien would never saddle her to someone completely objectionable, he would be all the more determined to see her married after the shocking scandal of her abduction.

The predictable hopelessness of her future suddenly crystallized into a hard, bitter seed that took root in her consciousness, and she felt an unexpected tear in her eye. Back to her sheltered life, she was destined to go. Back to being protected, being pampered, being treated as the china doll that could not be dropped or broken or taken out of its beautiful presentation box.

She turned her face to the wet, salty breeze, catching a bit of foam on her cheek as she did and filling her lungs with the headiest and most delicious air they had ever known.

The china doll that could not be allowed to truly *live*.

In that moment, Lady Nerissa de Montforte found herself more depressed than she'd been since Perry, whose indecision and waffling had set Lucien to the meddling that had made everything go wrong, had broken their betrothal.

Movement, at her shoulder. She turned and looked up and there was Captain O' Devir, clad in a clean dry shirt and white breeches. He had enough height that he blocked out the sun behind him, and it occurred to her that he probably chose to stand where he did, just to shield her from its bright and burning rays.

Maybe he was just a little bit of a gentleman, after all.

"Well," she said, almost to herself. "At least there is nothing *indecisive* about you, Captain O' Devir."

"Beggin' yer pardon?"

"I'm just musing."

"Indecision on the part of a ship's captain will get him and his men killed. No room for it at sea. Here." He brought one hand out from behind his back, and she saw then that he was holding a large straw hat adorned with a bright blue ribbon. He presented it with a bow and a flourish, as though she were a queen and he was laying the world at her feet.

"You'll have to forgive Midshipman Cranton," he said amiably. "I saw him headed topside with this and knew he intended it for you. Couldn't let him one-up me, y'know."

"Wasn't it his to give?"

"He has duties to be about, and being a lady's maid is beneath his training."

She smiled and took the hat. "But not beneath yours, I see."

He laughed, and something in his intense, long-lashed violet eyes struck and warmed a part of her soul, threw sunlight on that hard, bitter seed that was her life, her future, and caused it to open. In that moment, she realized she was actually glad—well, a little bit glad, anyhow—to see him. That the depression she'd felt a few moments earlier had lifted with his arrival. Well, fancy that. This rough and virile Irishman had, with no obvious intent, made her react to him as a woman does to a man, which was both foolish and impossible, of course—he was far beneath her in class, totally unsuitable, and besides, he'd abducted her and was her enemy.

Wasn't he?

No. Don't even think it, Nerissa. Don't.

But she *was* thinking it. Thinking that his mouth was sculpted and sensual, firm and commanding and not always hard, and she wondered what it would be like to be kissed by that mouth even if it was beneath hers in class, totally unsuitable, and yes, possessed by her enemy.

Nerissa Louise de Montforte, what in the name of the living God is wrong *with you?*

It must be the sea air. Hunger. The stress of being abducted. Or maybe that fall down the stairs had addled her brain.

When she made no move to put the hat on, he stepped closer and gently did it himself. His fingers, rough, scarred and calloused, brushed against her skin as he tied it beneath her chin and it was only after he spoke that she realized, much to her humiliation, that she'd been holding her breath.

"You can breathe now, Lady Nerissa," he said softly. "I'm really not about t' ravish ye."

Your eyes say otherwise, she wanted to say. *And I don't believe I'd detest it as much as I think I might.*

She had to get away from him. Her brain was out of control, her heart fluttering and tripping all over itself, her skin hot and flushed. She felt vulnerable. Exposed. Afraid that he could very well read her mind. She did not trust her thoughts. Did not want to hear them.

"Nerissa," he murmured, his head cocked slightly to one side as though seeing her for the first time. A smile tugged at the corner of his mouth. "Nerissa, who's not seasick despite never bein' aboard a ship, Nerissa who loves the taste of the sea on her lips and tongue, Nerissa whose eyes sparkle as she looks over the rollin' swells, whose spirit is comin' alive beneath me eyes because she's in her element, she is. Nerissa. I should have known."

"That's Lady Nerissa, to you," she snapped. "And known what?"

"Your name. Don't ye know? It means 'sea nymph.'"

"It's taken from a character in a Shakespeare play," she shot back, uncomfortably. "The Merchant Of Venice."

"A sea sprite. Uh-huh. Explains everythin', it does."

She stood up. Her knees were weak and she gripped her hands together to keep them from shaking. "Thank you for the hat, Captain O' Devir. And now, if you don't mind, I would like to go back to the cabin to ... to rest."

"Stay up here and enjoy the fresh air. 'Tis good for the soul, it is."

"You won't bother me?"

"Am I botherin' ye?"

Yes, in ways you can't even begin to imagine. She saw the twinkle in his eye. *Or maybe you can.*

She looked away. "No," she said, unable to meet his gaze. "You are not."

She sat back down. She really didn't want to go back to the cabin and be cooped up there when out here, her spirit soared and her blood sang and she felt wonderfully, gloriously, alive.

"Were ye comfortable last night?"

"Comfortable enough."

"I'll have someone bring ye somethin' to eat, if ye're up to it. Ye must be hungry."

"Thank you." She watched a young boy go forward to ring the ship's bell, presumably to signal the end of a watch. "And how is the poor man who fell from the rigging yesterday?"

He looked at her, his eyes warming in appreciation that she even cared. "Well now, thank ye for askin', lass. He's doin' well. Couple of cracked ribs, but he'll live to do it again another day, I wager."

You were very brave to jump in after him, she wanted to say. *You could have drowned, yourself. And I wish I could get the memory of you out of my mind. Your body hard and soaking wet beneath your clothes, your muscled arms and shoulders outlined beneath the dripping fabric. That knowing wink.*

He was looking at her in a way that made her very, very aware of him as a man.

And very, very aware of her unwarranted response to him.

"Maybe I'd better go back to the cabin," she said. *If only for my own good.*

He looked at her thoughtfully. She had a feeling he knew exactly why she wanted to put distance between them. But he said nothing, only nodded, and offering his arm, escorted her aft.

Chapter Eight

Ruaidri had found plenty of ways to keep himself occupied and away from his hostage for the rest of the afternoon. He'd discussed their mission with Lieutenant Morgan and his officers over coffee in the wardroom. He'd gone down to check on the hapless McGuire, who was nursing two busted ribs and a blow to his pride. He'd have liked to have set the hands to gun drill until he was satisfied that these American tars under his command were every bit as sharp as the British ones with whom he'd once bitterly served, but out here in the English Channel where the Royal Navy was thicker than fleas on a cat, he had no desire to call attention to their presence as he awaited their Saturday rendezvous. Instead he ordered sail drill, pushing the men hard and rewarding them with extra grog. He watched Lieutenant Morgan give young Midshipman Cranton his evening instruction in navigation. He ate his own now-cold supper standing up, watching the sun sink beneath the horizon and choking down the dry eggs and blackened toast. Night closed in. The stars came out. Restless, he made his way to the quarterdeck rail.

Nerissa.

Sea nymph.

As captain the quarterdeck was his domain, forbidden ground to all but the highest of command. Ruaidri wanted to be alone. He needed to think, because he hated the English, had to keep a clear head, and the young Englishwoman who even now slept innocently in his cabin was getting under his skin in ways that rattled him.

Nerissa.

Sea nymph.

Oh, for the love of Christ. There were times when his Irish soul ran to the poetic, the fanciful, the stuff of spirit. Useless shite in a sea warrior. He had no time or use for such sentimental rubbish. What was he thinking, that just because she'd been given a name that would forever tie her to the sea, that she was his destiny?

It was just a name.

Coincidence.

He sent his mind in the other direction, toward his loathing of the English in an attempt to focus on what was important. It had been years—seventeen of them, actually—since he'd been a young lad back in Connemara. He'd followed his late father into the fishing trade, he, Deirdre and their mam forcing a meager living off land owned by a distant Englishman. Lord This or That, he did not remember, did not want to remember. But the memories of that awful day were still with him. He, young and strong and proud, rebellious even, and thinking himself invincible. But nobody was invincible when it came to England's insatiable thirst for men to sail and fight its warships, men who were expendable, men who weren't given a choice in the matter, simply a cudgel in exchange for any resistance.

He had, of course, resisted. But he and the other lads with whom he'd hidden that day when the British man o' war had come into the bay had been betrayed by one of their own and he had, through the ringing in his ears, the pounding in his head after he and the cudgel had made each other's acquaintance, been dragged off with the others to the waiting warship, the desperate cries of his little sister, only nine years old, fading off behind him.

He'd been called "Roddy" then, a childhood name that the lads had given him as an acronym for his initials. Or so they said. In reality, it was because such an English-sounding nickname was guaranteed to stoke both his Irish temper and his fists, and they liked a good fight as much as he did. He couldn't fight his way out of the nickname though, and eventually the name had stuck.

And stuck for far too long.

It was an arse of a nickname, and not at all suitable for the direction his life had taken in the years since he'd ended his days as the Irish Pirate. He was a commissioned naval officer now. He'd needed a name that called for more dignity, one that shed any ties to Englishness, one that left his painful past behind. One that begged for a return to his roots. Ruaidri, his da and mam had named him some thirty-two years ago. A good, strong, Irish name, after the ancient kings of Connacht.

His own.

Aye, he might have forgiven Christian for leading that press gang all those years ago because he was only doing his duty, but he had never forgiven the English in general or the Royal Navy in particular for the years of hell spent aboard one warship after another, where he'd learned about the tail end of the cat, the bos'n's free hand with punishment, sadistic young shites that were the midshipmen, lieutenants who aspired to be captains and captains who fancied themselves one step down from God himself.

He hated the English.

God, he hated—

"Captain O' Devir?"

Her voice startled him from his reverie. He turned and saw Lady Nerissa de Montforte, she of sunshine and sea nymphs, standing a few feet behind him in the darkness. He scowled.

"I'm sorry to disturb you, Captain. Are you quite well?"

"Aye, of course. Why wouldn't I be?"

"You looked so sad, standing there."

"I'm fine," he said a bit more curtly than he intended. "What can I do for ye?"

She cleared a silky hank of long blonde hair from her eyes. "My pride has lost the battle with my appetite, I'm afraid. I come to you in defeat."

"Ye're hungry?"

She sighed. "Famished."

"I sent down supper. Did ye not eat it?"

She looked down, unable to meet his eyes, and he suddenly understood. No doubt she couldn't stomach whatever his cook, who was as useless as tits on a bull, had sent her. Spoiled aristocrat. He bet she'd never had to live on the broth of potatoes, fish and onions just to quell the screaming of a hungry belly. He bet she'd never had to....

The thought died in his head. She was a lady. A feckin' *lady*, for Christ's sake. L-A-D-Y *lady*. She couldn't help the circumstances of her birth any more than he could help his own. It was not her fault she'd had more of absolutely everything in one day of being the daughter of an English duke than he'd had in fourteen years of being the son of a poor Irish fisherman.

He sighed, feeling like a sack of shite.

"Dirty spoon again?" he asked, trying to strike a note of humor.

She shrugged and joined him at the rail, not too close, but near enough that they could converse. He found his gaze resting on her small hands. On the fancy white lace that fell from her elbow, fluttering over her wrists and emphasizing her fine bones and innate elegance.

"Slimy gruel?"

She would not meet his gaze and he sensed that she herself was aware of her own ridiculous demands and was ashamed.

"Maggots," she whispered, looking down. "They were in the bread."

Of course they were, he wanted to say. *Hard tack is full of them. You pick 'em out and dunk it in your lobscouse, shove it into your gob and wash it all down with your grog so ye don't remember how bloody awful it is. What the divil's the damned problem?*

Lady. L-A-D-Y lady.

That was the damned problem.

"I'm beginnin' to regret taking you and not yer brother," he said in exasperation. "Ye're a pain in the arse."

She stiffened. "Well, I didn't *ask* to be here."

"Aye, and the sooner ye're gone the better."

"I could not agree more. But in the meantime, you could at least ensure that I don't starve to death."

"Nobody's starvin' ye. Ye're just damned picky."

"And you are callous and rude."

"No argument there." He glared at her. "Will ye eat an egg or two?"

She glared back. "Boiled?"

"God almighty—"

"Because I'm certainly not expecting them to be coddled and served in a china egg-cup."

"Well, then, 'tis glad I am to hear it, because high expectations will only lead to disappointment and the divil only knows we've failed yer high and mighty ladyship in everything else."

"Not everything," she said beneath her breath.

"Oh?"

"Your objectionable language aside, you *have* been a gentleman," she allowed with pointed reluctance.

He made a sound of hopeless frustration and gazed out at the horizon, thinking he'd heave the ship to in the morning so Cranton could catch her a fish for breakfast. No worms in that. Nothing to complain about and the damn thing would be fresher than anything she'd find on her plate back in that fancy townhouse she must inhabit in London.

"I've been a gentleman, but saints alive, woman, ye push the limits of my patience, ye do."

"Well, you push the limits of mine. You have abducted me. Held me against my will. You have ruined me, ruined my life, and ruined any chances I might've had to marry a man of my own choosing."

"Oh, the drama," he said. "It can't be as bad as all that."

"It is as bad as all that. But what would you know? You don't move in my world. You have no idea what you have done to me in bringing me here, what it will cost me. I am ruined."

He risked a glance over at her. Her face was in profile, beautiful in the starlight. He wished he were not the gentleman he was trying to be, because his instinct was to slide an arm around her back and pull her close, to cajole away her anger, to kiss her senseless beneath Lucy and Susan and the grand union flag at the masthead and the canopy of stars that stretched across the zenith above.

"Do ye like fish, lass?"

"What?"

"We'll catch ye one for breakfast tomorrow. A big one. Nice and fresh, best ye'll ever have."

"A fish?" She raised a brow. "Will you prepare it yourself?"

"I might, if it'll make ye happy." He looked down at her. "Of course, ye don't know if I'm any better a cook than that useless looby who's charged with feedin' us all now, do ye? On the other hand, 'twould be hard to bollocks up a fish."

"You are going to cook me a fish."

"I could."

"And why are you smiling, Captain O' Devir?"

He hadn't realized he was. Another thing she did to him. Charmed him right out of his melancholy, kicked out the darkness that was English hatred and Josiah's death and Dolores Ann's betrayal and filled it with sweet, warm sunshine, even when she was being prickly.

"Am I?"

"You were."

"Well, lass, I was just thinkin' how nice it is to be standin' here with a pretty girl and enjoyin' a bit of life before her lauded brother catches up to and kills me in the most gruesome manner a body might imagine, before the Royal Navy finds a way to try and annihilate me, before I head back to America with her brother's explosive." He looked down at her. "Puttin' it all in me memory bank, I am. Moments like this don't last forever."

"And what makes you think you'll be so successful?"

"Eye on the prize, Lady Nerissa. Eye on the prize."

He realized he was looking at her lips, wondering what they would feel like beneath his own, what they would taste like.

Maybe it's not the explosive that's the prize but you, Lady Nerissa, yourself.

Now where the divil had *that* thought come from?

"You shouldn't be so blithe about my brother, you know. Any of them, actually. They are famously protective of me."

"Perhaps too much so, Lady Nerissa?"

"Whatever do you mean?"

"Ye're beautiful, likely heavily dowered, from one of

the oldest and most noble families in England. And yet, ye're not married."

"No, I am not."

"Why not? Those same overprotective brothers? Have they turned or frightened away all suitors, finding them unworthy of their little sister?"

She was quiet for a long, long moment. "I was affianced, once." She took a deep breath, raised her head and looked out towards the horizon where the moon, a giant glowing orb behind a few bars of cloud, was just climbing up out of the sea. "His name was Perry. He was the Earl of Brookhampton, our neighbor, and we knew each other from childhood."

"What happened?" He sensed the sudden withering of her spirit and it was all he could do not to take her hand. "Did he die?"

"In a way, yes, he did."

Ruaidri waited, letting her take her time. He itched to reach out and tuck that errant strand of hair, now silver in the rising moonlight, behind her ear.

"My brother, Lucien...."

"The one that is going to slit open me belly and strangle me with me own bowels?"

She gave a wan smile, responding to his attempt to lighten the moment. "Yes, that one." She sighed. "Well, Lucien is—*was*—very manipulative. He found great sport and satisfaction in arranging circumstances such that each of my brothers were coerced into marriage. Happy marriages, yes, but his arrogance in believing that he knew best for them and for others, was maddening."

He said nothing. Out of the corner of his eye he saw Midshipman Cranton materialize from out of the darkness to go forward and ring the bell, signifying the end of the watch.

"Lucien managed to get my three brothers married, and when Perry kept dragging his feet, unable to muster the courage to set an actual wedding date, he took matters into his own hands. He bought an estate in Spain. Arranged things through his solicitor so that it appeared Perry had inherited it from a distant relative. Told himself that absence would make the heart grow fonder, that if he were away from me, Perry would realize how much he missed me and would return all ready and eager to finally get married. But Perry never knew, of course, that Lucien was behind it all. Neither did I. Off he went to Spain, as Lucien intended. What Lucien did not intend was for the ship he was on to be attacked by an American privateer and the English prisoners sent to a French gaol."

"Yer brother sounds like he needs a good toe in the hole."

She smiled a little, obviously finding amusement in that. It was probably the first time anyone had ever dared speak the truth about the duke. Perhaps she found it refreshing.

"Anyhow, everyone thought Perry was dead, that he'd gone down with the ship, but he wasn't dead, just badly injured. By the time he came to his senses, the French gaolers did not believe him to be the English earl he claimed to be. He did not make for a compliant prisoner, so they beat him and put him into solitary confinement. It pretty much destroyed him, that prison. My brothers—and your brother-in-law, Captain Lord—got him out in a daring rescue and at first, he couldn't wait to hurry up and set a date for our wedding. But his incarceration changed him. He suffered wounds to his soul that were far deeper than anything he sustained physically." She looked down at her hands, her eyes tragic. "Of course, he learned that it was Lucien who manufactured the whole Spanish estate thing, and who could blame him if he could not forgive. I'm not sure I could, either. I'm not sure I *have*. Perry wanted nothing more to do with my family. He ended the engagement several months past, and I haven't seen him since."

She spoke so matter-of-factly that Ruaidri had trouble believing that her feelings for this man had been as warm as she claimed them to have been. He was used to women who wore their hearts on their sleeves, their emotions, needs and desires on display for all to see. This cool, elegant woman beside him ... did she lack that warmth, or had breeding and class choked off any expression of emotion she might otherwise have shown?

"Ye think he broke yer heart, don't ye, lass?"

"Of course he did."

"Yer heart isn't broken, Lady Nerissa."

She looked up then, frowning. "How dare you presume to know what is in my heart."

"Yer heart wasn't broken, because ye never really loved him the way ye thought ye did, did you?"

"What?"

"Ye stand here beside me and relate this tale of woe t' me with a dry eye and all the feelin' ye might use to describe a bucket of sand. I think there's more to ye than that, and I think that this man, Perry, would have made ye miserable. He wasn't good enough for ye."

"How dare you, Captain O' Devir!"

"Well, I'm standin' here, lookin' at you. Ye're made pretty enough to make a man weep, you are, and if this piece of shite couldn't make up his mind and sweep you off to the altar, he sure wouldn't have made ye a strong husband. Is that what ye'd have settled for? A wishy-washy nob who not only couldn't make up his mind, but was also gullible enough to be taken in by yer brother's schemin'?"

She just looked at him, mouth agape. To deny his conclusions would have screamed of falseness; to her credit, she did not.

"He was," she finally admitted, looking back out over the sea, "...indecisive."

"And you wanted that in a husband?" He snorted. "Doesn't seem he was worth a broken heart. Don't tell me ye're pining for this blatherin' idiot. Why, did he ever even kiss ye?"

"Captain!" she gasped, outraged.

"Well, did he?"

"Of course."

"With passion?"

"He was a gentleman. He ... he abided by the rules of propriety."

"Bollocks."

She gasped, her eyes widening.

"He was an arse. When are ye goin' to get good and angry about what he did to ye? If he loved ye as ye deserve to be loved, he wouldn't have dragged his feet, he'd have had a ring on yer finger and you in his bed before ye even had time to consider the difference between a kiss of passion and a kiss of 'propriety.'" He shook his head. "Ye don't throw gold overboard. Ye don't hold a diamond up to the light and wonder whether it's the real thing when it's blindin' ye with its brilliance. Indecisive piece of shite."

"You did not know him!"

"Why are you defendin' him? He took, arguably, the best years of yer life with his wafflin' like a one-footed duck."

"Lots of people are indecisive ... unsure."

"Not in my line of work, they aren't. Indecision will make a person dead, very dead. Oh no, I may be many things, Lady Nerissa, but I can assure you I'm not indecisive."

"And your point?"

"My point is, the good Lord gave ye a face and form to bring a man to his knees. Yer earl was an idiot. I barely know ye, but I can tell ye right now that if I were to kiss ye, it would sure as hell not be a kiss of *propriety*."

"Of course it wouldn't. No matter what you pretend, you are anything but a gentleman."

"Aye, 'tis true. But I could show ye what a kiss ought to feel like. Taste like. Make ye *feel* like."

Her head jerked up, her fingers went to her throat, and in the darkness, he could see the twin stains that suddenly bloomed on her cheeks. "Captain, what makes you think I want you to kiss me?"

"Everythin' about ye." He unclasped his hands from behind his back and reaching out, finally tucked that errant strand of hair behind her ear, noting that she did not flinch or push his hand away. "The way yer eyes look suddenly intrigued despite the protests of yer tongue. The fact that ye haven't slapped me. The fact that when I suggested it, ye swayed toward me just the slightest bit." He cocked his head, letting a little smile touch the corner of his mouth. "Ye'd enjoy it, you know."

"You are arrogant and audacious."

"And I could kiss ye senseless."

"You think *far* too highly of yourself."

"I think I can make ye forget that idiot ye almost married."

"I shall never feel again, what I felt for Perry. And if I did, it would never, not in a million years, be with *you*."

He grinned down at her. "I'd like to challenge that."

She turned from the rail to face him, her eyes flashing. She had been jilted by this complete arse of an earl, had been manipulated by the even bigger arse that was her brother but she was no simpering miss, and if the idea of kissing him completely repulsed her, she would have fled.

And yet here she was, still standing here.

"Ye're not gettin' any younger," he prompted.

"And you're not getting any less arrogant."

"Aye, don't hold yer breath on that one."

She stood there glaring at him.

Ruaidri O' Devir was nothing if not decisive. He took her into his arms and kissed her.

Chapter Nine

What on earth was she doing?

But as he pulled her close, as she felt the warmth of his strong, very manly hand graze her cheek, as he caught the annoying bit of hair that refused to stay in place and gently tucked it behind her ear, Nerissa knew she was doing exactly what she wanted to be doing.

Doing something because it pleased her. Intrigued her.

Excited her.

Kiss me, Captain. Because you are correct, you know, discerning my situation and my feelings in a way that is almost eerie. Can you read my mind, or are you just a cunning judge of circumstance and character? I don't care that you're the enemy. I don't care that Lucien will indeed strangle you with your own entrails. I don't even care that you're Irish.

There was nothing chaste and polite about the kiss, though he discreetly turned her so that his own big, powerful body, all the bigger, all the more powerful now that it had moved so close to hers, blocked her from anyone watching on the deck. She felt herself go all liquid inside before he even reached out and took her hand, thumbing her knuckles and rubbing a little circle on the tender underside of her wrist before pulling her up against himself. She struggled to draw breath, her knees going shaky and weak as he drew her closer still, never letting go of her hand, pinning it between their bodies and alarmingly close to the front of his breeches. She felt trapped, somewhat panicked, but the moment was fleeting. In the next instant his other hand had come up to caress her jaw, to graze her cheekbone with the rough pad of his mariner's thumb before pushing through her hair to cup the back of her head and hold her close.

Nerissa was unprepared for the jolt of raw electricity that coursed through her when his lips finally claimed hers. It was lightning forking out of the sky on a summer night, dangerous, intense, full of burn and energy and force. No polite kiss of propriety was this, as Perry's had always been, oh, dear Lord, no; this was almost savage in its intensity, masterful in its authority, and warm and hard and delicious and completely overpowering. She heard a moan deep in her own throat and suddenly realized that her hand, still caught in his, was pinned up against something hard and that it was his ... his....

Dear God above!

Shaken, she pulled back and hit him. Hard. Not the way a well-bred lady should hit a scoundrel who had taken just a little too much liberty with her, but a stout, well-aimed clout across the side of his jaw given with such force that her brothers, who had taught her how to land a punch, would have been cheering her to the skies. Hard enough that it hurt her knuckles, hard enough that he might even have a bruise in the morning, hard enough that she felt the pleasure of her own strength and indignation.

He didn't crumple to the deck of course, something that would have brought her great satisfaction.

Instead, he laughed.

"Told ye I knew how to kiss a lass, right an' proper," he said simply and offering his elbow, gave her a charming smile that reached all the way to his intense, absurdly long-lashed eyes. "And now that we've settled the matter once and hopefully not for all, why don't we go find you those eggs."

"And you accuse my betrothed of being an ... an arse," she said.

"Former betrothed." He began to walk, and she was forced to go with him.

❧

Nerissa was hard-pressed to call on every aspect of her breeding, her upbringing, her training and her nerves to try and adopt a demeanor that said she had not been affected by Captain O' Devir's kiss, and as a de Montforte she had it in her to do just that. *Valour, Virtue, and Victory* was the family motto. And yet, this man—unfairly virile, maddening, brooding one moment, laughing the next—had done things to make the blood in her veins go up in steam and her heart to forget how to beat. The back of her neck was suddenly hot and again, she felt that coiled sensation deep in her belly and centering between her legs, a sensation she knew was reserved for a woman's husband—not an arrogant Irishman who fought for a losing cause, who showed her none of the deference her class and gender demanded, who wasn't afraid of Lucien.

Who wasn't afraid of Lucien.

Imagine that.

"He'll strangle you on your own entrails." She had said it only partly in jest. Lucien would, when he caught up to

Ruaidri O' Devir, find a way to make him pay for abducting his little sister, for ruining her reputation and chances of ever making a respectable marriage, but Lucien's style wasn't exactly vulgar; no, he would not strangle the captain with his own entrails, he would likely have him condemned on kidnapping charges and ensure that his best friend, the brilliant barrister Sir Roger Foxcote, got him a date with Tyburn and the public gallows. Lucien would not stay and watch the life being choked out of his sister's abductor, though he might give the spectacle a passing glance from a gleaming coach; it would be beneath him to do anything more than that. He would not revel in it, but see it done and then ruthlessly set about marrying her off with a speed that would make her head spin.

It never occurred to Nerissa that Captain Ruaidri O' Devir might be a match for the mighty duke who was her brother.

And it never would. Mere mortals were not on equal footing with gods.

The captain, still beside her, stopped at the cabin door, pushed it open, and led her inside.

"Wipe the scowl off yer face, Sunshine," he said. "It's unbecoming."

"You took a liberty with me."

"You all but asked me to."

"You were ... vulgar."

"What, by showing ye the effect ye have on me? By forcing ye to listen to yer own body?" He gave a little laugh. "'Twas only a kiss. Not like I stole yer virtue or anythin'."

He deposited her in his cabin and left her stewing in her own confusion as he went off to find her the promised eggs.

It was only a kiss.

Oh, no, it wasn't. Not to her it wasn't. "Only a kiss" was the way she remembered Perry's kisses—chaste, polite, lukewarm, dutiful. But *this* man's kisses had set her blood on fire, had made heat singe her veins and dampen her skin; he knew what he was about, this aspiring, ambitious Irishman who fancied himself a real naval captain. How dare he.

Maybe she would strangle him herself, if not with his own entrails, than with a length of line. This was a boat. Or rather, a ship. Plenty of rope to be had.

❧

The gleaming black coach, its door emblazoned with the Blackheath coat of arms, pulled up outside of the Admiralty early the next morning. Footmen in elegant livery moved quickly to open the door and let down the steps for His Grace. A buzz of importance surrounded his arrival. Moments later, Lucien De Montforte, looking thunderously grim, was stalking from the coach and heading straight for the building.

Lawrence Hadley the Third turned from the window, girding himself for the coming encounter. Moments later, the expected knock on the door came. It swung open to reveal a clerk who was visibly nervous.

"Admiral Hadley, His Grace the Duke of Blackheath..." the clerk trailed off and quickly retreated.

The duke stalked in, not bothering to wait for an invitation, and fixed Hadley with a black stare that promised a gruesome and painful death if information wasn't immediately forthcoming.

"What is being done about my sister?" he demanded harshly, getting straight to the point.

Hadley poured a glass from a crystal decanter and offered it to the duke; it was ignored.

"The frigate *Happenstance* is weighing as we speak, Your Grace. I can assure you that we—"

"Why isn't Captain Lord in charge of this affair?"

"The First Lord of the Admiralty did not feel it prudent to put Captain Lord in command of this operation, Your Grace." Hadley downed his drink. "I know that he has served you well in the past, he is indeed one of our finest officers, but given his wife's relationship to this rascal that abducted your sister, we have chosen another to see to her rescue instead."

Blackheath pinned him with a glare that could have melted the ice off a winter lake. "And how long will it take for this frigate to reach Saint-Malo?"

"Barring any interference from the French and a favorable wind, I should hope some time tomorrow."

"And yet the rendezvous is not until Saturday."

"Indeed, Your Grace. But the Royal Navy does not, of course, deal with traitors, especially on their terms. It is our belief that the superior size and firepower of the frigate *Happenstance* will cow this rogue into relinquishing her ladyship and that all will end peacefully and with the least damage to both her reputation and person—"

"Your belief had better be correct, Hadley, or I'll see to it that your naval career sinks faster than one of your ships, do you understand me?"

Hadley spread his hands in a gesture meant to placate. "Your Grace, the Navy is well used to dealing with threats and I am certain we have the situation well under control. In fact, my son himself is commanding the frigate *Happenstance* and will sail to France, under a flag of truce if need be, in advance of the exchange to try and resolve this with force and cunning. I can assure you, he's a talented officer and, having been raised in America—I was posted there for a time, you know—he knows how these scoundrels think. I have complete faith that he will secure the release of Lady Nerissa and blow this rogue right out of the water. Now please, let the Navy do its job, and—"

"The damned Navy had better do its job or you'll rue the day you ever met me, do you understand?"

"Yes, Your Grace. I can assure you—"

"Get to work," snarled the duke and without another word, shoved the chair back and slammed out of the room.

Chapter Ten

Ruaidri had brought her the eggs. Left her alone in his cabin. Thought about spending the night in the remaining boat, slung out on its davits over the stern, and instead decided to try and snatch what little rest would be afforded him in the same place he'd snatched it the previous night.

Outside the cabin door on the open deck, his head pillowed on his uniform coat, a sea cloak serving as a blanket.

He slept fitfully and woke up stiff and sore while the deck was still dark, but let no man say that Captain Ruadiri O' Devir of the American Continental Navy was anything but an officer and a gentleman. He would not give his men anything to talk about by sharing a cabin with his captive.

Instead, his presence outside the door behind which she slept, ensured that both her safety and her honor were guarded by someone who held both in the highest of esteem:

Himself.

He was up and on his feet before dawn, walking the stiffness out of his legs, paying a visit to the recovering McGuire, and finding a drop-line so he could catch her the promised fish. As the sun's golden glow began to peep above the eastern horizon, he ordered the ship hove to. He had spent his earliest years as a fisherman. It didn't take him long to catch her a fish and true to his word, he quietly carried it down to the galley, filleted it, and throwing some butter into a cast iron frying pan, cooked it for her himself.

He didn't know why he was going to such effort. He told himself that no gently bred woman would go hungry on an American ship, but he wondered if it was more than that. More than feeling a bit sorry for her. More than feeling guilty that his own actions had indeed ruined her life. Maybe it had nothing to do with any of that, and everything to do with his own damned pride.

He was still thinking about that kiss he'd claimed.

He'd been unable to *stop* thinking about it.

Truth be told, his reaction to it had rattled him a bit ... and not much rattled Ruaidri O' Devir.

She was English, Anglican, aristocracy, part of a hated race, and the fact that his body had responded to her with lust and longing confused the living hell out of him. No good could come of even allowing himself to think past that kiss. She was his hostage. His bargaining tool for the explosive he'd crossed the Atlantic to get, and he could not let himself be sidetracked by any thoughts of a romantic entanglement.

And he needed sleep. Jesus, Mary and Joseph, he needed sleep.

Carrying a plate with the still-steaming fish, he opened the door to his cabin, giving his eyes a moment to adjust to the gloom. Faint light came in through the stern windows, made shadows play on the decking, and he heard the timeless creaking and settling of the ship's timbers all around him.

There. The girl was sitting at his table, her head pillowed on folded arms, her gown shimmering in the faint light and spilling down over her feet to the deck planking. She was fast asleep.

He moved as silently as a cat toward her and stood there for a moment in the early morning light, his eyes drinking in her beauty. When he had first met her, her pale ivory hair had been carefully pinned up and piled high, her face fashionably pale, her hands in gloves that probably cost more than his entire wardrobe. Now, slumped over his desk with her hair spilling over her arms in wanton defeat, she looked like the innocent young woman she was. Vulnerable. Beautiful. Freed, somewhat, from her constraints.

Lust stirred in his loins.

She was someone's little sister.

The thought clubbed him just beneath his breastbone. He had a sister, and if some rogue had dared to capture her, he would move hell and earth to find and kill the wretch. This woman's brothers must be frantic with worry. Sick with fear for her. He tried to ignore the pang of guilt; they were English and this was, after all, war. There was much about war that was unpleasant, and even more that was necessary.

She is someone's little sister.

"God almighty," he swore, and was standing there wondering whether to wake her with breakfast or leave her there sleeping peacefully, when she made a little sigh in her sleep and stirred.

She raised her head, and her eyes, clear and beautiful in the early morning light, found his.

"Captain O' Devir ... I did not hear you come in."

He put the plate down on the table in front of her and moved away, not wanting her to know he'd been gazing wistfully down at her, admiring her beauty, softening—a dangerous thing, that—as he thought of her family.

Instantly, he made his tone gruff. Irritable. "Aye, ye'd not have heard me, because I'd a mind to keep quiet.

Here. I brought ye breakfast. Caught and cooked it meself, just as I promised."

She looked up at him, blinking.

And then she smiled, a true and radiant thing that lit him up from the inside out, and Ruaidri felt everything inside of him melt.

He turned away, quickly, before she could see that that smile had completely undone him. He took off his hat, hung it on a peg, and rubbing at his eyes, blinked the fatigue from them and looked at her. Her face was open and earnest, and he saw that she had caught a bit of sun the previous day.

You are ruining her.

"You need sleep, Captain."

"I'll be the judge of what I need." Good lord above, he couldn't stay here. He plucked his hat back off the peg. "Get into bed, Lady Nerissa. Ye'll end up with the divil of a stiff neck and a backache as well if ye insist on sleepin' in a chair. I'll leave ye be. Enjoy yer breakfast."

She yawned and straightened up, pushing a hand through her hair. It rippled like silk down her back, and he felt himself beginning to harden beneath his breeches. "I can't sleep, Captain. Once I'm awake, I'm awake." She attempted a conciliatory smile. "You look exhausted. Where have *you* been sleeping? This is your cabin, is it not?"

"Outside yer door."

"What?"

"Well, someone needs to keep that motley pack of blackguards out there away from ye. Might as well be me."

"That's ridiculous. Sit down and have some breakfast with me."

"No, Sunshine, I caught and cooked that for you, not myself."

"There's far more here than I could eat in a week.

Please, have some. And thank you. It was very kind of you to go to such an effort on my behalf."

"No effort a'tall," he said, unable to conceal the growling of his own stomach as she cut the piece of fish in half and pushed the plate toward him. He pushed it back.

"Ladies first."

She ate. No complaining about dirty flatware, weevils, gooey gruel. She was happy and he had made her so and that made him, for some strange reason, happy as well. When she was finished, she pushed the plate and the fork across the table to him and he took it, standing up to eat so that she would not have to relinquish the chair.

He finished the meal and decided it was past time to leave.

"You should get some rest, Captain."

"I'm fine. Just need some coffee."

Her pale blue eyes darkened with what looked like concern. "You went and caught me a fish, cooked it yourself, brought it to me and you won't even sleep in your own bed. That isn't right." She watched him head to the door. "Why don't you just sleep here? It's not like my reputation isn't already in tatters. Grab an hour or two. I can go out on deck and keep company with Midshipman Cranton if it would make you feel better."

He grinned. "Plan on murderin' me in me sleep, lass?"

"If I planned on murdering you, I'd make sure you were awake so that you'd feel every horrible bit of it." Was that actually a hint of a grin on her sweet, haughty face, or was his own exhaustion playing tricks on his mind? "Besides, that honor will be my brothers'. No need for me to kill you when the four of them will be drawing straws over it."

He laughed, shrugged out of his uniform and put both his hat and the coat on the peg. He sat down on his bunk. Out of the corner of his eye, he saw her turn her face away, probably expecting him to show himself to be the barbarian she surely thought him to be by undressing in front of her. He leaned over to remove his shoes. Through a wildly curling tendril of black hair that fell down over his forehead, he could see her face still in profile, but her blue eyes cut over to look at him, just briefly, and he smiled privately to himself. He wished he could give her more to look at. If she were a lass like Dolores Ann, he most certainly would....

Sudden fatigue came crashing over him. Still clad in his waistcoat, shirt, breeches and stockings, he lay back against the sheet. Even in here the bedding felt damp, perpetually imbibed with salt air. He didn't care. He turned his head on the pillow, looked sleepily at his beautiful captive, and gave her his most blinding smile.

"'Tis dreamin' of that kiss, I'll be," he said, with a pointed sigh.

Her smile vanished and in the gathering light, he saw the quick stains of color on her cheeks.

"Go to sleep, Captain O' Devir," she said tightly and rising, went to sit at the windows at the stern, putting distance between them.

The rising sun painted the curve of her forehead, her pert nose and her lovely chin, and the strikingly beautiful image of her cast-in-light profile was the last Ruaidri knew before sleep claimed him.

❧

Nerissa drew her legs up tightly beneath her skirts and leaned her side against the stern windows.

She tried to concentrate on the sea below, the way the early morning sun caught the tossing waves and made them sparkle, the way the salty foam glittered like diamonds on a canopy of blue. Through the open windows she caught the odors of saltwater, hemp, varnish and now, something frying as forward, breakfast was prepared. Sounds above as the deck was holystoned; the endless, timeless, creak and groan of timbers, of masts, of the hull itself. The song of the wind and sigh of the tumbling waves, Lieutenant Morgan's voice somewhere outside, sunlight, now, high enough above the horizon that its pale light was starting to fill the cabin, movement out of the corner of her eye as the captain's blue uniform coat swung back and forth with the roll of the ship.

And Ruaidri O' Devir.

He lay several feet away and fast asleep. She had purposely avoided looking at him. Instead, she had tried to concentrate on the shipboard sounds around her, the smells, the morning light, but her brain only noted these things in passing; it only noted them, because the primary and most pressing object of its attention was the lowly Irish scoundrel lying motionless, virile, vulnerable, just a few feet away.

She would not look at him.

She could not *help* but look at him.

She turned her head, resting the opposite cheek against her knee and telling herself it was only so that she wouldn't get a stiff neck by gazing so long out the windows. It just *happened* that Captain O' Devir was in her line of sight, now. She didn't *intend* to look at him.

But she did.

She didn't intend to quietly get to her feet, either, and move soundlessly across the cabin, but she did.

And she didn't intend to stop near his cot and stand there looking down at him in a curious mixture of fascination, resentment and wonder, because this same man who should be her greatest enemy at the moment, this man whose background and class were so far removed from her own as to make him beneath her notice, this man who made the blood warm her veins and something to sing like a bird inside her when she thought of his kiss, was someone who should be reviled.

But she did stop near his bed.

And she did not revile him.

Instead, she stood there quietly looking down at him as the deck on which she stood rolled gently beneath her feet. He lay on his back, one arm resting on his chest, his head rolling slightly back and forth with the motion of the brig. Up close, it felt deliciously wicked to study him. To note the way his long black lashes swept his high cheekbones, the boldness of his nose and brows, the Celtic look about his mouth and chin and the dark bristles that shadowed his jaw. His hair curled in wild abandon around his face and then fell away, framing shoulders that were wide and imposing even at rest, and she watched his arm, the hand lax, the fingers well-formed and strong, rising up and down atop his chest in time with his breathing.

Something softened in her heart.

You are beautiful, Ruaidri O'Devir.

And I hate you for it.

She ached to reach out and touch his jaw, just to see what it felt like. Was it harsh and wiry? Stubbly and hard? What did his skin feel like? Would his lips be firm beneath her fingers, even slightly parted as they were in sleep?

She did not touch him, of course.

She was a lady. Ladies did not go around touching men in their sleep; they did not go around touching men, full stop.

What do you have to lose, Nerissa?

The thought hit her with sobering, and suddenly wicked, freedom.

What do you have to lose? Your reputation just by being here is in tatters. This will be the biggest scandal to hit London in decades. You are already ruined. People will assume you've been violated by this entire ship and its wild, wicked captain, so really, what do you have to lose?

Nerissa gazed down at her captor and began chewing on her lower lip.

You have nothing to lose. You can't lose something you've already lost. Lucien, in trying to quash rumors and scandal, will marry you off so fast that your head will spin when you get back to England. These are your last days of freedom ... of making decisions as Lady Nerissa de Montforte, even if you are *this man's prisoner.*

She began to reach out, her fingers stretching toward that shadowed cheek ... that dangerously beautiful mouth....

And paused.

What on earth are you DOING?

She drew back, resolute, and retreated back across the cabin to the stern windows, leaving Captain O' Devir to his dreams.

❧

Captain O' Devir's dreams, however were far from pleasant.

He was not a sound or heavy sleeper and Dolores Ann was close. She was there, her bright, bawdy smile beckoning him, her hand reaching out to slip beneath the bottom edges of his coat and find him in a quick, hard caress that left him groaning before she teasingly flitted away.

Delight, she'd called herself. It was what everyone called her save for her family, who didn't know her for what she really was.

A strumpet.

A teasing, careless flirt who hitched her wagon to the hero of the moment, a bawdy opportunist who lusted after the star that shone brightest without thought or care for whom she hurt.

He knew that, and yet he'd loved her anyhow.

Knew it and had asked her to be his wife.

In his sleep, Ruaidri flipped over onto his side and tried to make Delight go away but she did not, of course.

She was there and now, so was Josiah, and the two were meeting for the first time at a patriot gathering as Ruaidri introduced his bride-to-be to his friend and fellow captain.

Josiah, smiling his slow, easy smile with the extra space between his front teeth giving him an innocent little-boy deviltry that made him all but irresistible to the fairer sex. Josiah who had just won the accolades of the people of Boston and the gratitude of its leaders for capturing a British sloop full of munitions and powder that the patriots desperately needed. Josiah helplessly gaping at Delight's ample charms, while she herself lit up like a firefly in a hot June night. The two had had eyes only for each other.

Ruaidri had been drawn away in conversation with John Adams and when he returned a few moments later, already knew it was too late.

"Dolores, come away," he murmured, forgotten. "I should get ye home to yer mother."

"But Roddy, your friend Josiah here was just telling me about the way he ran straight through the British blockade and once on the other side of it, captured that sloop! He's a hero, Roddy! He's your friend. Aren't you happy for him?"

"I told yer father I'd have ye home before dark. Let's go."

A bright burst of her laughter and no, he didn't want to see it but he did—the light, evocative touch of her fingers against Josiah's wrist, the playful toss of her head, the flirtatious giggle.

And Josiah's slow, lopsided smile.

Best to get them away from each other, he thought with bitter savagery. Best to do it now.

He took her arm and began to lead her away and as he did, he glanced down at her and saw that she was looking back over her shoulder, coyly batting her lashes at the man Ruaidri considered to be his best and most loyal friend.

Chapter Eleven

Somewhere beyond the wooden door that separated the quiet, private world of *Tigershark*'s cabin from the busy deck outside, Nerissa, still on the window seat, heard the chime of a bell signifying the end of a watch. Moments later a knock came on that same door, and it opened almost immediately.

She was glad she had retreated to her spot on the window seat because Captain O' Devir, surely anticipating the wake-up call in his sleep or so accustomed to four-hour snatches of rest that he would have opened his unfairly gorgeous eyes even without the knock on the door, immediately sat up, rubbing his forehead as Midshipman Cranton walked in.

"Good morning, sir."

"The weather, Mr. Cranton?"

"Sunny skies. Some clouds off to the west, could be a storm in the offing, but still well enough away, I expect."

"Our course?"

"Southwest on the starboard tack, the French coast visible in the distance with the glass."

Captain O' Devir, looking tired and anything but refreshed, swung his feet out of the bed and padded across the cabin to the table where the old coffee pot stood. Nerissa watched him pick it up, upend it, and swear beneath his breath when only a few cold, very cold, drops tumbled out and into his mug.

"Where's that cheeky little wretch who's supposed to be my cabin steward?"

"Helping Cook prepare lunch, Captain."

"Tell him to get his sorry arse in here now or he'll be wearin' the coffee ye're about to get for me on his damned head." He handed the pot to Cranton. "Be quick about it. And bring an extra cup for the lady, too."

Only then did the young man's gaze slide to Nerissa. A faint blush spread over his cheeks and she could all but see him checking her over for damage to either her person or her spirit. The fact that she had been in here while the captain had taken his rest was troubling the youth, and why not? He probably thought it scandalously improper. Nerissa's own face flamed. To address the issue would only make it worse and add to her humiliation. She offered a smile and a helpless shrug of her shoulders; it was all she could do.

"Will that be all, sir?"

"Aye, Mr. Cranton. And the quicker you are with that coffee, the better mood I'll be in when ye see me on deck."

The young midshipman wasted no time in retreating and Nerissa, one brow raised, looked at Captain O' Devir and shook her head.

"Are you always such an ogre to your crew?"

"I am always an ogre until I have me first cup of coffee."

He stood up, hands in the middle of his lower back, and stretched, first one way, and then the other. He looked delightfully rumpled, sleepy-eyed, and while she might not consider him handsome in the classical sense, he was nevertheless the most virile and devastatingly attractive man Nerissa had ever met.

He rubbed at his stubbled jaw and slanted her a

wicked, teasing look. "Had a dream about you, y'know. Dreamt that ye slid into bed with me and kept me nice and warm. Dreamt of yer lips against—"

"Captain O' Devir, I do not care to know the content of your dreams."

"Ah, looks like someone else is out of sorts until her mornin' coffee, eh?"

"I do not drink coffee."

"Well, ye won't be drinkin' tea while aboard an American ship, Sunshine, for reasons both practical and political. So if ye want a good hot beverage to perk ye up, ye'll have to take coffee. Soak some hard tack in it and it makes both more palatable."

"I am going to starve to death while I'm here, I just know it."

"I'll catch ye another fish. Can't have a dead hostage now, can I?"

"You'll be dead enough when my brother Lu—"

He laughed, his eyes sparkling with merriment. "Yes, yes, I know, we've already sailed those seas, lass." He picked up the pitcher, poured some water into a bowl, pushed up his sleeves to expose well-muscled forearms sparsely covered with black hair, and grabbing a square of linen, dipped it in the water and began to wash his face. His shirt was wrinkled beneath the waistcoat, and she wondered if he'd slept in his clothes so as to be in readiness for anything unexpected, or because he was trying to preserve her eyes from the sight of him in undress.

She had grown up with four brothers; she knew, of course, that the male anatomy was greatly different from her own, knew that beneath the span of cloth that connected Captain O' Devir's wide shoulders there would be plenty of hard, defined muscle, just like in his arms; there was no paunch beneath that white waistcoat with its gold buttons, no jowliness to that watchful face with its quickly changing expressions; he would be lean and fit and beneath the skin, his muscles would be hard to the touch, and the minute she had this thought, she was both horrified and furious with herself.

Why are you thinking of touching *him?*

"I'm predictin' today will be a bit more excitin' than the last," he was saying, grabbing a small brush and smearing lather on his cheeks and jaw before picking up a long razor and setting to work before a tiny, cracked mirror. She stared; she had never seen a man shave before and her brothers, she assumed, were always shaved by their valets.

"What do you mean?"

His striking violet eyes met hers in the square of glass, breaking her fixation. "Yer brother will have received my ransom note by now and things should start to happen. Knowin' the Royal Navy as I do, they won't meet me on my terms but will try and set some of their own. Goin' to miss me, Sunshine?"

"No."

"Come now, not even a wee bit?"

"No."

"Eh, well. Wish I could say the same, but it's been rather fun havin' ye aboard and tryin' to get under yer skin."

"I am glad I was able to provide both entertainment and amusement," she said dryly.

"'Twould have been better if ye'd allowed yerself to enjoy that kiss, too."

"Do you ever relent?"

"Never." His eyes were gleaming above his beard of soapy lather. "And I'll be kissin' ye again before I send ye home, I will."

She flushed and looked away, suddenly feeling very warm beneath her clothing.

"Lookin' forward to goin' home?" he asked, his voice serious now.

"With both anticipation and, if I may be honest, dread."

She met his eyes in the tiny mirror. His gaze had lost a bit of its merriness and now fixated on hers. "Why's that?"

She shrugged. "As long as I'm out here, I can pretend that the whole of London isn't turned upside down looking for me. I can pretend that my reputation isn't going to be in ruins, that my name won't be the highlight of every scandal sheet, every newspaper, to come out of a London press. I can pretend that my brothers and family are going about their business, enjoying their children and not worried sick about me." She sighed. "Right now, the real world seems very far away."

"Aye. The sea, she'll do that to ye."

He was just wiping the remaining bits of lather from his clean-shaven cheeks and jaw when the door opened and a young lad came in. His hair stuck out in every direction, ill-fitting clothes hung from his lanky frame, and a colorful bird with a beak that looked like it could take off her finger in one bite, was watching her balefully from his shoulder.

Nerissa stared balefully back.

"Got your lunches, sir," the boy said. "Cook made fried pork. Brought you a fresh pot of coffee, too, as well as two cups." He glanced curiously, unabashedly, at Nerissa. "Begging your pardon, m'lady, but most of what we've got aboard is a bit the worse for wear. I found the cup with the fewest amount of chips and cracks in it."

"Thank you," she said, and favored him with a smile that soon had him blushing as red as the plumage on the back of the bird's head. "And what is your parrot's name?"

"Take that bird out of here before it sh—" the captain caught himself—"before it makes a mess or says somethin' it shouldn't. There's a lady present, Joey."

"Says something it shouldn't?" Nerissa asked,

looking with renewed interest at the boy's pet. "Can it talk?"

"Aye, m'lady. Ol' Scups here has quite the vocabulary. The crew's been teaching him a new word every week. In fact—"

The captain took the tray from the boy's hands, slammed it down on the table, and with a jerk of his chin, indicated the door. "Words that aren't fit for a lady's ears."

"I have never heard a parrot talk before," Nerissa said wistfully. "Surely whatever it has to say won't curl my hair or turn it purple now, will it, Joey?"

"Well—"

At that moment, there was a call from the lookout high in the tops. Immediately Captain O' Devir dropped the facade of gracious host and became the commander of a warship that he actually was, motioning them both for silence as he listened intently.

The door opened. "Mr. Morgan's respects, sir, but Wiggins up in the main top just spotted a sail about five miles off to the northeast. Frigate, sir. British colors."

Captain O' Devir was already reaching for his uniform coat. He drained his coffee and grabbed his hat. "Later, Sunshine," he said, striding for the door. "Don't wait lunch on me."

She watched him go. Joey followed, the parrot still on his skinny shoulder, leaving her alone in the suddenly-quiet cabin with nothing but her thoughts and a tray of untouched food.

A Royal Navy frigate, flying the Union Jack.

Help, it seemed, had arrived.

In her bones, she knew that ship out there was here for her. The English government had wasted no time in setting about getting her back, and she knew her formidable brother had probably pulled every string in his hand of marionettes to bring about her timely rescue.

Knowing Lucien, he was probably there aboard the ship and Captain O' Devir had just seen his last sunrise.

She got up and went to the windows, feeling a sudden weakness in her knees as she looked out over the sea. What would this day hold? An end to her time as a captive? A peaceful exchange? A terrible sea fight where brave men fought and suffered and God forbid, died?

No. She did not want to see Ruaidri O' Devir die.

He was a rogue and an audacious scoundrel, but she didn't hate him *that* much.

In fact ... she didn't hate him at all.

She turned and spied the tray that had been left on the table. Resolutely picking it up, she used her elbow to open the cabin door and stepped out into the sunshine.

The captain had not had his meal. If he was going to die today, the least she could do was ensure he did so on a full belly.

Chapter Twelve

"Can we outrun them, sir?"

Ruaidri, the heavy telescope braced through the ratlines, was studying the distant frigate. He gauged her speed, noting her sail trim and her course. She was a formidable looking bitch, bristling with guns and manned by the Navy that had stolen him from his homeland, forced him to work its ships, insulted, abused, scarred and shamed him. He felt the old anger rearing up, bile burning in his stomach. He knew the prowess of the British seamen. He knew the strength of their ships, the tenacity of their fighting spirit, and he knew that while his little brig might be well-built and fast, she would be the inferior of a frigate if it came down to a fight.

"She's piling on more sail, Captain. I'd say she's seen us."

"Noted, Mr. Morgan."

Was it just a random patrol out there, or was this England's answer to his audacious demands? Either way, he would call the shots, not they. The exchange between Lady Nerissa and the explosive would take place in Saint-Malo as he'd demanded, when he'd demanded, not out here on the open sea where he would be at a disadvantage.

He shut the glass and handed it to Midshipman Cranton. The French port of Calais—and safety—lay ten miles to the southeast. The wind was out of the west, the frigate, her shape subtly changing as she began to come about, well to the northeast.

"Get all hands to their stations," he said. "Decks sanded down, guns loaded up with grape and chain, nets strung and the boats lowered. Clear the ship for action, Mr. Morgan."

"Think he'll attack, sir?"

"Of course he will. He's British, isn't he?"

The frigate was still changing tack, presenting her broadside as she maneuvered to take full advantage of the wind. She would try to catch them before they could reach the safety of France, he knew. Try to either engage them or cut off their escape route before they could reach a safe port. Ruaidri's thoughts flashed to Lady Nerissa. Her safety was more important than anything else under his command, with the exception of the mission he'd been sent here to undertake. He would send her deep into the hold, well below the waterline, where the brig's stout timbers would offer her the most protection. Joey and that damned parrot could accompany her and keep her amused while the rest of them were getting blown to bits.

Nearby someone cleared his throat, and Ruaidri was roused from his reverie by a presence at his shoulder.

It was the subject of his thoughts. She had brought the food out, the tray held carefully in her hands to prevent the motion of the ship from spilling anything.

"What is happening, Captain?"

"We might see some action in a bit," he said with deliberate non-concern. He nodded toward the distant ship. "'Twill be a while before they're in range, maybe another half hour or so. Ye can stay up here for a short time longer, then it's belowdecks with ye, Sunshine."

"Are we in danger?"

"Of course not."

"Will we be?"

"Not if I can help it."

She nodded, once, her lovely blue eyes troubled. Her knuckles looked very white as she gripped the tray, steadying herself against the motion of the brig and trying to keep her balance.

He took pity on her. "Go sit and eat, lass. Might be yer last meal here and it looks a damned sight better than the rest of the shite Cook's been sendin' up."

She set it down on a nearby deckhouse, steadying it with one hand. Her eyes were wide as she noted the hurried preparations on the part of the seamen, the sense of quiet urgency around them. "I brought it for you."

"Well, now, did ye?" He looked at her quizzically. "Why is that?"

"You didn't get the chance to eat it earlier."

He looked at her, one brow raised, then took the tray from her and escorted her away from listening ears. "What's the *real* reason?"

"I noted how quickly you left the cabin. I can see the trepidation in your men's faces, I know you consider that ship out there to be an enemy. You are either going to be captured or killed, Captain O' Devir, and if either comes to pass, I'd like you to at least go to prison or your just reward on a full stomach."

He laughed and shaking his head, plucked the coffee mug from the tray, lifted it to his lips, and regarded her from over its rim. It was good and hot and black and bitter, just as he liked it. "Are those the only two outcomes you foresee, lass?"

"What other possible outcomes could there be?"

"Well, we could emerge victorious, for one." He took another sip of the coffee. "Or I could elect to run."

"You won't run."

"I won't fight, either, if I don't absolutely have to. Not with you aboard."

"Am I worth that much to you, Captain?"

Yes. Yes you are. "Ye're worth that much to this brother of yours who wants to hang, disembowel, or behead me with a dull knife, which makes ye worth that much to the Royal Navy and England itself."

Something in her face fell; what did she want him to say?

His first lieutenant was hustling past, a hint of ginger in his wake. Ruiadri hailed him. "Mr. Morgan! Brace up that main topsail a wee bit more, see if we can get some more speed out of her. Lively, now."

"Aye, sir!"

He turned back to Nerissa. "Besides, ye're a lady," he added, his gaze sliding back to the distant frigate. "I've no wish to subject ye to the horrors of men injured, dyin', pleadin' for mercy as they're hacked to pieces in front of ye."

"I see." And then: "Will you be safe, Captain?"

"No more or less so than anyone else aboard this ship."

She nodded, and her eyes darkened with what looked like worry before she looked away.

"Here now, what's this?" he said. "Ye'll not come to any harm. Ye may despise me, Lady Nerissa, but I'd give me life before I let anythin' happen to ye."

She wouldn't look at him. Instead, she walked to the rail and leaned against it, looking out over the sea toward the frigate that was surely coming for her. Quietly, she said, "It's not my own safety that concerns me."

He joined her, standing close enough that they could converse without their words being overheard. Softly, he asked, "Whose, then?"

She just looked pointedly at him, then looked away again, her mouth a tight line.

"Ah," he said, and because her hand was so close, he reached out and covered it with his own.

She did not pull away.

Instead, her fingers—slender, soft and colored like the inside of a seashell—wound gently around his. She kept them that way for a long moment, gripping his hand with surprising strength and leaving him to wonder if hers would be the last female touch he ever encountered. One never knew, really, going into battle.

"I don't despise you," she said. "Despite the fact you abducted me, starved me with the worst food I've ever been exposed to, and provided me with no change of clothing, you have been nothing but a gentleman toward me and I would hate to see anything happen to you."

He cocked his head and looked down at her. "What's this? Have ye come to care about me, lass?"

"Certainly not." She let go of his hand as though his skin had burned her.

The moment lay between them, still pulsing with life and bare, raw honesty. His gaze was drawn once more to her hand. A hand whose fingers had just entwined with his in fondness, in friendship, or maybe just in worry.

He thought of where he'd like that hand to be.

"Ah. Just wonderin', then."

"Stop wondering, then. I don't care about you. I just don't want anything to happen to you."

"I could get blown to bits today, y'know. Won't be anythin' left of me for yer brothers to kill. Just think of it, Lady Nerissa! I could die this mornin', perhaps in your arms ... and ye'll always lament the fact you didn't tell me you cared about me."

"Would you stop it?"

"'Twould be a lot to lay on yer conscience, now, wouldn't it?"

"*Stop!*"

He laughed, seeing the swift bit of color that washed across her cheeks, and glancing aloft, satisfied himself that the ship was getting as much as it could out of the set of the sails. But not enough, even with the topsail adjusted to make better use of the wind. Even without the glass, he could see that the frigate was gaining on them.

She followed his gaze, and by the sudden expression in her eyes, he saw that she saw it, too.

She looked up at him. The wind caught a tendril of her hair and sent it across his face, tickling his nose. "What do you want from me, then?"

He raised a brow. "Want from ye?"

"Well, since you seem quite convinced that you'll be lying in pieces soon enough."

"Ah. Well, Lady Nerissa. Let me think about that." He grinned down at her, but there was an earnest wish behind his words that his cavalier manner could not disguise. "If I were to die today, I couldn't ask for more than the memory of yer lips against mine. A kiss from a pretty lass to send me into battle. Aye, that's what I'd be wantin' from ye."

"A kiss?"

She stared at him. The color blossomed in her cheeks once more but before she could speak, the sound of thunder came rolling across the water from well astern.

She turned, eyes widening. "What was that?"

"Yer friends back there are demandin' that I heave to."

"Will you?"

The moment was lost. He would not get his kiss from a pretty lady to send him into battle, after all.

"Hell, no."

She paled as she realized the impending gravity of the situation.

Ruaidri pushed back from the rail, beckoning with a

crooked finger for Midshipman Cranton and ordering him to take her below. "You think about what I'd like," he said, inclining his head, and relinquishing her to the youth, headed for the helm. "In the meantime, I've got a battle to fight."

❧

"Come, your ladyship. They'll be within range of us pretty soon and the captain wants you to be safe below."

Reluctantly, Nerissa allowed Midshipman Cranton to guide her toward the hatch that led below where presumably, she would spend a terrifying tenure wondering if she was going to die, if those she was beginning to know and like were going to die, if the British rescuers on the pursuing ship—which might, for all she knew, include her brothers—were going to die.

Her thoughts were troubled as they descended into the darkness. Now she rather wished that she had given Ruaidri O' Devir what he'd asked for. A kiss. It would cost her nothing but might mean everything to him. But she, in her stiff pride, had denied him that.

So little that he had asked for.

So very little.

The gloom was thickening as they went deeper into the ship, the sounds above fading and a quiet stillness of creaking timbers and dank air that absorbed all sound, blanketing all. The midshipman paused. "I'm sorry to be leaving you, Lady Nerissa, and sorrier still that it's in darkness without a lantern, but I promise that Joey will join you shortly and one of us will be back for you just as soon as we can be. I'm needed on deck."

"I will be fine, Mr. Cranton."

It was too dark down here to see him nod, but she

sensed the brief movement in the darkness and a moment later, he was gone.

So she was supposed to stay down here like a good little pet and keep out of trouble. She was supposed to stay down here and wonder what was going on above, wonder what would become of her, wonder if she would survive any more than anyone else, especially if one or more shots from that frigate found *Tigershark*'s hull and sent her straight to the bottom.

Trapped in darkness on a sinking ship?

No, it was not where Nerissa intended to be.

She knew better than to bother the captain or appear on deck, but she sure as salt wasn't staying here. Waiting until Midshipman Cranton's footsteps faded back into the silence, she picked up her skirts and slowly feeling her way along a bulkhead, retraced her steps.

A muffled roll of thunder told her that the pursuing frigate was closer now, and again, she thought of the Irish captain's sharp, angular face with his bold black brows and ever-changing eyes, his intent focus, that deep despair that cloaked him in a way she could not quite fathom.

I wish I'd given him that kiss.

Too late, now.

The next time she saw him, he might be dead.

A dim glow of light shone ahead of her, fainter than the first breath of sunrise on a distant horizon, but it was enough to tell her where the companionway was. It wasn't easy to ascend in the darkness but she managed, and soon found herself on the next deck. Here, the sounds of impending battle were unmistakable; heavy cannon being wheeled into place, men shouting orders, running feet on the deck above.

She turned, and stifled a scream.

"What are you doing, Lady Nerissa?"

A man stood there, gaunt, sunken-cheeked, with the

most soulful eyes she'd ever seen. He wore a blood-stained leather apron and his hair was a dingy shade of brown more than halfway on its journey to gray and receding from his brow like an outgoing tide. He looked familiar, and she suddenly realized who he was: the surgeon who had come up from below to accompany the sailor whom Captain O' Devir had rescued after falling from the rigging.

"You startled me," she said, a hand on her bosom.

"Likewise."

"I suppose you're going to tell me I cannot be here. But I'll tell you right now, Mr...."

"Jeffcote."

"Mr. Jeffcote, that I will not suffer being hidden away in the darkness, wondering if I'm going to live or die, while the world comes apart all around me."

"Nobody's forcing you to stay there. The sick bay's safe enough, I reckon. And if we come to battle, I expect I could use some help comforting the men."

"Comforting the men?"

Above, another ominous boom, this one louder, and a chorus of jeers from above as the American crew taunted their pursuer.

"Aye, comforting them. Holding their hands, like, if they need a leg cut off or a splinter cut out. Giving 'em water or rum, fetching me bandages, making yourself useful. You up to that, my lady?"

"I have no experience with such matters, but yes ... I am willing to help you, Mr. Jeffcote."

"Come along, then," he said, passing a weary hand over his balding pate. "You can start by making bandages. I've a feeling we're gonna need 'em."

Chapter Thirteen

The young Scottish lieutenant of His Majesty's frigate *Happenstance* saluted as he approached his captain. "We'll be in range soon, sir."

"We're in range now, Mr. McPhee. Fire a bow chaser. If they know what's good for them, they'll heave to."

Lawrence Hadley the Fourth stood on his quarterdeck, hands clasped behind his back as he rocked imperceptibly back and forth on his heels. He watched the great fore-and-aft mainsail of the fleeing American brig like a bull fixated on a giant white cloth. Faintly, his mouth turned up at one corner, defying its owner's attempt to appear unflappable. He wanted that ship and the glory its capture would bring him with a desperateness he could taste, and when word got back to England, this would surely win him a knighthood, if not a peerage.

The likelihood of American ships in these waters was low.

The likelihood of this particular American ship being commanded by the audacious sod who'd dared abduct the fair Lady Nerissa was high.

Either way, she was a fine brig and would make an even finer prize once her crew was either dead or in gaol and the vessel herself sent to the auction block. The money she would bring him, the glory—

"What are the chances, sir, that he's our man?"

Hadley was roused from his reverie by the presence of his second lieutenant. "I'd say they're damned good, Mr. Dewhurst. The only Yank I know of in these waters is that wretched scoundrel John Paul Jones, and that isn't Jones." He studied the fleeing vessel with a calculating eye, then glanced at the gun crew running out a larboard gun. "In fact, get the royals on her. I haven't got all day to waste in a game of tag."

"Aye sir." Dewhurst turned to bawl the order, and immediately, men began to scurry aloft.

But even without the royals, they were gaining, the distance between the two ships closing.

Closing....

Forward, he could see McPhee supervising the gun crew ... saw them run the muzzle of the great black beast out through its port and heard the accompanying rumble of wooden wheels against the deck. A moment later a crack of thunder echoed back to him as the gun barked out its demand, and he waited impatiently for the enemy brig to heave to in response.

But she did not.

Indignation caused him to clench his fists. He could, and would, blow that ship to smithereens.

They were beginning to overtake her now, their head-rig starting to obliterate his view of the brig's stern. Two hundred feet separated them. His Royal Marines were waiting with muskets high above in the tops. Dewhurst was waiting for him to give the signal to load up the larboard battery.

McPhee was back.

"She's not heaving to, sir."

"I can see that, Mr. McPhee." Outrage that the rebels would openly defy a king's ship made him unusually curt. He had left England in haste, confident that if he could find the American ship on board which Lady Nerissa was imprisoned, his presence alone would cow the damned rebels into surrender. After all, he mastered a Royal Navy frigate—a ship that had more muscle than three of those brigs combined would ever hope to have—and sailors who belonged to the finest navy in the world. He had expected to range up on the American ship and effect an immediate lowering of her colors. Not this. Not sheer, open defiance. He set his teeth, furious. "Load up the larboard battery with chain and run out. If she won't heave to, we'll bring down her rigging and *force* her to."

"Do ye think she's the same ship that's got the Lady Nerissa sir?"

"Well, it's obvious by her build and flag that she's American, she's fleeing toward the safety of a French port, and my intuition in such matters is usually correct. In fact—What the *devil*?"

A collective gasp went up as a sudden flash of blue-green, its wearer struggling in the grip of two sailors, suddenly appeared on the brig's quarterdeck.

"Is that—"

"Oh, my God...."

"By Jove, sir, it's a woman!"

The Yankee brig had slowed as she began to turn toward the wind, her topsails luffing. Hadley barked an order for his own ship to do the same and to range up beside them.

"Ready on the larboard guns in case this is a trick," he snapped to McPhee. Fury burned through his veins at the sight of the struggling figure in teal. "I want Featherston's marines ready to fire down on that bastard the minute I give the word. In the meantime, prepare to board."

He seized a speaking trumpet, strode to the rail, and all but slammed the instrument to his lips. "I am Captain Lawrence Hadley of the Royal Navy frigate *Happen-*

stance and I demand that you heave to and prepare to receive boarders!"

The other vessel was as close to the wind as she could get without heaving to and showed no signs of heeding Hadley's demands. He was just considering whether to fire into her when he saw movement on her quarterdeck, and a lean but powerful figure dressed in a blue and white uniform stepped forward wearing a tricorne and a belt that bristled with weapons. His brows were black and bold, and he was taller than any of his nearby officers or men. Just behind him, Hadley glimpsed the bright blue-green gown that marked the lady's form, her hair covered by a large round hat as she struggled in the grip of two pigtailed seamen. Bile rose in his throat at the thought of what the rebels had done to her. At how they were treating her. The two seamen shoved the girl forward and she fell heavily against the tall officer, who immediately snared her and crushed her face to his chest to restrain her; in the next instant, he plucked a pistol from his belt and drove it into the rounded felt crown of her hat.

"Saints alive," breathed McPhee. "He'd kill her right in front of us."

"He won't kill her," Hadley shot back. "She's his insurance, the only thing standing between himself and my guns."

"Do you want me to—"

"Greetin's right back at ye, ye poxy shiteballs!" came the voice of the tall officer across the water. "This is the American Continental brig *Tigershark*, and I'm her captain, Ruaidri O' Devir. Ye got somethin' to say to me, or should we let our guns do the talkin'?"

"He's a bloody Irishman," snarled Hadley, under his breath.

His second lieutenant, Dewhurst, pressed close. "And a goddamned rebel. He'll hang for this."

"Permission, sir, to go rig a noose from the foreyard, myself!" said Tuttle, the youngest of the midshipmen.

Beside him, McPhee, trying to maintain a quiet professionalism in a moment that was growing increasingly tense, leaned close. "I believe Captain Featherston and his marines can get a clear shot at that bastard, sir. Do you want me to give the order to—"

"You fire on him with his gun to the girl's head and it will be the last damned move you ever make," hissed Hadley in a voice that turned McPhee's face white beneath his freckles. He raised his speaking trumpet. "Heave to, you rebel, and release her ladyship to me *now*."

"Eh, now, Captain! I'm not as dumb as ye likely think me," called the Irishman, all but suffocating the girl as he drove his pistol hard against her hat. "I'm guessin' ye're the poor sod sent to negotiate with me, eh?"

"I do not negotiate with rebels!"

"I'm no rebel, Captain, but a commissioned officer in me country's navy, just as you are."

Hadley saw red. "You don't have a country, and when I am through with you, O' Devir—"

The Irishman's challenging smirk was visible even without the aid of a glass. "Let's cut with formality," he called. "You want Lady Nerissa, and I want the explosive. Ye got that for me, Hadley?"

"Send Lady Nerissa across on your boat and I'll send the explosive."

"Well, now, I appreciate yer offer, Captain, but those aren't me terms and if I send her across, I'll have to trust yer word as a gentleman that ye'll send the explosive in return. I was in yer Navy once, did ye know that? I know how ye do things." He tightened his forearm over the girl's back when her struggles began anew. "Ye'll be forgivin' me if I don't place much trust in anyone in yer Navy." His mocking smile faded and the eyes that met Hadley's across the water were ruthless and hard. "Now, if ye're done wasting me time, I'd like to be on my way."

"You send Lady Nerissa across right now or I shall be forced to fire on you!"

"Unless ye have that explosive and are prepared to make a fair exchange, I'm afraid that's not happenin', Hadley. And you and I both know that if ye fire on me, the chances of Lady Nerissa being hurt by either yer guns—" he waved his pistol "—or mine, are pretty feckin' good."

"How dare you threaten—"

The Irish captain's face went hard. "Ye were instructed to meet me under my terms, at Saint-Malo. Do so on Saturday mornin', and we'll talk then." Just as quickly, the darkness in his face was gone as he grinned and touched his hat in a mocking salute. "Top o' the mornin' to ye, Captain!"

He turned away, the struggling figure in aqua fighting him all the way, and Hadley felt sick to his stomach as the rebel brute raised his hand and brought his pistol down hard on the girl's oversize hat. She went limp, and was quickly dragged off by several seamen before disappearing from sight.

His voice trembling, Hadley crooked a finger towards Captain Featherston of the Royal Marines.

"Put a ball right in the center of that bastard's back," he ground out.

The marine raised his musket but the moment was lost. Ruaidri O' Devir had already walked away, swallowed up by his men, and the brig was falling back off the wind and beginning to gather way.

Hadley felt impotent rage burning behind his eyeballs; he could do nothing, and that treasonous rogue out there knew it. Worse, his charging out here ahead of a tangible plan and backed by nothing but his own British arrogance that an inferior ship in an inferior "navy" from an inferior country would defy him, had left him humiliated.

"Stay in pursuit," he muttered, taking a deep and steadying breath.

"He struck her," McPhee was saying in horror, his voice hollow. "Captain, he *hit* a woman."

"So he did. And when I get hold of him, I'll give the lady herself the honor of hanging him."

Chapter Fourteen

"Fine young lady you make, Cranton!"

"Aye, he looks damned fetching in a dress, don't you think, Captain?"

"You can pull the stuffing out of your bodice now, *Milady*, hahaha!"

The men, laughing, wolf-whistling at the red-faced Midshipman Cranton, and clapping their clever captain on the back as they went below, were met by the surgeon and Lady Nerissa de Montforte, garbed in the midshipman's uniform, as they were coming up from a sick bay that had not seen one casualty of the sea battle that never happened. Lady Nerissa took one look at Midshipman Cranton, who went even redder as he pulled a wadded-up stocking out of his bosom, and her jaw dropped.

"Well, Mr. Cranton," she said, brows raised. "When you told me you needed my gown so as to clean the sea stains and tar from it, I had no idea that you had ... uh, other uses for it."

Loud guffaws met her remark.

"Really, Captain O' Devir," she said, turning to the grinning Irishman. "Your so-called Navy has some odd ways of amusing itself."

"Odd ways that saved all of our hides," cried a nearby seaman. "Three cheers for our captain!"

"Hip hip, huzzah! Hip hip, huzzah! Hip hip, huzzah!"

Nerissa, confused, could only stare at them all. They'd surely lost their minds. "I expected there to be a sea fight, and I'm very glad there was not, but how did you manage to avoid getting blown to the ends of the earth, Captain O' Devir?"

He just shrugged, his eyes hungry and dark as he took in her long, willowy form, her legs clearly outlined in Midshipman Cranton's skinny breeches. "Well, Lady Nerissa, ye're the most valuable person on this ship and that countryman of yers back there knows it. He wouldn't dare fire on us with you up here on deck."

"But I *wasn't* up here on deck."

"Aye, precisely. But that piece of sh—... ehm, that blaggard back there, didn't know that. Ye'll stay in Cranton's uniform so he doesn't find out."

"What? What are you all talking about?"

Lieutenant Morgan, chewing on a piece of dried ginger, was the one who clarified it for her. "Captain O' Devir would never risk your life by having you up on deck where musket or cannonballs could be flying, so he had Cranton here pretend to be you."

The youth rubbed the back of his head. "Didn't need to hit me quite so hard, sir," he said good naturedly. "I nearly didn't have to fake being knocked out cold."

"My heavens," Nerissa said, as laughter greeted the youth's remark, and immediately the sailor's teasing resumed.

"Still think you make a fetching young lady, Mr. Cranton!"

"Can I call on you, my lady?" asked Tackett the sailing master, making an elegant leg to the blushing youth. "I'd love to run my fingers through your hair...."

"Hell, I'd love to run mine through his cleavage."

"Hahaha!"

"Shut yer gobs, ye rogues," said Captain O' Devir. "That's an officer ye're talkin' to. Give him some respect."

More guffaws, because it was hard to give a man any respect when he stood before them in a lady's gown, red-faced, fuming, and reaching into his bosom to tear out the other stocking.

He flung it down. "My apologies, Lady Nerissa," he said, looking like he was about to take a swing at the sailing master. "You should not have to listen to such talk."

She couldn't help but be caught up in their high spirits. "I have brothers," she said, smiling. "There's not much that will offend me, I can assure you."

More laughter.

"Besides," she added, "I think you should be commended for your bravery. I don't see any of your crewmates or fellow officers here, volunteering for such a thankless job."

"Aye, give him a medal!"

"And some pins for his hair!"

Laughter, jeers, back-slapping. Cranton reached for his sword, only to remember it was absent.

Nerissa touched his shoulder. "Pay your friends no mind," she said gently. "While I may not be happy about being held prisoner here, I am most grateful to you, Mr. Cranton, for saving lives on both this ship and theirs. You made quite a sacrifice ... and at great expense and humiliation to yourself, as well."

"Thank you my lady." He grinned foolishly. "But it was the captain's idea, not mine."

Their commander, still eyeing Nerissa with a wolfish gleam in his eye, only shrugged off the praise. "'Tis right she be, Mr. Cranton. Now go get out of that gown and back into a proper uniform."

"Aye, sir!"

The youth fled, tripped over his hem, and landed in the arms of his shipmates, whose laughter roared forth anew.

The crew's guffaws ringing behind them, Nerissa and the captain returned to the deck and found their way to the stern to watch the frigate's progress. She lay a half-mile off, doggedly pursuing them but making no further move to overtake or fire on them. Nerissa breathed a sigh of relief. No blood had been shed. Nobody had been killed or captured. She was still here, still a hostage, yes ... but nobody had been hurt and that was more important than anything else. Suddenly aware of Captain O' Devir's presence beside her, she looked up at him. His eyes were dark with that same restless hunger she'd seen in them just a few minutes before.

"You're a clever man, Captain O' Devir," she said, meeting his gaze and feeling an answering heat that centered itself between her thighs. "You managed to avoid a sea fight and bloodshed with a simple ruse, and nobody got hurt."

"Aye, well, we're not out of the woods, yet."

"No, but for now ... is it fair to say you've given us all a breather?"

"Aye, lass. 'Tis fair."

They stood gazing at each other, and Nerissa felt the warmth between them, a current of like-mindedness, and she knew that he was thinking very much the same thing that she was.

They were at the stern of the ship, with nothing but the taffrail and ocean behind Nerissa's back. And, the frigate. Still the frigate. Captain O' Devir glanced over his shoulder to ensure they were unobserved by the crew and moved close to her, his body shielding her from anyone on deck who might happen to notice how close he stood to her. "Ye know," he said, his eyes hot with challenge, "I never did get me kiss."

She swallowed the sudden dry spot in her throat. "Given that you didn't end up in battle, I guess you didn't need the kiss after all."

"A matter of opinion, Lady Nerissa."

"A matter of fact, Captain O' Devir."

"A matter that needs rectification."

"A matter best settled away from curious eyes," she said as he reached out and gently tipped her chin up, grazing the soft skin there with his rough and callused thumb. She shuddered despite the warmth of the day and took a deep and steadying breath, hating her body for the way it so wantonly responded to this man who was wrong for in every single way she could possibly think of.

His head was lowering to hers, his powerful shoulders blotting out the mast and the great sails behind them. She tried, feebly, one last time to head off what she knew was coming.

"Careful, Captain. You wouldn't want your men to see you kissing Midshipman Cranton, would you?"

"I'm past carin' what anyone thinks," he said and reaching out, took her into his arms.

❧

"I am going to be ill," Captain Lawrence Hadley choked out, watching the captain of the American ship sidling up to one of his midshipman. He dug the telescope into his eye, his voice strangled with rage and disbelief. "Abuse of a gently-bred young woman, mocking a king's ship, treason against the Crown and now cavorting with his young lads. He's a damned *sodomite*!"

"Poor Lady Nerissa ... sir, what will we do?"

"Yes, Captain, we have to save her!"

Yes, he did indeed have to save her or there'd be no

saving *him* from the Duke of Blackheath—if his superiors, starting with his own father, didn't have his head, first. But what could he do? He could not fire on the American brig and risk injury to Lady Nerissa no matter how much he'd like to blast that Irishman into a thousand pieces. He would, too. Just as soon as the time was right, and there was no chance of the young lady being injured.

"Why don't we just meet him as he proposes?" Lieutenant McPhee asked, reasonably. "Seems like it would be the best solution."

"Because I have not been given the explosive," Hadley muttered. "Because I'm not going to be given the explosive. Because Admiralty is not going to relinquish that explosive to an enemy, no matter who his hostage is or how important she may be. Deception, not negotiation, is the only weapon in my arsenal."

"So ... what now? Do we have another plan?"

"I thought the presence of a frigate of the king's navy would be enough, and it damn well should have been!"

Obviously, it had *not* been.

McPhee appeared to chew on the inside of his lip, his brown eyes deep in thought.

"Maybe Admiralty won't be putting the explosive on the bargaining table," he said slowly, "but if we were to go back and fetch the inventor, Lord Andrew, maybe the Yanks will accept him instead."

Hadley turned and looked at him, studying him for a long moment. Then, he shook his head. "The Duke of Blackheath will never permit that."

"I'm sure Lord Andrew is free to make his own choices, and what manner of man wouldn't trade himself for his own wee sister?"

Hadley nodded slowly, watching the brig that, were it not for the lady's presence topside, would have been his an hour ago.

"Besides, sir ... we're near the coast of France. Plenty of places for O' Devir to duck in and hide, and plenty of French ships to give him protection from us. We now know what his ship looks like, we know he has the young lady, all we have to do is make all haste back to London, convince Lord Andrew to return with us, and arrive at the meeting place on Saturday with him. O' Devir would be a fool not to accept the inventor in the formula's stead." He grinned. "Why settle for the product when you can have the source?"

"Hmm. And of course, after the lady is safely in our hands, we do what is necessary to retrieve Lord Andrew as well, preferably before these rascals can even leave the rendezvous place with him."

"Seems reasonable to me, sir."

Hadley nodded once, pretending to consider his lieutenant's plan. "You are a clever young officer, Mr. McPhee," he said. "You will make a fine captain some day. Your idea has merit."

"Shall I give the order to change tack, and make all possible haste, then, back to England, sir?"

"Yes, Mr. McPhee. Do it, and do it now."

He raised the glass once more for a last look at the man he was determined to kill at all costs. Through summer haze, salt spray, and distance, he could just see the Irishman standing on his own deck. The slim young midshipman was in his arms, and the two were kissing.

Kissing.

Hadley made a noise of disgust and turned away.

At least Lady Nerissa de Montforte was safe as long as O' Devir's tastes ran to young boys.

Chapter Fifteen

Nerissa drew back, eyes wide as Captain O' Devir finally released her mouth, grinning at the expression in her eyes, his hand still alongside her jaw. She felt him pass his thumb across her lips as though to seal in the kiss that had just about robbed her of the ability to stand, to breathe, and certainly to think. She inhaled on a deep shudder of confusion and unconsciously, licked the taste of him from her lips with one slow swipe of her tongue. Salt spray. Coffee. She could still feel the imprint of his powerful arms around her, the press of his masculinity against her own hips. In her own nether regions, desire flared.

Her emotions were in turmoil.

She glanced around his shoulder. The crew was busy about their duties; nobody had noticed the stolen kiss.

And she had enjoyed it. Welcomed it—though everything about her breeding, her upbringing, and her situation dictated that he was entirely unsuitable. But none of that mattered. None of it mattered, because she was drawn to him like a bee to a flower, a mare to a stallion, and she wanted him to kiss her again despite the fact she should never, ever have let him kiss her in the first place.

"Well," he murmured, watching her with a clever,

knowing smile, "Given that ye didn't hit me this time, I'm thinkin' ye must have liked that."

"I'd be a liar if I claimed otherwise." She moved away to put distance between them. "Some things make no sense, Captain."

"Maybe they're not meant to."

"What do you mean?"

"Suitability and desire don't always go hand in hand. We're not suited, t' be sure. But our bodies don't know that, do they? Unsuitability doesn't dampen the fact that everythin' in my body and blood and brain that makes me a man, is desperate to have ye ... to claim more than a kiss." His voice grew husky, and his eyes intent. "*To take ye to me bed.*"

She flushed at his brazen words, images rearing up in her mind of what it would be like to be in bed with him, his body dwarfing and all but crushing her own, his powerful arms lowering himself to her to complete *the act*. Oh, how was she to react to such a declaration? How, when her brain told her that he could never be for her but her body—oh, her treacherous, willful body!—found him hopelessly, devastatingly attractive despite all the reasons logic told her it shouldn't? Flustered, she smoothed Mr. Cranton's coat down over her hips, suddenly far too aware of the indecency of her legs so clearly defined by the breeches and too late, realizing that the simple movement of smoothing the fabric over her hips drew Captain O' Devir's eye and made the purple in his irises darken even more beneath their absurdly long fringe of lashes.

"And why would you want me, Captain O' Devir?"

"I'd have to be a feckin' dead man not to want ye. I admire yer pluck, lass. Yer courage. Yer resilience. Aside from an initial fuss, ye've accepted your lot here with little complaint and plenty of fortitude. There's a lot to be said for that."

"Well, going into histrionics and railing about my fate aren't going to change it or save my reputation."

"But ye didn't count on wantin' to kiss me, now, did you?"

"I have nothing to lose at this point, do I?"

"No, but ye've got everythin' to gain."

"How so?"

He laughed, and it wasn't just humor, but something dark just beneath the surface, something restless and dangerous and riding a narrow edge. Something full of challenge. "What're ye goin' to do when ye get back to England, lass?"

"Do?"

"Aye, do."

"Why, I suppose I will ... rest for a few days ... perhaps accept the calls of my closest friends ... write in my diary of this awful experience—"

"Awful?" He raised a black eyebrow.

"I've been abducted, nearly seen a man drown, almost been in a sea fight, and been kissed by a man who is altogether ... *unsuitable*."

"Ye needed to be kissed, and still do. Ye need to be kissed until yer lips are bruised and yer head is swimmin' and ye can't think of anythin' but the feel of a man's arms around ye and the anticipation of what comes next. Ye've never *had* a proper kiss in your life, have ye?"

"Of course I have!"

"No, ye haven't."

Her chin came up. "I'll remind you, Captain O' Devir, that I was affianced once. I can assure you I've been kissed."

"Well now, that both answers and poses a question, it does. Ye're young, probably heavily dowered, as lovely as Ireland is green and probably have men fallin' at your feet like flies. Affianced once but no more, and still not spoken for. Why not?"

She felt the inevitable shame. The anger. The freefall of her heart as the events of the last months washed over her. "I would rather not talk about ... my affairs."

"Why not?"

"Because it's none of your business!"

"Aye, 'tis right you are. None of me business." He smiled that hard, razor's edge smile, sighed, and appeared to relent.

Nerissa turned her face away to look over the waves.

"Why not?" he persisted, purposely bumping her with his elbow.

Frustrated, she turned to deliver a rebuke but he was grinning, and she realized he was intentionally baiting her and that getting her hot and flustered was, in some way, a victory for him.

"If you really must know, Captain, I ... I have been holding out. Hoping that Perry would change his mind. Come to his senses. I loved him, and I don't want to talk about him or any other potential suitors."

"Why not?"

"Don't you have any other words in your vocabulary besides those two?"

"Can't think of any at the moment."

He was still looking at her, one brow raised, waiting. "We could talk about you and me, if ye like."

"There is no 'you and me.'"

"There could be, if ye wanted it as much as I do."

"We are ill-suited. You said it yourself. I'm English. My father was a duke. What was yours, Captain?"

"A fisherman."

"I was raised by nannies and dance masters and French tutors and music instructors and an overly controlling brother. Who were you raised by?"

"Me lovin' mam and a pack of village lads who taught me how to speak with me fists."

"Are you even literate?"

"I'm a self-made man, Lady Nerissa. I may not've had yer fancy schoolin', but I can assure you I can read a book, write a poem, plot a course and carve a ship out of a piece of wood."

She sighed and her shoulders dropped. "I'm sorry. I did not mean to be hurtful. I am just ... I am just so confused, and when I'm confused I get frustrated and when I'm frustrated my temper gets short and when my temper gets short I say things I regret."

He cast a glance at their distant pursuer, then back at her. "What are ye confused by?"

"You."

"Ye shouldn't be. I'm a simple man."

"The feelings I'm developing for you are not ... simple."

"What feelin's?"

She just shot him a quelling look, unwilling to give him yet another victory.

"I suppose you've never been in love, have you, Captain? Never had your heart broken?"

He looked back again at their pursuer and for the briefest of moments, a shadow crossed his face. "Ah, well, there might've been a time or two. But I'm over it, I am. No sense lookin' back."

"And no pretty girl in some distant American port waiting for you? No woman wearing a ring on her finger, praying for your safe return?"

"Not a one."

They stood together for many moments, Nerissa looking down at the sea driving past below, wondering what it was about this man that encouraged her to lay bare her soul, to confide things in him that she would not have shared with the closest of her friends. She'd known him for less than a week and already she felt more comfortable in his presence than she ever had in Perry's. He irritated her, he forced her to look deep inside her heart, he challenged her and humored her and rattled the base of the lofty pedestal on which she had spent her life, and she sensed an underlying loyalty in him that she guessed was utterly unshakeable.

"Ye've let yer man Perry go now, haven't ye, lass?" he asked gently. "And ye're feelin' guilty about it."

Sudden tears sprang up behind her eyelids and she swallowed the lump in her throat, looking down into the blue, blue sea.

"Am I right, Lady Nerissa?"

"Yes, Captain. I believe you probably are."

"Why don't ye just forget him?"

"I ... think I have."

"No ye haven't. And ye certainly haven't forgiven him."

"*I haven't forgiven my brother.*"

There. She'd said it. And now the tears were spilling over because no, she hadn't forgiven Lucien. Not for his manipulations that had cost her Perry, not for his choking over-protectiveness, not for what—or whom—he most certainly had planned for her the minute she was back on English soil and under his *protection* once more.

Ruaidri O' Devir seemed to read her mind. "Stop yer pinin', lass. Maybe he did you a favor, this brother of yers. You can do a lot better than some sorry lad who doesn't have conviction, who didn't love ye enough to offer for ye the minute ye came of age."

"Perhaps I can, but Lucien will waste no time in finding me a husband the moment I get back to England." She wiped at a falling tear and willfully pulled herself together. "I will not love the man he picks out for me. I may not even like him. But that's the bane of being a rich noblewoman, isn't it? I am of no more value than a pedigreed broodmare. My worth is what lineage and dowry I can bring to another man's family. I doubt I'll have much choice in the matter, especially after ... this."

Out of the corner of her eye, she saw that the teasing smile had left his face and there was a penetrating sadness there.

"So that's your world, then."

"Not just my world. My cage."

"Well, *mo nimfeach mara beag* ... while it must be nice to have money and all its trappin's, to have privilege and status and all the finer things in life, I must say I'd want no part of that kind of world." He laid his hand over her own. "And I think the man who ends up with you is more blessed than the one who finds the pot o' gold at the end of a rainbow, and I'm not talkin' about any feckin' dowry, either."

She said nothing for a long moment. "There are times that I wish my life was different, too. That it offered more ... freedom."

He looked out over the sea. "I could give you that, ye know."

Startled, she looked up at him. "What are you saying, Captain O' Devir?"

"Stay here with me. Sail the seas, be free of balls and teas and social visits and expectations and the course yer brother will set for ye. Choose yer own path in life."

"Stay here with *you*?"

"Why not?"

"Stop saying that?"

"Saying what?"

"Saying, 'Why not!'"

He shrugged. "Well, it was just an idea."

Her palms suddenly felt cold, even as her heart began to race with the thrill of possibility. "I can't stay here with you and you know it."

"Don't see—" he grinned—"*why not.*"

"Ohhhh!"

"Think about it. We get on well. I want ye in my bed. If ye're honest with yerself, ye want me in yours. Makin' love to me wouldn't be the trial it might be with someone who was *suitable* but repellent. Ye'd have no obligation to produce an heir. No obligations to an ancient family or a society that ye obviously ache to escape. Ye'd be loved and treasured and cared about, never set aside once yer purpose—whatever the divil that is—is fulfilled."

"What are you saying, Captain O' Devir?"

"That I'd marry ye, if I could. Give ye that freedom ye crave."

Her mouth opened and shut, but nothing came out. Nothing.

"If I could," he said again.

Finally, she managed, "I can't stay here with you. I don't know anything about you, except that you're Mrs. Lord's brother."

"What d'ye want to know?"

"Everything! Nothing! I can't believe we are having this conversation!"

"No reason ye can't stay. Ye just said yerself that there's nothin' to go back to."

"I'm not—"

"Tell me what ye want to know about me."

She tried to catch her breath. To collect her thoughts. Time was passing too fast, this situation rapidly escalating out of control.

"I can't stay with you, certainly not as your mistress and you're right, we could never marry. Besides, you ... you have no p-prospects! No way to support a wife in the style to which she might be accustomed—"

"I'm an officer in the Continental Navy, Lady Nerissa, and a damned good one at that. I can assure ye that my prospects are actually quite good. Especially if I return home with that explosive."

"It's not a 'real' Navy!"

"Try tellin' that to the people who are payin' me to be here. Try tellin' it to my men, who serve this ship and trust their lives to my skill and judgment. Try tellin' it to that sack of shite trailin' us back there if he decides to bring a fight to me. The fact that England doesn't recognize her former colonies' declaration of independence doesn't negate its existence."

She just looked at him. "How did you even end up in this ... *navy?*"

He deliberately let his elbow touch hers as he leaned on the rail and followed her gaze down into the blue water swirling in their wake. "When I was but a lad in Connemara, I was press-ganged. I spent the next ten years of my life as little more than a prisoner, servin' a king who's not mine and fightin' for a country I loathed."

"I'm sorry," she murmured, not knowing what else to say.

"Aye, well, it's done and o'er with, now."

"I suppose it's too much to hope that, having once found yourself in a similar situation as you've put me in—that is, of being held against your will—you will be all the more sympathetic to my plight."

"I'm fierce sympathetic," he said, looking down at her, "and it pains me that these are the measures I've had to resort to. But, when opportunity comes a' knockin', one would be a fool not to answer the door."

He glanced up at the trim of the sails and then forward, always the captain even in a moment of leisure. In the near distance, Lieutenant Morgan stood with young Cranton and the even younger Joey taking measurements with a nautical instrument of some sort. He must have seen something in Captain O' Devir's eyes, for he immediately left the two youngsters and approached, deliberately averting his gaze from Nerissa and saluting his superior.

"Mr. Morgan, 'tis time to tack. Please see to it."

"Aye, sir."

The officer moved smartly off to carry out the order.

"So, how did you escape?" Nerissa asked.

"Several years back, I jumped ship in Boston. I hung around for a bit, got the lay o' the land, and convinced some backers to give me command of a sloop. I did a bit of smugglin', seein' as how the English were starvin' Boston into submission. Or tryin' to." He laughed. "Lads like me, we kept the city in food and drink. Ran arms, procured gunpowder. Probably saved a lot of lives." He straightened up. "Come, let's walk."

He offered his arm and she took it, grateful for his strength as they headed forward.

They passed a sailor down on his knees repairing a large, salt-stained sail, who touched his fist to his forelock as they passed. "Good morning, sir!"

Captain O' Devir nodded. "Mornin', Sanderson."

They continued on, past big, deadly-looking guns standing sentinel on deck, past a barrage of ropes and rigging that looked so complex Nerissa wondered how anyone could even remember their names, let alone their functions. "'Twas during that time that I fell in with Sam Adams, Dr. Warren, John Hancock and a group of prominent patriot leaders. Friendships were formed, trust earned, though I'll be the first to confess that I started thinkin' so highly of myself that I made what was nearly a fatal mistake."

"Which was?"

He grinned. "I got caught."

"By the British?"

"Not just the British, but my own brother-in-law, Deirdre's husband. He outsmarted me. But I was soon free again, lickin' me wounds and injured pride, takin' stock of me life and thinkin' about what I wanted out of it. I went back and forth between Boston and Ireland a few times since, but I keep going back to Boston and findin' ways to make a nuisance of myself." He grinned. "Better than starin' at sheep back home."

"Two of my sisters-in-law are from Boston. Another, originally from Salem."

"Are they, now?"

"Yes."

"And have they turned into fancy English snobs?"

She might have stiffened, if the teasing smile wasn't back on his face. "No. They are wonderful, and I adore them."

"Well, I suppose England owes us, then. Three American lasses for three rich Englishmen in exchange for one English lass for a poor, unsuitable Irishman."

"I have *not* said I will stay here with you, Captain O' Devir."

"No, ye haven't, but I'll keep working on ye."

"And what about you? Why aren't *you* married?"

The teasing grin faded as quickly as if someone had stabbed him in the heart and his face, so open and carefree just a moment before, closed up, his eyes becoming guarded. "Ah, well, 'tis the sea I'm married to, Sunshine. And as to why it's that and not another, that's a conversation for another day."

The space between them went suddenly cold. Nerissa felt him withdrawing from her, defenses being thrown up like walls around a castle, impenetrable, unbreachable. She felt suddenly bereft. Awkward. Angry at her inadvertent blunder.

"You did say I could ask you anything," she reminded him, trying to regain what they'd had just a moment past, but the friendly openness between them was gone.

"Aye, so I did."

She pushed back from the rail. "I think I need to get out of this ridiculous uniform and back into my gown." she said, heading back to the stern cabin.

"Ye don't want to get back into that. It's filthy, now. Ruined."

"Well, I can't live in this."

"No, ye can't. You're not an officer, not even crew." He beckoned to the man who knelt on deck, mending the sail. "Sanderson!"

The man stood up, saluting. "Sir!"

"The lady needs clothes. Probably more than that sail needs mendin'. Fashion a jacket for her from one of the midshipmen's dress coats and a skirt or petticoats or whatever the divil women wear out of some sailcloth, would ye?"

The man went bug-eyed with horror. "Well now, sir, that's not something I've ever done before, and I—"

Captain O' Devir shot him a hard glare and the man instantly quieted, his hand raising in a quick salute.

Nerissa, her head high, stalked off and Ruaidri O' Devir watched her go. He could feel her indignation and he was sorry for it.

But there were some things he wasn't prepared to discuss.

Some things he wasn't prepared to remember.

Some things he wasn't prepared to relive.

Chapter Sixteen

The afternoon passed. Nerissa went back to the cabin, still garbed in Midshipman Cranton's uniform. Ruaidri tapped into his men's unspent and restless energy over what had nearly been a fight with the British ship and set them to drilling the guns, promising an extra measure of rum that night to the gun captain and crew who managed to fire, swab out, and reload his gun the fastest. He tried not to think about Lady Nerissa and how hurt she had looked when their conversation had reached its awkward end. He would have liked to have sought her out, made her laugh and kiss her senseless until she forgot both her innocent question and his own rather abrupt response to it. But he would not go chasing after her, not when he had a ship to run and the respect of fifty tough and hardened tars to maintain.

And so he stayed on deck for another hour, watching the British frigate fall farther and farther behind the closer they got to the French coast, finally turning tail and retreating when some sails off to the south proved to be French ones. Fuck Hadley. He was no coward but he was no fool, either, and Ruaidri knew they would meet again.

But not, he hoped, until Saturday, the day after next.

When the exchange would take place. When he would get the explosive and high-tail it back to Boston as he'd been sent here to do. Where he would say goodbye to little miss Sea Nymph, his *nimfeach mara beag*, and never see her again.

He should be feeling a sense of triumph, of accomplishment, at the thought.

Instead, it brought him only a desperate ache.

I don't want her to go.

He wished he could marry her. It was impossible, of course—too much separated them when it came to culture and class. The very idea was ludicrous, though not so much that his mind didn't keep flitting back to the idea despite his best efforts to direct it elsewhere. She was a gently-bred noblewoman who should never have been put into a position of being alone with a man. When he'd scooped her up off that London floor, he hadn't thought that far ahead—an opportunity had presented itself and he had grabbed it. Now, he realized just how much he had taken from her and her family with that one impulsive action. The scandal would be tremendous, outrageous, forever damning. The world, the society papers, the people amongst whom she lived and breathed ... all would think she'd been compromised. She could never be expected to make a decent match after this. She would be forced to live out her life as either a spinster or wife to a man who would not love her any more than that wanker Perry had, who would forever view her as damaged goods.

He could offer for her, but she would surely refuse him and he wouldn't blame her one bit. And yet ... he could love her. He was already half in love with her, and to fall the rest of the way wouldn't take much. He sensed a free and wayward spirit beneath the trappings of breeding and convention that complemented his own, and he had seen her kindness in her concern over McGuire when he'd gone overboard, the careful way she treated the blushing Cranton, the gentleness in her manner, her thoughts, her very soul. He had ruined her—and he owed her, no doubt about it.

I should have waited, and taken the brother. The inventor. I did it all arseways, didn't I?

He sighed and cast a last glance at the horizon. Hadley's frigate was gone. The evening was settling in, the moon coming up in the east. Things were in motion, wheels would be turning, and Saturday's exchange was well on its way.

The thought brought him no joy.

Another night spent sleeping outside his cabin, restlessly craving the woman who slept so innocently beyond the door.

That thought brought him no joy, either.

❧

Captain Lawrence Hadley had beaten it back to London.

"You know damned well, Larry, that I don't have the explosive and I certainly wouldn't offer it to the enemy even if I did have it," Lawrence Hadley the Third said to his son as they sat in the elder's office early the next morning. "But the Duke of Blackheath and Lord Andrew are due to arrive within an hour. I've got a meeting with the First Lord of the Admiralty about this in less than fifteen minutes, Admiral Elliott Lord and his brother at noon. We've got to think of something to stall that Irish vermin."

"Father, we don't have time to waste. He struck her with his pistol. I saw it with my own eyes."

"He *struck* her?"

Startled, both Hadleys turned toward the door, which had been left ajar to catch the breeze coming in down the hall ... and through which the mighty Duke of Blackheath and his brother had just come, some forty minutes early for their appointment.

Admiral Hadley got to his feet. "Your Grace, Lord Andrew, I thought our meeting was for ten o' clock—"

"*He struck her?*" the duke roared, and the walls themselves seemed to shrink from his fury.

"Your Grace, you have my full assurance that the Navy is putting every resource at its disposal toward bringing Lady Nerissa home safe and sound, with no expense or vessel spared—"

"No expense spared? What is this—this *buffoon* doing here in your office when he could be out rescuing my little sister? Is this the best the Royal Navy can bloody do?" The duke stalked towards the suddenly hapless younger Hadley, who knew that Blackheath was so well-connected that the First Sea Lord of the Admiralty himself was probably in his debt. "If you were in a position to see her, you were damn well in a position to save her! *Why did you leave her?*"

"With all due respect, Your Grace, I had O' Devir in range of my guns," Hadley said defensively. "I expected him to surrender to me; I had a king's frigate under my command, I could have blasted him out of the water three times over. I would have, too, but he brought Lady Nerissa topside and made sure I could see her, knowing full well that if I fired on him the risk of her being injured was substantial."

"*Why did you leave her?*"

"O' Devir was adamant that he would not talk business unless we did so under the terms of his demand, which is to meet at the French port of Saint-Malo tomorrow afternoon to make the exchange."

The duke stood there staring at him, his nostrils quivering with a rage so tightly controlled that Hadley felt a cold trickle of sweat beginning to slide down the groove of his spine.

"Your Grace, if I had stayed there, keeping this rebel's ship in sight, I dare not think of how much more he might have hurt the lady just to taunt me or punish me for staying vigilant. I—"

"Cease your damned prattle! I don't want to hear excuses! You went in there without a plan, with nothing to offer O' Devir in trade except your own foolish arrogance in thinking he'd be cowed because you had a bigger ship than he did. Is that not so, Hadley?"

Hadley flushed darkly.

Swearing under his breath the duke stalked to the window, where he stood looking out at the surrounding buildings, his fists clenched at his side as he tried to get his temper under control. Hadley let out a pent-up breath. The duke was angry, yes, but beneath that anger was a debilitating worry, a visceral panic over the fate and future of the little sister he loved.

"So you saw him strike her," he said softly, his voice trembling like a volcano about to explode. "And you left her there alone with this ... this rebel, this pirate, *this murderer*."

There was a moment of uncomfortable silence.

"I saw no recourse, Your Grace. I can assure you that I am as worried as you are—"

"*You cannot be one iota as worried as I am,*" snarled the duke, turning and impaling Hadley with a glare so black and deadly that the naval captain took a step back. "She is not *your* sister!"

"Lucien, easy," said Lord Andrew, laying a restraining hand on his brother's arm as Blackheath returned his anguished gaze to the street. "We will sort this out."

"I actually have an idea," Hadley said, drawing himself up. "It is not without risk, but I think it will work."

Blackheath looked at him with disdain.

"We bring Lord Andrew to Saint-Malo and let him

trade himself for his sister. And then rescue *him* once the exchange is made."

"We cannot give O' Devir the explosive," the elder Hadley said, vehemently shaking his head. "That is quite out of the question."

"*You* cannot give him the explosive, Admiral, because I haven't yet sold it to you," Lord Andrew countered, warming to Hadley's suggestion. "It is still mine to do with as I wish, and if I want to trade it for my sister, that is my prerogative.

The admiral's mouth fell open in horror that this aristocrat, whose blood was as ancient and blue as the ocean itself, would betray his country so, even if it was to rescue his sister.

"However," continued Lord Andrew, "that is not my intent."

All three men stared at the young inventor.

"It is unthinkable, of course, that I hand over the explosive," Lord Andrew continued. "However, your son's plan has merit." At the thunderous fury rising in his brother's face, he merely shrugged. "Why settle for the explosive when you can have the man who actually knows how to make it?"

"You're not going to share that information with him, are you?"

"Of course not, Admiral Hadley," Andrew said in disgust. "I'll stall him. Put him off. Once Nerissa is safe and I'm on his ship instead, I'll go below. Plead seasickness or something, anything to get me off the deck so you, Hadley, will have no reason not to fire on that brig and bring these pirates to heel. It could work, you know."

"Aye, it could."

"Your Grace?"

The duke's eyes, black, bottomless pits of pain, met his brother's. "I'd rather we just send over a false explosive. I don't want either of you in such danger."

The younger Hadley shook his head. "I doubt O' Devir is such a fool that he wouldn't test it first, and if he finds it to be inferior to his expectations and we've not held up our end of the bargain, there's no telling what he'll do to Lady Nerissa. No, Your Grace, I think this is the best way of handling this situation ... and I can assure you that I will not fire on that brig until your sister is safely upon my ship and Lord Andrew is well off the enemy's deck."

Lucien's mouth tightened. "Very well, then, Hadley." He let his black stare pierce the other man. "But the moment you've captured that vermin, you will bring him to me. *I* will be the one to decide his fate, not your guns. Do you understand?"

"Sir, I cannot—"

The duke's fist came down hard on the senior Hadley's desk. "*Do you understand?*"

"Yes, Your Grace. You make yourself very clear, indeed."

Chapter Seventeen

Morning.

An evening spent by herself, an unpalatable meal brought by Joey who'd sat and demonstrated some of "Ol' Scup's" vocabulary until Nerissa couldn't help but laugh at the parrot's raunchy command of the English language, the captain coming in briefly to retrieve a chart, and another long night in darkness lit only by a swinging lantern while she lay awake and pondered Captain Ruadri O' Devir and the way he made her feel.

Intrigued. Outraged. Fascinated. Incensed.

Open to possibilities that were too scandalous to even consider.

Stay here with me.

Early sunlight sought out the gloom of the cabin. Tomorrow was the scheduled rendezvous. Today would be her last full one aboard the brig. What would this day bring?

Tigershark's motion beneath her was oddly comforting, and soothed her restlessness in ways that she hadn't expected. Up and down, up and down, while the heavy wooden planking beneath her feet seemed permanently set at a forty-five degree angle.

If my brothers could see me now.

She was rather glad they could not. She already

feared for her captor's safety once Lucien caught up with them. And while Captain O' Devir might have confused and even angered her with the abrupt and unexpected way in which he'd pulled back in answer to her innocent question, the idea of harm coming to him filled her with a sharply unbearable ache. A worry that she hadn't expected.

The sun rose higher. She got up and made her toilet as best she could at the crude little washstand, ran her fingers through her hair and tried to restore her appearance with the help of the bit of mirror above it. She ached for a real bath. A comb. Lavender water and silk against her skin, edible food, a decent bed and Ruaidri O' Devir.

Ruaidri O' Devir.

She pressed her fingertips into her eyes and took a deep breath. *Oh, what is the matter with me?* She walked over to the little ship model wedged into the bulkhead and picked it up, fingering the smooth, lovingly-crafted hull, the carefully-strung rigging. It was a work of art, something exquisitely beautiful made from materials that were quite primitive, and she wondered, now, if that rough, common man out there, he who wore the uniform of an organized navy but was as wild and untamed as the windy, rain-soaked moors of his native land, had made it.

Behind her the door opened. Her instinct was to hurriedly put down the little model, but she had nothing to hide. Boldly, she met the eyes of the man standing in the doorway, his face in shadow beneath the brim of his tricorne hat, his tall, powerful body silhouetted by the light from behind him.

He didn't seem to know what to say.

Neither did she.

He walked into the cabin and wordlessly removed the hat. "Mornin', Sunshine."

"Good morning, Captain."

"Got some business to attend to," he said brusquely. "I'll try not to disturb ye."

She shrugged. It was, after all, his cabin. Wordlessly, she watched as he went to the desk, pulled out the chair and sat down. Flipped open the log book and sharpened a quill, dipped it in ink, and set it to paper. Her eyes drank in the sight of him. She had missed him. Hadn't been able to stop thinking of him. Now, she itched to move closer, just to see if he truly was able to read and write as he claimed or if he was just going through the motions to fool her. But his hand was quick and sure, his intent conveyed to the page in decisive flourishes and quick, repeated dips of the quill into the little bottle of ink, over and over again in almost an agitated motion. No man who was illiterate would write like that. She stepped closer. Came up behind him and looked down. He wrote with his left hand. His words were clean and sure, his spelling sound. No illiteracy here. She smiled.

"You're an enigma, Captain O' Devir."

"And why is that, Sunshine?"

She looked down at his entry, preceded by the date and followed by the weather and sea conditions. *Spoke the British frigate* Happenstance, *Captain Hadley. No shots exchanged. McGuire still in sick bay.* Succinct and to-the-point.

She took a deep breath and let her hand drop, lightly to his shoulder. To the gold epaulet that capped that bulging expanse of muscle, the silken thread soft beneath her fingers. He raised his head. Put the pen down.

What am I doing?

"No longer angry with me?" he asked softly, tilting his head to look up at her.

"I was wrong to pry. Besides—" she shrugged. "You're a male."

"Aye, last time I checked."

"And males sometimes prefer to keep things inside. I should know ... I've spent my life living with four of them."

He corked the bottle of ink, wiped the pen and pushed the log book aside so that his entry could dry. "We all have things we don't like to talk about. Things that cause pain simply by givin' them voice. Things we're ashamed of, even."

Her hand was still resting on his gold-threaded epaulet. Propriety demanded that she remove it. Her own will told her to let it stay and besides, the captain was making no move to dislodge her touch.

"So where do we go from here?" she asked, her fingers beginning a slow kneading of his shoulder beneath the dark blue cloth until she felt the great muscles relax.

"Is there a 'we?'"

"There is as long as I'm still aboard this ship." Mustering her courage, satisfying her curiosity, she let her hand wander closer to his neck, gently rubbing the stiffness out of his muscles as she gazed down at his wildly-curling black hair. He had tried to tame it into a queue, but the thick, spiraling tendrils had a mind of their own, springing out of the queue, curling around his ears, his forehead, his face in wild abandon.

"Tomorrow's Saturday and it'll be here before a body knows it," he said softly, and leaned his cheek, rough with the day's bristle, against the back of her hand. It was a gesture of acquiescence. Trust. Encouragement.

"Yes."

"I had a thought last night," he said quietly. "Thought I'd bolloxed this up good by abducting the wrong de Montforte, that I was wrong to take you and not yer brother. And maybe I was. I regret the scandal this will cause ye back home, regret that it might well indeed ruin ye, but there's one thing I don't regret,

Lady Nerissa, and that's having had the chance to know ye."

She looked down at his epaulet. "It has been ... an adventure," she allowed. "I'll not soon forget it."

He turned his head slightly, just enough that he could look up into her eyes. "Ah, but will ye forget *me*?"

She was silent for a long moment. Her hand still rested against the base of his neck, a curling black tendril of his hair brushing her knuckles. She was just about to remove it when he quietly reached up and laid his own hand over her own, keeping it there.

"Will ye, lass?"

She met his gaze with resolution, and felt something huge and painful grip her heart. "I will never forget you, Captain O' Devir."

For another long moment he remained quiet. He reached out and shut the log book and just sat there staring at it. His mouth was tight. She could almost hear him thinking. At last he turned in his chair so that he could look up at her, and she saw then that his eyes reflected the sudden, unreasonable sadness she felt in her own heart.

"Can't say as if I'll ever forget you either, Lady Nerissa."

"This—this friendship, or whatever it is we share ... it is an unexpected complication, is it not?"

He smiled. "A complication, but given the circumstances, not unexpected."

"Tomorrow, I will be reunited with my family and you will sail back to America. Should you make it back across the Atlantic with the explosive, or even without it, your life, Captain O' Devir, only stands to get better. Mine on the other hand ..." she made a helpless, defeated little sound that wasn't quite laughter, but a reflection of the hopelessness her future held. "Mine will be one of uncertainty, memories and longing." At his look of deepening regret, she hastily added, "And don't think for one instant it's all your doing. It was destined to be that way the moment you brought me aboard and showed me there's more to life than genteel boredom. That my heart still knows how to beat, that I am capable of responding to a man, perhaps even ... even to have feelings for him." She looked unflinchingly into his eyes. "Soon, Captain, we will have parted, never to meet again." She looked down. "Of course I will miss you."

He let another long moment go by before he finally spoke.

"I could give ye somethin' to remember me by," he said softly.

He turned fully around in the chair, taking her hand and bringing it down to his lips until they feathered against her knuckles. His gaze met hers, his intent clear.

".... Something more than ... just a kiss?" she whispered.

"Aye, lass. Something more."

She did not move away. Did not show outrage or insult, but simply closed her eyes as his tongue came out to touch her knuckles, first one, then the next, moving down her hand all the way to her little finger. He turned her hand over and kissed the underside of her wrist.

Nerissa's eyes opened wide.

Captain O' Devir merely smiled and looked up at her through his long, long lashes. And then his lips moved down the heel of her hand, past her palm and out to the tip of her little finger and once there, pulled it deeply into his mouth and sucked it, hard.

Nerissa flushed, the breath catching in her throat. Sensation gathered in her nipples, between her legs. And now Captain O' Devir was getting to his feet. Unbuttoning his long blue and white uniform coat, taking it off and putting it over the back of the chair he'd just vacated. He turned and reached for her.

She all but plunged into his embrace.

Desire flared like fuel on a bonfire ... her female body responding to his tough, hardened male one which made her feel deliciously small and protected, which smelled good, which felt good, which *was* good as she allowed herself to be pulled close to it and his arms, thick, brawny, hopelessly powerful arms—a man's arms—went around her.

A man's arms.

She felt herself growing warm and wet between her legs as she pressed herself against him. The bar of his forearm was an iron vise around her back, his hand against her shoulder blades and now following the curve of her spine, cupping her buttocks, and pressing the length of her up against his own. Oh, damn him, damn herself, how she wanted him. Craved him. Ached for the touch of his skin against hers, the feel of him against her, inside her, all around her. He was giving her that but it did nothing to soothe that craving and only made it worse, pushing her toward something she sensed but did not understand. She caught her lip and pressed her forehead against his chest, flushing hot with longing as his finger traced the seam of her bottom through the breeches and moved purposely down to that insatiable place between her legs, wiping it, pressing it, through the breeches. Nerissa sank down against his fingers, the craving becoming unbearable. His hands drifted to her hips, pulling her back onto unsteady feet. She did not protest. Her eyes drifted shut, and a soft moan came from deep within her throat as she wound her arms around his neck and raising herself on tiptoe, met his lips with her own.

This was not a tame, chaste kiss like the ones she'd known from Perry. Oh, no ... this was a harsh, demanding, take-no-prisoners onslaught of his mouth against her own, his body against hers, fierce and unrelenting and driving her head back even as his hand, again rubbing her bottom through the breeches and causing her to go dizzy with sensation, forced her closer and closer until she was pinned against the hard swelling in his breeches. The feel of that thick, rigid flesh against her own femininity, his mouth forcing her lips apart until his tongue drove between her teeth and sought her own, the brutal strength of his arm behind her back, all hazed together in a whirling blur of sensation and she pressed her breasts hard against him, pushing her fingers up into the wild, unruly locks of his hair.

She pulled away, her body throbbing in places she hadn't known existed, her breath coming in hard pants through her mouth and the ache between her legs crying for his touch.

Was it possible to get any closer to another human being?

Of course it was.

And she knew it as well as he did, and wanted it with a desperate certainty that didn't bear questioning.

"Captain O' Devir—"

"Ruaidri," he said hoarsely, nuzzling the hair at her temple, the top of her cheekbone.

"Rory?"

"Ru-ah-ree," he repeated impatiently, his tongue coming out to touch, to taste, the delicate skin of her ear and trace its shell-like perfection.

She was back in his arms again, his jaw rough with stubble beneath her fingertips, his hair coarse and wiry as she plunged her hand up through his wildly curling mane and freed it from its queue to spill around his broad, powerful shoulders. Her fingers explored the feel of his cheeks and jaw. His hands roved down her back, framed her hips, and she suddenly grabbed for his shoulders as he lifted her as easily as if she were an empty jar. She pulled her legs up, wrapped them around his hips as he walked and locked her arms around his neck, watching the deck now moving beneath her from over his shoulder.

"Y' ought to hate me, lass."

"I ought to, but I don't."

"I'm not in the business of ravishin' beautiful young women, even if they are English."

"Sometimes a woman wants to be ravished, Ruaidri. Just once."

"Do it right and a woman'll want to be ravished a whole lot more times than just once."

"Maybe we only have 'once.' We will never see each other again, after tomorrow."

After tomorrow. Why did those two simple words and the thought of being back with her brothers, back in her quiet, predictable, ordered world, cause her heart to feel as though someone had just speared it with a dull knife?

After tomorrow.

He carried her to the stern windows, stopping along the way to retrieve a bottle from a drawer in his desk and two tin mugs, both hopelessly dented. The sensation of being in such huge, powerful arms made her a little breathless, made her feel small and sheltered and deliciously protected. Holding her against himself with one hand, he put the bottle and mugs down, yanked the light canvas cushions from the stern seat and tossed them to the deck flooring. He set her down, unbuckled his sword belt and put it aside. She took off the midshipman's jacket. A moment later they were both lying on the cushions, stretched out alongside and facing each other.

She propped herself on one elbow, gazing into his unfairly beautiful, long-lashed eyes that made him look innocent and harmless. She had seen the rough edges that made up his character, she had sensed the restless, predatory coil just below the surface. There was nothing innocent or harmless about this man, this man she sensed was as dangerous as any of her brothers.

Propping the side of his head in one hand, he

reached out and grasped a long blonde hank of her hair, smoothing it between his fingers. "I want to make love to ye, lass."

"I ... want you to, Ruaidri."

"Ye know what it entails, don't ye?"

She blushed but forced herself to be bold. "I know ... certain things. And I've been ... touched before."

"Have ye, now?" He was smiling with just one corner of his mouth.

"Of course it was nothing more than a touch. And it might have been quite accidental, really. I'm a lady, Captain."

"I see. Do ladies lack the same desires that other females have?"

"I'm not an 'other female,' so I don't know."

"Hmph." He let go of her hair and with one finger, traced the curve of her jaw, down to her throat, causing her to suppress a little shiver of desire. "Well, I've never taken a highborn English lady to me bed, but I can tell ye right now, Lady Nerissa, that ye've got the same parts an' pieces as any other whether she be an Irish barmaid or an American seamstress, and I know very well how to make those parts an' pieces work. To sing together in harmony, to bring ye such pleasure that ye'll think ye've died and gone to heaven."

"Confident, aren't you?"

"Always." He smiled, and uncorking the bottle with his teeth, splashed spirits into each of the two mugs. He raised his own. "To you, Lady Nerissa. And unforgettable memories."

"To ... us," she murmured, and boldly bringing her mug to her lips, tipped it up, took a sip—and felt fire raging all the way down her throat, as though she'd swallowed a razor.

She slammed the mug down, gasping, sucking in breath that was afraid to enter the same space that that

—*liquid* had just passed through. Tears streamed from her eyes. As she coughed and gagged, Ruaidri also sat up, pressing the mug back into her hand, laughing as he bade her to take another sip.

"I'm not drinking that foul stuff!"

"The second sip'll be easier. Ye've already broken ground with that first swallow."

"What *is* this?"

"Irish whiskey." He took another swig from his own mug. "It won't kill ye."

She could feel the path of fire all down the back of her throat, down her esophagus and all the way to her stomach. But she was a de Montforte. She was not going to be cowed by a bit of Irish whiskey. Resolutely, she took another sip, grimacing behind the mug itself.

"You are correct," she allowed, resisting the urge to cough. "The second swallow isn't so bad. Probably because my throat is now lined with scar tissue from the first one."

"Puts hair on yer chest," he said, grinning.

"I don't want hair on my chest."

"What *do* ye want on yer chest, Lady Nerissa?"

Startled, she met his gaze as she was about to take another sip of the whiskey. "I—I don't know how to answer that."

He put the bottle down, reached out, and took her hand, covering it with his own, dwarfing its petite bones and fine white skin with his own strong, callused fingers and the broad expanse of his palm. She looked down at that hand, noting how tanned it was against her own, the little black hairs sprouting up on its back and how it looked so sun-bronzed against the white cuffs of his shirt. It was a strong hand, a working man's hand, nothing like the elegant, well-groomed hands of her brothers and others of the aristocracy.

She wondered what rough, working hands like that, would feel like against her skin.

Against—

"So we were talking about breasts," he reminded her.

She flushed, because that was exactly what she was thinking about. "Chests."

"Chests, breasts, tits, nipples."

"Don't be coarse."

"Take my hand, Lady Nerissa. Unfold my fingers. Stroke each one. See how strong they are against your own. See what they feel like."

She sat up, reached out and took his hand. It was warm and hard, everything about it suggesting strength. She spread the fingers out, examining them. Clean, but not pampered. The nails short, also clean. The nail of his forefinger was half-gone and what remained was discolored. It was not a pretty hand, not a beautiful hand, but holding it in her own warm grasp and examining the knuckles and tendons, feeling the strength and rough power in that single part of his body, did things to the pit of her belly and made the breath come a little faster in her lungs.

She turned the hand over. Traced the creases of his palm, examined the white line of a scar in the fleshy area between his thumb and forefinger.

Interesting, the male hand. She had grown up with four brothers and she had never known how fascinating the male hand really was.

"Now," he said, still keeping his hand motionless in her own, "lift my hand and put it where ye want it to be, Lady Nerissa."

"What?"

"Chests, breasts, tits, nipples."

She blushed wildly and felt a sudden tingling in those nipples, as if they were begging for exactly what he'd just suggested. Sensation stabbed between her legs and she felt an embarrassing dampness down there.

She moved closer to him. And still holding his hand, she tentatively placed it against her left breast.

The sensation was immediate. If the whiskey had burned a path down her throat, the feel of Captain O' Devir's hand imprinting her breast, even through Midshipman Cranton's shirt and waistcoat, was like a conflagration in comparison.

"Hold it there," he said, watching her face. "Hold it there until ye get brave."

"And this isn't?"

He laughed. "Nah. Brave is unbuttoning yer waistcoat."

"What about your hand?"

"Put it down. Unbutton yer waistcoat, if ye dare. Then take my hand and put it where you *really* want it, Lady Nerissa."

His eyes were smiling and full of challenge but he did not move his hand, letting her take control, letting her explore at a pace that was not overwhelming. She lowered his hand to his lap and placed it over his knee. Oh, why was it suddenly so warm in here? The air struggling to get into her lungs? She unbuttoned the waistcoat ... and peeled it off.

Their gazes met, his expectant and faintly laughing, hers wide, shy, eager and nervous.

But no, she would not be nervous. She trusted this man who could have taken full advantage of her during her stay here but hadn't, this man who caught fish for her breakfast and needled her until she didn't know whether to laugh or scream, this man who was about to give her a memory she would never forget. He wanted to make love to her. She would let him. And it was likely to be the one and only time she'd ever get to experience pleasure from a man of her own choosing, because tomorrow was coming, tomorrow would be here soon, and after that they would never see each other again.

She pulled the shirt out from the waistband of her breeches.

He drummed his fingers, once, against his bent knee, reminding her that his hand was there to be retrieved.

She reached out once more and took it. Brought it to the bottom of her shirt hem, lifted it with her other hand, and placed it there. He frowned, briefly, as he felt her stays.

"Have you been wearing this damned thing all this time?"

She just shrugged. "It's not as if I have my maid here to remove it for me."

Leaning close, he pulled free of her, unbuttoned her cuffs, pulled the shirt over her head and sat there gazing at her—the tiny waist, the boned stays pushing up to the perfect round globes of her breasts, their white, creamy crests. Pointedly, he looked down at his own hand, resting once again atop his knee and looking darkly tanned against the white breeches.

She reached out and took it, placing it against the pushed-up swell of one breast and pressing it there. His palm was deliciously warm against the pale white flesh, his large hand and rough fingers all but encompassing the creamy swell, and she felt that moist heat deep in the junction of her thighs growing wetter.

I want you to touch me, Ruaidri.

Could he read minds, too? His eyes had darkened beneath their bold black brows, the color becoming almost luminous; he looked at his hand there on the swell of her breast and thumbed the high swell once, twice, until Nerissa shuddered.

"You must think me terribly shameful," she said quietly, closing her eyes.

"No. What I see is a woman who deserves more than she's been given. A woman determined to show the world in her own way that she can make somethin' out of adversity." He got up, went around behind her and kneeling, his breath warm against the nape of her neck, unlaced her stays with a deftness that even Hannah, her maid, would have been hard-pressed to match. Moments later, she was sitting on the deck flooring in nothing but Cranton's breeches and the gaping undergarment, letting in cool air, letting in wicked thoughts and desires that could and would not be ignored.

He returned to his spot on the cushions, sat down, and, a smile tugging at the corner of his mouth, once again let his hand dangle suggestively over his knee. He drummed his fingers once against his kneecap, reminding her of where she wanted them, reminding her that he *knew* where she wanted them.

"A beautiful, passionate, kind-hearted woman," he added. "But not shameful."

She met his gaze, then quietly shrugged out of the gaping corset before dropping it to the decking.

"Once we do this, there's no goin' back," he said.

"There was no going back from the time you picked me up off that floor back in London, Ruaidri O' Devir. We might as well follow this course to its end."

She took his hand and again placed it over her breast. Their gazes met. His mouth turned up at one corner and he finally began to stroke the neckline of her chemise, savoring the softness of her skin, his rough, calloused thumb rubbing her nipple through the thin, gauzy material until a whimper rose deep in the back of her throat.

"I like that, Ruaidri," she whispered.

"I know. I like it too." She leaned into his touch and shut her eyes against the exquisite sensations as he drew small circles with fingers, flicking his thumb back and forth over the nipple until it grew engorged beneath the fabric and sent lightning bolts of sensation radiating out from her nether areas. "I like watchin' the pleasure on yer face. Watchin' the wonder in yer eyes as you experience this for what I'm assumin' is the first time."

"Yes ... it is the first time."

And will probably be the last.

He moved closer to her, sliding his hand now up beneath the chemise. She moaned as it found her breast, the calloused fingers scratchy, erotic and warm, her nipple swelling hard as he caught it between thumb and forefinger and gently rolled it back and forth, around and around until she began to gasp.

"I didn't know this could feel so good," she breathed, catching her bottom lip between her teeth and biting down to contain the building pleasure-pain between her legs.

"'Twill feel a lot better before we finish." And with that, he gently forced her backwards and down, down upon the thin cushion with the weight of his body as he pressed up against her, with the force of his kiss as his lips met hers, with the firmer, more commanding, more demanding touch of his fingers flicking over her nipple, tweaking it, until she was pressing hungry lips against her own and arching upwards into his touch.

He tasted of Irish whiskey, his tongue warm and demanding, thrusting hard against her own and filling her mouth. She opened her own mouth wide, unable to get enough of him, her body working into a frenzy and her breath hot against his stubbled cheek as his hand moved to her other breast and began to work that one, too. She drove her hand into his hair, holding his head to hers and trying to find an anchor, her body blind with need. Hot breaths, mingling. Hot mouths, grinding. The world beyond them went away. And then, just when she thought she might die, he tore his mouth from hers and began raining kisses down her neck, down into the hollow of her throat where her collarbones met, down along the neckline of her chemise. She opened feverish eyes, saw his wild black curls filling her view, tipped her head back on a silent moan as his mouth moved closer and closer to the tightly budded, blushing nipple.

"Ruaidri," she whispered, not knowing what she wanted, or how to get there.

But he knew. He knew, because he pulled down the gaping neckline, freed her breast and pushed it up to his mouth and a moment later she felt his wet tongue swirling around the engorged nipple, sucking it deep into his mouth, sucking, sucking harder, until she began to whimper uncontrollably. She pressed her lips against his shoulder, catching the fabric of his shirt between her teeth as a frenzied sob of pressure built and built between her legs.

"Do ye want me, Nerissa?"

She could not do more than moan, to push her face against his shoulder as his hand left her breast and roved downwards, over the frayed edge of her chemise, to the button closure of her breeches. A quick tug and they were parted, her hot sex bare to his thrusting fingers, which quickly became soaked in the moisture of her desire.

He drew back, looking at her, his fingers stilling as he brought her right to the very edge of the precipice and held her there.

And then he eased her back down to the cushions, slid both hands under her hips to catch the breeches and pulled them down, down, down from her buttocks until she lay bare from the waist down beneath him, her womanhood wet and hot with want for him.

He reached out and parted her with one hand. She raised herself on her elbows and lay quivering beneath him.

"You," he said softly, as he gazed down at her pale ivory curls, "are beautiful."

Flushed and damp, she could only look up at him,

her lips bruised from when she had bitten them only moments before.

"And ye'll remember this afternoon forever, Nerissa." She saw his throat move as he swallowed. "We both will."

And with that, he coaxed her back down so that she lay on her back, one breast still free from the chemise and wet from his mouth; he pinched the nipple, gently rubbed it with his hard, raspy fingers, and kissed it ... once ... twice ... three times before he drew up the cropped bottom of her chemise to expose her belly and there, began to brush kisses down her abdomen.

Nerissa tensed, knowing he would find her slick moisture, wondering if it would put him off, but no, that rough warm palm was pressing hard against her hip, his thumb caressing the faint hollow of her pelvis, now moving closer to her wet center and oh, oh dear God above, now pressing between the wet petals, rubbing up and down the slit and smearing her own moisture from top to bottom.

She bucked upward, sobbing, her hips squirming beneath his touch, her legs instinctively longing to clamp around his hand. She opened her eyes only to find the cabin spinning behind his dark head, a shaft of light coming in through the stern windows touching the edge of his shoulder. His mouth drifted further down, into the hollow between her ribcage and hips, wet kisses, hot kisses. She felt his lips brushing into her wet curls now, and all the while his thumb was still down there moving back and forth, back and forth, in a slow, languorous stroke.

He raised his head then, and looked directly into her eyes with an intensity that brooked no argument.

"I'm goin' to taste ye, Nerissa," he said.

She had no voice, and could do nothing but nod weakly.

He moved lower, found her grasping hand with his own and locked fingers with her, pushing the hand out to her side, locking it there, letting her squeeze his hand and crush his fingers as his mouth moved through her curls, nuzzled warmly into her cleft, and he began to lick her with the point of his tongue. He parted her between thumb and forefinger, exposing her to the cool air, and in the next delicious moment he had covered her with his mouth, sealed her with his lips, invaded her deepest recesses with his tongue while she writhed on the cushion beneath him, her fingers clenched around his as release began to build.

"Come for me, Nerissa," he murmured, against her warm slit. "Let go."

"I don't know ... I can't ... I—*ohhhhh*...."

His tongue had found and stabbed into some hidden part of her that his fingers had exposed like the pit of a forbidden fruit, the seat of her pleasure, the spot from which all sensation radiated. He began to lick it, to flick at that stiffly engorged bud with his tongue, to pinch it with his fingers until and with a sobbing scream, Nerissa bucked up and off the deck, climaxing against him over and over again in vicious, desperate waves as he sucked and mouthed her without stopping.

The violent spasms washed over her ... one ... two ... three, with receding aftershocks that left her drained of energy and shaken by their very force. The captain lay there for a moment, his head resting on her hip bone, his own breath laboring to get in and out of his lungs and blowing hot against her abdomen. Tentatively, she reached out and stroked his thick, wiry curls, the hard, wide span of his shoulders, knowing there should be more, wondering why he had not availed himself.

"What about ... you?" she asked softly.

"This was never about me." He reached a hand out, stretched it along her leg, and made a sigh of contentment. "I took ye from England as an innocent, untouched virgin," he said. "Tomorrow, I'll be sendin' ye back. Not so innocent anymore, but certainly untouched, and most definitely still a virgin."

"Untouched?"

"Aye, untouched. Some day ye'll marry, Lady Nerissa. You don't think so, but ye will. I have made it such that what happened between us this afternoon, will remain our little secret. Always."

Chapter Eighteen

Haze lay thick atop a shimmering sea, and in the distance the French privateering stronghold of Saint-Malo slumbered in the sun. It was three hours before noon and the heat of the day was already oppressive on deck, the sails above gasping limply in what little breeze was to be found.

"We're early, Captain Hadley," said Lord Andrew de Montforte as the frigate's commander finished conversing with Lieutenant McPhee and joined him at the rail. "I would not expect them to be here just yet."

"As they will not expect us. Which is why we are, indeed, early. I intend to retain whatever advantage God sees fit to give us."

The inventor, his dark auburn hair queued beneath a black tricorne, steadied himself against the shrouds as he stared out over the sea in nervous anticipation. He was unnaturally pale, this youngest of the de Montforte brothers, a bit "affected" if Hadley's observations were as keen as they usually proved to be.

"Does a brig have two masts, Captain?"

"It does, my lord."

"Because I think we've found our man." Lord Andrew handed him a telescope. "Look there."

Hadley raised the glass to his eye. Sure enough, her

pennants just visible above the trees of a low headland, were two masts. Square-rigged. A brig.

Memories of Lady Nerissa being struck down by that sodomizing pirate assailed him. He would avenge her, and he'd do it in front of this brother, too. Impress the hell out of him. There were worse women that an enterprising young captain in the Royal Navy could take, than a heavily dowered noblewoman.

The haze continued to drift, pushed aside from a coming breeze out of the south that was gathering strength by the moment. Ruffles appeared on the surface of the ocean. Above, the great rectangles of sail began to swell and at their bows, the water began to foam.

"Douse the main," Hadley ordered as Lieutenant McPhee appeared beside him. "We don't need to be coming in this fast."

His orders were repeated and moments later, men were hastily climbing the shrouds to beat and fist the great sail into submission against its yard.

The frigate slowed, losing some of the way she'd so eagerly seized. Hadley impatiently beckoned Captain Featherston of the Royal Marines close.

"I want your best marksmen in the tops in case this is a trick," he said. Marines aloft, their muskets trained down on the American brig, also gave him an advantage should O' Devir try to hurt Lady Nerissa again but he wasn't about to voice that particular concern in front of her clearly worried brother. "And load up the guns. Both batteries. Don't run them out, just get them ready."

"Aye, Captain."

The frigate continued her slow slide around the headland, past a thin, sandy beach fronted by cliffs and waters that were the color of cobalt in the sun. He was aware of Lord Andrew nearby, eagerly watching their progress. He wished his lordship would go below for his own safety as much as he hoped he'd stay topside so he could witness, first-hand, the saving of his little sister.

A King's frigate versus a puny American brig?

An officer of his Majesty's Royal Navy against an Irish pirate?

He snorted. There would be no contest.

They rounded the point and there, her larboard guns all run out and facing them, and figures holding muskets in her tops as well, was the brig.

"So much for the element of surprise," said Lord Andrew nearby.

"I could blow that bastard to bits," Hadley ground out. "The only reason I'm holding back is because I dare not risk injury to Lady Nerissa."

Lord Andrew only nodded, and his throat moved as he swallowed. He was clearly nervous.

A ginger-haired man in an officer's uniform moved to the rail and called across the water.

"State your business!"

Hadley grabbed a speaking trumpet. "I am captain Lawrence Hadley of His Majesty's frigate *Happenstance*," he shouted, incensed that he had to go through this farce with a gang of pirates, treating them as though they deserved the respect and dignity of an opposing navy when they were nothing but wretched, rotten, treasonous *rebels*.

A tall figure, now familiar to him after their last encounter, suddenly appeared on the brig's quarterdeck, his face in shadow beneath his tricorne. He was clad in blue and white as was the supposed "officer" beside him, and his air of arrogant authority, of competence and command made Hadley fantasize about having one of his marksmen in the tops above, put a ball through the blackguard's heart.

McPhee, beside him, echoed his thoughts. "Tom Crosby of the Marines ... he can shoot the beak off a seagull at seventy feet. Ye know what I'm thinking, Captain?"

"I'm thinking I'd very much like Crosby up there to drop that rascal in his tracks," gritted Hadley.

"And *I'm* thinking that if you give that order, his second-in-command will never hand over my sister," said Lord Andrew darkly. "I'm full prepared to trade myself for her. I'll put them off as long as possible about the explosive. Let's just get this over with because I'm sick with terror about her."

Across the short expanse of water, the pirate—and a pirate he was, for Hadley could not bring himself to think of him as anything but—was raising a speaking trumpet to his own lips.

"Top o' the mornin' to ye," he called in a deliberately taunting tone, as though rubbing it in that he, a lowly Irishman, was calling the shots with a King's frigate. "Still doin' things yer own way, are ye, Hadley? My instructions were to meet in a tavern on land. But no matter, I'm in an accommodatin' mood. Have ye brought me the explosive?

"I've brought you its inventor, Lord Andrew."

"Fair enough." The Irishman beckoned to someone behind him, who turned and disappeared below. "I was forced t' serve many years and most of me youth in yer damned navy, Hadley. I don't trust ye. Heave to and send a boat across with Lord Andrew, and I'll send Lady Nerissa over in return. Any tricks and the girl dies. Understand?"

"There will be no tricks," Hadley ground out as Lord Andrew's knuckles went white on the railing beside him.

"Good, because there's a French frigate on the other side of this headland to make sure ye don't try anythin' underhanded. A little insurance, if ye will. After the exchange, you'll sail off to the north and I'll remain here, supported, if need be, by that French frigate as well as the nearby presence of John Paul Jones ... another officer in the Continental Navy ye so despise."

Lord Andrew, who had been tensely watching this exchange, whirled angrily around. "Are you going to let that fool go on or can we close this supposed deal and get my sister back?"

Hadley quelled his irritation. He didn't need or want some young nobleman telling him how to conduct this operation.

"Ready the boat," he snapped to Lieutenant Dewhurst, who was tensely watching this exchange a few feet away. "Lord Andrew will be going across. He will not be staying any longer than it takes to open fire on that damned brig, beat them into submission and get him back."

"What about this French frigate? And John Paul Jones?" Dewhurst asked.

"There's no damned frigate, and if Jones were nearby he'd be here, not hiding. It's obvious that Irish bastard is bluffing." Hadley turned to Lord Andrew. "When I open fire, my lord, I expect you to head belowdecks. We'll try and board them so as to take the ship quickly and with the least threat of injury to yourself. Even so, stay below, in the deepest part of the hold you can find, until firing ceases and they surrender the ship to us. At that point, we'll come across to retrieve you."

"Understood."

The boat was readied. Across the hundred or so feet of sparkling blue water that separated the British frigate from the smaller American brig, Hadley saw movement behind O' Devir. He grabbed his telescope and caught his breath. There. It was Lady Nerissa.

Lord Andrew saw her too. He saw his baby sister, her hair caught in a simple tie of crude leather beneath a brimmed hat and wearing what looked like sailor's breeches and a naval jacket. She was white with fear but otherwise appeared unharmed, *thank God*, and even from this distance, he could see how her gaze tracked to that blasted Irishman as though he was some sort of a god instead of the man who had abducted her, struck her, and probably—

No, he would not think of that, he could not, he would not, it was too painful.

But Lawrence Hadley and Lord Andrew de Montforte weren't the only close observers.

High above in the foretop, the keen-eyed Tom Crosby of the Royal Marines was also gazing intently down at the enemy deck. Except he wasn't looking at Lady Nerissa, obviously compromised and hurt by this band of scurvy rascals and derelicts. He was looking at the proud shoulders of the Irish captain, calculating distance and windage and the slight breeze that was coming over his right shoulder as he balanced the musket against the shrouds, drew in his breath, and took careful aim at the figure standing down there on the opposite deck. He was good at what he did. Very good.

O' Devir would not see another sunrise.

"Boat's ready, sir!"

On the quarterdeck below, Hadley nodded to Lord Andrew. The inventor, carrying a satchel, walked to the entry port and, accompanied by Lieutenant Dewhurst, began to descend to the boat below.

In the maintop, Crosby's finger began to itch and his breathing became as focused and intent as his eyes, tracking the long muzzle of the musket with deadly purpose.

Lord Andrew and Dewhurst pushed off from *Happenstance*'s main chains and began to make progress across the sparkling water.

The Irish captain of the American ship watched them wordlessly, his mouth a grim line beneath the shadow of his tricorne.

Tension rose.

And suddenly Hadley saw movement beyond the trees and knew immediately what it was: the masts of the French frigate that had been no bluff at all, and an impending ambush.

"Dewhurst, return *now*!" he roared.

He saw O' Devir, just in the act of motioning Lady Nerissa forward to the rail, turn in surprise as he too saw the jib-boom of the French frigate sliding around the headland, its ports all open and guns run out with deadly intent. The captain of the French frigate, who cared naught for any agreement between the American brig's captain and the commander of the Royal Navy frigate, saw nothing but the fine English ship sitting in the bay like a plum waiting to be picked.

"*Get below!*" shouted O' Devir, waving her frantically back, and high above in the tops Royal Marine sniper Tom Crosby saw Lady Nerissa freeze—and then run, not towards the hatch that would take her to safety below but toward the Irishman himself. O' Devir was already turning to intercept her, and Crosby knew he could never let her reach him.

"Top of the morning indeed, you bastard," he muttered, and sighting down the barrel at the broad blue back he squeezed the trigger, watching in grim satisfaction as O' Devir went down like a stone and the world erupted in chaos.

Chapter Nineteen

"Bloody hell! Bloody thundering hell, who fired that shot?" howled Hadley, seconds before fire and flame flashed from the American brig's forward guns, the delicious image of O' Devir being shot down on his own deck darkened only by the fact that it wasn't his orders that had brought it about. Someone's head was going to roll.

Its captain down, the brig was in chaos. And now, in full view as she came around the headland was the French frigate, determined to make a prize of them.

"Don't even *think* of it," snarled Hadley and turning, shouted, "Ports open, lads, and give those Frogs a taste of British hospitality!"

His was the finest and best-trained Navy in the world, and Hadley had spent many months drilling his men until they could load and run out in half the time it took any of his peers. One moment, the French frigate looked to be the victor in a well-crafted ambush; the next, a broadside was flashing all down the British ship's side, tongues of flame and choking smoke throwing death and destruction on the other ship, caught by surprise and now trying desperately to come about.

"Load up and hit her again, lads!" he shouted, hearing screams through the smoke as an answering roar from the French guns found its target. And there, from off in the smoke, the smaller American brig was still barking out her own impudent reply, some unfortunate junior officer trying to rally his men and pull order out of chaos following the death of that blasted rascal he called a captain.

Hadley took off his hat, wiped his brow and smiled as he saw Lieutenant Dewhurst and Lord Andrew, followed by the boat crew, scrambling back aboard to safety before his attention was claimed once more by the matter at hand.

"Fire!" he shouted hoarsely, eyes stinging as the French ship's masts poked above the black, acrid smoke and tongues of fire pierced the gloom. Beside him, Midshipman Rawlins suddenly clasped his chest, coughed, and fell to his knees, blood bubbling from his mouth; the pop of musketfire and the roar of the frigate's guns deafened him and desperately, he found time to hope that Lady Nerissa had managed to get below even as he ordered his carronades into position. "The smashers," the big, blunt-nosed guns were named, and they did their work with cruel ruthlessness; within moments, the French ship was turning tail and running, just as Hadley expected it would do once it got a taste of His Majesty's finest.

"Cease firing!"

The French ship was piling on sail, its cowardly captain wasting no time in making his escape. Grim-faced, Hadley looked at the dim outline of the American brig through the clearing smoke and saw that his work was far from done, here.

"Ram and board them," he said with savage triumph. Adjusting his sword belt, he went to the rail, intending to be one of the first onto the American's decks.

"*Prepare to ram!*"

The jib and topsails filled. The helm was put up, the

sleek frigate turned her long jib-boom away from the wind and slid down on the American brig, its shots, coming frantically now, doing little damage as she gathered way and came at them, bows on.

"Fire the carronades, sir?" asked Lieutenant McPhee, eyeing the big guns with hope.

"No, I don't want carnage and can't risk the lady being hurt. We will board and take her that way."

"Aye, sir."

Men ran to the weapons chests, girding themselves with pistols, cutlasses, boarding axes and pikes, and still the frigate moved down on the brig, oblivious to the smaller vessel which continued firing to no avail. With a crashing groan, *Happenstance* impaled her long jib-boom in the American ship's rigging and held fast.

"Boarders away!"

The Yanks might have had a smaller ship but as Hadley ran across the forecastle, up and onto the hopelessly tangled bowsprit and dropped lithely down onto the brig's decks, the Americans came at him and his men like a mob of howling Indians. Steel clashed against steel, pierced flesh, sprayed blood across the decks. In the tops above, Hadley heard mustketfire as his Marines fired down, trying to pick off the Americans; a giant, gap-toothed seaman came at him with cutlass swinging and a blow from McPhee's own sword countered it, saving his life a moment before a hole bloomed on the giant's chest from a well-placed shot from Tom Crosby, still firing down on the deck from the main top. The man pitched forward, dead before he even hit the deck.

"Strike, damn you!" he heard McPhee yelling, "Strike you filthy rebels!"

He fought his way to the lieutenant's side, his coxswain at his back, his eyes stinging from sweat and smoke and his brain dimly registering the fact that someone on the brig was still firing. And now the rebels were being beaten back, shaken by the loss of their captain and unable to match the ferocity of the British seamen who outnumbered them three to one.

"Strike, damn you!"

A shout ended on a gurgle of blood nearby as one of the rebels went down under McPhee's sword. Hadley tripped over a ring bolt and ripping his pistol from his belt, fired at a smoke-smeared form that came at him, knife raised. The firing was more sporadic now, the heart going out of the bastards, and finally, almost desperately through the melee and smoke came the hoarse voice that would end the slaughter.

"We're striking!"

Hadley looked up and saw the American colors being lowered from the brig's gaff. His ears ringing, his chest heaving and a muscle twitching with fatigue somewhere in his shoulder, he blinked the smoke out of his eyes, took off his hat and wiped his forehead with the back of his sleeve.

The young ginger-haired officer, his coat sleeve ripped and oozing blood, came toward him, holding out his sword in both hands. His face was as white as the belly of a mackerel as he picked his way over broken spars, bits of cordage and debris, an upended gun, and bodies ... of the helmsman ... of two pigtailed rebel sailors ... of O' Devir himself, lying motionless on the deck where Crosby's well-placed shot had brought him down.

"Lieutenant John Morgan, sir." His gaze cut soberly to the downed figure of his captain as, tightening his mouth, he presented his sword to Hadley with sober reluctance. "I'm in command of the American brig *Tigershark*. The ship is yours."

❧

As the world had exploded in smoke and flame around them, the quick-thinking Midshipman Cranton had grabbed Nerissa's elbow, dragged her below at a dead run, and locked her in the hold to keep her safe. There she had spent the battle alone and in the dark, the minutes dragging by like hours.

Every thunderous crash of the guns, every thud of the frigate's iron striking their hull, every scream from above amidst the clang of steel as men fought hand-to-hand for their lives, had pierced her soul until she could do nothing but huddle in the dark, her head buried in her arms, trying to block out the sounds of carnage above. She heard Lieutenant Morgan shouting orders, Cranton repeating them, even as her heart had prayed and her ears had strained to hear a dear voice, an Irish voice, to no avail. *Oh God, oh, God, why don't I hear his voice?* Musketfire, thuds, the screams of dying men. Nerissa shut her eyes and rocked back and forth, unable to make herself any smaller, unable to blot out the memory of the French frigate coming around the bend, betraying them in its captain's eagerness to make a prize of his British counterpart ... unable to blot out that last image of Ruaidri O' Devir, desperately waving her back to keep her safe even as a shot had rang out from the British frigate and he'd gone down right in front of her a split-second before Cranton was tearing her away and toward the hatch.

It was a long moment before she realized that above, the fighting had stopped. She took a shaky breath and raised her head. Beneath the ringing in her ears, she could hear the mad pounding of her heart in the deafening, frightening silence.

Footsteps. Someone approaching from out of the gloom. It was Midshipman Cranton, his eyes downcast and blood oozing from his chin. Just behind him was a

Royal Navy lieutenant with pistol trained on the boy to make sure he did exactly as he was told.

She should have been desperately relieved to see the familiar uniform of her countrymen.

Instead, she pushed a fist against her mouth to quell her rising panic. "Captain O' Devir," she managed, reaching for Cranton's arm as if it were an anchor. "Please, tell me how he fares."

The youngster would not meet her eyes, and only glanced resentfully at his British counterpart as the other jabbed his pistol against his ribs in a silent order to get moving.

Cranton wordlessly offered his arm. Nerissa gripped it hard, willing her feet to move. She felt the heavy, uncertain motion of the brig beneath her as it rolled in the swells, saw Royal Navy officers striding past as they searched the ship. She concentrated on each breath she drew into her lungs, each step that brought her nearer and nearer to a truth she could not bear to face. A truth that awaited her topside. They emerged on deck and into hot, blinding sunlight. Carnage and unspeakable destruction met her gaze, and she could do nothing but stand there blinking in shock, unable to process the reality of what she was seeing with what her imagination had thrown at her during the endless horror of waiting below.

The Royal Navy frigate, looming over *Tigershark*'s decks and locked to her in a tangle of spars and rigging. Upended guns, some spattered with blood. The jib, its stay severed, flapping in the wind like a piece of laundry. Jagged pieces of spar and hull scattered across the deck, stains of blood, a severed arm. Nausea rose in her throat as a sinking numbness fought horror. And the dead and wounded from both sides lying in twisted agony where they had fallen, a few still moving, groaning, most silent and still in grotesque attitudes of death. The similarity of the uniforms, both sides in blue and white, made it hard to tell who was who, and pressing clammy knuckles to her mouth to quell her rising hysteria, Nerissa's gaze roved the deck, searching for the one man she knew she would not find standing.

Cranton, already being led away by a Royal Navy officer, gave her a look that spoke volumes, then turned away.

Ruaidri ....

She felt his absence, his loss, immediately.

Knew that the vital force, the confident, larger-than-life energy that was Captain Ruaidri O' Devir was no more.

A buzzing started in her ears and the numbness began to take over. A Royal Navy officer was talking to her but she never heard the words, only saw his mouth moving. Never in her life had she felt more suddenly *alone*, as if someone had reached into her chest, wrapped cold fingers around her heart, and ripped it, still beating, out of her chest. Bile rose in her throat and she began to shake. *Ruaidri? Ruaidri, where are you?* She didn't want to look for him amongst the bodies; she could not *not* look for him. The English officer had moved to block her view as best he could. She tried to see around him. His mouth was still moving, his voice underwater, and he was saying something about keeping her gaze downcast so that she wouldn't see things a lady should never have to see, something about being safe now that they were here, that they had come for her. A short distance away his captain was speaking with a grey-faced Lieutenant Morgan. His order to round up the rebels and start herding them below was the sound that finally penetrated Nerissa's traumatized senses, and tears welled up in her eyes as the initial shock gave way to the sheer agony of reality.

The dead, needlessly cut down all because of her—and that wretched explosive that Andrew should never have invented. Men, good men, on both sides, men who were young and full of promise, men who should have lived to see tomorrow, men whose mothers would be grieving their losses for the rest of their lives.

Ruaidri ... oh, Ruaidri....

She stood frozen, the vomit rising in her throat as she determined to be brave, to be strong, to be a de Montforte in the face of the carnage all around her ... and there was the British captain, the business of surrender completed and now in the hands of his subordinates, striding with the confidence of the victor across the bloodied, littered decks toward her. She could see it was all he could do to contain his triumph. Was she supposed to be *grateful?*

He stopped and bowed before her. "Lady Nerissa?"

She stared at him, her mouth trying to find and form words, anything—

"Lady Nerissa, I am Captain Lawrence Hadley ... are you all right?"

Coming up behind him and wearing civilian clothes was a beloved and familiar figure.

"*Andrew*," Nerissa choked out on a broken sob, and as her brother sprinted the last few steps toward her, finally succumbed to the horror. She fell to her knees, weeping. She felt his arms go protectively around her, shielding her from the carnage, his dear voice close as he held her in his arms and the tears streamed down her cheeks in great, gulping sobs.

"She's in shock," she heard the British captain say above her head as though she wasn't even there, and in that moment she hated him—for imposing himself into her world, for doing this to the dead and wounded lying all around her, for his air of self importance, for the barely-concealed triumph in his eyes, for the way he was acting so genteel and chivalrous when he had been the instrument of such unspeakable horror. She cried bitter tears into Andrew's sleeve, her nose running helplessly, and then Hadley himself was kneeling down and filling her view, his gaze searching her form with too much familiarity.

"Lady Nerissa," he said, more intently this time, "have you been harmed?"

She cried harder, burying her face against the inside of Andrew's shoulder so she wouldn't have to look at that hated face.

"Not now," her brother said from above, his voice tight with authority. "You can see she's been harmed, in spirit if not in body. No one of the fairer sex should have to see what she's seen, heard what she's heard, suffer what she's suffered." He held her close, his hand stroking the back of her head. "You're safe now, Nerissa," he murmured. "Everything's going to be all right. You're with me now, and no one will ever harm you again."

I was safe with him, *too ... safer than I'd ever felt in my life.*

"Ruaidri," she choked out, the tears overwhelming her such that she couldn't catch her breath. "Where is he?"

Hadley, again. "Who?"

"*Ruaidri*!" she shouted in a voice that was anything but a lady's, and burst into fresh tears.

Stunned silence from both men as they realized she had used her captor's given name. Not "that rogue," or "that scoundrel" or even "O' Devir," but Ruaidri, a strange and very Irish-sounding name that had rolled off her tongue with more ease and familiarity than either of the men, exchanging glances above her head, were comfortable with. Andrew got to his feet, pulling her with him. Hadley gave her an assessing, penetrating look, then stepped back to finally allow her a view of the deck behind him.

Nerissa's heart stopped beating. She took a step forward, another, and stared, mute. At the blue-and-white clad body sprawled face-down on the quarterdeck some twenty feet away. At the wildly curling black hair lying in a reluctant queue between the broad, powerful shoulders, the cocked hat upside-down on the deck nearby. At the spreading stain of blood beneath him that turned the white breeches crimson and trickled first to starboard, then to larboard, then back to starboard in confusion as the brig rolled beneath them in shared agony.

Her world tilted and swayed and she knew, suddenly that she was going to be sick.

"That ... *animal* will never harm you again," the British captain was saying, unable to keep the triumph from his voice. "You are indeed safe now, Lady Nerissa."

She wrenched free of her brother's arm and made it to the rail just in time to spill a very unladylike spew of vomit into the merciless sea below.

Chapter Twenty

Fuck, Hadley thought, in silent rage. He'd seen the look of stunned devastation on Lady Nerissa's face. He'd seen her go white, then gray, before she'd run to the rail to puke her guts out. He'd heard of hostages falling in love with their captors or at least, taking their sides in things and defending them vehemently. Thank God he'd gotten to her in time. A hot bath and some decent food in her stomach, some skillful handling of both her and her brother, and he could hopefully undo the damage that O' Devir (may his Irish carcass rot in hell) had wrought. Indeed, if he played his cards right, he could paint himself as both savior and hero and emerge from this debacle with Lady Nerissa's affections transferred squarely to *him* in undying gratitude.

But he could not shake the thought that was foremost in his mind. Had O' Devir compromised her? Had his way with her? Taken her innocence?

Tight-lipped, he looked at her standing there at the rail, her brother rubbing her back and offering a handkerchief so she could wipe her mouth. She had recovered somewhat, her shoulders set and stiff with pride, but she kept her back to him in silent, pointed rebuff as though *he* was the one who had done something wrong.

Or maybe, he told himself hopefully, she just didn't want to look at O' Devir's corpse.

He did, though, and turning, allowed himself that indulgence. It would not do to smile, of course, and he schooled his face into a look of sober respect as he drank in the delicious sight of his dead rival. He was good at masking his emotions. He always had been. But triumph swelled his heart, and that triumph would sustain him when he eventually went to the grateful Duke of Blackheath to ask for the lady's hand.

"Squall coming in from the west, sir."

It was McPhee. Roused from his thoughts, Hadley followed the lieutenant's gaze. Sure enough, dark, angry-looking clouds were piling up atop the distant horizon—no surprise, given the day's heat.

"Finish up here. I want to get Lady Nerissa back to England as soon as possible before this scandal can blow sky-high." He clapped his first lieutenant on the shoulder and grinned, unable to keep his good mood under such tight wraps any longer. "Any promising young lieutenant craves the chance to command, eh, Mr. McPhee? You will sail this brig back to London. She's so new the worms haven't even found her bottom yet. The rebels, if nothing else, build fine ships—she'll fetch a good price at auction for us."

The young Scot's gaze flashed around Hadley's epauletted shoulder. "Er, heads up, sir."

Turning, Hadley saw the lady, head high and eyes flashing, coming back toward them. He smiled and inclined his head. "Are you ready to depart, Lady Nerissa?"

"No, I am not ready to depart. In fact, I am staying here," she said flatly, and he sensed that beneath her veneer of strength she was about to shatter and doing her best to hide it, as her breeding and the expectations that accompanied it, demanded. "Being the gentleman you are, I'm sure you intend to offer me the use of your own quarters, Captain Hadley, and I have no wish to put you out on my account. My things are here. I am comfortable here and to be honest, I've had quite enough for one day. More than enough. I don't fancy a move to your frigate or anywhere else."

Hadley raised a brow, his mouth twitching in irritation. *Of course she wanted to stay here. It was where her memories with O' Devir were.*

He bowed deeply. "My dear Lady Nerissa, I can assure you it is no trouble at all to give up my cabin. It is, indeed, what any gentleman would do, and without complaint."

She was unrelenting. "I am staying here."

Hadley looked to Lord Andrew for support. The younger man shrugged as if to say that women were women, and there was no use arguing with them.

Especially *this* one.

Hadley tried another tack. "I hope, Lady Nerissa, that your 'things' here aboard this brig include ... er, more suitable clothing for a young lady of your station, than what you are currently wearing?"

Wrong move.

Oh, so wrong....

Her pale blue eyes hardened but she still managed to freeze him with an icy smile. "I have my gown, Captain. Salt spray and tar have ruined it. One of Captain O' Devir's men was to make me some petticoats out of sailcloth so that my wearing of his midshipman's garb would not be so offensive to easily-bruised sensitivities such as yours. In fact—"

"Nerissa, please," said Lord Andrew, his hand on her arm. "He's only trying to help. And I concur with him. I want you off this ship. What happened to you here, and what you've seen today is something I'd like to separate you from sooner rather than later."

"I'd say sooner," Hadley said, with a baleful look at the swelling storm clouds.

The beautiful china-blue eyes pinned him with contempt. "I will stay here."

He could not force her, as much as he'd like to. It would only make her resent him all the more, and alienate the brother who might be instrumental in making his case to the Duke of Blackheath for the lady's hand in marriage. A bit of scandal—not too much, but just enough to make her undesirable to the more eligible bluebloods who'd be his competition ... he, painting himself as the hero who had saved her in order to win over the duke ... oh, he could deal with her resentment toward him. It wouldn't take much to win her, and he could start by letting her have her way, at least, for now.

Once they were married, things would, of course, be different....

He bowed solicitously. "Very well, Lady Nerissa. You have, indeed, been through enough. I have given command of this vessel to my first lieutenant here, and he will see to your comfort and well-being on the short trip back to England." He turned to the officer. "Keep us in sight, Mr. McPhee. Any trouble, signal to us."

"Aye, sir."

"Lord Andrew?"

"I will remain here with my sister. I'm sure I can find a cabin somewhere now that what remains of this ship's crew and officers have been either killed or imprisoned in the hold, below."

Hadley had had enough of treating these rebels as though they actually deserved the respect of a sovereign nation's navy. "Begging your pardon, my lord, but you give these traitors to our king and country far too much honor. They have no navy, despite their silly uniforms and customs copied, I must say, from our own Navy, and they most certainly have no 'officers.' They are a nothing but a bunch of pirates and will be dealt with severely upon our return to England."

Lord Andrew said nothing, though Hadley saw a flat hardness come into his eyes that wasn't much different from what he'd seen in his sister's.

"Both of you, go back to the frigate," Nerissa said. "I wish to be alone."

"You can't be left here unchaperoned."

"At this point, does it even matter?" she retorted and again, Hadley sensed the brittleness beneath the facade of steel. "I'm ruined. At least give me the dignity and space in which to heal without doting, overly concerned men interfering in that process."

Lord Andrew looked wounded, but he exchanged a helpless look with Hadley. "Nerissa, this goes against everything I—"

"Please, Andrew. I'll lock the door. I'll be safe, and neither of us have to tell Lucien about any of this." She glanced at the lieutenant. "I'm sure Lieutenant McPhee can post a guard outside if it makes either of you feel any better."

"Most certainly my lady, I would be happy to do that," piped up the young lieutenant.

Lord Andrew debated with himself for another moment or two but in the end, the distant squall decided him.

"I won't leave you," he said. "But I will give you your space. I'll take one of O' Devir's men's cabins, you can have the main one, and the matter is settled."

❧

Lieutenant McPhee might have been young but he had three sisters who fancied themselves constantly in and out of love, and he prided himself on being a quietly observant man.

He knew women, better, he suspected, than either

Hadley or Lord Andrew did. It did not escape his notice that Lady Nerissa carefully avoided looking at O' Devir lying dead on his quarterdeck while Hadley and her brother were watching her, but she didn't fool him. He saw the way her stricken gaze went straight to the scoundrel when Hadley and Lord Andrew weren't watching her, saw the way her eyes filled up with fresh tears as they all walked past the body as though it wasn't even there, saw the way her steps faltered, so imperceptible that her own brother, chatting with Hadley at his side, had not even noticed. McPhee felt for her. He saw his captain piped over the side and back to the frigate, quickly got her ladyship settled in the brig's main cabin and her brother in one of the officer's ones, and returned to the pressing business of ensuring the brig was seaworthy.

It was his first real command. He would make it count.

Forward, a complement of the frigate's men, wielding axes and working against time and nature, had finished cutting her jib-boom free of the brig's rigging and the two ships began to ease apart. Midshipman Walters was overseeing the hasty splicing and replacement of standing rigging and nearby, a carpenter was hard at work patching a hole above the waterline. Hadley had spared him only a dozen men, but it would have to be enough.

He paused next to Walters. "You were brave today in battle, Philip. I will make note of it to Captain Hadley when we return to the frigate."

"Thank you, sir." His voice dropped and he glanced around to ensure others were out of earshot. "I was terrified."

"A normal and healthy response when it comes to self-preservation, laddie," said McPhee, wryly. "You've done a good job clearing the decks of debris, but I'm afraid we'll have to deal with the dead bodies sooner rather than later. The men, they're a superstitious lot, especially with a storm off to windward."

The midshipman nodded.

"Prisoners all secured below, Mr. Walters?"

Of course they were, but McPhee, relishing his first command, was leaving nothing left to chance. The rebel crew, sullen and defeated, had been rounded up and herded below where they would be imprisoned in the dark hold until they got back to England. There, they would be sent to Mill Prison or some other hell hole where they'd spend what was left of their lives wishing they'd met their end here today instead. The brig would be auctioned off to fetch a hefty sum that would line all their pockets, and if the discreet, wolfish gleam in Hadley's eyes had been anything to go by, the courtship of Lady Nerissa would begin as soon as the captain managed to break through her resentment.

McPhee shook his head. The lady had been through enough, and Hadley hadn't even had the decency to give her time to sort herself out before trying to impress her. Opportunistic sod, he thought, then put the thought out of his mind. It wouldn't do to criticize, even in the privacy of his own mind, his commanding officer.

"I need to oversee that new jib before that storm hits," he said. "In the meantime, Mr. Walters, I'm afraid you'll have to play undertaker. The men are already uneasy about the dead rolling around in their own blood, and the sooner they're disposed of, the better. I want their attention on sailing the ship, not imaginary ghosts."

"Aye, sir."

Three of those men were nearby, tightening deadeyes on the jury-rigged main shrouds and glancing nervously over their shoulders as if expecting the dead to rise up and murder them. "You, there!" said Walters importantly, aware of McPhee beside him. "Smith, Bates and Dobson! Come with us. We need to dispose of the dead."

The three men knuckled their forelocks to this youngster who was half their age but better bred than they could ever hope to be, and went to the nearest corpse, a pigtailed rebel with receding blond hair whose considerable girth was stuffed into a tightly buttoned waistcoat. His eyes were open and staring, and they remained so as Walters ordered the seamen to pick him up, walk him to the side, and throw him over into the embrace of Davy Jones.

"See ye in hell, you blasted rebel," muttered Bates in the expectant silence before his words were punctuated by a splash below.

Above, an uneasy wind began to move through severed and intact standing rigging, tickling the British colors now flying from the brig's gaff.

"Make haste," McPhee said tensely, looking impatiently forward where a small crew was fighting against time to get the new jib strung.

"Think she's seaworthy, sir?"

"She'll do. Get rid of that next body. We haven't all day to sit here and discuss the weather."

"Aye, sir. Put up a good fight, those Yankees did."

"Aye, at least they stayed and slugged it out with us, which is more than can be said for those cowardly Frenchmen. You three finish up here. I need to oversee that jib before the squall hits."

Lieutenant McPhee moved off, picking up his pace as he cast a worried glance off to the west. Walters, looking unhappy about this unpleasant task to which he'd been assigned when his visions of glory as the acting second-in-command surely spelled something far different, led the way to the next corpse, its arm nearly severed at the elbow and blood congealing around the gaping mouth.

Bates, a big burly topman who wasn't afraid of the

devil himself, took off his cap. "This un's one of our'n, boys. Poor ol' Joe Ames, by the look of him."

Walters averted his gaze from the bloodied mouth. "Wrap him in sailcloth and lay him under the gunwale. He can get a proper burial once we're back in England."

The wind was strengthening and the day began to go darker by degrees. Ames was quickly swathed in sailcloth, dragged beneath the shelter of the gunwale, and left behind.

They moved on to the next body.

"Well now, this 'un sure ain't one of ours," muttered Bates, gazing down at the remains of Ruaidri O' Devir in awed fascination.

His two shipmates joined him. "Aye, hard to believe he had all of England afraid they'd be the next one to be kidnapped. A regular John Paul Jones, eh?

"Don't look like much of a threat, now," said Bates, and drawing back his foot, kicked the body, hard, in the ribs. "That's for what ye did to the fair Lady Nerissa, you piece of shit."

A groan of pain came from the dead man and with an expletive Bates jumped back.

"Jay-zus, Oi thought 'e was supposed to be dead!"

"Nearly shit your pants, did ye?" said Smith, laughing.

Walters had gone white. "Sure looked it."

Bates, embarrassed, recovered his swagger. "Beggin' your pardon, sir, for tellin' ye how to do your job, but Oi think ye should put a bullet in 'is skull and finish him off. After what we all saw him do to that fine lady a few days back it's no less than 'e deserves."

Walters, not quite thirteen and easily influenced by the suggestion of an older man even if he was just a seaman, puffed himself up and reached for the pistol in his belt. "A fine idea, Bates," he said importantly. He checked the flint, cocked the pistol, and lowering his arm, took aim on the back of the dark head.

"Don't do it, sir," said Smith, gently pushing the midshipman's arm away so that the pistol pointed harmlessly at the deck. "Not without Mr. McPhee's permission. He might not take kindly to it."

Bates, enjoying his stab at authority, was not to be deterred. "You pillock, what are ye, daft in the head? Don't listen to him, Mr. Walters. Don't ye remember what this bastard did to our lady? Don't ye remember how 'e struck her down right in front of our eyes? He don't deserve mercy." He spat on the Irishman's back and kicked him again. "Shit, if Oi had a knife on me Oi'd cut his balls off myself, listen to him scream, *then* put a bullet in 'is brain. Nobody harms our fine English ladies, 'specially some filthy boglander dog like this one."

The kicks had roused O' Devir. At their feet, he was trying to push himself up, swaying and trying desperately to keep his balance; he managed to raise himself up on one hand before he passed out and fell, rolling onto his back and lying still once more.

"Go get Lieutenant McPhee," said Smith to Midshipman Walters, trying to protect the young officer from what could potentially be a court martial. "He'll want to know about this."

Walters began to leave, glanced at Bates' florid, bullying face, and thought better of it. "I will stay here with the prisoner. Bates, *you* go and get Mr. McPhee. *Now*."

Moments later, Lieutenant McPhee was hurrying aft, Bates lumbering along next to him.

"What is this? He's alive?"

"Aye, sir," said Walters. "Bates kicked him in the side and he groaned."

"What?"

"Aye, sir, watch, Oi'll show ye—"

"There is no need for that, Bates," snapped McPhee, his own foot flashing out to stay the seaman's before it could connect with the defenseless man's ribs. "Have you no mercy or common decency?"

"None, sir," said Bates, smiling and folding his arms. "Told the lad to put a bullet in the rascal's head and give justice to the young lady, Oi did. Wish 'e'd had the stomach to do so, after what this Irish maggot did to poor Lady Nerissa."

"Two wrongs don't make a right, Bates, and we are not such savages in the Royal Navy." McPhee knelt down, turned O' Devir's lolling head toward them with a hand on his jaw, and pushed up an eyelid.

"He's dead, sir," said Dobson, finally speaking.

"He's not dead, we all saw him moving!"

"Well, if 'e wasn't dead then, 'e sure as shit is now," said Bates, "In fact—"

"Shut up, Bates," snapped McPhee, his eyes angry as he looked up at the bully. He let O' Devir's eye slide shut. "Just shut the hell up, would you?"

Others were leaving their assigned tasks and gathering around, murmuring in excitement as they looked down at Lieutenant McPhee and the dead man they'd all been sent to apprehend.

McPhee, frowning, picked up the man's wrist. He lay a thumb against its inner surface, feeling for a pulse.

"Can't see how 'e can be alive, sir. 'Bleedin' from 'is leg like a slaughtered pig, 'e is."

Smith stood looking down at them. "Or was. Looks like some poor bloke thought he could save him with a makeshift tourniquet. What is that, someone's stock?"

"Don't know, too much blood and I ain't untyin' it."

McPhee, his face grim, quietly laid the Irishman's wrist over his chest. "He's alive indeed. And that bleeding must be stopped or he will be dead, within the hour unless I miss my guess."

"Thought you all wanted him dead."

"*Captain Hadley* wants him dead. But I suspect he'd be just as happy to keep him alive until he can get him to England, take credit for his capture, and present him to the Duke of Blackheath on a silver platter."

"We're the Royal Navy. We could kill 'im now and ain't nobody would ever know," Bates persisted.

"I would not take that honor away from the Duke of Blackheath," murmured McPhee, rising to his feet. "She's his sister to avenge, not ours."

"Aye, pity the poor bloke who has to deal with *that* devil. O' Devir'll wish we'd killed him now."

Laughter.

"Cease your damned prattle," McPhee said, raising his head to watch the men forward, still wrestling with the jib. "Nobody's killing anyone. Mr. Walters, have your men take him below, find the Yankee surgeon if they have one, and have him do what he can to save this man's life."

"Aye, sir."

"And see to the rest of the dead. That storm will be on us within a half-hour. I want us out of here and away from a lee shore. We have no time to lose."

McPhee moved off, leaving Walters in dubious command once more.

At their feet O' Devir was struggling once more to regain consciousness, his eyes opening to regard the darkening sky above with blank confusion.

"Where ... where is she?" he murmured, eyes rolling in pain.

"Who?"

"*An bhean* ... The lady...."

Walters cleared his throat. "She's—"

"Ye rotten bastard, ye had yer way with 'er and now ye want to know where she is?" Bates puffed himself up, thinking how good it would feel to kill such an obvious menace to society in general and British ladies in particular. "Ye're a piece of shit, O' Devir," he said, bending down, "and Oi'm gonna enjoy seeing ye hang."

The Irishman managed to raise his head. "Nerissa...."

"Ye're not fit to speak her name, ye buggering piece of offal," Bates snarled, and before Walters could intervene, he grabbed the rebel by a fistful of hair and in one brutal motion, slammed his skull down hard against the deck. O' Devir went lifeless once more, and in disgust, Bates let him drop to the deck with an ugly thump just as the first drops of rain began to spatter all around them.

Walters stood there, open-mouthed and blinking.

Bates turned on him. "Shall Oi throw him overboard now, *sir?*"

Stunned by such a display of savagery, trying to regain his usurped authority, Walters shook his head. "No. You, Bates ... go see to the rest of the dead. Smith and Dobson, help me get him down to his surgeon. And bring your pistols just in case those rebels down there try anything."

He cast a nervous glance forward. McPhee's back was turned and he was motioning angrily to the men fighting to get the new jib strung. He hadn't seen, thank God, what had just taken place. Bending, Walters himself slid his hands beneath the Irishman's shoulders, lifted his upper body, locked his arms around his chest and stood, his arms groaning under the man's dead, muscled weight as Dobson and Smith hoisted up the torso and bloody legs. O' Devir's dark head pitched forward onto his chest, his arms swinging as the three made their way toward the hatch.

Pray God you didn't just kill him, Bates, thought Walters on a note of panic.

McPhee's wrath would be bad enough.

He didn't even want to consider Hadley's.

Chapter Twenty-One

Why, oh why, am I crying?

Nerissa, still clad in Midshipman Cranton's uniform, sat on the cot in what had been Ruaidri O' Devir's cabin, overcome by exhaustion, confusion, awful memories of what she had seen above, and yes, grief.

She reached out and placed a palm over the wool blanket that covered the bed. Images of the recklessly brave Irishman rose in her mind. His bold black brows, his outrageously long lashes, his hard mouth and equally hard features. *I did not know him, really. He made me laugh and he showed me pleasures I did not know existed, but that was all. He kidnapped me. He might have hurt Andrew.* She felt a fresh wave of hot, salty tears welling up in her eyes, tumbling down her cheeks. *He meant nothing to me, really. So why am I crying?*

Because you loved him, said a little voice inside her head.

Rubbish. Or was it? How could she love a man she'd only met a few days before? A man who was ill-suited to her, unacceptably so, really. A man who carried secrets, who was Irish Catholic, who claimed captaincy in a non-existent navy in a non-existent "country."

A man who was brave enough to leap into the sea to save one of his own, bold enough to make an outrageous demand of the most powerful country in the world, unconcerned enough to laugh at the idea of Lucien catching up to and killing him, thoughtful and kind enough to catch and cook her a fish.

A man who had made both her heart and her body come wonderfully, vibrantly alive.

A man.

A real man.

And you're surprised you're crying?

Beyond the salt-glazed stern windows she could see dark, ugly clouds moving toward them. The brig was already feeling it, her motion increasing as she took the building swells on her larboard quarter. Nerissa wondered if those hungry waves had already received Captain O' Devir's body. He would want that, she thought, on a fresh wave of tears. There was at least some dignity to it. The idea of him being brought back to England only to be scorned, laughed at, probably dissected by doctors in training and finally, to be hung in a cage at the mark of high tide to deter other would-be pirates was too much to bear. Did they even still do that?

What did it matter.

You were a good man, Ruaidri O' Devir, she whispered. And true to his word, he had left her maidenhead intact, saving her for a husband she knew in her heart that she would never take.

You were a good man, Ruaidri O' Devir, and you left me with a beautiful memory that no one will ever be able to steal from me. And yes I'm crying, and these tears are for you because I did, I see now, start to love you.

A knock sounded on the door. "Nerissa?"

She dried her eyes on her sleeve, ran fingers through her hair, and went toward the door. But really, there was no use trying to hide her feelings from Andrew. They had always been close. He would understand.

"I came to check on you," he said, moving into the cabin. "You all right?"

"No, I am not," she said, "and you of all people should know it."

"There's something I need to tell you."

"Hadley's intending to court me, isn't he?"

"Damned if I know, but Lucien would never allow it so don't waste a moment's worry on it. No, Nerissa, that's not I came down here to tell you."

She went back to the cot and sat heavily down. "Oh, out with it, Andrew. I'm too tired and too upset to play games."

He came and sat beside her. Took a deep, bracing sigh and took her hand. "That villain who caused all this, Ruaidri O' Devir—I have no wish to upset you even more, Nerissa, but ... he's alive."

"*What?*"

"I'm sorry."

She stared at him, blinking, her mouth agape. Then her lip began to tremble, her body to shake, and the tears flowed down her cheeks in fresh abandon.

"I don't understand," she whispered. "He looked to be dead...."

"Yes, well, rats, cockroaches and parasites are also hard to kill, aren't they?"

She looked over at him, her eyes suddenly flashing. "How dare you say such an awful thing!"

"What?"

"You heard me!"

He stared at her, saw the anger in her eyes and suddenly it dawned on him why she'd been crying. The truth hit him like a punch to the stomach. "Oh, damn it all," he muttered in disgust. "I knew it."

"Knew what?"

"That you were in love with him. For God's sake, Nerissa, what is the matter with you? You've always been a bit on the wayward side, but this really takes the cake."

She rounded on him. "None of us get to choose

whom we fall in love with, Andrew, and you of all people should know that. You might've married someone of your own station, but Charles and Gareth certainly did not, and that doesn't make their love for their wives any less valid or our sisters-in-law any less worthy just because they're not of blue blood!"

"*Marriage?!* Who said anything about marriage? Dear God, don't tell me you're going to marry him!"

"I would indeed if he were to ask me!"

"Has he?"

"No, but if he did—"

"Nerissa, he's *Irish*."

"I don't care if he's from the damned moon!"

"And he hit you. He—" Andrew made a noise of impotent rage and pain, his lips suddenly trembling—"*hit you.* How can you have such feelings for a man who'd abuse you?"

"What on earth are you talking about?"

"Don't pretend you don't know! Even Lucien's found out about it. Everyone knows that he struck you down with a pistol and then buggered—" he flushed, swearing under his breath—"I mean, had his way with a young midshipman. I find that rather hard to believe, but enough of Hadley's people saw it that they're out for blood."

"Struck me down? Buggered a midshipman?"

Andrew flushed again at her use of the word 'buggered.'

Nerissa shoved a loose strand of hair off her forehead and turned to look askance at her brother. Is that what they'd all thought? That Ruaidri had actually harmed her? No wonder he was so angry. "Oh Andrew, you poor, deluded fool. Captain O' Devir would never hurt me. What Hadley and his men saw was Midshipman Cranton dressed up in my clothes and pretending to be me on the deck. Ruaidri—"

"Oh, so it's Ruaidri now, is it?"

"Yes, *Ruaidri* predicted that Hadley would never fire on us if he perceived me to be in danger, so Cranton took my place on the deck; he was never harmed, either. It was all an act." As he stood staring at her, she tucked her fingers into the crook of his arm and said gently, "Ruaidri had actually sent me below and deep into the hold so that I'd be safe just in case Hadley did open fire."

Andrew shook his head. "And the young midshipman he was bug—er, kissing?"

Nerissa shook her head in exasperation. "Honestly Andrew, for someone as intelligent as you are, I'd have thought the identity of that young midshipman would be quite obvious."

He lowered his head to his hands and rubbed with infinite weariness at his forehead.

"Bloody hell," he muttered. "Bloody, thundering hell."

Nerissa's own mind was already changing course, racing along on a new and decisive tack. "Enough of that. What am I doing sitting here? He needs me." She got to her feet. "Take me to him, Andrew. Please."

"What are you, insane?" he asked, recovering. "You go and raise suspicions about your feelings toward him and there's no telling what that young lieutenant up there will do, let alone Hadley, who clearly has his own cap set for you. Sit down while we think this through. In fact, I'm inclined to just leave this all for the time being and let Lucien sort it out when we get back to England."

"Lucien will never, not in a million years, allow me to marry Ruaidri."

"He will never, not in *two* million years, allow you to marry him—but he might at least endeavor to save his life just to make you happy."

"And if he won't?"

"For God's sake, Nerissa, do you have to make this so complicated?"

She glared at him.

"Until we get home, I would advise you to pretend you have nothing but contempt for O' Devir. I wouldn't trust Hadley not to kill him if he thinks he's a threat to his own plans for you."

"So you won't let me go to him."

"Do what you want. But I'm telling you it's unwise."

Nerissa collapsed back to the cot, digging the heels of her hands into her eyes. Ruaidri was hurt, in pain, maybe even dying and for his own safety she couldn't even go to see him? Fresh tears began leaking from her eyes at the hopelessness of the situation.

Andrew let out a bone-weary sigh of resignation and put his arm around her back. "You care for him that much, then, do you?"

She nodded, unable to speak.

"Well, he's not the man I'd have chosen for you, Nerissa, but as you say ... we don't get to pick whom we fall in love with."

She reached into his pocket, found a handkerchief, and dabbed at her eyes.

"You say he's alive ... I saw him, Andrew. There was so much blood, I can't even imag—" she raised a hand as though to stop the awful memory and the thoughts that logically followed it, in their tracks. Steadying herself, she tried again, her voice tight and controlled. "Is he all right?"

"He's unconscious, but alive. One of Hadley's marksmen got him just above the back of the knee. He's lost a lot of blood. Too much, really. His own surgeon is working on him now with McPhee himself holding a gun on the poor doctor to make sure there are no escape attempts." His eyes were grave. "I wouldn't get your hopes up, Nerissa."

"That Ruaidri won't make an escape attempt?"

He smiled sadly, acknowledging her faith and hope in a fellow who was surely as mortal as the next, her inability to see what he felt was obvious. "No, Sis. That he'll survive this night."

There was a sudden fiendish howl of wind from outside, a flash and crack of thunder that shook the ship as heavily as the broadsides had done earlier in the day. *Tigershark* leaned hard to leeward, her great timbers groaning, and beyond the stern windows the sea, gray and angry now, appeared at an angle as rain began to pelt the heavy glass.

Above, Midshipman Walters's high-pitched adolescent voice yelled an order, yelled it again in a futile attempt to be heard over the wind.

"Too young and too unsure a lad for such an important position," Andrew mused. He braced himself against the roll of the ship. "I hope we're all safe. I'd like to see Celsie and little Laura again before I leave this earth."

But Nerissa was thinking that if Ruaidri was in command, neither Andrew or anyone else would have anything to worry about. She wondered how poor Midshipman Cranton, Lieutenant Morgan, and the rest of *Tigershark*'s crew were faring, locked down there in the pitch-black hold while the ship groaned and fought her way through increasingly heavy seas and this, after being wounded by Hadley's frigate only hours before.

Hours?

It was getting darker and darker beyond the stern windows and dimly, it occurred to Nerissa that the loss of light wasn't just due to the storm.

"What time is it?" she asked.

"Getting late," her brother replied. "Have you dined?"

She shook her head. "I have no appetite."

"I wish I could claim the same. I'm famished."

"There's good wine and spirits in that small cupboard," she said, nodding toward the paneled bulkhead. "Maybe some cheese. We could feast. Get foxed."

"You need to pull yourself together, Nerissa."

"I am together."

"Just because you've stopped crying doesn't mean you're all right."

More desperate calls from above, and poor, out-of-his-depth Walters trying vainly to be heard over the wind. "Get McPhee!" he was shouting. "I need him up here, I've lost track of the frigate in the darkness!"

"Heads will roll," Andrew said, going to the cupboard and pulling out a round of cheese. He found a knife, cut off a wedge, and offered it to her. "Want some?"

"What I want is to go to Ruaidri."

"We've already discussed that. You can't."

"I must."

"He's unconscious. He won't know you're there."

"How do you know he's unconscious? Have you seen him?"

Andrew broke off a chunk of the cheese and popped it into his mouth, chewing hungrily. "I confess I had a look at him to satisfy my curiosity, if nothing else." He took another bite. "Please have some cheese, Nerissa. You need to eat."

But Nerissa just went to the stern windows and looked out over the darkening sea, and the last thing on her mind was food.

Ruaidri O' Devir might not survive this night.

And if he did, he would never survive what awaited him in England.

There was only one way to save him. It was a daring plan and it would take more stomach than she'd ever had to demonstrate. Once she carried it out she would be a fugitive, with no going back.

But Nerissa was a de Montforte ... and she knew what she had to do.

❧

"Hell of a place to die, down here in the darkness."

"I don't like the feel of the ship. She's laboring. Those Britons are having trouble keeping her on her feet in this squall."

"Aye, well, better to die here than at the end of an English noose."

The hold was hot and dark, already unpleasant with the scent of some forty nervous, beaten, and injured men all confined in such small space. Some were still bleeding from the short, brutal fight with the English frigate. Others were sweating profusely in fear and misery. The youngest of the lot, Joey, sat stroking his parrot, his mind filled with images no child should ever have to see or remember. Nobody had brought them food. Nobody had even brought them water.

"So much for getting that explosive," Lieutenant Morgan said, bracing himself against a bulkhead as the brig leaned hard over. "But we gave it our best shot."

"We might've done it, if that cowardly scrote Hadley hadn't shot our captain in the back before the fight even started."

"Didn't quite shoot him in the back, now."

"Shot him when his back was turned and he was trying to save the lady, and in my book that's the same damned thing."

They could feel wind buffeting the ship and around them, the sound of water surging against the hull and finding its way in through the oakum that made the seams, working now in the heavy seas, watertight.

"Damned cowards," said one of the topmen, picking at a bandaged finger.

"I don't know who I'd like to have a go at first, that bloody Frenchie who betrayed us or Hadley."

"Don't quite matter now, does it? We're done for."

Nobody said anything, remembering the faces of friends and shipmates they'd never see again. Remembering their own actions and wondering what they could have done differently. Remembering their captain dying in his own blood as poor Tackett, shot through the chest as he'd torn off his neckerchief and tried to tie off the bleeding, fell dead beside him. Neither had even had the chance to fight.

"Think he could've saved us?" young Cranton asked.

The smell of ginger filled the close, hot space as Morgan tried to combat his seasickness with the contents of his pocket. "He was clever and tough. Ruthless, when he had to be. If anyone could have done so, it was him."

The moments ticked by, only the sound of their breathing marking the passage of time.

At length, Cranton spoke. "He sure had his secrets, though. Carried them to the grave."

"Aye."

The ship rolled and yawed, tilting sickeningly.

"He ever tell any of you what he did?" Morgan asked.

"Not me."

"Me neither."

The voice of the helmsman's mate was a murmur in the darkness. "On the way across the Atlantic, he used to stand with me deep into the night after I'd relieve Tackett at the helm. We had a good chin-wag about a lot of stuff. Women. Politics. Shipbuilding. Hopes and dreams."

"Did he tell you what horrible thing he supposedly did?"

"Not in so many words. But I kind of guessed it."

The ship yawed again, and someone in the close space vomited.

"Fuck you, Moore."

"Christ, if the stink down here was bad before, ye've just made it unbearable."

Moore puked again.

"So what did he do?" Cranton drew his knees up and wrapped his arms around them, trying to filter his air through his sleeve. "What dark and awful secret did he take to the grave?"

It was a long while before the helmsman spoke. "He murdered his best friend." And then, in the stunned silence, he added, "and it was over a woman."

Chapter Twenty-Two

It seemed as though Andrew would never leave.

Eventually, though, her deliberate yawns got through to him and bidding her a good night he opened the door, exchanged a few words with the sentry that McPhee had posted just outside, and found his own cabin.

Nerissa wasted no time.

She wolfed down what was left of the cheese to replenish her energy, waited for five, ten, twenty minutes until she was sure her brother was safely back in his own cabin, and set to work rooting around in Ruaidri's desk. Her stomach clenched at the thought of what she was about to do, what she intended to do, though she saw no way out of it. *Oh, God give me strength!*

There. A glass paperweight, smooth and green, tiny bubbles inside it frozen in space and time. A shamrock dominated its center.

A shamrock. She hoped that it, along with her own determination, would be the instrument to save an Irishman from the gallows.

She hefted it in her hand, getting the feel of its weight. The glass molded itself to her palm, lent strength to her fingers and her own resolve, and grew warm.

I can do this.

I have *to do this.*

She found a knife, hacked at her gown, pocketed the strips. Then she went to the door and quietly pulled it open, one hand on her stomach, the other discreetly behind her back.

"Good evening, my lady," said the sailor who stood there. "What can I do for you?"

"This storm ... It is making me unwell. I need some fresh air."

"I'll go with you."

"No, no, I'm quite all right. I fear that I may be sick, and I would be dreadfully embarrassed to cast up my accounts in front of you or anyone else."

"I'm sure I've seen much worse."

"I'm sure you have, but I do have my sensibilities, sir, and I am asking you to respect them." She gave a moan to add emphasis to her nonexistent *mal de mer*. "Is the storm waning?"

"It is, but we've become separated from the frigate. I'm sure well find them at first light."

"We're all alone out here on the sea?" she squeaked, pretending a frightened gasp.

"You are under the protection of the Royal Navy, milady. There is nothing to fear."

"And was that awful—" she gave a sudden, quivering sob, wondering if she had a career on Drury Lane —"Irishman, properly disposed of? I would dread to have him rising up from the dead and ravishing me."

The seaman eyed her askance. "You haven't heard?"

"Heard what?"

"He's not dead. Wish he was, though, for what he did to you. No gentleman should ever strike a lady."

And no lady should ever strike a gentleman, but this one is prepared to if you don't let me pass.

"He's not dead?" She widened her eyes and clutched

at her chest in feigned terror. "Oh, dear God in heaven help me!"

The sailor drew himself up. "There is no cause for alarm, milady. The rogue is barely breathing and his own surgeon just spent an hour trying to patch him up. Not worth the bother if you ask me."

Nerissa pretended to shudder. "And where is he now? Am I safe up here on deck?"

"McPhee put him below about twenty minutes ago with the rest of his scurvy bunch of pirates. He won't harm you, milady. The lieutenant himself is guarding the hold."

"The lieutenant himself? Why, I do feel much safer, sir ... but since he's the one now commanding this ship, I would have thought he'd have assigned such a task to one of the midshipman. Is that awful Captain O' Devir so very dangerous?"

"Not so very dangerous at the moment, but very, very important."

She appeared to consider that. "What about that young man with the cherubic curls? Walters, I believe?"

"Walters has the deck. If you turn and look in that direction, you can see him in the darkness. Again, you are quite safe, my lady."

She nodded, remembering she was supposed to feel seasick, and passed a hand over her brow. "I need to get some air," she said and began to move past him, but she knew he was going to be difficult; his eyes were on her, and he wasn't going to let her out of his sight. Certainly not long enough for her to slip below. The minute she disappeared, he would raise the alarm, thinking she'd fallen overboard in the still-heavy seas.

She felt the heavy, reassuring weight of the paperweight with its little shamrock in her palm. *You can do this.*

I can't!

You can, because you're doing it to save his *life.*

The guard was right behind her. She pretended to trip, and pulling off a nonexistent necklace, let it fall to the deck.

"My choker!"

"Eh?"

"My choker! It was a gift from my brother for my twentieth birthday. Oh, do help me, sir, I fear I've lost it in the darkness!"

She began to sob and sure enough, the sentry put down his pistol, dropped to his knees, and began to search with his palms on the wet, salt-sticky deck, eager to be the one to save the damsel in distress.

The damsel, though, raised her hand, uttered a silent prayer for strength and forgiveness, and gave a little cry as she brought the paperweight down hard on the back of his head.

The feel of the impact in her palm and up her arm was awful, and the nausea that suddenly flared in her stomach was not feigned. She allowed herself a moment of horror as she looked down at the man's prostrate form, both awed and sick at heart that she had actually struck someone down. She sucked her lips between her teeth, pulled from her pocket one of the strips that she had cut from her ruined gown, and hastily tied it around the fallen man's wrists. A second piece secured his mouth in a gag, and bending down to make sure he was still breathing, she picked up his pistol and left him there on the deck in the darkness, hoping that squeaky-voiced Midshipman Walters would not come back here to check on him.

Walters himself was at the tiller, conversing with the helmsman. Neither had heard a thing over the roar of the sea as it creamed past the ship in the darkness.

Gripping the deckhouse, skirting a mast, Nerissa crept quietly behind them, thankful for the sound of wind and wave, the trusty Irish paperweight still securely in her hand. It was slippery and she told herself it was only salt spray, and not the sentry's blood.

There, in the darkness, was the hatch that led below. She knew the layout. A short companionway ladder, which she easily descended in breeches and coat. Lantern-light behind a cabin door.

Andrew.

She bit her lip, then reached into her pocket. Found a strip of her gown. Quietly, carefully tied the door shut against its neighboring latch so that he would be safe—and unable to interfere.

Another hatch, and finally the hold, where McPhee would surely be on guard.

The ship was pitch black. She paused for a moment to get her bearings. Around her, the quiet was eerie and frightening, the sound of the sea rushing past outside, muffled. She wished she had a candle, though the risk of carrying one and being discovered was too great. She would have to rely on her memory, and her senses.

I'm coming, Ruaidri.

I won't let you down.

Her palms moved along wooden bulkheads as she felt her way forward and steadied her balance. Great masts creaked in the heavy darkness. And there, a noise. Just below and somewhere in front of her; the sound of low voices and a man moaning in pain.

She had found the hold.

Which meant that McPhee was nearby.

Her gaze plumbed the darkness, but to no avail. She took a deep, steadying breath and held it, straining to hear something, anything.

And there, yes. Snoring.

McPhee, it seemed, was asleep.

She listened to the light, rhythmic sound of his slumber, trying to discern exactly where he was. She moved silently to her right. There, barely discernible in the pressing gloom, she could see a dim glow. Praying that the steady snores would continue, she crept toward it, the glow getting brighter as she moved around the base of the foremast, a bulkhead, and there, finally, the small space in which McPhee had crammed himself, his back molded to the curve of the hull, his cheek across his drawn-up knees and his feet resting on the hatch cover beneath which the American crew was imprisoned.

A musket and a pistol lay near his heel.

Nerissa swallowed hard and began to creep forward, bringing up the pistol she had taken from the sentry and training it on McPhee's still form.

He didn't move.

She crept closer, the agonized moaning coming from below that closed hatch causing her heart to beat a little faster. Was it Ruaidri? Or some other poor soul, desperately in need of medical attention and trapped like an animal in the darkness?

Three more feet and she would be able to touch McPhee.

She crept forward another few steps and holding her breath while keeping her gun trained on him, slowly reached down to retrieve his pistol.

His eyes opened and he jerked up, staring at her.

"Don't move," she said, hoping her voice didn't betray her quaking nerves. "I don't want to shoot you."

"Lady Nerissa?"

"Open the hatch."

"I can't do that."

"I can't shoot you, either, but I will if I have to. Open the hatch."

"You'll have to shoot me, then. And the moment you do, my men will be down here like a swarm of hornets."

"There are a dozen of you. And one less, if you make

me shoot you. There are, if I guess correctly, some forty Americans and one nearly-dead Irishman locked in that hatch below your feet. While we both place great faith in the Royal Navy, Mr. McPhee, even you will acknowledge those are pretty long odds."

"Do you know what you're *doing*?"

"Indeed, I have thought it out most carefully."

"You're the daughter of one of Britain's noblest, oldest families, a family whose very history is interwoven with England's itself. You are about to betray your country, your family, your navy!"

"Open the hatch. *Now*."

He let out a deep sigh, unfolded himself from against the hull, and reached for the latch that kept the square wooden door firmly atop the space in which the prisoners were kept below. She did not expect him to give up without a fight, and indeed he did not; as he undid the latch, he swung around in a lightning move and made a grab for her pistol and everything happened at once.

Her arm jerked up, the small weapon went off, and as the cover exploded off the hatch, a horde of Americans came bursting forth, intent on reclaiming their ship.

"Huzzah for you, Lady Nerissa!" shouted Lieutenant Morgan as he clambered up and past, knocking a stunned McPhee onto his back while seizing the British lieutenant's weapons. He went tearing out into the darkness, his shipmates, stinking of sweat and salt and blood, howling like Indians in his wake. One of them stopped to tackle McPhee, quickly binding his wrists with a piece of rope that Nerissa had found and now offered silently; the last strip from her gown secured his mouth, and then there was nothing but his eyes meeting hers from above the gag, the sounds of fighting from above, and down here in the darkness that was lit only by the dim glow of McPhee's small lantern, the yawning black hole of the hatch.

"Let this be a lesson to you, Mr. McPhee," she said, her fingers tightening around the lantern, "to never go to sleep on the job."

He shut his eyes and let his head fall back against the curve of the hull, no doubt already envisioning his own court martial and dishonorable discharge from the Royal Navy.

But Nerissa didn't care.

She was already climbing down the short ladder into this wretched small, hot space, already shining the light into what had been pitch blackness, already looking for *him*.

"Nerissa, *mo grá,*" he said weakly, from where he had been dragged to a corner and propped up against someone's jacket. "*Mo cróga, bean laoch álainn.*" He was still in the bloodied breeches, a clean band of linen wound just above one knee. "My brave, beautiful warrior woman." His eyes, deep and bottomless in the lantern-lit darkness, looked up at her through their absurdly long lashes, and she reached a hand, still smelling of gunpowder, down to touch his bristled cheek. He closed his eyes and held it there, reluctant to ever let her go, and she reveling in the warmth of his skin beneath hers, the knowledge that his heart still pumped his lifeblood beneath her hand.

"I could not let you die," she breathed, kneeling down beside him and offering him the strength of her own slim, lithe body. His face was ghostly from loss of blood, and she could see that it was an effort for him to even keep his eyes open, let alone press her hand to his cheek.

She sat down on the hard, blood-stained planking and gently gathered him in her arms, stroking his heavy curls as he rested his forehead against her shoulder.

"*Tá tú mo banlaoch*," he whispered. "My heroine. My savior...."

"Sleep, Ruaidri. The ship is back in your men's hands and you, my love, are safe in mine." She threaded her fingers up through his hair and gently caressed his scalp, wincing at the hard swelling she found there. She did not want to think about how he must have received it. She did not want to think of him being hurt, she did not want to think of anything but how grateful she was that he was alive and safely in her arms.

Hadley ... the Royal Navy ... Lucien.

Strength and a hard, ruthless confidence filled her heart. She had come this far.

She could deal with all of them.

Ruaidri's forehead grew heavy against her collarbone. He murmured something unintelligible and, with her hand still quietly caressing him, finally gave himself up to the demands of his body and slept.

Two decks above, Lieutenant Morgan was in command of the American brig *Tigershark*, and her proper colors were once again flying proudly at her gaff. The dead—including Bates, who'd been taken down by a well-aimed shot to his groin from young Midshipman Cranton—were buried at sea and what remained of the British prize crew was rounded up and herded below to the same hold that had so recently imprisoned the Americans.

When that British crew arrived, resentful and angry, they found Lieutenant McPhee bound and gagged, and in the hold itself, the boy that Captain O' Devir had presumably buggered. He was holding the Irishman in his arms, his lips buried in the thick, curling black hair that lay like a mantle over the wide span of his uniformed shoulders.

The midshipman's eyes lifted to regard the Royal Navy sailors and in that moment, to a man, they saw that it had been no boy that O' Devir had presumably been buggering.

It was Lady Nerissa de Montforte.

She had returned the ship to the enemy. She had betrayed them all and committed treason against her king and country.

For Nerissa, there was no going back.

Chapter Twenty-Three

It was Lieutenant Morgan and two brawny seamen who personally came down into the hold and helped their very weak captain to his feet, up the short ladder, and topside. For Ruaidri, his head swimming, his vision going light and dark and darker still as he fought to stay conscious, it was a journey through the gauntlets of hell on a leg that was on fire beneath his left hip. But he'd be pickled in vinegar if he allowed either of the seamen to actually pick him up and carry him. Injured or not, he was in command here and he would not show weakness when there were others who were injured just as badly, who were fated to die, or who'd lost their lives this day.

Nerissa stayed at his side, discreetly offering her arm so that he might steady himself. She knew. She knew, and he loved her for it.

They reached the quarterdeck, dark beneath the stars. As they emerged on deck, cheering erupted all around. Cheers for the strength of their captain, who was on his feet. Cheers for the fact he was back in command. And mostly, cheers for the beautiful Lady Nerissa, whose bravery and sacrifice had saved them all from Mill Prison, the gallows, or both.

If they were fond of her before, now she was their

heroine and savior—just as she was his. She had won their hearts.

"Three cheers for the captain's lady!" They all but swarmed her. "Hip hip, huzzah! Hip hip, huzzah! Hip hip, huzzah!"

Ruaidri heard the cheering as though from a great distance. He had not been up here since before the battle and now he paused, surveying the damage in the darkness. Only Nerissa beside him knew how heavily he leaned against her as the men went back to repairing rigging, sails and planking, scrubbing blood-stained decks and upending a heavy gun that lay on its side.

"Damage report, Mr. Morgan."

"Five dead, sir. Mr. Tackett, the carpenter's mate Pettengill, and three able seamen. Sears, Moody, and McCafferty. Brits threw them all overboard."

Ruaidri nodded once, measuring his breathing in order to fill his dizzy brain with the air it needed to keep him on his feet and get him through this grim task.

"Wounded?"

"Twelve, sir. One not likely to make it."

"I wasn't likely to make it either, but damn the eyes of anyone who says I won't. And the ship, Mr. Morgan?"

"Rigging cut up some, sir, but we're working on it. The Brits weren't aiming to damage her so things could have been a lot worse. They rammed and boarded us. Fought like tigers, our lads did, but we were outnumbered three to one."

"Outnumbered? What about Le Favre, that little maggot in command of the French frigate? Where was he durin' all this?"

Morgan shrugged. "Bolted as soon as things got hot."

"Bolted, did he? When I catch up to him he's goin' to wish his arse had been blistered in butter and set afire."

"Aye, if he hadn't gotten greedy and tried to take the English frigate, things would've turned out a lot differently. He ruined it for everyone. At the end of the day though, we got what we came for."

Ruaidri regarded him keenly. "The explosive?"

"Lord Andrew de Montforte, sir. He refused to leave his sister and *she* refused to leave us." He quickly filled his captain in on what had happened. "Someone —" he cast a pointed look at Nerissa—"locked His Lordship in his cabin, but we freed him and brought him below. Figured he could help Dr. Jeffcote with the wounded while we tried to decide what to do with him."

Ruaidri just stared at him. Lord Andrew de Montforte? Here? Now?

It was all he could do to contain his grin. "Well, now, things have just got a whole lot better, they have. Thank ye, Mr. Morgan. Time to beat it back to Boston, then."

"Boston?" He'd all but forgotten Nerissa standing quietly nearby. "We're still going to Boston?"

He looked at her as if she were daft. "Well of course we are, lass, what did ye think?"

"I *thought* you would release Andrew, maybe in France or Jersey ... that you'd let him go because he's my brother—"

Ruaidri just stared at her. Had he missed something here? Were they both reading the same page? Inhabiting the same earth? He bit back a wave of sudden nausea. Damn his dizzy brain for its inability to think. Damn his weakened body when the ship and the situation in which they found themselves needed everything he had to give. He was close to either puking or passing out or maybe both, and now this? Fire burning up his leg and the musket ball that Jeffcote had dug out of the back of his lower thigh now a grim souvenir in his waistcoat pocket, he straightened up, cursing the sudden look of dismay on Nerissa's face as she realized her brother would not be spared, and certainly not released.

"For the love o' God, woman, I didn't come three thousand miles just to feck around in the English Channel. I have what I was sent here to get, and my orders are to deliver him and his secrets to John Adams."

Her face had gone flat. "So you'll go through with this, then. Take him away from his family, his wife and baby girl, and bring him to the rebels."

He felt suddenly wearier than he'd ever imagined he could be. "This is a discussion for another time, Nerissa."

Her mouth tightened. Her fingers dropped from his arm, and he was left to stand on his own, weaker than a newborn kitten and just as unsteady on his feet. The world swayed and his skin went clammy. Morgan was looking at him critically, and Ruaidri turned away to lean against the deckhouse, thankful for the darkness that hid his body's violent shaking from the crew. What had Jeffcote said? That the ball had nicked a blood vessel which, if not for poor old Tackett and his quick thinking with an improvised tourniquet, would have killed him? Damned if he knew. He certainly didn't remember anything between shouting for Nerissa to get below as the world had blown apart, and waking up on a bench in the surgeon's quarters, a bandage around his thigh and the smell of death and suffering all around him. Thank the living Christ they hadn't taken his leg.

And now he'd upset the one person in the world for whom he'd have given that same leg if only to spare her a single ounce of pain.

"Mr. Cranton," he said, using all his strength to raise a hand and summon the midshipman. "Go get Lord Andrew and tell him I fancy a chat with him. Settle him in my cabin with some refreshments. I'll be in to speak with him shortly."

"Aye, sir."

He bent his head, suddenly nauseous, the wind blowing hair that was damp with salt spray and probably blood, around his face. Gone was the ribbon with which he'd queued it when he rose this morning and in its place, a hard, painful, goose-egg. He rubbed distractedly at it and looked over at Nerissa, feeling the accusatory weight of her stare.

He met that stare, unwilling to back down. Unable to back down.

"What do you possibly have to say to my brother?"

"I haven't decided yet."

She made a sound of angry disgust, turned and stalked off.

A wave of vertigo caught him and he briefly shut his eyes, trying to keep what blood was left in his body in the places where it was most needed. His gaze lit on the compass, tried to make sense of it in the darkness, and failed. He glanced up at the trim of the sails, saw they were drawing well, and swaying drunkenly with sudden dizziness, caught himself before he could topple off to the side and end up as a sorry mess on the deck.

He missed Nerissa's strong, slim arm.

But there was time to miss it later. They were not out of danger. Not by any stretch of a leprechaun's luck.

Placating her was going to have to wait.

"A night glass," he said, and Morgan handed one to him.

Ruaidri opened it, struggling to hold up the heavy instrument in arms that were failing him. Sweat dappled his forehead. Cranton was materializing from out of the darkness and impatiently, Ruaidri motioned to the young officer.

"Yer help if ye please, Mr. Cranton."

"Aye, sir."

Cranton turned and bent, and holding the instrument to his eye while balancing it against the youth's shoulder, Ruaidri scanned the eastern horizon. Darkness lay heavily all around them, but he had the night vision of an owl and the glass, its image inverted, was almost redundant.

Morgan pressed close. "Is he out there, Captain?"

They all knew who 'he' was. In a few hours, dawn would be lighting up the sea and as the light strengthened, Hadley would see that his prize had gone missing —and he'd come looking for her with a vengeance.

"I don't see him, Morgan, but that doesn't mean a thing." He shut the glass, swaying on his feet. "We can't linger here."

"Your orders, sir?"

"Wind's decent out of the east. Slap as much canvas on her as she'll carry without rippin' the sticks out of her and let's get the hell out of Europe. 'Tis time to go home, lads. Time to go home."

Sudden cheering erupted all around. Weak, dizzy, and white with pain, Ruaidri pushed himself off the deckhouse, impatiently motioning for Morgan to help him to his cabin where Lord Andrew and his next battle surely awaited him.

One skirmish won, he thought, the next about to begin.

❧

Lord Andrew, slouching in Captain O' Devir's chair with a glass of Irish whiskey in his hand, stared morosely out the darkened stern windows and contemplated the absolute mess in which he and Nerissa now found themselves.

The absolute mess that *she* had brought about.

His wife Celsie back home at Rosebriar with little Laura and surely worried sick about him. Nerissa ruined, a traitor to England and now, God help them, in love with a rebel who was destined to die when his leg turned gangrenous, the Royal Navy returned, or Lucien caught up to him. *Lucien.* His brother wouldn't give O' Devir a chance to even explain himself before he executed him. Andrew raked a hand through his hair. A fortnight ago his life had been secure and orderly, full of hope and excitement as he'd planned for the explosive's demonstration and finally, recognition for his achievements. Now the world was turned upside down.

And why?

The explosive, of course.

That damned explosive.

He tossed back another swallow of the whiskey. Had he ever come up with an invention that didn't cause mischief, upend people's lives and in general, prove to be a thoroughly useless addition to the society it sought to improve?

The explosive. He was beginning to rue its existence, just as he had rued that damned aphrodisiac he'd accidentally discovered. His inventions were supposed to better the world, not make it worse. The aphrodisiac though, had led him to Celsie. The explosive, on the other hand ... it should never, ever have been invented. Whether it ended up with the Royal Navy or the Americans, its existence would lead to nothing but death, destruction and misery, and he'd sure seen enough of that today to last a lifetime.

Death, destruction and misery.

O' Devir bleeding out on his own quarterdeck. English dead, American dead, severed limbs and battered corpses. Soon-to-be grieving widows, mothers, children and lovers. Lives wrecked, bodies broken, dreams shattered and futures destroyed. Such was war. There was nothing patriotic about it, nothing justified and certainly nothing noble, and sitting there contemplating the darkness beyond the windows, Andrew suddenly realized that he wanted no further part of any of it. That no invention, solution, substance or creation to ever spring forth from his brain and hands would ever contribute to the suffering or death of another human being.

The formula for that explosive ... he would take it to the grave.

There is enough misery in this world. I will not add to it.

He sighed and looked at his pocket watch. Nerissa's abductor wanted a meeting. Andrew just wanted to find some quiet place to be alone.

He thought back to that moment in London, when he'd briefly met the man. O' Devir had struck him as a fool and a braggart, assured of his own effect on the fairer sex and spoiling for a fight. The kind of man that put a brother's hackles up on behalf of his little sister, the kind of man that other men recognized as a danger, a heartbreaker, competition, and one they would want as far away from the women in their lives as it was possible to get him.

Another swallow of whiskey. Damn, damn, and triple damn.

From outside came the low murmur of voices. The door opened without even the courtesy of a knock, immediately offending Andrew's lordly sensibilities—until he remembered that he was the guest in this man's quarters, not the other way around.

O' Devir stood there, Nerissa at his side and her lips tight with anger.

Trouble in paradise already?

For a long, assessing moment, Andrew locked gazes with the Irishman's. The arrogant scoundrel who'd leaned against the wall in that London townhouse and perused his little sister with a predatory gleam in his eye was not the same person who stood before him now. This was a confident man, a worthy man, a *warrior*, still garbed in the uniform of battle, his blue and white coat stained and torn, one bandaged leg of his snowy breeches cut off at mid-thigh and heavily soaked with blood.

Lord Andrew put down his glass.

So this, then, was the man for whom Nerissa had betrayed her own country.

This was the man that his little sister loved.

Andrew got to his feet and went forward, warily extending a hand.

"Captain Ruaidri O' Devir of the American Continental Navy," the Irishman said, extending his own hand and getting straight to the point. The hand was ice-cold and clammy, but his grip was firm and hard. "'Tis a pleasure to meet ye under my real identity."

"Lord Andrew de Montforte," he said, his own grip equally firm.

The Irishman moved toward the table, picked up the bottle of whiskey and uncorked it, one black, arching brow raised.

"Care for a top up?"

"Yes, thank you."

Potent amber liquid splashed into Andrew's glass, and it was only then that he saw that O' Devir's hand, the fingers calloused and the knuckles criss-crossed with scars, was white and shaking.

The Irishman noted the direction of his gaze. "Ye'll forgive me, m' lord," he said, pouring and half-raising his own glass as he sat down on the cot a few feet away. "I've had better days."

"You have done much that demands forgiveness, Captain. I'm not sure I know where to start." He took a sip of his own drink and glanced at his sister, who stood there uncertainly. "It would be best if you left us for a bit, Nerissa."

"Why, so you two can beat the stuffing out of one another?"

O' Devir sipped his drink. "Wouldn't be a fair fight, now, would it?" he said, swirling the liquid in its glass.

"Indeed, I'd never take advantage of a fellow who's just lost enough blood to float his own warship."

What makes ye think I'd be the one at a disadvantage?"

Andrew raised a brow, but he caught the humor in the other man's eyes and knew it was all in jest, perhaps only to set Nerissa, who was looking increasingly worried, at ease. "Pray God we never make each other angry enough to find out. Nerissa? If you please?"

She folded her arms. "And just where am I supposed to go?"

O' Devir's smile grew fond. "Go find Mr. Cranton, *mo grá*, and tell him I'd like him to bring ye round to the wounded. Seein' a lady's pretty face and hearin' her gentle voice will be good medicine for them."

"You two won't kill each other?"

"Not tonight."

Biting her lip, Nerissa gave them each a last lingering look and left, closing the door behind her.

"Well," said O' Devir. "Tha' 'twas easy."

"It won't always be. Better start planning now how you're going to handle her."

"I'd never presume to try and figure that out, Lord Andrew."

"Andrew. Just Andrew. If you're going to wed her, we might as well dispense with formalities."

"What makes ye think I'm goin' to wed her?"

"Refuse, and I won't let you leave this cabin alive."

"Ehm, right." The other man, lips twitching, took a swallow of whiskey, then sat reflecting upon the contents of his glass. "And what about this eldest brother of yers? Will he give consent? I'm told I'd better keep my entrails in good condition as they'll end up being his chosen instrument of my strangulation."

Andrew guffawed, choking and nearly spilling his drink.

"I had a feeling she was only blaggardin'."

"No, she was not. Though Lucien will see to your dispatch in a much less messy way than strangling you with your own entrails."

"Pistols or swords?"

"Both, probably."

O' Devir sighed. "I suppose I'll have to put up a fight for the sake of pride and appearances."

"I wouldn't bother, as it will only prolong the inevitable outcome. My brother is one of the most dangerous men in England."

The Irishman lifted his glass and smiled. "Ah, but we are not in England, are we?"

Andrew returned the salute. "Indeed, sir, we are not." He had deliberately goaded, perhaps even insulted the man, trying to gauge the depth of his self-restraint. He was both satisfied and relieved that O' Devir had not risen to the bait. His sister would be safe with a husband who could control his temper. He would certainly need that ability, married to one such as her.

"Of course, I should kill you anyhow," Andrew murmured, contemplating his own drink. "You abducted my little sister. You've probably had your way with her, and most certainly, have ruined her. Her life will never be the same."

"No, it will not."

"*Have* you had your way with her?"

"I'm an officer in the Continental Navy, not a pirate."

Andrew eyed him levelly. "So you haven't."

"The only reason I'm even goin' to *answer* that question is because ye're the lass's brother and deserve one. But no, I haven't." He ran a hand through his hair, as black and wild a mane as Andrew had ever seen, and sighed. "Got too much respect for her, I do."

The two men drank, quietly sharing the silence. The lantern swung to and fro with the motion of the ship. O' Devir had gone silent and glancing over at him, Andrew saw that he was discreetly leaning against the ship's inner hull, his eyes drifting shut. So the illusion of strength, then, was an act. His future brother-in-law was weaker, far weaker, than he was letting on and Andrew knew that if he wanted to get anything more out of this conversation he should probably try and bring it to a close sooner rather than later.

"Anything else I should know about you, O' Devir?"

The Irishman's eyes opened. "Lots." He gave Andrew a level stare. Here, too, he did not back down or look away. "You interested in hearin'?"

Andrew rubbed his jaw and thought about that for a long moment. "No," he said finally. "No, I am not."

Still that steady gaze. "I've done terrible things."

"What you've done in the past does not concern me as much as what you'll do in the future—and how you treat my little sister. I won't plumb your secrets, especially as you seem quite willing to confess them."

"I killed a man."

O' Devir was regarding him with flat challenge, daring him to take up this gauntlet.

"I know all about it." And at the Irishman's raised brow, he added, "Lucien had you investigated."

"And he'd still see me wed to yer sister?"

"I consider myself a damned good judge of character, O' Devir, and I can sense enough about yours that the particulars of Mr. Brown's unfortunate death are of little interest to me."

"I love your sister. And she might not be lovin' me back if I were to tell her the particulars that ye're not so eager to hear."

"You haven't told her?"

"Not yet. Things happened rather quicker than I expected, they did. I'll tell her in good time." He looked up at Andrew with eyes that were resolute. "I'd give my life for her, ye know, and consider it an honor doin' it."

"I don't doubt that."

"I won't break her heart like that other ball of shite did."

"If you do, my brothers and I will hunt you down to the ends of the earth and kill you."

Outside the stern windows, the sea sparkled in the moonlight. O' Devir was leaning his head back against the inside of the hull again, watching the thin line of the ship's wake through distant, half-shut eyes.

"For her own safety, you can never bring her back to England again, you know. Not after what she did today."

It was a long time before the other spoke. "I'm not worth the sacrifice. She shouldn't have done that."

"Well, she obviously thinks you are, and she did do it. In releasing your men to retake the ship, she betrayed her country. That's treason. A capital offense. Not even Lucien will be able to save her from the gallows once the truth comes out."

"It doesn't have to come out. The only witnesses to her action who are likely to talk are those locked below in the hold."

"But you won't kill them to keep them quiet."

"Certainly not. I'll set them ashore at some French port, and off we'll go to America."

Andrew stared down into his whiskey. "Well, we all make our own beds, carve our own paths in life, do we not? My sister knows her own mind and she is not, and has never been, rash. She knew there would be no going back to her country, her birthplace, her home ... the family that she loves. And still, when faced with the choice, it was to save your life over everything she holds most dear." Andrew looked at the other man gravely, growing increasingly concerned about his pallor. "You'd better not die on her, O' Devir. Don't let her sacrifice come to naught."

"Not plannin' on it."

"Yes, well, there are lots of things we never plan."

"Aye. And speakin' of plans, just so ye know, mine was to abduct you, not her." O' Devir pushed away from the inner hull against which he'd been leaning and seemed to come back to himself. "Things just sort of happened the way they did, and I took advantage of it. Never meant to cause yer family any pain, just carryin' out the mission that Adams sent me to complete, which was to get that explosive." He looked flatly, almost beseechingly at Andrew. "I wish ye'd give me that formula. I really don't want to bring ye all the way back to Boston."

"I can't. I won't."

"She'll find that hard to forgive, if I don't set ye free somewhere safe."

"Blame it on me, then. After all, I'm the one refusing to relinquish it. Not like you have a choice, if its procurement is your sole reason for being on this side of the Atlantic. Besides—" Andrew's smile was wry —"I'd just as soon stay here and keep an eye on things, at least, until you two tie the knot. And the sooner the better as far as I'm concerned."

"Ye want it done that quickly?"

"Yes. By her actions, she's denied herself the big, formal ceremony in England she'd otherwise have received. No, O' Devir ... there is no reason to wait. Best to wed her quickly and quietly, and if you know of a place or a person who'll do it, all the better."

"Back to Saint-Malo, then. As good a place as any and better, probably, than most."

The Irishman's skin had gone waxen, tiny droplets of sweat gathering on his brow, and Andrew began to wonder if he'd even last the rest of the night. "You look like hell. You even up for a transatlantic crossing?"

O' Devir snorted in amusement. "Never felt better." And then, sobering. "Are you?"

"Never made one."

"'Twill be rough, I expect. Storms this time of year comin' out of the Caribbean."

"It's not like you're giving me a choice, O' Devir."

"I gave ye a choice, but ye're just as stubborn as I am."

"Probably more so."

"Guess we'll have plenty of time to get to know each other over the next few weeks, eh?"

"Indeed, and don't think I won't be watching you." Andrew drained his whiskey and rose to his feet. It was time to go. "You seem to be a fellow of courage and strength, Captain O' Devir. I may have given you consent to wed my sister but I can promise you that if you hurt her in any way, shape or form, you're as good as dead. I'll see to it myself."

The Irishman got up and moved painfully to the door to see him out. "I can assure ye, Lord Andrew, that yer fears are unfounded."

"They damn well better be." Andrew paused with his hand on the latch. "I bid you good night, Captain. And I suggest you get some sleep. Blood takes time and rest to replenish, and you've vowed not to break my sister's heart. Dying would be an immediate way to accomplish that, and I forbid it."

O' Devir smiled wearily. "Good night—and soon enough, good mornin', Andrew. 'Tis been a pleasure."

"*Get some sleep.*"

The door closed behind him.

Finally alone, Ruaidri stood there for a long moment leaning heavily against the door. He was so weak he felt sick to his stomach. The cabin was making a slow revolution both around and inside his head and he despaired of even making it back to his cot. *I should have told him*, he thought. *Should have told him what happened with Delight ... and with Josiah Brown.*

Should have told him....

But hadn't he said he'd known? How much did he know?

Staying alert, staying on his feet, and staying focused during the arse-grilling he'd just been dealt had depleted him of what strength he'd had left. He opened his door to order Morgan to change course, staggered back toward the bunk, collapsed face-down across it ... and knew no more.

❧

"Ships don't just vanish into thin air, Mr. Dewhurst," said Captain Lawrence Hadley, scanning the southern horizon beyond *Happenstance*'s plunging jib-boom. He swung the glass starboard, desperately hoping for a bit of white above the horizon that would at least give him hope that his prize, *Tigershark*, had survived that brief, vicious squall.

"No sir, they don't. But they do occasionally vanish beneath the surface of the sea, especially during storms like that one we just fought our way through."

McPhee, whom he'd left in charge of the prize, was a competent seaman and a level-headed officer. It had blown hard all night and the American brig might've sprung a mast following the damage to her rigging, or simply got separated from them. He told himself that was all it was, and that her absence would be short-lived.

He could not contemplate the very real possibility that she'd gone down in the storm. Not with one, but two de Montforte siblings aboard. The blame would, of course, be laid on his doorstep for allowing the two aristocrats to stay aboard the brig when they'd have been so much safer on board a Royal Navy warship. But no fate that awaited him should that brig not turn up in

London under McPhee's command—and it very well might—would come close to what the Duke of Blackheath would do to him if he did not bring his brother and sister back safe and sound.

Cold sweat ran down his back.

They were alive and the ship was fine and would be waiting for them in London. He was worrying too much. Letting his imagination get the best of him.

"Even so, prepare to tack, Mr. Dewhurst. We'll beat down to as close to the coast of France as we can get, do a few passes where we last saw *Tigershark*, and keep our eyes peeled for signs that she went down. Flotsam. Spars, canvas, and—and the like."

He could not say "bodies."

"Aye, sir."

He was the picture of calm as he stood at the rail, but only he knew of the sudden burning in the pit of his stomach, the restless agony of his bowels as nerves began to get the better of him.

The American brig did not appear on any horizon.

She did, indeed, seem to have vanished.

And in England, both the lords of Admiralty and the Duke of Blackheath waited.

Chapter Twenty-Four

Morning broke bright and clear, and as the day progressed with no sign of the British frigate HMS *Happenstance*, the brisk easterly was happy to stay in their good graces by speeding them out into the Channel. By the time the shadows were growing long across the deck, Nerissa, her fair complexion protected by a straw hat as she sat in the shade of the mainsail, had found plenty of time to contemplate the enormity of what she had done.

Given the chance, would she have sacrificed all that she had ever known and been and was, to save Ruaidri's life all over again?

Of course she would have.

A hundred times over. Even if he was unrelenting in his mission to bring Andrew or the formula back to the Americans. He had his duty, she supposed. And from what Andrew had told her over a shared lunch of stewed beef and hardtack, her brother had no intention of abandoning her anyhow.

At least, not until she and Ruaidri were married.

Eventually, the British prisoners in the hold would find their way back to England, carrying the news of her betrayal with them, and that weighed heavily on her.

I will never see Blackheath Castle ever again. I'll never see De Montforte House in London again. Maybe not even my brothers and my sisters-in-law. I will be in disgrace, a hunted fugitive, and my actions will cost my family as much as they will cost me. Perhaps even more.

Her gaze went to the closed door to Ruaidri's cabin.

But he *is alive and once again in command of this ship. He is alive because of those very actions of mine, and I would not take them back for all the birthplaces and comfortable memories and family pride in the world.*

The brig cut swiftly through the swells, the water rushing beneath her keel and falling away in great sheets of foam. She was a good sailor, Lieutenant Morgan told her, constantly searching the horizon with a telescope (and he had two more men aloft, also keeping watch for Hadley's frigate), and she had outrun a powerful British warship before. Though *Happenstance* did not appear on the horizon the distant sails of a man o' war's did, but the leviathan was beating to the northeast and by the time she could come about, the American brig, had the other ship even seen her, would have shown a fleet pair of heels and been long gone.

Night approached, and the shadows began to fade. Nerissa's anxious gaze went aft, toward Ruaidri's cabin. He had not emerged all day, though she'd seen young Joey going in and out a few times as well as Mr. Jeffcote, the surgeon. How she longed to go to him herself, but Andrew had already made it quite clear that he would tolerate no impropriety until they were safely married. Seeing Captain O' Devir in possible dishabille, he said, would not do.

The evening meal was served. Nerissa dined on deck with Andrew, Lieutenant Morgan, Midshipman Cranton, and the new sailing master, who regaled them with exaggerated stories of mermaids, sea monsters, and where he was convinced the lost city of Atlantis lay. His voice droned on while the sky went from purple to black, the brig's long jib-boom just visible far, far ahead against the stars. Nerissa stole another worried glance toward the stern cabin. Why had Ruaidri not come out all day? She longed to go to him, to check on him, to ensure that he had everything he needed, that he was not growing feverish or uncomfortable. Most of all, she just ached to touch him—and to be touched by him.

The stern lantern was lit, and *Tigershark* continued westward through the Channel. Morgan called for the main topgallant to be set, and the ship picked up speed through falling darkness. Someone far forward began to sing, and a few drunken voices joined the lone crooner.

It was a happy ship, once more.

"I'm going to bed," Nerissa announced, and Andrew saw her to the cabin he'd insisted on for her and bid her goodnight. She waited for his footsteps to fade. Before ten minutes had passed, she was silently making her way topside through the darkness, and easing open the door to Ruaidri's quarters.

All was quiet. A lantern swung from a hook, throwing a soft, shifting glow over the small space that drew shadows with the motion of the brig. Slowly, Nerissa turned to look toward the cot, expecting to find her captain asleep, fearful she might find him dead.

He was neither, but sitting up in bed, a book lying across his lap—and he was watching her with a knowing smile.

"I thought ye'd never come."

"You put a lot of faith in my ability to sneak around this vessel undetected. I waited until it was dark."

He put the book down and began to swing his legs off the bed, his face going suddenly gray with pain. He offered a weak smile and fell back, the smile spreading as Nerissa marched up to him, picked up his legs, and gently swung them back up into the cot.

"You're staying right there, Captain O' Devir," she said sharply, if only to take her mind off what it had just felt like to touch his long, well-muscled legs and feel their heavy weight in her hands. "Don't you even try to get up, do you hear me?"

"Got no reason to go anywhere, now that ye're here."

"How are you feeling?"

"As sick as a small hospital." He patted the space beside him, invitingly. "I'm too sore to get up. Come sit with me, Sunshine."

He must have fallen into bed exhausted, not even taking off the clothes she'd last seen him in. Now, her gaze went to his breeches, the left one hacked off above the knee and soaked with blood so dark it looked almost purple. The stocking was long-gone, the leg itself ghastly to behold. Raw bruising, swelling, and just peeping out from above the back of his knee, stitches, ugly black things that would leave a scar; he must have ripped off the bandage sometime during sleep which, judging by the look of him, had been restless and tormented. She shouldn't be thinking about how fine a leg he had, the calf well-defined and long. She shouldn't be gaping at the sparse black hairs that ran the length of that leg and wondering what they would feel like beneath her fingers. The man was hurt, in pain. She felt suddenly guilty.

He grinned knowingly. "When I'm stronger, ye'll find yourself in more trouble than ye can handle, lass."

She laughed. "Sometimes I wonder if you can read minds."

"Not minds, just faces. And yers is an open book."

He reached a hand out toward her. She moved close to the cot and took it in her own. For a long moment neither said a word, content to just be in each other's presence.

"Still angry with me?"

"Of course I am."

"We had a good talk, yer brother and I."

"I was afraid of that. But since you're both still alive, I'm assuming you emerged as something more than enemies."

"Well, ye should know that I've made my intentions clear to him."

"Intentions?"

"That I *intend* to take you as my wife."

Her heart leapt within her breast and she moved away, suddenly flustered. "Was he holding a gun to your head, loaded with his new explosive?

Ruaidri smiled. "I'm sure he would have, had I not asked for ye."

"Why *did* you ask for me?"

He pretended to look wounded. "Come now, lass. Why do you think?"

"Because you were grateful that I pretty much threw my life away in order to save yours?

His eyes grew sad, and this time, there was no pretense. "I wish ye wouldn't have done that, Nerissa. I'm not worth it, though those who serve this ship certainly are. 'Twas a rash move on yer part and there's no goin' back."

She sat down on the edge of the cot, her hips snugged comfortably against the outside of his thigh. "It was not a rash move. I thought long and hard about what I intended to do, and I did it knowing full well what the consequences would be."

"Tell me why ye did it."

"No."

"Tell me."

"No!"

"Did ye do it because ye felt sorry for me?"

"No."

"Did ye do it because ye wanted to thwart Hadley?"

"No."

"Did ye do it because ye didn't want to see young

Cranton and the rest, die in a British jail or at the end of a British rope?"

"No."

"Ye've said the word 'no' five times now, Nerissa. For yer next response, the answer had damn well better be 'yes.'"

He looked steadily over at her, the lantern throwing the shadow of his long lashes across his irises. In the gloom, he was pale and waxen beneath his mariner's tan, his face and the pillow against which he lay, a stark contrast to the darkness of his hair. He reached out and took her hand once more.

"Did ye do it because ye love me?"

Outside, the sea washed softly away as the brig cut through the long ocean swells. A warm breeze drifted through the open stern windows. Here in this small, private space, the world ceased to exist and there was only them.

She looked steadily into his waiting gaze.

"Yes."

He shut his eyes and sank back into the pillow, and she realized that despite his teasing demands he had, at least figuratively speaking, been holding his breath as he'd awaited her answer. An answer, it seemed, that was very important to him.

His thumb stroked the back of her hand. "Say it, then. Say it so there's no confusion and no doubt in either of our minds why ye did what ye did, and say it because there's nothin' on earth I'd rather hear, nothin' on earth that would make me happier than yer response to the next question I'm goin' to put to ye—and the response to that one had damn well better be *yes*, too, Nerissa."

She knew what the question would be. Her blood firing with want, with need for this man, she twisted around and, pulling her hand from his own, gently laid her fingers and palm against the bristly black shadow that had come up to cloak his jaw.

"I love you, Ruaidri O' Devir."

He just looked at her, his eyes as deep as the sea beneath them.

"I love you," she repeated, when he said nothing. "You are entirely wrong for me, not the man my brothers would have chosen for me, but you are my world and if I had to betray my country and those who serve it all over again to save your wretched Irish hide, Ruaidri O' Devir, I would. Again and again and again."

He was still gazing intently at her, his grip becoming a little more intense. "Are ye ready for my next question, Nerissa?"

Mindful of his leg and the pain he was in, she carefully, gently, eased herself down until she lay close alongside him, her head nestled against his shoulder and her eyes looking up into his.

"Ask me, then."

He moved his head slightly and let his lips rest against her forehead, where they lingered a long, tender moment before he pulled back and, with a finger beneath her jaw, gently tilted her head up to his so that she was forced to stare into his eyes.

"Will ye marry me, Lady Nerissa de Montforte?"

"Yes." Her gaze was unflinching. "Yes, I will marry you, Captain Ruaidri O' Devir."

He made a sound of gratitude and contentment and the arm against which she lay curved around her back, drawing her close up against him, dwarfing her with its size and power.

"Soon?"

"As soon as you're ready." She blushed a bit. "And able."

"France then, after we drop off our prisoners."

"And Andrew ... he has given his consent?"

"Andrew's a fine lad. Even if he'd just as soon run me

through for stealin' ye from that London townhouse, I'd still say he's a fine lad. Aye, he's consented, even encouraged our union, but has made no demands on whether it's to be in a Protestant church or one of my faith. I'm a Papist, Nerissa. That won't change."

"It doesn't need to change. We both pray to the same God. And that same God will bless and recognize our union no matter what church we take our vows in."

"Kiss me, Nerissa."

She inched up closer to him, leaned over his chest, and boldly cupping his face in her hands, enjoying the feel of his cheekbones and the roughness of his jaw, she lowered her mouth to his.

Injury and loss of blood might have rendered him weak but the strength of his kiss, the urgency with which his tongue came out to plunder her mouth, and the feel of his hand sliding beneath the lapels of Midshipman Cranton's coat to gently knead her nipple were enough to set her blood on fire.

Unexpectedly, he drew back. "I'd take ye now, if I could." His lips brushed her forehead, and she felt the weight of his cheek against the top of her head as he rested it there. "But I made a promise to yer brother that I'd respect and honor ye, and I'm a man who always keeps his word."

"Andrew would never know." She took a deep, steadying breath. "I can't wait until we find a priest, Ruaidri."

"I can't either. But we'll have to."

"Why?"

He dropped his fingers from her breast, smoothed her jacket and claimed her hand once more, his eyes resolute. "There's nothin' I'd like more than to make love to ye right now, Lady Nerissa de Montforte, even though it would likely kill me. But yer to be my wife and ye deserve my love and respect. I will wait." He touched her cheek and smiled. "And so, *mo grá*, will you."

She sighed and gently settled back against his chest. He curled an arm around her to hold her close. She watched the lantern swinging back and forth, back and forth, hypnotic in its timeless motion. Her eyes grew heavy and with the sound of her captain's heart beating steadily beneath her ear, she finally fell asleep.

Chapter Twenty-Five

They were married the following day.

Early that morning, *Tigershark* discharged her prisoners at the privateer-friendly French port of Saint-Malo and sent a boat ashore containing Lieutenant Morgan and Midshipman Cranton, both looking very official in their dress uniforms. They returned with a priest named Coutanche, a nervous little man who spoke rapid French and went wide-eyed when he learned the bride was none other than Lady Nerissa de Montforte, sister of the English Duke of Blackheath.

He was chattering like a squirrel as he was hoisted aboard the ship, growing more and more panicky by the moment. "Oh, I don't know if I can perform such a wedding, this duke will not be happy, oh, *non*, I cannot—"

"*I* am representing my family in my brother's absence," said the well-dressed auburn-haired fellow who came forward to greet him. "The bride is my sister, and you will perform this marriage or you will answer to *me*."

"And-and-and ... you sir, are?"

"I am Lord Andrew de Montforte." His expression firm, he turned and headed aft. "Come with me. The groom is in his cabin."

As they walked aft, the young nobleman discreetly pressed a piece of folded paper into Coutanche's hand indicating that he should immediately pocket and post it. The priest did so, overwhelmed by the presence of nobility even if they were English. Wondering what he was being drawn into, Coutanche was shocked and not a little horrified to be brought into the captain's cabin and there, introduced to a gaunt, pale fellow in the uniform of the Continental Navy who proved himself to be Irish the moment he opened his mouth.

"Pleased to make yer acquaintance," the captain said with a briskness that belied his sunken, exhausted eyes. He was in a blue and white uniform with gold epaulets, his waistcoat and breeches as white as sea foam, but he made no move to get out of the cot in which he lay. "We're ready to begin."

As for the lady, she was shockingly garbed in the uniform of an American midshipman and appeared to be quite comfortable in it.

Coutanche stood there staring, his mouth opening and closing soundlessly. He hoped this English duke wouldn't find his way to France and make him suffer for this sacrament he was being asked to perform. An aristocratic lady, marrying a John Paul Jones? And one who looked to have a foot in death's door, at that?

"Well, get on with it," Captain O' Devir said impatiently. He swung from the cot and stood, the threat of his height and powerful build tempered, somewhat, by the fact that he swayed on his feet and gripped the back of a chair with a shaking hand. "The day's wastin' and we have places to be."

The priest withdrew a well-worn Bible from a leather satchel and there, in the small cabin of an American warship and witnessed by Lord Andrew de Montforte and Lieutenant John Morgan, he nervously performed the sacred rite that would bind these two together forever. As he left, he wondered if the Irish captain of this trim vessel would survive the rest of the day, let alone his marriage night. He'd seen butcher shop carcasses with more color and life in them than the pale, waxen-skinned master of the American brig.

Not my business, he thought. *Not my concern.*

The whole affair took less than an hour. Coutanche was rowed back to shore, *Tigershark* quickly weighed anchor, and filling her sails with a stiff wind out of the northeast howling down-Channel, the American brig stood northwest and turned her prow toward home.

It was only then that Coutanche remembered the folded note that Lord Andrew had silently passed him.

❧

Lady Nerissa de Montforte might have been garbed in Cranton's best rig, but Ruaidri had done all he could to give her the best wedding day he could. His bride's gown had been hopelessly ruined and the petticoats and jacket he'd asked the sailmaker to make were not yet finished, but even so, she deserved all he could give her. As they'd sailed south toward Saint-Malo, he'd ordered his own copper tub brought up from below so she could savor a bit of pampering on her special day. No hot, scented bath had the Lady Nerissa enjoyed. No perfumed rosewater or finely-milled soap, no soft towels or any touch of the luxury to which she was accustomed. No, her bath had been seawater warmed by the galley fire and a rough bar of soap, and her towel had been rougher still.

And she had not complained.

And now they were finally on their way, the wide open Atlantic opening up before them as Brest and the coastline of France fell away off their starboard quarter.

Ruaidri, who'd also enjoyed a well-needed bath, lay

now in his cot, cursing the weakness of his body and thanking the One who walked on water once for sparing him what he'd thought would be an inevitable fever.

He had much on his mind.

"Go to England and bring me back that explosive," John Adams had said. *"Your country is dependent on you. Godspeed."*

Yes, he'd crossed an ocean to bring an explosive rumored to be more fantastic than anything anyone had ever invented, back to America. He had risked his life and lost his heart. He'd carried out his mission, but he'd never dreamed that his bounty would include not just the explosive, but a wife.

A wife he had yet to tell his deepest secret and darkest shame to.

A wife who knew nothing about Josiah.

Or Delight.

Maybe there was no need to tell her. It was all in his past, anyhow. His past as Roddy, not Ruaidri. He would leave it there.

No harm done.

He got up, limped to the stern windows, and scanned the horizon. No Hadley, no sails, nobody in pursuit. Just sunlight on clear blue swells, the ship's wake trailing back toward a Europe he was desperate to see the arse end of.

The effort of just moving this far exhausted him, and he cursed what little blood still remained in his veins. His head swimming, he took off his uniform jacket and lay back down on the cot. His gaze fell on the ship model he'd made as they'd crossed the Atlantic to get here. Maybe it was time to start another, perhaps of *Tigershark* herself. But no. Even the idea of carving a model hull made him feel tired. How long would it take for him to get his energy back?

The door to the cabin opened and Nerissa came in,

her cheeks pink and fresh from the stiff wind that drove them steadily westward. She paused, looking at him lying there in the cot.

They were alone, the two of them, for the first time as man and wife.

"You should sleep, Ruaidri," she murmured, her eyes darkening with concern.

"I'm tired of sleeping."

"You want to heal, don't you?"

"I'm fine."

She raised a brow and turned, going to check her reflection in the tiny mirror above his washstand. His gaze traveled down her proud shoulders and back, her tiny waist, her rounded bottom in Cranton's breeches. He didn't care what she was wearing. She looked delicious, and he felt himself beginning to harden as he watched her try to comb her pale, windblown hair into some sort of semblance, tidying herself for her man as women had done since time began. He wondered if she was nervous. If the idea of consummating their marriage filled her with as much unease as it did him. Would his body be able to perform the task to which it would soon be called? He grinned wryly. *The head and heart are willing*, he thought ... *but oh, do I have the strength to pleasure her as she deserves?*

Time would tell.

Or he'd die trying.

There was a knock on the door. Andrew came in, frowning as he saw Ruaidri lying weakly in his cot. "You look like hell," he said flatly.

"I'm fine."

Nerissa turned from the mirror. "Andrew, don't you have some place to be? Something else to do?"

He actually had the good grace to blush. "I suppose you'd like some ... privacy."

"I suppose we might," she said, a touch of impatience in her voice. "You have protected me long enough, dear brother. But you have given me to Ruaidri here and that is now his task, not yours."

"At the moment, he's not fit to protect a fly from a spider, let alone—"

"I'm fine," Ruaidri insisted, yet again.

Nerissa sighed and crossed her arms. "And just what do I need protecting from, Andrew?"

Andrew's color deepened. "Right. I understand. I'll ... leave you two to it, then." He moved to the door and there, paused to look one last time at Ruaidri. "Remember my warning, O' Devir. Be gentle with her."

Ruaidri raised a brow. He supposed he ought to take offense at such a remark and a few short years ago when he'd been younger, his temper hotter and his moods more volatile, perhaps he would have. But Andrew was her brother, a family member who loved her very much, and having been in a similar situation with his own sister not so very long ago, Ruaidri knew just how hard it was to turn and walk away, leaving your little sister in the care of a man who was anything but a brother and who had every intention of making her a woman.

Yes, he understood.

He smiled. "Ye have my word on it, Andrew," he said reassuringly.

With a last warning glance at *Tigershark*'s captain, Lord Andrew left the cabin.

And Nerissa and Ruaidri were alone.

❧

"Well," she said, not quite so confident now that her brother had gone. "I suppose I should ask, 'now what,' but I think I know what comes next." Her voice wasn't quite as strong as it had been moments ago. "You ... you *will* be gentle, won't you, Ruaidri?"

He sat up, wishing he had the strength to go to her, to lift her in his once-strong arms and carry her to the cot, to the stern cushions, even down to the deck flooring. But the effort of standing for his nuptials for even a few moments had taxed his strength and even sitting up was exhausting. "Are ye frightened, lass?"

She shrugged and looked away. "A little."

"Come sit beside me, Nerissa."

She licked her suddenly-dry lips and moved hesitantly across the cabin, eyed the empty space beside him and at his urging sat down, as stiff as a canary frozen on its perch.

"'Tis a confession I have for ye, lass," he said, aching to reach out and touch her but forcing himself to keep his hands to himself for the time being.

"A ... confession?"

"Aye." He leaned back against the curved hull and looked at her. "We haven't known each other for long, but in that short time, have ye ever known me to be frightened of anythin', Nerissa?"

"No...."

"Have ye ever known me to be worried about anythin'?"

She gave a little smile. "No."

"Have ye ever known me to be insecure, uncertain, or lackin' faith in meself?"

"Never."

"Well, here's my secret, then." He smiled, looking a bit sheepish. "I don't know if I can do this... and that makes me all of the above, especially frightened."

"Do ... what?"

"Come now, lass. What do ye think?"

She turned a bright, blushing pink, the color suffusing her cheeks and making him want to kiss her maidenly shyness away.

"I wasn't aware that the ... the, um, marriage act required any particular acts of strength."

"It is what one makes it. But alas, since I've lost so much blood, I'm weak and faint, easily fatigued ... no good to you as a husband today, tonight, maybe not for the next few nights."

There. A slight crease between her brows, a frown. "Do you mean that we ... we won't be doing ... doing *that*, today?"

"I don't know if I can." He sighed, looked up at her through his lashes, and let them droop. He was glad she could not see the smile he wore on his heart. Maybe she'd take up the challenge. Maybe she would not. He hoped she would. "But ye're welcome to try, lass."

"Would it be dangerous for you?"

"Don't know. We could try it and see, I suppose."

He heard her swallow, hard. A long silence ensued, before she finally asked in a little voice, "What do *you* want?"

"To make ye happy."

She moved a little closer to him. He opened his eyes and smiled as she took his hand, her fingers warm and gentle around his own. Let her think he was that debilitated. Perhaps he was. But by letting her explore him and take the lead in this act, to plumb the limits of what he was capable of, it would give her confidence, alleviate her fear and awkwardness ... and if he were honest with himself, allow him the chance to save his own pride for not being more assertive in bed on his own wedding day. The devil knew he wanted to be. *God* knew he didn't have the strength.

Above, Morgan's command to set the t'gallants drifted down and he felt *Tigershark* lengthening her stride like a racehorse being let out to the buckle. His eyes drifted shut once more, defying his will to keep them open. Beneath him, he could feel the long swells driving in from the open Atlantic, could feel the ship's eagerness to get home. All was right in his world, whether or not they consummated their marriage this afternoon. All was—

His eyes opened as he felt a slight, uncertain touch at the corner of his mouth and he found himself gazing up into her steady blue ones.

"Having four brothers, I know a little about masculine pride," she said softly. "Though very little about the marriage act, save for what I've gleaned from my sisters-in-law. But if you find yourself so weak, Ruaidri ... maybe I can do the work."

"Work?"

"Well—" she blushed once more "whatever it is that we're supposed to do to consummate our marriage."

"We don't *have* to do anything," he said cajolingly, secretly hoping the part of her that was a rebel would take such a challenge and run with it. "If you don't want to."

"What would *you* like?"

He looked up at her, his smile spreading. "I would like you to lean down," he murmured softly, "and get right up close to me ... yes, like that ... and put your lips against the corner of my mouth that you just touched ... and kiss me."

She moved a little closer to him and shyly, obligingly, did as he asked, her very nearness forcing away the air that lay between them until their bodies were nearly touching. He wanted to drown in the sight of her. Her beautiful, eager face. Her guileless, pale blue eyes with the slightly down-turned corners. Her high cheekbones and full, smiling mouth, the lips so pink and pretty.

"Kiss me, Nerissa," he said, lifting a hand to touch her arm, to run his fingers down the inside of her wrist, to draw little circles there with his fingers until a faint wash of color spread itself across her cheekbones at the teasing sensations it evoked.

Nerissa lowered her head, and slowly put her lips against the corner of his mouth.

For her, it was a mystery solved, a heady answer to tender exploration and quiet yearning. She nuzzled his skin, found it slightly rough despite the fact that his servant had come in to shave him earlier. He still tasted of the wine they'd shared after the binding words had been spoken and everyone had drunk a toast to the new Captain and Mrs. O' Devir. She could smell his shaving soap and clean hair and skin, freshly washed in the same copper tub that she had used earlier. She could feel the warmth of his big, broad hand still gripping her wrist. The scent of him—all tough male, sensuality and desire despite his words protesting he didn't have the strength—caused a little flutter of sensation deep between her legs. More sensation in her nipples and in the pit of her belly. Emboldened, she pressed her lips to his and guided by instinct, let her tongue slip out to lightly touch the corner of his mouth, to taste it, to trace the shape and texture of his lip until he made a noise of satisfaction deep in his throat.

"Ah, love," he murmured, and releasing her wrist, reached both hands up to thread his fingers through her hair, loosening the pins that held up the heavy tresses, grazing the side of her neck with a warm, raspy thumb, and finally, cupping the back of her head to hold her gently down against him.

She angled her head, adjusting her position so that she was kissing him fully now, his lips hard against hers, his tongue coming out to find her own, to push against it, to taste her as she was tasting him. She heard a moan come from her own throat, felt the pressure against the back of her head holding her in place and urging her on. She lowered herself further, her nipples just grazing his chest. Though there was plenty of fabric between them, the sensation was like lightning striking her there, and she heard her breathing becoming heavier as his fingers drifted through her hair, pulling it down and around her shoulders, following it out to its ends until the back of his wrist just grazed her nipples through the fabric.

"Do you want me, Nerissa?"

"I want you, Ruaidri."

"Tonight, you will take the lead, and yer body will tell ye what to do. Tonight, you will do with me what ye will, explore me at your own speed and comfort level, and if I survive it—" here, he smiled up at her in a slightly cajoling way—"I promise you that the next time ye'll have more man than you can handle, Sunshine."

"What if that 'next time' is later on this evening?"

"Minx," he murmured, still pulling gently on her hair.

"Tell me what to do, Ruaidri. I think I know ... but I don't want to hurt you."

"Ye won't hurt me. Just ... don't expect much from me."

"Is that a challenge to yourself, or to me?"

"Both, I think. Unbutton my waistcoat, lass. Don't be shy."

She kicked off her shoes, drew her legs up, and sidled closer to him, her hair hanging down around her face and just brushing the buttons of the garment he'd asked her to loosen. He was not fragile, she told herself. Weak from loss of blood, bruised, battered and most fortunate to be alive ... but definitely not fragile.

Her fingers fumbled as she found the top button of his clean white waistcoat, pushed it through the hole, then moved down to the next one ... the next ... and the next. Her knuckles brushed the fine linen shirt just beneath, her gaze lingered at the skin at his throat, tanned and masculine and showing a few wiry strands of black hair. Unconsciously, she licked her lip, wondering how warm that bit of skin would be against her mouth. What it would smell like. What it would taste like. Another button, now, and she could feel the hard strength of his breastbone against her fingertips, the heart beating strongly just beneath.

Images of him lying on the deck in a pool of blood suddenly assailed her. Hadley's triumph. Andrew's empathy. She, running to the rail to vomit, shattered by the horror of what she had seen. He had come so close to dying. Indeed, she had thought him dead. Everyone had. But no, that heart was still beating and for a moment, she opened her hand, flattened her palm against his breastbone, and just absorbed its beat up through her skin, her hand, her wrist, letting its energy go all the way to her own heart.

She didn't realize her eyes were leaking tears until his voice brought her back to the present.

"Nerissa."

Startled, her gaze flashed to his, found him quietly watching her.

"Nerissa," he repeated, looking up to her. "Why do ye cry? We don't have to do this if ye aren't ready ... I'd never force ye, y'know."

The tears ran harder and again she saw the blood beneath his leg, mixed with seawater and rolling back and forth with the motion of the ship, and she could not speak.

"I'm sorry I'm not the man ye might've chosen ... sorry I'm just a sailor, sorry ye didn't have the grand weddin' ye deserved—"

"I'm crying," she choked out, "because I keep thinking of you lying in your own blood, and how I'd thought this heart I feel beneath my hand had stopped ... and that you were dead."

His gaze softened. "Don't think about it," he said, reaching up to thumb away her tears. "I'm very much alive. Weak as a kitten, I'm afraid, but 'twill take far more than an English musketball to do me in."

She gave a jerky little nod without speaking, and his hand drifted down to anchor hers against his breastbone. Against his heart. For a long moment they just stayed like that, she trying to get her sobs under control, he quietly covering her hand with his own.

"The best way to forget things we wish we'd never seen is to make new memories," he said quietly. "We have our weddin' night—or rather, afternoon—and the rest of our lives to make those memories." He gazed up into her eyes, willing her to hear what he was saying, to forget the dreadful things that she had seen. "Now, love, since ye're so concerned about my heart, lean down and kiss me again but keep your hand there, and feel it beat harder, feel it beat stronger ... feel it beat just for you and you alone."

She leaned over him, found his lips with her own and, with her hair falling down around their faces like a canopy of ivory silk, kissed him. The weight of her body pressed her hand down further against his chest and as she lost herself in the kiss, as his tongue plunged into the honeyed recesses of her mouth, she did indeed feel his heartbeat begin to thud, thud, thud against her palm.

She broke the kiss, breathing hard.

"Finish undoin' me, Nerissa," he said softly. "Ye've got a lot more buttons to go before you get me out of this waistcoat."

She nodded, her fingers fumbling, undoing the button just beneath his heart, the one at the apex of his ribs, the ones that trailed down his belly, the ones that were close, very close, to the waistband of his breeches. She paused, staring at her fingers. The front of his breeches. The white fabric was curved and hard, bulging with the part of himself that made him a man—and that would soon make her a woman. What did it look like? Feel like? What would his response be if she were to touch it?

There. The last button of his waistcoat was undone. He sat up in the bed and she helped him out of it, allowing him to lean into her own strength as she eased him back to the cot. There wasn't an ounce of fat on him, but lord, he was heavy. Solid. Full of muscle. He looked up at her and smiled, his eyes going foggy for a moment.

"This is madness," she said, worried.

"'Twill be fun."

"You just lost what little color you had left."

"I'll get it back. I'm lyin' down again, aren't I?"

Indeed he was, his hair black against the pillow, the wild, spiral-curling mane spread out beneath him and giving him the look of some Celtic savage.

"Are you sure this won't kill you?"

"If it does, mine will be the most envied death in the history of Mankind. Now take off yer clothes, Nerissa. Slowly. I want to watch yer fingers push the buttons through their holes and think about them touchin' me."

She obliged him, trembling in anticipation as she shed the midshipman's jacket. The waistcoat beneath. She pulled the long, loose shirt free of the breeches into which she'd tucked it and sat beside him, shyly biting her lip.

"If I had the strength," he said, his gaze roving appreciatively over her form and lingering on her breasts through the light linen shirt, "I would not be asking ye to do yer own undressin', lass. But I'm enjoyin' watchin' ye, I am, all the same."

He looked down at himself for emphasis. Nerissa followed his gaze and tried not to stare. She had thought him full and bulging before. Now....

She swallowed hard, her skin suddenly prickling with heat.

"And if I had the strength, I'd shed me own clothes as well," he added. "But today, that task is yers."

She nodded. "So I should take your shirt off next, I imagine?"

"If ye like, lass." His smile deepened, and a twinkle came into his eye. "Or, ye could leave my shirt on and unfasten my breeches."

She darkened with color. She wanted to lie with him, skin to skin, beating heart against beating heart, and she wanted nothing to stand in the way of that—not fine lawn shirts, not breeches, not anything.

"Can you sit up?" she asked, hating to make him move, dreading that same unfocused look he'd got when he'd sat up a few moments past.

"I can," he said, and she curved her arm around his back, supporting him. She pulled his shirt from the waistband of his breeches and he bent forward so she could pull the garment over his head. He straightened up and for a moment he sat there smiling at her, letting her look her fill of the splendid, inverted triangle of his powerfully-muscled shoulders and chest, the smattering of wiry black hair across his pectorals, his hard, defined abdomen. The little black hairs seemed to gather near his navel, tapering to an arrow that led to the waistband of his breeches and disappeared.

Nerissa's fingers went to her mouth and above them, her gaze met his. A Greek statue could not have come closer to perfection than Ruaidri O' Devir did. The back of her throat went dry even as the ache between her legs intensified, and she felt liquid heat down there, reminding her of her own body's response to this man that she had married.

My husband, she thought, in a bit of awe.

Mine.

The unfocused look was back in his eyes once more.

"Are you well, Ruaidri?"

"Faint in me head," he said as casually as he might note the weather, and settled back once more. He smiled up at her, the bulging muscles of his shoulders and upper arms clearly defined against the pillow. "But I'm fine, lass. Ye can't hurt me."

She moved up closer to him, arms on either side of his as she twisted to straddle him, and lowered her head. Her lips grazed the bridge of his nose, the smooth expanse of his forehead, the dark eyebrows, the purple bruising beneath the hair at his temple where he must have hit when he fell. She closed her eyes, nuzzling his hair and wishing she could kiss away every bit of pain and suffering that awful day had brought him.

It was a moment before she realized that he was touching her, his fingers brushing her neck, drifting down the base of her throat and to her breasts, hanging loose beneath the shirt. She paused, her lips still in his hair, enjoying the sensation of his touch. How warm were his hands as he plumped the weight of her breast against his palm. How delicious was his thumb, the edge of his nail, as he traced the perimeter of her areole. She shivered with want and longing and gave a little sigh against the damp skin of his temple.

"Oh," she breathed, biting her lip.

"Ye're beautiful, lass," he said, his breath whispering against the side of her neck, and gently pinched her nipple. "Ye're beautiful, and I'm the luckiest man on earth right now."

The gentle pinch became a persistent, relentless roll between thumb and forefinger, back and forth, back and forth, until the nipple grew hard and engorged and a fine layer of perspiration broke out along her forehead. She ached to reclaim his lips, but to do so might dislodge his hand, oh, his wonderful, delicious, warm and masterful hand, and she dared not move. Her breathing grew ragged. Her skin grew hot. Her arms began to tremble as she balanced there above him, her weight on her hands on either side of his torso, her hair hanging down over one shoulder to brush and puddle on his chest. Little gasps of delight rose in the back of her throat, becoming a sigh as his hand drifted to her other breast.

"Ruaidri," she murmured, trying not to squirm. "Ohhhh...."

"Take yer shirt off, *mo grá*. I want to see you."

She pulled back and did so, tossing the garment aside. She saw his gaze drop to her breasts, saw his eyes darkening with desire. He twisted his hips, perhaps to ease the swelling beneath the drop front of his breeches as he gazed at the high, pert globes and the blushing pink nipples that seemed to harden all the more beneath his appreciative stare.

"Ye haven't killed me yet, lass," he said hoarsely, "but I've definitely died and gone to heaven."

She lay back down beside him, facing him, their breaths warm and mingling. She could feel the heat radiating from his body, warming her like a blanket and making her want to burrow into its very source.

He reached out, his fingers atop her shoulder, and gently traced her curves—the firm muscles of her upper arm, the hollow of her elbow, the deep indentation of her flat, tiny waist, the feminine rise of her hip and the downward sweep toward her knees. He was smiling softly as he drew her with his hand, warming her flesh and setting it on fire, and she finally couldn't take the sweet torture anymore. Boldly, Nerissa reached out and, finding the button of his drop front breeches, undid it.

He sprang out into her hand, a thick, solid ridge of hard male flesh, warmer than she expected, larger than she could have imagined, but as unyielding and hard as a steel hammer beneath the warm, humid skin. She looked down at him, fascinated. Here was the armament of a man, a warrior, one who made no secret of the fact that he wanted her and wanted her badly.

"May I ... touch it?" she asked, looking up into his eyes.

"Have at it, lass."

She raised herself up on an elbow, gently pushed him down on his back, and with both hands, gripped the sides of his waistband and began to pull the breeches over his hipbones. She froze, remembering his wound, seeing the black thread that marked the stitches, but he only smiled. "Stop yer worryin', Nerissa. I won't break."

Gently, she eased them off. She undid and stepped out of her own. Moments later they lay side by side and naked, he splendid in his masculine perfection, his legs as long, hard-muscled and perfectly formed as the rest of him. His arousal sprang thick and hard from its bed of black hair, his testicles heavy against the sheet of the cot.

"Oh," she said softly, as she sat there looking. And then she reached out and hesitantly touched him with light, questing fingers.

He groaned, and let his head fall back on the pillow.

She squeezed closer to him. How velvety-soft was the male skin over its own iron-hardness. How lively it was beneath her fingers as she gently tested its rigidity, traced its shape, fingered and stroked the giant ridge of male flesh with increasingly confident fingers. He filled her hand. He was warm and thick and hard. She squeezed him, encouraged by his soft words of love for her, and let her thumb move over the blunt, triangular head. Once, twice, and a third time, this last causing a creamy seed of moisture to ooze from its slit. She looked at it for a long moment and then at her husband, lying there so rigidly still, his hand clenching and unclenching the sheet on which he lay and his eyes all but rolled back in his head.

"Are you in pain, Ruaidri?"

"No, lass."

"Why do you look as though you are?"

"Because I'm holdin' back ... tryin' to conserve me strength so that what I have, is yours." He opened his eyes then and in them was a crystalline desperation, something feral and untamed, and she shivered in recognition of it. "I'm weak, Nerissa. But I'll be stronger tomorrow, and stronger the day after that, and stronger, still, as each day falls behind the next."

She touched her thumb to that pearly drop, smearing it across the slit and around the head and causing him to leap in her hand. "What are you saying?"

"That if I were myself, I'd rise up and throw you down to the bed and take you as an eager, driven-mad husband should take his wife, that is, with no quarter and no holdin' back. I can't, though. I'm faint, I'm dizzy, I'm weak. But not so weak as I can't do other things to pleasure ye. Turn around, lass, turn so that ye're facin' the other way, and put yer belly here, so that I might kiss it."

"You want to kiss my belly?"

"I want to kiss yer belly, and yer c—" he paused, re-thinking words that he'd been about to say—"lady parts," he said. "Help me, Nerissa. I'm hungry for ye."

Somewhat shocked, she drew her feet up, pivoted, and lay back down again until her knees were against his forehead, her own mouth shockingly near his arousal, which, if at all possible, looked even bigger than it had a few minutes ago; it had taken on a veiny, purplish cast, and with increasing boldness, she reached out and resumed exploring it with her fingers.

"Easy there, lass," he said roughly. "Not yet."

"Not yet?"

"No. First, this."

"This" turned out to be the blade of his hand sliding between her knees, parting them, the rough pads of his fingers skating over the soft, downy flesh of her inner thighs until she squirmed and sighed and moaned with the sheer pleasure of the sensation. Between her legs she felt moisture, a desperate craving for his touch, for fulfillment, as he moved toward the warm, liquid center of her.

"Oh, Ruaidri," she breathed, as his fingers slipped

between her slick petals and his thumb dragged up and down, over and through her most inner flesh and the damp curls that framed it. Sensation began to gather deep inside her, searing her with its intensity, building in force, and she heard little noises of anguish coming from her own throat. She tried to contain them, biting savagely down on her lower lip, shuddering with each delicious stroke of his fingers. The pleasure-pain built. Her heart hammered wildly in her chest. Desperately, she reached for his organ, thick and swollen and so close to her lips, but he grunted a refusal and caught her hand with a muffled "not yet." Not yet? And then her thoughts sizzled away as he threw a strong, heavy arm over the rise of her hips and dragged her closer to him, now tipping her onto her back, his heavy black mane dragging over her pelvis as he sought her, now, with a hungry, desperate mouth.

Instinctively, she tried to clamp her legs together, but his hand was there anticipating it. Gently, insistently, he pushed her thighs apart, wider and wider still, until cool air was sweeping against her hot, moist folds and making her tremble and shudder and flush. A moment later, it wasn't cool air against her; it was his mouth, fully open and hungry for her, his lips sealing her, his tongue working against her folds and the hard, swollen bud of her center, rasping back and forth, circling it, suckling it, until Nerissa, unable to hold back any longer, bucked upward on a helpless cry of abandon. He caught her scream with his fingers, never complaining as she bit down, sobbing, on them, only licking and stroking her with his tongue until her spasms peaked yet again and she convulsed all around him.

He drew back, slowly. She lay flushed and gasping beside him, her hair damp against her cheekbones.

"You ... you said you didn't think you could do this," she managed. "Oh, my God...."

"I haven't done it." He licked his lips, pointedly savoring the taste of her as he gazed into her eyes. "'Tis why I told ye to slow down, lass."

She sat up, shoving her damp hair off her brow. "I want you to feel like you've made me feel, Ruaidri." She reached out then and stroked him, knowing, instinctively, what he needed. But this time there was no reason to hold back, to save her virginity, to take steps to prevent a baby. This time he was her husband and she wanted to know him to the full extent of the word. "Will you let me?"

"Aye, lass. Ye're ready now. Good and ready. Don't hold back."

He smiled and lay back down, his male organ rising up out of its bed of black hair, swollen and ready for her.

As she was for him.

Still tingling with sensation, Nerissa gently straddled him. She let her knees take her weight and, guided by his hands which had come up to frame and hold her hips, gingerly eased herself down against his shaft. She felt it, thick and hard, pressing there against her slick inner lips, waiting for entry, waiting to push through her maidenhood and make her a wife. She felt it and wanted it, and shifting her weight, reached down to take it in her fingers ... to rub its head within her soaking-wet folds until her husband tipped his chin back and gritted his teeth and made a half-primal sound of agony. Her heart was pounding in anticipation.

Ruaidri had opened his eyes and was watching her, his expression one of anguished intensity. "Do it slowly, lass," he murmured. "'Tis your first time ... ye're tight and firm ... 'twill hurt."

"I don't care." She leaned down and placing her hands on either side of his head, her thumbs caressing his cheekbones, looked him in the eye. "I don't care, because I love you, Ruaidri O' Devir, and none of us are leaving here until you make me a proper woman."

She raised herself up on her spread knees, placed the swollen, blunted head against her entrance, and biting her lip, began to ease herself down.

"Relax," he said softly. "Let yer legs go wide and it won't hurt so much."

She did, the raw contact of his genitals against hers causing sensation to build within her all over again. She held him steady, his rigid tumescence sliding slowly, into her ... deeper into her ... oh, it felt alien and yet perfectly natural and there, oh there, was resistance even as she feared her body could never accommodate the sheer width and size of him.

"No turnin' back," he said, gazing up at her.

"None wanted, Captain O' Devir."

He gripped her outer thighs, and with a hard groan, drove himself up and deeply inside of her.

She cried out, the pain catching her by surprise. He looked up at her, watching her carefully, allowing her to get used to the sensation of his being inside of her, deeply inside of her. For Nerissa, it felt as though he could not rend her asunder any more than he already had, and she felt warm liquid running from her, running onto him, and knew that it was her own maiden's blood. He let go of her hips and reached out to take her hands, threading his fingers through her own and gazing steadily, intently, up at her as she sat speared and shaking on his arousal.

"Are ye ready, Nerissa?"

"I'm ready," she said in a little voice.

"'Twill get better again, I promise. Better than it's ever been."

"You promise?"

"I promise."

"And you, Ruaidri? How do you feel?"

"Faint. But I'll be damned if that stops me," he said with a grin, and then, still holding her hands, their fingers interlocked, he began thrusting his pelvis up, trying to get her to join him in the rhythm.

"Ohhhhhh," she said on a deep and anguished shudder. She closed her eyes, and the deep, searing penetration suddenly moved from pain to pleasure, the slippery friction of it going deeper, withdrawing, deeper, withdrawing, beginning to build a climax within her once more.

It didn't take her long to find the same rhythm. Her breathing quickened, her blood ignited as she rode him deeper and deeper toward his own release. Her head fell back, her hair swinging with every thrust, her fingers locked with his as the joyous agony rose within her yet again, rising, rising, now peaking as her senses exploded and the spasms convulsed her once more.

And still he thrust, once more, twice, until at last, with a guttural cry, his body went stiff beneath her and she felt the warmth of his seed pulsing into her womb. She leaned down and wrapped her arms around him, holding him as he came, anchoring herself as her own convulsions shook her to the core.

It was a moment before she could breathe again.

"Ruaidri," she said, and realized that he'd gone still, his hand lax within her own.

She pushed back and off of him.

"Ruaidri?" He lay motionless beneath her, his eyes rolled back in his head.

"*Ruaidri!*" she cried, feeling him still locked inside her, shrinking now, sliding out. She grabbed one limp, heavy wrist, chafing it with panicked desperation. "Ruaidri, oh my God!"

Oh dear God she'd killed him! Killed him!

She tried to get up, felt him slide out of her on a rush of moisture, and finally gained her feet, rushing madly to find clothes and run for help. She had just managed to get one leg into her breeches when there was a movement from the cot and her husband turned his head to look at her, an amused little smile tugging at one corner of his mouth.

"Well, that was a first," he murmured, his grin spreading. "But I quite enjoyed it. Took things to whole new heights, it did. Jay-zus. What are ye doin' half-into yer breeches and lookin' like the world's just come to an end, Nerissa?"

"*What?*" she howled, frozen.

"I said, what the divil are ye doin', lass?"

"I was going to get help!"

"For what?"

"For you!"

He roared with laughter. "I passed out. Felt good. Incredible, in fact. Never happened to me before ... must be the loss of blood."

"I thought I'd killed you!" she nearly screamed, sobbing with relief. "And you're lying there laughing about it!"

"Best release I've ever had," he said with a happy sigh. And then, noting her outrage and relief, he moved over on the cot and reached for her. "Get out of those damned breeches, Nerissa, and come join me."

"Come join you? You just scared the living daylights out of me."

"We'll do it again soon," he said. "And maybe you'll get used to it. In the meantime, I'm knackered. And freezing-cold. Care to warm a body up, Sunshine?"

He grinned over at her. When he looked at her like that, it was impossible to stay angry with him. Besides, she thought grudgingly, it wasn't his fault that he'd passed out. He'd lost a lot of blood. What was left had gone to his male organ instead of his brain, and had done him in.

She glared at him, but her anger was short-lived. She stepped out of the breeches and returned to the cot. He reached out to snag her around the waist. She climbed up beside him and nestled her back against his chest, his abdomen, his thighs. He molded himself to her, enclosing her protectively with his own body, and it felt good. Blissfully, blessedly, *good*.

She sighed with contentment. He wrapped a possessive arm over her upper body and pulled her up even closer, his chin buried in her hair, his breath warming the back of her head. Eventually that arm grew lax, and before his warm, heavy weight was sagging into hers, she, too, was asleep.

Chapter Twenty-Six

Several days later ....

Hadley had gone back and scoured the area where he'd put McPhee in command of *Tigershark*. He had studied the currents, sailed with them in search of flotsam and debris, circled the area once, twice, three times, and finally admitting defeat, had made sail for London. Surely, McPhee was waiting for him there. Now, he watched the banks of the Thames become more and more clogged with buildings, wharfs, and vessels unloading their wares, the refuse and dirt of the great city reaching out to encompass everything it touched. He was the picture of calm as he stood on his quarterdeck, barking orders to proceed under topsails and jib alone as he waited for a pilot to come meet him, but to his eye was a spyglass and only he could feel his heart pounding as he anxiously scanned the sea of vessels that clogged the Pool of London.

The American prize brig, *Tigershark*, was not amongst them.

Dewhurst tried to offer a bit of hope. "Maybe they got delayed by the storm," he murmured, though a sideways glance at his face showed his own doubt and silenced him immediately.

"They're not here. Damn it to hell, *they're not here*."

His lieutenant kicked at an imaginary deck seam. "Might've lost some rigging and got delayed," he offered.

"Might've gone down," Hadley snapped.

"Might've been retaken by the French. After all, that frigate was right there in the area."

"Does it matter? That brig's not here. She's missing, and with her, Lady Nerissa and Lord Andrew de Montforte." His eyes bleak, he slapped the glass shut with the palm of his hand. This could mean the end of his career. There would be an inquiry, of course—he had lost an American prize that would have brought a tidy amount at auction and he had made a bad decision, a very bad decision, in allowing Lady Nerissa—at her own insistence—to stay aboard the prize brig. And why? Because he was trying to win her favor? Her heart? How was he going to explain *that* to his superiors back at the Admiralty?

And God help him, *how was he going to explain it to the Duke of Blackheath?*

His insides twisted and turned and he felt a sudden urge to defecate.

"See to our anchoring, Mr. Dewhurst, he muttered, and putting the glass back in its rack, stalked off.

❧

Hadley had good reason to be nervous. At the very moment his bowels were emptying at the thought of facing the Duke of Blackheath and telling him of his siblings' absence and possible—if not likely—loss, Lucien de Montforte himself was arriving at the Admiralty.

Footmen leaped down to steady the fretting horses,

to open the door of his gleaming black coach and to put down the steps for His Grace. Wordlessly, the duke strode beneath the great portico and into the austere building itself where a clerk, recognizing him, raised his eyebrows and immediately began to look like a penned sheep circled by a wolf.

"Is Lord Sandwich in?" the duke asked.

"I'm sorry your Grace, but he stepped out for just a moment, and should return shortly. Would you care for some refreshment? Some—"

"Show me to his office. I will await him there."

"Your Grace, I can't just bring you into the office of the First Lord of the Admiralty, I could lose my position here and...."

His voice fell off as the duke's cold black eyes settled on him, pinning him to his chair and sucking every ounce of courage from the blood that ran suddenly cold through his veins. Without raising his voice, without moving a muscle, the duke merely said, "If you value your position that much, then it would behoove you to grant my request because I can *assure* you that the strings of Admiralty are not controlled by those you *think* control it." The hard mouth was unbending. "Do I make myself clear?"

"Y-yes, your Grace, very clear indeed." He rose to his feet, managed a clumsy bow, and led Lucien de Montforte to Lord Sandwich's office. "Make yourself comfortable, Your Grace. Some coffee, perhaps? Tea? Refreshments?"

The noble profile turned to gaze out windows grimy with coal smoke. "I am quite comfortable. Send the earl to me when he arrives. That is all."

That is all.

The young officer bolted. He had been grateful when his own connections had landed him this position at the Admiralty, away from seasickness and foundering warships and tyrannical captains who thought nothing of beating their junior officers over the breech of a gun. But at that moment, he would have traded hell and high water to be out on a ship ... anywhere but within the reach of the mighty Duke of Blackheath.

He had just returned to his desk when the door opened and two well-dressed young men came in, their faces grave and bearing a similarity in profile to that devil he'd just left back in Lord Sandwich's office. One, clad in the uniform of an Army officer, was tall and taciturn with blond hair tied back in a neat queue; the other's hair was a tawny golden-brown and his blue eyes were dark with worry.

He drew himself up. "Can I help you?"

The same lordly attitude, the same expectance of being obeyed. It was there in the Army officer, just as it had been in Blackheath. "I am Major Lord Charles de Montforte, and this is my brother Lord Gareth. I understand our brother the duke is here?"

"Yes, he is. If you'll but wait here, I'll—"

"Take us to him immediately," Lord Charles commanded. "This is a matter of grave importance to my family and possibly even the security of England herself."

The clerk took a deep, bracing sigh. If it wasn't one, it was three. He was going to lose his position over this, to be sure. Maybe he'd find a berth on a Royal Navy ship and there, serve out his days waiting to get his head blown off.

In the meantime, the pale blue eyes of the major were regarding him with growing impatience.

"Come with me," he said, and led the two brothers to Lord Sandwich's office.

❧

John Montagu, the fourth Earl of Sandwich and currently serving his third stint as the First Lord of the Admiralty, returned from lunch in a bad mood. As he entered the Admiralty, he saw the young officer at the desk beckoning madly to him.

"What is it, Fleming?"

"The Duke of Blackheath and his brothers, sir. They're here."

Sandwich's thin mouth, perpetually down-turned these days, tightened in a frown beneath his long, hooked nose. "Where?"

The young man grew visibly uncomfortable. "They demanded to be put in your office, my lord." As Sandwich's brow went dark, he began to stammer. "I-I told him that that was not possible, th-th-that I would lose my position over it, but he said that you and I both would lose our positions if I didn't grant him his wishes and he's in there now, sir, waiting for you—all of them are."

His mood souring all the more, Lord Sandwich stalked down the hall toward his office, the heavy joint of beef he'd consumed over lunch beginning to sit rather uncomfortably in his stomach. He knew all about the abduction of Lady Nerissa, was doing everything he could think of to get her back. Damn the Americans, the most worthless race of men on earth. This was going to put him into his damned grave. What more could he possibly do to appease Blackheath that he hadn't already done?

Better think of something. Life will surely get worse than it already is if you don't.

He pushed open the door to his office and saw the three brothers there, the resemblance between them all quite unmistakable. Bows were exchanged, but Blackheath allowed no time for pleasantries. A muscle twitching in his cheek, he looked coldly at Sandwich and then, reaching into his pocket, produced a folded piece of vellum and slapped it down on his desk.

Lord Sandwich pulled out his chair and sat. He glanced up, once, at Blackheath through watery, pale blue eyes, thinned his mouth and unfolded the paper.

"This was delivered to me an hour ago," the duke said icily. "Earlier this morning, Rear-Admiral Hadley informed me that my siblings were safe and on their way back to England aboard the American prize-brig *Tigershark*." Blackheath's eyes were blazing-cold. "*Is someone lying to me, Sandwich?*"

The earl rubbed wearily at the bridge of his nose. He was already dreading whatever words lay on that vellum. "We received dispatches from the cutter *Mosquito*, which spoke Captain Hadley's frigate in the Channel following a brief squall. Captain Hadley informed *Mosquito*'s master that he'd taken the brig after a brief skirmish and left Lady Nerissa and Lord Andrew aboard, but that the storm had separated them. He was on his way back to find them. I can assure you, Blackheath, that no one is lying to you."

Sandwich kept the rest of that thought to himself. *They wouldn't dare*.

"Then read the damned letter," Blackheath said coldly, slamming the heel of his hand down on the vellum. "Read it and explain to me *what the bloody hell is going on here*."

All three de Montforte men were waiting. Lord Sandwich pulled the paper toward him, smoothed it flat and began to read:

My dearest Lucien,

I don't have time to go into details as we will be shortly underway, and it is only by virtue of the fact that he is currently quite incapacitated and his crew lacking his own canny suspicions that I am able to slip this note off to you. Whatever you may or may not have heard, Ruaidri O' Devir, captain of the American brig Tigershark *and abductor of our beloved sister, is alive. Not well, but alive and back in command of this brig, and given the sheer stubbornness of his will, I expect him to make a full recovery. By the time you receive this, he will have been united in marriage to our sister and* Tigershark *on her way back to Boston with the prize she came here to get—that is, me. Rest assured that we are safe, and so are the secrets of my invention which I will never disclose, not even under threat of death. As for O' Devir, I have given my consent to this union and am confident that he will be a good husband to our sister. There is so much to convey, and so little time to do so ... I must go, but wanted to spare you further worry as to our safety and well-being. Please give my love to Celsie and know that I'll be home just as soon as I can manage it.*

Yours,

—Andrew, Saint-Malo, France

Lord Sandwich rubbed at an itch beneath his starched, rolled and powdered bagwig and pushed the vellum back toward Blackheath. So *Tigershark* was once again in the hands of the Americans and on her way to Boston, carrying not only two de Montforte siblings but the most important military discovery to come along in the last two centuries ... a military discovery that *had* to stay here with England at all costs.

"What are you going to do about this, John?" the duke demanded, his mouth taut with fury.

Not, "Are you going to do anything about this." It was already assumed that he was going to do something about this, and that he would do it yesterday instead of tomorrow. Given Blackheath's famously protective stance toward his family, Sandwich knew it was less about England's military security and more about the fate of his two siblings that was the force behind Blackheath's cold, deadly anger.

'Struth, what a colossal mess. Things surely couldn't get any worse.

But in the next moment, the clerk knocked on the door to tell him Captain Hadley of the frigate HMS *Happenstance* was waiting outside, and Sandwich suddenly knew that yes, they could indeed get a whole lot worse.

And did.

Hat under his arm, the naval captain entered, his face paling beneath its tan as he saw the three de Montforte brothers already waiting in Sandwich's office. The First Lord of the Admiralty rounded on him.

"Your father assured me you were the man for the job, the man he most trusted to bring Lady Nerissa safely home," Sandwich thundered, taking out his own stress on the hapless captain. "Where is she?"

Hadley opened his mouth, his elbow now crushing the hat to his side. "My lord, I—" he glanced nervously at the duke and his equally intimidating brothers. "Her ladyship insisted on staying aboard the prize after we captured her. I put my first lieutenant, a good man, sir, a fine sailor, in charge of her to sail her back to London. Lord Andrew stayed with her."

"What about O' Devir?"

"Cut down on his own quarterdeck, my lord."

"And you know this for a fact?"

"I saw his corpse with my own eyes. One of my own marines delivered the fatal shot."

"And where is that damned brig now, Hadley?"

What color remained in the captain's face swiftly dissolved, leaving his cheeks the color of tallow. His gaze flickered to the window, down to his feet. "I don't know, my lord."

"*What?!*"

"She was with us as we headed back to England. A storm came up. Night fell. We became separated. I went back to look for them, but ... but they were gone." He met Sandwich's furious gaze, but could not muster the courage to look at Blackheath.

Sandwich let him squirm for a few moments, then picked up the vellum and held it out. "Read this."

Steeling himself, Hadley did. Twice. He looked up, frowning. "I don't understand ... the Americans must have found a way to retake the brig." He straightened up, the color returning to his face. "With your consent, my lord, I will head right back out in pursuit, surely they can't be more than a couple days ahead of us, and I—"

It was the Duke of Blackheath whose cold voice cut through Hadley's words.

"No, you've already cocked this up well and good, you incompetent ninny," he snarled. "You're done. *Done*." He rounded on Sandwich. "Maybe if *you* had sent more of our fleet to North America instead of concentrating them here for fear of an invasion by the damned French, vermin like this damned O' Devir rascal would've been blown to bits long before he could have even *thought* about crossing the damned Atlantic and threatening us in our own waters."

"We will find him, Your Grace."

"Yes, you will. In fact, you'll assign the fastest warship in the damned *Fleet* to finding him, you'll put a commander on board who knows what the bloody hell he's doing, and you'll have her outfitted and ready to chase down this—this *parasite*, immediately. I expect you to set about doing this the moment I leave this office, and *you* can expect to accommodate a passenger. *Me*. Do I make myself understood?"

Lord Sandwich kneaded a weary brow. He understood.

Chapter Twenty-Seven

The crossing took nearly six weeks.

For Nerissa, it was a time of getting to know the enigmatic man she had married. Of learning that he had an aversion to salted fish, that he was a stern but fair captain who never, no matter what the crime, resorted to the lash, that he was a tough, stubborn, and respected commander whose single-minded drive to get them back across the Atlantic as quickly as possible had the miles falling away behind him.

She learned that he enjoyed making things, and she watched another exquisite, perfectly scaled ship model come to life beneath his big, scarred hands in the rare moments when he'd find time to relax in their cabin. He learned that she was happier when she had something to do, and he began to teach her the rudiments of navigation. She learned that he despised tea, harbored a private guilt about how his most recent actions would affect his sister, and that most of the swear-words in the vocabulary of Joey's parrot had come from him. Late at night, they lay in the narrow cot, talking about the differences in their childhoods, their countries, their shared hopes and dreams after a session of gentle love-making, and fell asleep wrapped in each other's arms.

And he grew stronger.

Stronger by the day.

In the early days of his recovery, a member of the crew would bring a chair up on the quarterdeck for him. There he would sit when standing became too exhausting, calling for endless sail drills, gun drills and musket practice, until the men under his command were as fine a fighting unit as any captain in any navy could hope for. During those times Nerissa stood quietly nearby, admiring the sheer, pig-headed determination he showed in denying his injury mastery over him, denying anyone to pity him or think any less of his capabilities as a commander for it. He might have collapsed the moment he returned to the privacy of their cabin but on deck, no man would have perceived any weakness. He led with a quiet, firm resolve, and the men trusted him. Respected him. Perhaps even liked him.

Even Lord Andrew.

He was not the man the youngest de Montforte brother would have chosen for his baby sister, but even he could not deny the glow to her cheeks and the warmth in her eyes when she was with her new husband. He noted the way her gaze followed him as he went about the business of commanding the ship, the way she tenderly saw to his comfort as he slowly regained his strength. And he saw the way he treated her, with free and easy abandon instead of the status-conscious, fawning deference to which she was accustomed ... and that in itself gave her a certain liberty to be the person she had never really had the chance to be: Herself.

And she was blossoming. Thriving. Looking more beautiful and more fulfilled than he had ever seen her.

Andrew, despite missing his own wife and daughter with a desperate ache, was happy.

Now the vast Northern Atlantic was behind them. Boston lay only two or three days ahead of *Tigershark*'s plunging jib-boom and somewhere off to starboard was the distant coast of Canada. On this chilly morning, the October sun was just dragging itself up out of the east with grudging weariness, wanting like everyone else to stay asleep under the warm blanket of the horizon as the days got shorter and colder. The morning filled with thin light, revealing Nova Scotia far, far off the starboard beam—and something else off the larboard one. Above, the voice of the maintop lookout suddenly pierced the early-morning quiet.

"Deck there! Sail off the larboard quarter ... looks to be a cutter!"

Ruaidri rubbed cold hands together, cupped them around his mouth and tilted his head back. "Colors, Mr. McGuire?"

"She's British, sir!"

Every man on deck immediately stopped what he was doing and looked out to sea. Nerissa had just come out with a mug of hot coffee, and now she too watched in apprehension as her husband moved to the rail and carefully selecting a spyglass, raised it to his eye.

Andrew, seeing her go still, took her hand. "Well, this might get interesting," he said, and Nerissa could not tell if he was happy about the appearance of the British cutter or wishing it would disappear. She knew her own feelings. There was nothing to be gained for either her or Ruaidri by the presence of a British warship. Nothing.

She remembered their tangle with Hadley's frigate back in the Channel, the blood and death and destruction. The blood went cold in her veins and she drew the heavy boat cloak that Ruaidri had given her closer around herself, trying to take comfort from his lingering scent. "We're off the Canadian coast," she murmured. "Ruaidri says there are plenty of Royal Navy ships and Loyalist privateers based in Halifax. Oh, Andrew ... I do hope there isn't a sea fight. I can't take another."

Andrew squeezed her hand. "I don't think he'll fight unless he has to. His mission is to get me to Adams."

"He'll fight if they challenge him."

"Let's hope they don't, then." He took her coffee mug, stole a sip, and handed it back to her. "Because I've had quite enough of sea battles, myself."

The minutes ticked by. The wind played with the black, frizzy tuft of the Irish captain's queue as he studied the distant ship for what seemed like a long time. Finally, he swung the instrument to sweep the horizon, smiled, and shut the glass. A brisk westerly was blowing over the starboard beam, chopping up the water like firewood and sending spray high over the jib-boom to spatter the jibs, staysails and forecourse. He said something to Midshipman Cranton. The midshipman saluted and hurried off. Rubbing his hands together for warmth, Ruaidri strode casually over to the two de Montforte siblings, the limp that had been such a part of him several weeks back, now gone.

"Cold day, eh?" he asked, as if that warship out there that was even now coming about to point her prow on them, was of no concern to him whatsoever.

Nerissa could not conceal her anxiety. "I'm hoping it's not going to get a whole lot warmer."

"What, no faith in me, Mrs. O' Devir?"

How could she answer that? If that British ship out there caught up to and captured them, Ruaidri was as good as dead and so, after her unspeakable act of treason, was she. Maybe Andrew would have some clout, but enough to save all their lives? Maybe hers. Certainly not her husband's.

"Very well then," she admitted. "I'm nervous."

"Why?"

"Because that ship out there is a lot bigger, faster and stronger than we are."

"So it is. But that ship is alone. And we, my dear—" he slid an arm around her waist and walked her a few steps away, where the mainmast no longer obscured her view—"are not."

His strong arm steadying her, he pointed far out to sea. The deck seemed to drop out beneath her feet as *Tigershark* cut through a succession of heavy swells, and Nerissa was grateful for her husband's solid strength. Salt lay thick in the air, making her skin moist and clammy and the deck sticky beneath her feet. But what was he looking at? The sea was restless and undulating, the wind pushing up lofty peaks that broke and spilled over into trails of lacy foam. The brig rose and fell, rose and fell, and with each swell that forced her high, Nerissa finally saw them—two ships, several miles out off their larboard bows, appearing and disappearing near the horizon.

"I see two ships," she said.

"You see two *American* ships," he said triumphantly. "A schooner and a brig. I'm guessing our British friend will decide the odds are against him and run like the divil himself is on his tail."

"He won't want to take them as prizes?"

"If they were merchantmen, aye. But those aren't merchantmen." He grinned. "They're privateers, armed to the teeth and more than a match for him. He'll turn tail and run for it, unless he's an utter fool."

Tigershark crested another swell and there they were, clearer now that she knew what she was looking at. Ruaidri handed her the glass. "If ye look closely, ye'll see the schooner is piling on sail. Ah ... and there goes the brig, doin' the same."

Far off, the shape of the British ship lengthened as she came about. Ruaidri, it seemed, was correct; her captain was no fool. A bright orange flash burst from the distant schooner as she fired a gun demanding the Briton to heave to, and a moment later, the heavy roll of thunder came rolling across the water. The brig, a half mile behind her, was hastily dropping her topsails as she, too, prepared to give chase.

Ruaidri was grinning.

"Mr. Morgan!" he called, and a moment later the lieutenant was at his side. "We've got more wind than we know what to do with. Get the t'gallants on her and let her fall off two points. We'll run down on the enemy and lend our own guns to the chase, should those two out there need them."

"Aye, sir!'

Moments later, men were swarming aloft to set the topgallants, *Tigershark's* huge fore-and-aft mainsail swung out over the sea as she was given more rein, and she was eagerly galloping down on the cutter, now fleeing with her tail between her legs.

They were closing the distance fast.

Another flash of orange followed by the roll of thunder came from the schooner, now well off the starboard bows as she bore down on the cutter like a greyhound on a rabbit; behind her, the brig changed tack and began to swoop down on the quarry from the other side, leaving her little place to go.

"That fight'll be over before we even get to join it," Ruaidri said with a sigh. But he was smiling, his eyes bright with admiration. "Given who's in command of that schooner, though, I'm not surprised. He's a bold lad, that one."

"You know him?"

Ruaidri's smile spread. "Oh, aye, I know him well."

His predictions proved true. The cutter gave a brief but futile account of herself, gunfire was exchanged, and moments later, the British ship was striking her colors.

"Got to love the privateers," Ruaidri said, watching the distance between *Tigershark* and the three ships speared on her jib-boom diminishing as the brig ate up the distance between them. "Nothing whets the appetite for battle more than prize money."

By the time they came up on the two American privateers and the British cutter, the brig had sent a boat over to her and was in the business of procuring her surrender. The schooner, though, lay hove to in the pitching seas and waiting for them. Ruaidri was in as high spirits as Nerissa had ever seen him. But then she looked again at the American schooner and the breath caught in her throat.

She was still learning about ships. She knew that a schooner had two masts with sails rigged fore and aft, whereas a brig's two masts had square sails on the foremast and a fore-and-aft sail on the main. Other than that she might have said that they all looked pretty much the same. But there was nothing "the same" about that schooner that lay there waiting for them. A sleek black hull with a white stripe lined with gun ports bisecting her sides. Sharply angled masts that were raked backwards instead of being affixed upright. A long, jaunty jib-boom, sinful lines, and a low, lean hull that sat so low in the water that it was almost one with it, made this schooner very, very different from anything Nerissa might have ever seen or even imagined.

Breathtakingly beautiful. Almost too pretty to be a fighting ship, though one look at the guns pointing out through her ports told a different story altogether.

And while the ship itself might have been different, the man standing in obvious command and impatiently tapping a speaking trumpet against his thigh had something familiar about him. As they drew closer and she saw his features come more sharply into view, she saw what that familiarity was. He was tall and lanky, but there was a merriment in his eyes and something about his mouth and the way he smiled that were known to her; known to her, because her own husband shared them.

The man raised the speaking trumpet to his lips. "*Dia duit ar maidin, mo col ceathrar!*" "Sorry we didn't wait for you to join us, but she was about to run."

"*Tá do long álainn. Tá sí cáiliúil,* Brendan!" Ruaidri called back. "And your arrival was timely. *Go raibh maith agat.*"

"Think nothing of it, Ruaidri. You'd have done the same for me, I'm sure. Permission to come aboard?"

"Quite happily granted."

A few moments later, the schooner's captain, accompanied by a slight young figure in coat and breeches whose swelling chest and flare of hips instantly corrected Nerissa's initial assumption about her gender, was climbing aboard. The man doffed his tricorne to Nerissa, revealing rich, tousled chestnut hair and a face that probably melted hearts from here to Boston and back. The way the young woman was gazing up at him, Nerissa guessed that hers was one of them.

"Welcome aboard, Brendan," Ruaidri said warmly. "'Tis grateful I am that you two showed up when ye did. Things were about to get hot, and while I'll never run from a fight, I've got somewhere to be."

"Continental Navy now, are you?"

"Aye. On a mission for John Adams."

The man named Brendan smiled. His voice was rich and melodious, and while its accent wasn't as pronounced as Ruaidri's, it was just as Irish. He had an easy charm about him, an engaging kindness in his eyes and manner that immediately put a person at ease. Now, he slid his arm around the slight young lady who'd come aboard with him and pulled her forward. "*Stóirín*, meet *mo col ceathrar* from Connemara—Ruaidri O' Devir. Ruaidri, this is Mira ... my best friend, my best gunner, my beloved—" his laughing, honey-colored eyes warmed as he gazed down at his companion's grinning, upturned face—"my wife."

The other woman wiped a palm on her breeches and

stuck out her hand in greeting. "Heard much about you, Ruaidri," she grunted, tipping her head to one side and studying him with bright green eyes. Her accent was American, her thick, dark hair caught in a braid that hung the length of her back. "So ye're the dreaded Irish Pirate, are ye? Aye, there's a family resemblance."

"No longer the Irish Pirate, but a commissioned officer in the Continental Navy." Ruaidri proudly pulled Nerissa forward. "And while we're on the subject of introductions, this is my wife Lady Nerissa and her brother, Lord Andrew de Montforte. Nerissa, Andrew? I'm pleased to introduce to you the famed American privateer, Brendan Merrick."

The schooner's captain bowed gallantly over Nerissa's hand. "I would say I'm pleased to make your acquaintance, Lady Nerissa, but indeed we have all already met." He grinned. "So instead, I'll just say that it's a pleasure to see you again."

Andrew stepped forward, frowning. "We've met?" he asked, studying the other man's face. "I'd have remembered."

"It was back in '74, at a ball thrown by your brother the duke to send Lord Charles off to Boston. I was in the Royal Navy then, and commanded one of the ships that brought your brother and his regiment over to America. I wouldn't expect you to remember me. It was a long time ago now, you both were quite young, and there were many people there. Welcome to the family, my lady."

"The family?"

Ruaidri pulled her close. "Brendan," he said grinning, "is my cousin."

"Cousin? Nerissa repeated, wondering if the world, as large as it was, could get any smaller. But a moment later she found out that indeed, it could.

"So *you're* Lady Nerissa," said the rather odd young woman whom Ruaidri's cousin had married. She folded her arms and cocked her head, her pale green eyes sparkling with mischief. "You and I, we ain't never met, but I know your family well."

Nerissa was taken aback. "How could you know my family?" she asked, bewildered. This unlikely woman was not the sort of individual likely to be rubbing elbows with the English *ton*.

"I know 'em because yer brother, Lord Charles, stayed in my town after he got hurt at Concord back in '75. Stuffy and oh-so-proper, your brother, but I forgave him for being a Brit after he fell in love with my best friend, rescued her from a shitty—" Nerissa blanched at the woman's language—"situation, and took her off to England to marry her. I miss Amy, I do, but she's better off there than here."

"*You're* Mira? *That* Mira?" Nerissa was gaping. "Amy's best friend from back home?"

"Aye, that Mira, the only Mira, as the world ain't big enough for two of us." She laughed at the stunned expression on Nerissa's face. "Amy and I still write to each other, and she's told me many a time about how welcome ye made her feel, how ye taught her how to move in your world, how much of a friend to her ye've become. Sure does make me breathe a lot easier, knowing the family she married into treats her a hell of a lot better than the one she was born to. Pleased to finally make your acquaintance, Lady Nerissa." She stuck out a tiny hand as her husband and Ruaidri moved to the rail and began talking ships. "And you too, Lord Andrew. What the hell are ye doing in America?"

Nerissa just stood there blinking. She had heard her sister-in-law speak of her best friend Mira, but never in her wildest dreams had she ever thought to meet her, or pictured her to be quite so ... unconventional.

It was Andrew who found his voice. "We are here, Mrs. Merrick, because I am as much a prize of war as that cutter your friend out there has just boarded."

"Oh, him? He ain't my friend, he's my brother, Matt." She peered closely at him. "What do ye mean, prize of war?"

"Captain O' Devir is delivering me to your John Adams."

"Why? What the hell does Adams want with an English nob?"

Andrew sighed helplessly. "I am sure the 'English nob' is of less interest to him than that which the English nob has invented. In my case, an explosive."

"Amy told me about your flying machine."

"Then she probably also told you that it failed. But the explosive ... I fear both Captain O' Devir and your John Adams are wasting their time with me. I will not, even under pain of torture and death, disclose the formula for how to make it."

"Aye, well, that's a problem," the young woman said. "But who wants to talk about stuff like that when it only puts people's hackles up? We were just headed back to Newburyport when we saw your sails at first light." She turned to Nerissa. "I know what it's like to be a girl, and I know what it's like to be onboard a ship and wanting nothin' more than a hot bath, warm, dry clothes and a nice big bed to sleep in. Come stay with us in Newburyport, even for a couple of nights. I'd like to get to know ye both, and hear all about how Amy's doing."

Nerissa glanced toward her husband, who was deep in discussion with his cousin over at the rail. "Ruaidri? We have been invited to visit the Merricks in Newburyport."

Ruaidri glanced uncertainly at Andrew, and Nerissa knew he was weighing whether to take Mira up on the offer or to proceed with all haste on to Boston.

"Yes, come stay with us," Brendan added, clapping a hand on his cousin's shoulder. "Faith, it's been ages since we last saw each other. We've lots to catch up on."

Ruaidri sighed, and capitulated.

An hour later, a prize crew was put aboard the cutter with orders to sail her back to Newburyport. American colors were run up her gaff and shortly afterwards *Tigershark*, accompanied by the beautiful schooner *Kestrel* and the newly-constructed brig *Eveleen*, was heading west.

None of them could know that a mere day's sail to the east, beyond the tossing waves and the flat horizon, another British ship was rapidly gaining on them.

A frigate, sleek and fast, commanded by one of the Royal Navy's finest officers.

A frigate carrying the Duke of Blackheath, who was determined to find his siblings—and kill the Irish rogue who had abducted his little sister.

Chapter Twenty-Eight

Newburyport, Nerissa decided immediately, was beautiful. She had heard much about this bustling Massachusetts seaport situated at the mouth of the mighty Merrimack River from both her brother Charles and his wife Amy, whose family here in Newburyport had cared for him after he'd been gravely injured during the battle of Concord. Mira had been Amy's best friend, and Nerissa felt like she knew her already, having heard many accounts of her actions and exploits from her sister-in-law. Mira's brash, open manner, though, made it easy for a person to think they'd known her forever. She was shockingly open, coarse, unintentionally funny and warm. Nerissa smiled, thinking of how things had come full circle, and how she had found a connection to her own family back home, and maybe even a friend.

Small world, it was.

The Merricks were most hospitable, and Mira had been right. Nerissa, like the others, had enjoyed a hot bath after arriving at their stately Georgian home, and there had been no greater bliss after a month at sea. Fine milled soap, hot, steaming water and soft, fluffy towels ... a proper gown instead of the midshipman's uniform ... floors that weren't moving, walls that weren't creaking, and tasteful, genteel furnishings. It wasn't Blackheath Castle but the Merricks, Nerissa decided, were doing quite well for themselves.

The house itself was spacious, and Brendan and his wife shared it with not only a dozen cats, but Mira's father Ephraim Ashton, a crusty old sea captain who, Nerissa decided, must have suffered hearing loss from the close report of too many cannon over his lifetime. Any hearing loss he hadn't suffered was certain to be inflicted on others, as he was loud, cantankerous, argumentative with his daughter and quite happy to let Nerissa and Andrew know just what he thought of the British.

Her ears were grateful when he went to bed. Even Andrew, clad in a borrowed banyan, his eyes drooping after his own hot bath and the splendid feast that had been served earlier, seemed to let out a sigh of relief.

Now, they all sat around a fire in the great hearth, letting the stuffed turkey and roasted yams settle as refreshments were brought around. Outside, the wind gusted around the windows. The silence was heavenly.

"Don't mind my father," Mira muttered, getting up to stab at a few half-burned logs with a poker. Sparks showered up into the great chimney, and she stuffed a fresh log beneath the graying, charred chunks of wood that were doing their best to warm the room on what had turned into a cold, wet and windy night. She went back to the sofa and sat down next to her husband, snuggling up against him in an open, unfettered display of relaxed affection that would have been quite shocking in the sort of company Nerissa was used to keeping. "He's all bluster and perfectly harmless."

She had shed her boyish seagoing clothes and made as pretty a lady in an embroidered short jacket and dark plum wool petticoats as Nerissa supposed any colonial woman could be; a miniature of her handsome husband hung suspended from a ribbon around her neck, her dark brown hair was swept up atop her head, and her green eyes were bright and completely unapologetic at such an open display of love for her man.

Her husband didn't seem to mind, either. He just hooked an arm around his wife's shoulders and snuggled her close. Sparks popped in the hearth. Andrew's eyes lost their battle to stay open and he quietly drifted off in his chair. Nobody disturbed him. Talk moved to ships, the war, and politics. The wind moaned around the eaves outside. There was something lonely about the sound and unbidden, Nerissa thought of home.

Of Blackheath Castle, three thousand miles away. Of dear Charles and Amy, of Gareth and Juliet, of Lucien and Eva and Andrew's poor wife Celsie, who must be worried sick about her husband. And her little nieces and nephews and even her dog.

Oh, how I miss you all.

She wondered if she would ever see them again.

Movement beside her. She looked up to find her husband eyeing her keenly. "How ye keepin', lass?"

"Still a little under the weather," she confessed.

He picked up a cup of hot mulled cider from the tray that the housekeeper had brought in and set it on the little table beside her. "Here. Drink up. Ye didn't eat much at supper and unless ye want me to start worryin' about ye, ye'll have a go at some of this."

"Still not feeling well, lass?" Brendan asked, his warm amber eyes concerned.

"I'll be all right," Nerissa said, not wanting anyone to worry about her.

"Hasn't got her land-legs back yet," Ruaidri said, coming around behind her to lay a reassuring hand against the inside of her shoulder. His fingers were cool against her neck, soothing, and she leaned slightly into his touch. "Ye'll be fine, won't ye, *mo grá*?'

"If you say so," she said.

Brendan plucked a tiny cake off the tray and washed it down with cider. "My cousin's right. It takes time for the body to make the adjustment from sea back to land. I'm sure you'll be fine by morning."

So said the two sea captains, who surely knew about such things. Mira, however, just eyed her speculatively and reached for her own drink, a little smile playing around her mouth. "It won't cure whatever ails ye, Lady Nerissa, but if ye like to ride, I've got horses. Once this gale blows itself out to sea, should be a fine day tomorrow for a blistering gallop along the beach and a ride around town. I'd love to show ye Newburyport. Your brother, too, if he's inclined. Sound good?"

If nothing else, it would take her mind off her family back home. "I would enjoy that, Mira."

"Good. We'll play it by ear as to the time. We don't hold with formalities around here."

Unless someone came in during the day to do cleaning and other domestic work, she didn't hold with servants either, aside from a matronly housekeeper who seemed to do duty as both cook and family friend. Which left Nerissa with the dilemma of how to lace her stays, style her hair, and go about the business of dressing and undressing herself—all tasks that, up until the moment she'd been abducted, had been done by her maid. How did one go about being a lady in this place? But Mira had no maid, and *she* seemed to manage....

And if Mira can manage, so can you. Your life as a pampered pet is over. You wanted to be freed from your cage, to really get the chance to live. You have it, now, and if truth be told, you're doing quite well.

Lucien, of course, would not approve.

Don't think about him.

Brendan leaned forward and poured himself another mug of hot cider. "So tell me more, Roddy—"

"Ruaidri," her husband interrupted. "I stopped being Roddy three years ago."

"Faith, old habits die hard," his cousin said with an apologetic smile. "So tell me more about what you've been up to since we last saw each other what, three years ago now? Four?"

"Four, I believe. Went back home after that business here in Boston, got bored, ended up back here and when John Adams tapped me on the shoulder, I answered the call. Had nothin' to lose and everythin' to gain."

"Happy in the new navy, then?"

"Aye." Ruaidri pulled his chair closer to Nerissa and took her hand. He looked over at her, his eyes all but undressing her and promising untold delights later on when they finally ended up in the big, soft bed that awaited them upstairs. "I've come out on the lucky end of things, I'd say. Could've done without the injury, but I'm still here and ready and willin' to make plenty of trouble if they need me to." He told them about the fight with Hadley's frigate and how the ship had been taken and his men imprisoned below. "But for the courage and cunning of my lovely Nerissa here, I'd have been swinging from Hadley's yardarm or a rope at Tyburn. I owe her my life."

Nerissa picked up her cup of cider and stirred it with a stick of cinnamon. But as she took a sip, her stomach rolled under an unexpected wave of nausea and she quickly put the cup down. Dear lord, how long would it take her to get her land-legs back?

Mira was eying her closely. "So what'd ye do, Lady Nerissa, to save the day?"

"Just 'Nerissa,'" she said, her hand on her belly. "If you're not inclined to stand on formality, I'm not either."

The other woman grinned. "Right. So what did you do?"

"Not much," she said. "I simply freed Ruaidri and his crew so they wouldn't all die."

"She doesn't give herself enough credit," her husband said fondly. "I was near to dyin'. Took a musket ball in the back of my leg and must've hit my head when I went down, 'cause I remember none of it. The Brits threw me into the hold with the rest of my men after they took *Tigershark* as a prize, and this little lass here—" he lifted her knuckles to his mouth and kissed them—"betrayed both her king and country to save me. Knocked the sentry over the head, crept belowdecks to the hold, forced the prizemaster at gunpoint to release my crew and allowed us to retake the ship. I wouldn't be here if not for her."

Mira was staring at her with amazement and a new respect. "*You* did *that*?"

Nerissa idly stirred her cider, wishing the nausea would pass. "Well, I couldn't just let them all die."

"Nearly died anyhow," Ruaidri said. "A month and a half ago now it happened, and I still tire faster than a racehorse runnin' through mud."

Andrew, who'd been dozing near the fire, cracked open an eye. "You lost a lot of blood. It takes time for the body to build it back up. Count your blessings that you're even alive."

"It's been over six weeks," Ruaidri said impatiently. "How much longer does a body need?"

"As long as it takes." Andrew stood up, politely suppressing a yawn. "I beg your forgiveness for retiring early, but I'm done for." He bowed politely to the ladies and excused himself. Nerissa wondered if he wanted to write a letter home to Celsie before crawling beneath the covers of a real bed for the first time in a month and a half. She knew how much her brother missed his wife and daughter, but he'd been stoic about this whole thing and had not complained, perhaps, she thought ruefully, because he wanted to be near his little sister to keep an eye on her. She watched him go.

Brendan contemplated his cider for a long moment.

Andrew's footsteps receded and a door shut somewhere upstairs. Something was troubling the chestnut-haired Irishman, and now he looked up at Nerissa, frowning slightly. "A fine fellow, Lord Andrew," he said quietly. "But I've met your other brothers, including your oldest one, and he didn't strike me as a man to take kindly to the abduction of his two youngest siblings. I can't help but wonder, lass ... where is the duke in all this?"

The question was spoken without judgment or force, and yet it penetrated the armor with which Nerissa had girded her heart, armor that protected her guilt at feeling, somehow, that she was quite justified in fleeing England, fleeing Lucien, even. After all, he had made such a total cock-up of her life with the way he'd arranged it, arranged others within it—most notably, Perry—that there was a part of her that felt that her manipulative, Machiavellian older brother had got exactly what he deserved. Had he worried and fretted and sworn with helplessness after she'd been abducted? Was he tearing his hair out and suffering the grief that he had caused others, most notably herself? *Good,* a little voice in her mind had said. *Good*, because that's exactly what he deserved.

But here, three thousand miles away from home and all that was familiar, sitting in a strange, wooden-framed house amongst people she barely knew and everything—with the exception of her dear, beloved Ruaidri and Andrew, who surely wouldn't be with her much longer—she had ever known and loved gone, the little voice of her conscience was persistent and loud. A wave of homesickness assailed her, and she wished, oh, how she wished, that she had the same brazen and carefree manner that Mira had. She wanted nothing more than to just crawl into Ruaidri's embrace and let him hold her. Just hold her.

She cast a longing glance over at him. His freshly washed hair was a damp riot of wild, spiraling curls spilling across his broad shoulders, his jaw newly shaven. He had shed his naval uniform for civilian clothes—worn leather breeches tucked into boots and a dark gray coat open to show an embroidered waistcoat of sage-colored wool. He looked relaxed and at ease. He looked delicious. Oh, she couldn't wait to be in his arms, in a real bed, with a solid floor beneath them instead of a rolling deck.

The reminder that the floor beneath her wasn't moving made her remember all over again that she felt queasy.

"So you're recently married, too?" Mira asked.

"Six weeks."

"And you forgive this Irish rascal here for bringing your brother to John Adams?"

Brendan, his feet thrust toward the fire and his thoughts his own, raised his head. "Mira, *stóirín*—"

"It's quite all right, Captain Merrick," Nerissa said reassuringly. "I've spent a lifetime around people who have treated me like a fragile teacup. I am not fragile. I am not a teacup. In the past two months I've survived a fall down a flight of stairs, an abduction, a sea-fight, the near loss of the man I love, and a rigorous trip across the Atlantic filled with storms, saltwater, and food crawling with vermin." She smiled at the American woman. "Your wife's bluntness and candor are actually quite refreshing. They make me feel as though I'm being respected."

Mira grinned, and Nerissa got the feeling that beneath her rough manners, Brendan's wife was actually a very perceptive soul. "And look at ye, stronger, I expect, than ye were before ye met Ruaidri here and got subjected to such a barrage," she said, her eyes bright above her cup as she sipped her cider.

"Well, perhaps I'm stronger than I was two months ago, but that doesn't keep me from worrying about Andrew once Ruaidri turns him over to your John

Adams." She looked at her hosts. "Do you know the man?"

"I've met him," Brendan said. "He commands the utmost admiration, as does his wife. A credit to America, both of them."

"Is he likely to harm my brother in his attempts to get the formula from him?"

Mira guffawed. Brendan lifted a brow and Ruaidri, his lips twitching, stifled a yawn. "Saints alive, Nerissa, if I thought that Andrew would come to any harm at Adams's or anyone else's hands, I'd have left him back in France. Adams is a good lawyer and, as my cousin says, a credit to America, but even he's not able to get blood from a stone. I'd lay money on it that he'll try every which way but sideways to get Andrew to give him the formula, try again, and finally decide he's better off tradin' him for high-rankin' American prisoners held by the British than wastin' his time on somethin' Andrew will never give up."

Brendan shifted the position of his long legs. "Aye, lass. Adams is a good man. Your brother'll be on his way home to England before you know it."

Outside, a gust of wind hit the house, rattling the windows in their casements and causing a downdraft to push at the fire.

Nerissa stifled a yawn, but her husband's sharp eyes caught the subtle gesture.

"Time to call it a night, I think," he said, getting to his feet and collecting everyone's empty cider mugs. He set them on the tray so they could be easily carried back to the kitchen. "My poor wife has yet to gain her land-legs. She needs rest, and much as I wish otherwise, so do I. Maybe tomorrow ye can show us around Newburyport? Nerissa and I'll need a place to settle, and it looks like this one has a lot to offer."

"I should hope that existing family and friends would top that list of what it offers, *mo chol ceathar,*" said

Brendan warmly. "Besides, our wives seem to be getting on famously, and you can be in Boston in the time it takes to set your tops'ls. You could find worse places to settle, but none better."

Ruaidri, who'd noted his wife's well-concealed sadness earlier in the evening and correctly guessed the reason for it, laughed as Nerissa all but leapt to her feet. "Oh, Ruaidri—I would love it if we made this place our home. Could we?"

Ruaidri laughed. "Let's have a look at it tomorrow. Plenty of time to make up our minds." He wrapped a hand around her waist. Goodnights were said, and before they were even halfway up the staircase, he had lifted his wife in his arms and carried her the rest of the way.

She was asleep before he even peeled the covers back and gently lowered her down to the sheets. She might protest that she was no china doll, but in some respects, Ruaidri mused, he would always treat her as one—worthy of the utmost care and protection.

His care and protection.

How he loved her.

Loved her.

His eyes filled with sudden, unexpected emotion as he looked down at her, sleeping. They were safe here in Newburyport, with a solid roof over their heads and the end of his mission in sight. A nice little town, this one, and his cousin was right. They already had friends and family here. It was as good if not better a place than any to settle down and begin their lives together. Ruaidri stripped off his coat, breeches and waistcoat, and clad in just the long linen shirt, climbed carefully into bed beside his wife.

He was already growing hard, and he ached to make love to her.

And then he remembered her pushing her food

around on her plate and knew that her needs—a good night's sleep—were far more important than his own.

Curling his body around hers to keep her warm, he wrapped her in his hard, strong arms, buried his face in her hair and fell asleep to the sound of the wind whistling around the eaves as the gale built outside.

Chapter Twenty-Nine

Nerissa awoke several hours later.

The room was still dark, save for a single candle that had burned low on the highboy a few feet away. Outside, she could hear rain lashing the windows, hammering them in wet sheets of fury. It was a miserable night out there and she was glad they were here in a warm, dry house as opposed to what would be the damp discomfort of *Tigershark*'s cabin in such "dirty," as Ruaidri would call it, weather.

His warmth surrounded her, encompassed her, and she became increasingly aware of something hard pressing into her backside. She turned over and found him awake, his wildly curling black hair in sharp contrast against the pillow in the room's faint light as he lay on one elbow gazing down at her. He made no apologies for his bulging arousal, and she stretched her arm out beneath the blankets and found him beneath his bunched-up shirttail. He was rock-hard, and she gently stroked him as they lay quietly together.

"Mmmm," he murmured, with a sigh of relief.

"Why are you awake?" she asked.

"Why are you?"

"I'm hungry."

"No surprise there," he murmured, his voice deep

and warm in the near-darkness. He traced the curve of her cheekbone with his fingers. "You didn't eat much at supper, lass. Feelin' better, are ye?"

"Yes." She brushed her thumb over his velvety knob, loving the way he filled her hand. "But that doesn't explain why you're awake in the middle of the night."

"Maybe it's because I want ye."

"You can have me. Any time you like."

"Ye were asleep."

"I'm not, now." He grew restless as she continued to touch him, and her own blood began to ignite at the thought of him being inside her, filling her, loving her with all the strength in his big body and holding her protectively in his arms. The warm glow of the candle softened the hard, angular cast of his features and he smiled at her, drinking her in with his eyes before reaching up to clear a thick tress of long blonde hair away from her face.

He tucked it behind her ear. "I love ye, Nerissa O' Devir," he murmured softly. "Ye're the best thing that's ever come into me life. 'Til the day I die, I'll be thankin' the good Lord and every saint in heaven for sendin' ye to me."

"I love you too, Ruaidri." His arousal filled her hand, hot and heavy and hard. "Thank you for abducting me."

He laughed and used his body weight to dislodge her before she could bring him to climax, rolling her over onto her back. The covers tented above them, letting in drafts of cold air, and he quickly yanked the blankets up to try and hold the heat in.

Outside, the cold, autumn wind howled and a tree branch scraped against the window pane. Warmth, security, coziness, and the arms of her husband ... there was no place Nerissa would rather be, no place on earth that even her wildest dreams could ever have taken her, and she realized that despite the fact she was in a strange bed in a strange country three thousand miles from home, she was happier than she had ever been in her life.

He reached down, framing her face between his rough, calloused hands, and lowered his head to kiss her.

She eagerly received him, desperate for the taste of his lips, the heavy weight of his body pressing hers down into the mattress, that sweeping, delicious joy of being melded to, mated to, joined as one to, this man that she had married. His mouth drove hungrily into her own, forcing her head down into the pillow, covering and capturing her soft moans of pleasure as his tongue swept into her mouth and set her blood afire. She reached up and pushed her hands through his hair, clasping his head to hers. His curls tangled in her fingers, coarse and wiry and refusing to be tamed, much like the man himself.

"We must be quiet, Ruaidri," she whispered, as he pulled her shift up and ran his hands down her sides. He drove them beneath her hips and cupping her bottom, pulled her up against his erection, pressing and grinding against her until they were both breathing hard. "The walls ... they might be thin. I ... oh ... I would be terribly embarrassed if anyone were to hear us."

His shifted his weight, not yet entering her, then lifted a hand to tweak and massage her nipple until lightning flared between her legs and became liquid heat. A helpless little cry tumbled from her lips and he quickly kissed her to cover it. "Nobody will hear us," he murmured against the side of her neck, then kissed her again as he rolled the nipple, engorged now, between thumb and forefinger. "We'll make sure of it."

He moved lower on the bed, capturing the other nipple between his lips, teasing it with his tongue, flicking it into a peak of sensation. Nerissa tried to reach for him once more but he caught her hand, pushed it high over her head and anchored it on the pillow, all the while sucking at her nipple, drawing it deeply into his mouth and lightly nipping it until she gasped and twisted and pushed upwards with her hips, wanting him.

"Be still, lass," he murmured, looking up from the gentle curve of her breast with a little smile. "We're tryin' to be quiet, remember?"

"I'm—" she sucked her lower lip between her teeth as his hand strayed lower, grazing the flat plane of her abdomen, the little indentations where her lower pelvis met her hipbones, and finally, that desperate, almost painful spot between her legs that was already wet with desire for him—"trying."

"Then let me see if I can make it harder for ye," he teased, spreading her with his fingers and stroking her inner flesh until she moaned and twisted slowly on the sheet, her heels digging into the mattress, the blankets already spilling to the floor.

"Oh, Ruaidri ... I shall be so embarrassed if anyone were to hear us."

"The house is asleep."

She gave a little sob as he found her slick, hidden bud between thumb and forefinger and gently rolled it. "It won't be if you continue to do that to me. I can't keep quiet ... it's agony..."

He moved lower then, his mouth dragging down across her abdomen, his tongue coming out to dip into the little divot of her navel and to swirl around its perimeter, even as he still held her arm above her head, even as he still rubbed and stroked her into a heavy wetness. She turned her head on the pillow, dimly aware of the shadows moving across the ceiling, her breathing coming thick and hard as his lips dragged through her curls and he nuzzled that sweet, hot spot he was still massaging with his fingers.

"I love the smell of ye, Nerissa," he murmured

against her, his voice hoarse and savage. "I love the taste of ye. Ye make me crazy with need. Ye make me lose me fuckin' mind. Ye slay me, ye do my head in, and I wouldn't have it any other way."

With his elbow, he forced her legs wide, so wide that she felt the tendons straining, and pushed his mouth deep into her cleft, his tongue taking over where her fingers left off until the scream she was helpless to prevent rose like a crazy, unleashed beast from deep inside her. Just in time, he released her straining arm and offered the palm of his hand to her mouth and she bit down hard on it to contain her cries, tears of sweet anguish coursing down her cheeks as climax rocked her not once, not twice, but a sharp and undulating three times. And then, before the last waves could die away, he rose up above her, strong and virile, his arousal thick and swelling in his hand, and guided it to her wet cleft. She rose to meet him, sobbing in joy as she felt him shove deep inside of her with an almost brutal possessiveness, filling her with himself, stretching the walls of her womanhood, the delicious penetration finding more sensation deep inside of her and causing it to build once more.

His own passion built with the force and gathering momentum of his thrusts, and it occurred to her, with some distant part of her mind, that the bed was squeaking, that someone might hear, and then her husband drove himself deep inside her a final time, shuddering as he spilled his seed. His hot forehead dropped to hers. Her arms came up to encircle his broad, brawny shoulders. He lowered himself to his forearms and buried his face against her neck, his breath hot against her skin, her damp hair.

They lay there for a long moment, their bodies damp with perspiration, his thick, coarse hair pushing into her cheek.

"That wasn't quiet," he rasped, still breathing hard.

"Do you think anyone heard us?" she asked, mortified.

"Don't know. Don't care."

"I hope I didn't hurt your hand," she said a little sheepishly.

He just laughed and easing himself out of her, got up to fetch the washcloth that was neatly folded with the bowl and pitcher. He cleaned them both up, then went about retrieving the kicked-off blankets in the darkness.

"I'm cold now, Ruaidri. Come back to bed and keep me warm."

"I'm tryin' to find the blankets."

He tossed them over the bed and she sat up, helping to straighten them and tuck them in. A moment later, he slid in beside her and gathered her safely up into his arms. They lay there together, the faint nausea she'd felt hours earlier beginning to press on her once more, he gazing up at the shadows playing across the ceiling.

"How long does the land-sickness last, Ruaidri?"

"Should be gone by now, I'd expect. What, ye still feelin' poorly, lass?"

"Not quite poorly, just not ... not myself. A bit sick to my stomach."

"Do you want me to go find some ginger in the kitchens? 'Twill calm your stomach."

"No, don't trouble yourself. It will pass."

"Probably all that rich food we had at supper. Ye've been eating shipboard shite for the past month and a half; ye're not used to it."

"What time is it, anyhow?"

"Don't know, too dark in here to see the clock, but I'm guessin' it's comin' up on about five in the mornin'. 'Twill be a while before the sun comes up." He squeezed her hand. "Let me go find some ginger for ye."

She didn't want to send him out of this cozy cocoon even though she knew he'd do it for her, do anything for her, in a heartbeat. "No, Ruaidri. Stay here with me. Please."

He lifted a brow at the plea in her voice. "Come now, lass, what ails ye?"

"I just ... I just don't want to be alone." She suddenly felt small. Vulnerable. A bit ashamed, especially after the way they had just come together and made the rest of the world cease to matter. "I don't want you to leave me."

"Homesick?" he asked gently, sitting down on the bed beside her, and she felt his word pierce her heart. He knew. He understood. She thought of her family in a distant England she would probably never see again, and blinked back a sudden, unexpected sting of tears.

What is wrong with me?

"What's the matter, love?"

"I don't know."

He leaned over and wiped away the single tear tracking out of the corner of her cheek, down her temples and into her hair. "I'm here for ye, Nerissa. I always will be."

"I know."

"We'll make a home together. Here, if ye like. We'll be happy."

"I know," she repeated in a little voice, and felt a hot tear trickling out of the other eye, now.

He pulled her up against him, stroking her hair, just letting her rest in his nearness and strength as she wept quietly against his shirt.

"Things'll get better, *mo grá*. Do ye like it enough to make our home here?"

"I could live anywhere as long as you're there."

"Brendan's my cousin. And he tells me his sister Eveleen lives here, too. Only family I've got left except for Deirdre, and she's off in England. I wouldn't mind it, and it's close to Boston, too. Useful, in my profession."

"The wooden houses might take some getting used to."

"So we'll buy or build a brick one."

"And the winters here are colder than in England."

"No matter, I'll keep ye warm."

She smiled. "I would like that."

He eased her back down to the bed, pushing an arm beneath her back and rolling her up against himself to plant a kiss on her forehead. "I love ye, Nerissa."

She burrowed closer to him. "I love you too, Ruaidri. You make my life complete."

"Feel better now?"

"Yes."

And she did. All was, at least for the time being, right in her world. They lay there together listening to the rain tapping against the window and the wind beginning to die. She snuggled closer to him and idly traced the hollow beneath his collarbones with her finger, and it was then that a memory came to her, one that she'd put away at the time but now, in the close darkness, brought out to be examined.

"Ruaidri," she said quietly, "you were sharp with your cousin earlier. When he called you that odd name ... 'Roddy."

It was a moment before he answered. "Aye, maybe I was, a bit."

"Why?" She gazed over at him, confused. "Why this aversion to a name you once went by? I'm sure he meant no harm."

He put a weary arm over his forehead, and gazed up at the ceiling. "Ah, Nerissa. I suppose that if I tell ye I'm finally gettin' sleepy, ye'll still demand an answer."

"You have all morning to sleep in."

"And you have all day to get yer answer."

"But you know I'm impatient. And the fact that you're suddenly too tired to tell me makes me all the more curious."

He said nothing for a long moment, and even in the darkness she could see that the question pained him. She immediately regretted it.

"I'm sorry," she said, releasing him. "I can wait. Let's go to sleep, Ruaidri. You can tell me later."

"Might as well tell ye now."

"It was an innocent question."

"I know, love."

"You don't have to tell me if you don't want to."

"There are a lot of things I don't want to tell ye but should. My aversion to what was once my nickname is just one of them."

She moved up and over him, and rested her head on his chest. His shirt was damp and warm with his body heat, and beneath the fine fabric she could feel the little wiry hairs of his chest against her cheek, could hear the quiet beat of his heart.

"My da was a fisherman who came down from Mayo and settled in Connemara after he met and fell in love with my mother," he finally said. They named me Ruaidri, and a few short years later, my sister Deirdre came along. We scraped a living off the land, a better one off the sea, but it was a hard life, Nerissa, bein' Irish and servin' an English landowner."

"I remember you telling me that, once."

"Then I told you about the English comin' to our little bay, and the press-gang takin' me when I was still a young lad. There was no one to support me mam and little sister, as my da had died by then and they were left to the mercy of charity and neighbors. I never saw my mother again and when I next met Deirdre it was here, in America, and she was all grown up and married to the very man who'd led the press gang that took me."

She sensed his guilt that he'd not been there for his family but said nothing, instead just letting his heart beat against her palm.

"I was forced to serve the Royal Navy for years," he

said, his voice quiet in the darkness. "Worked my way up, and had I been born to privilege and wealth instead of poor Irishfolk, maybe I'd have been able to make lieutenant. But there was nothin' in the Royal Navy for me but scorn, contempt, and the lash. No chance for a fellow like me to ever get ahead or find equal footin' in a race who looked down on, would always look down on, a poor Irishman. In '74, I found a way off the ship I was servin' at the time in Boston, introduced myself to some wealthy Bostonians and convinced them to give me command of a little sloop. Smugglin', ye know ... a man can get rich off it, and I did pretty damned well. Knew the ways of the English, knew their strengths and weaknesses, knew the waters around Boston like the back of me hand."

"What did you smuggle?"

"Oh, anything that needed to be brought in. The English had shut down the port of Boston and nothin' was getting through. People were starvin'. They needed food, and when Sam Adams, Joseph Warren, and John Hancock approached me about runnin' guns and powder into Boston so that the rebels could be armed, well, I didn't have to think too long or hard about it." He looked up at the ceiling, the branches of the tree outside throwing moving shadows against the plaster. "I was called Roddy, then. A childhood nickname that grew out of my initials—R. O. D. Or maybe Roderick, the English version, I guess, of me given name. Hated the name, I did, but I was a tough, scrappy cub, hot tempered and easily riled to fisticuffs, and the lads liked to call me that because it was guaranteed to put my hackles up and bring on a fight. Figured out one day that it was easier just to let it go ... there were other things far more important to fight over than a name." He made a little noise of remembrance. "Like food."

Something in her heart hurt. It pained her to think of him as a child, hungry and thin, probably existing on fish, onion soup, whatever his family could eke out of a stingy land while she had never known an empty belly, poverty or want, a single day of her life. But she knew him well enough to know that pity would only irritate him.

"I don't see you as a 'Roddy,'" she said, instead. "I could never see you as anyone but Ruaidri."

"Well, ye didn't know me back in '75, and a damned good thing ye didn't Nerissa, as lookin' back, I didn't like the person I'd become. I was good at the smugglin', and I was good, very good, at twistin' the tail of the British lion, that hated country that had robbed me of my youth, my family. Vengeance felt sweet, and it was. But success and the huzzahs of the people to whom I smuggled food and arms ... it got to me. I was the local hero, and my head swelled with the knowledge that I was their savior, their Robin Hood. Someone started callin' me the Irish Pirate, and the name stuck. I reveled in it. I grew proud, boastful, cocky ... thoroughly unpleasant with my success ... obnoxious ... and careless."

"You got caught?"

"Aye, I got caught. And deserved it, I might say. Pride goeth before a fall and my fall was a long, hard, humiliatin' one. It was Captain Lord—the very fellow who'd led that long ago press gang, the husband of my little sister—who got the better of me one night durin' a smugglin' operation. Next thing I knew my crew was in the gaol and I was locked up aboard his frigate and the town was calling for his head—and the Royal Navy, for mine. 'Tis doubtful they'd even have given me a fair trial ... my fate was to die, and to die publicly. To make an example of me to the rebels."

"But you're here, now...."

"Aye, I ... escaped."

She heard the slight hesitation in his voice.

"Escaped?"

"Let's just say I had some help ... from the very man

who captured me. It was tearin' him up inside and he was about to lose the woman he loved—my sister—over it. So he found a way for me to escape with neither of us lookin' bad. We've forgiven each other, and while we might not be best friends, we get on all right, Christian and I."

"So why the aversion to the name 'Roddy'?"

"Because it was the name of my childhood, the name I associate with pride, arrogance, and a certain ugliness of character that brought about my downfall. I associate that name with humiliation and embarrassment. With youth. I'm a better man than that, Nerissa, and lookin' back on those times I'm filled with shame and disgust about how I behaved, crowin' like a rooster at sunup to anyone who'd listen. I've grown up since then. I'm no longer the person I was when I was Roddy. I wanted to leave all that in my past, so I scuppered it, along with the name that went with it ... and took back my real name. The one given to me by my da and mam. Ruaidri."

She lay there, her cheek pillowed on his chest for a long moment. He had never struck her as a prideful or boastful man. A confident one, yes, and one sometimes given to judgments that some might have thought impulsive, but a braggart? Ruaidri?

No, she couldn't see it.

But she could see something else, and her feminine intuition told her that there was more to this story than what he'd just told her.

"You're holding something back," she said quietly.

He said nothing.

"Aren't you?"

"The baring of one's soul is rather like stripping a bed, isn't it, lass? One sheet at a time."

"But there's something else. Something you don't want to tell me."

In the darkness, his face closed up, and his mouth

took on the firmness it did when he dug in about something. "Ye're a good lass, Nerissa. Aye, there's more ... but ye're here with me, in my arms, and we're both happy. Let's savor that. There are some things best talked about at another time."

"Was it about a woman?"

He said nothing.

"It was, wasn't it?"

"Nerissa, love... not now."

Not now. She frowned, feeling a deep and unfamiliar twinge of jealousy that twisted like a snake in her heart, a sudden presence amongst them that had not been there a moment earlier. So it *was* about a woman, then. A woman he didn't want to talk about. Anger made the skin on her back seem to prickle and she willed herself not to be a shrew, not to push him when he wasn't ready to be pushed, to just let the matter go so it wouldn't spoil things between them. But it stung, his reluctance to tell her. And she suddenly felt awkward, lying here on his chest while a few inches away, his brain was filled with memories of another woman that he would not discuss. Had he loved her, then? Loved this other woman as much as he claimed to love her? Nerissa felt suddenly excluded, and deep in her soul, cold.

Wordlessly, she pushed herself up and off his chest and lay stiffly beside him, both of them now staring up at the ceiling.

Moments ticked by. The branch continued to scratch against the windowpane, and somewhere in the house, a clock chimed the five o' clock hour, joined by another and another until all were going off in near unison.

In the darkness, he reached down beneath the blankets and found her hand.

"This is why I don't want to discuss it," he said. "Now ye're angry."

"I'm angry because you're my husband and you're keeping secrets from me. It hurts."

"We have a lifetime to get to know each other. And I don't want to talk about another woman right here, right now. I don't want her here in this bed with us, and her name's not fit to be uttered in the same room as yours. She's in the past, Nerissa. Leave her there."

"Did you love her?" she said in a tight little voice.

"Aye, I did. And she was right for Roddy. Suited him quite well, in fact. But not Ruaidri."

The snake that was uncoiling inside her heart twisted and turned some more. Nerissa didn't know why this hurt so much, why it should bother her, but it did. Was this unknown woman the real reason he no longer went by the hated nickname? Because she was associated with it?

"What was she like?"

"I don't want to talk about her."

"You can't even tell me her name?"

He sighed, released her hand, and with a sharp, irritated motion, threw back the covers, his feet already on the rug. He sat there for a moment, raking his hands through his hair, making his curls even wilder, frizzier. His breeches lay over the back of a chair and rising, he snatched them up and began to step into them. "I think I need to go take a walk."

She didn't know what to say. She didn't want him to go. She didn't want him to stay, either, if there was going to be a sudden coldness between them. She wanted things to be the way they'd been when they'd spoken of Newburyport and their future and he had held her when she'd felt unexpectedly wobbly, and she suddenly hated this unknown woman who had, as her husband predicted, come between them.

She sat up in bed, pulling the blankets up to her chin as she watched him dress in the darkness. "Come back to bed."

"I'm awake now." He reached for his waistcoat and began to button it.

"I'm sorry. I ... just can't stand secrets between us."

"You need to learn patience, Nerissa. There's a season for everything, and the sharin' of a person's past is one of them." He drew on his frock coat, rooted around in the pocket and found the piece of ribbon with which he'd earlier tied his hair, quickly securing it once more.

"Where are you going?"

"I told you, for a walk. There's an apothecary in Market Square, maybe they'll have something to quell your nausea besides ginger."

"At five o'clock in the morning?"

'Twill be five-thirty by the time I get there, and if they're not open for business yet I'll wait. Go back to sleep. I'll be back and maybe both of us'll be in better temper by breakfast." He came back to the bed and dropped a kiss on her forehead as he did every morning, but the usual tender warmth was gone and she could sense the penned-up frustration to which she'd pushed him. Anger gnawed at her insides and again, she felt the press of tears.

Wordlessly, he picked up his tricorne, opened the door and slipped out into the hallway. There were a few squeaks on the stairs as he descended them, a distant click of a quietly opened and shut door, and then he was gone.

The tears spilled over then, and a fresh wave of anger, this time, with herself.

Oh, what is wrong with me? Nerissa thought, and raised her fist to punch at her husband's pillow. And then she saw the impression his head had left on the white cotton. The tears coursing down her cheeks, she pulled it to her, buried her face in the hollow, and let it muffle the sound of her sobs.

Chapter Thirty

He had taken the coward's way out and he knew it.

Ruaidri stalked down the drive in the darkness, past a large anchor that lay nestled within a bed of wet autumn leaves, the night air wet and cold around him. The gale was blowing itself out, the worst of it far out over the Atlantic. Dawn was still a ways off and the scent of the sea lay heavily in the night air. He drew it deeply into his lungs, trying to clear his head.

You took the coward's way out, you sack of shite. You put her off, built a fence around that part of your life you don't want to talk about or share. You think you'll lose her if she were to know, don't you? Fool. Coward. She presented the perfect time and place to tell her what happened, the real reason you refuse to let anyone call you Roddy, the real reason you'll never again fight a duel or let yourself look back into the past or think too much about your life before it *all happened.*

Yes, *it*.

He reached the High Street and proceeded through the darkness, rain dripping from the branches overhead and tapping against his hat. Why wasn't life ever anything but complicated? If there was anything Nerissa should be angry with him about, it was the fact that he still planned to take her brother to Adams. A better man would set him free even at risk of his career, as

Christian had done for him and the woman *he* had loved. A better man would not be stalking all alone through a muddy street in the dark, past sleeping houses, but would be back in bed with his wife and facing the demons that both drove and repelled him.

All alone.

Not quite.

Ruaidri wasn't sure exactly when the churning anger —all of it toward himself—lifted enough for him to become suddenly aware of his surroundings, to realize that he was being followed. The hair on the back of his neck rose and he resisted the urge to pause and look around to find this threat, knowing instead that it was smarter to keep on, to pretend that he wasn't aware that he was no longer alone so he could keep an advantage. He considered his situation and his surroundings. The street ahead was empty, the night as silent as the tomb, and not even a dog barked in the heavy wet darkness. But his senses had come on high alert, and he knew with a certainty he didn't question that the presence he now felt was a hostile one.

He continued to walk, the rain, now a raw drizzle, cold against his face. He was not afraid. Newburyport didn't exactly look to be a place where footpads or highwaymen would thrive, and most common thieves were likely to be up to their usual mischief earlier in the night, when the taverns let out and sailors were reeling back to their ships, drunk.

No, this hostile presence was purposeful, and personal.

Intent.

Gaining on me.

There. A branch blown down by the gale, as thick around as his wrist and as long as his thigh. He bent down to pick it up, sensed a whoosh from behind and spun on his heel, the makeshift weapon already coming up to protect his face—

Bam! A wicked length of steel crashed down where his head had been not a second before, impaling itself in the wood Ruaidri still held in both hands. He shoved hard, using his attacker's momentum to send him staggering backward, the sword still buried in the wood and splitting it nearly in half.

Ruaidri broke the branch over his knee, kicked the useless sword and the wood in which it was impaled out of reach, and instinctively dropped into a crouch.

"Ye fuckin' bastard," he snarled, gripping the remaining length of the branch and trusting his life to its splintered, jagged end. It felt good in his hand. A worthy defense, an even better weapon. He moved to his right, trying to discern his attacker's weakness. "What the bloody divil ye tryin' to do, kill me?"

The attacker, dressed in a black greatcoat, calmly reached into his pocket and withdrew a pistol. "That is exactly what I am trying to do and I can assure you, you *parasite*, that I will not fail in my attempt."

"Who are you?"

"I am Lucien de Montforte."

Lucien de Montforte.

The Duke of Blackheath.

"Her brother," he said aloud, as the two circled each other. Oh, why was he not surprised?

"Yes, her *brother*. Surely, you did not think your offenses against my family would go unchallenged, did you?"

"I thought ye were in England, not skulking around out here in the dark at five in the mornin'. What kind of pervert are ye?"

A muscle twitched in the duke's jaw. "Even you should know that only a fool would go in blindly without noting the lay of the land or planning his attack. Another ten minutes and I might've knocked on your host's door and demanded the release of my siblings, but you rather made that all quite unnecessary with your unexpected appearance." He calmly produced a handkerchief and wiped the barrel of the pistol, his eyes as black as the night around them. "It was not hard to identify you, given the physical descriptions that have been given me."

Ruaidri eyed the pistol. If he were quick, he could disarm the duke and do it before either of them got hurt. But out of the corner of his eye he saw movement, and two shapes materializing out of the darkness, one dressed in the uniform of a Royal Navy officer.

A complication.

Nothing more.

Blackheath put the handkerchief back in his pocket. His smile was cold and deadly. "Where are my siblings?"

The duke had a still, deadly, urbane way of delivering his words, a deliberate calm veiled in steel and wrapped in a nauseating upper-class English accent that scraped at Ruaidri's nerves and made him think, fleetingly, of English superiority and Irish abuse, of class privileges, subjugation, and land ownership denied. The knowledge that this man considered him as lowly as a maggot and most likely saw him as less than human was enough to make him want to lunge in and finish this fight. And he could, too. The duke would be trained with sword and pistol, probably quite deadly. But he would fight like a gentleman, and for the first time in his life Ruaidri was glad that he himself was no such creature, that he was nothing but a cur who'd been raised in the dirt and had had to fight his way out of pubs and scrapes and everything in-between from the time he was a starving Irish lad in distant Connemara.

The duke would fight like a gentleman.

Ruaidri would not.

And suddenly Blackheath, his face all but indistinguishable in the darkness under his tricorne, represented everything Ruaidri had ever hated about the English, every slight that he as an Irishman had ever suffered, and he took a savage delight in throwing down a gauntlet of his own.

"Yer brother's me prisoner, and yer sister is back home—*in my bed.*"

Blackheath's smile faded and he raised the pistol. He put a hand over its pan, shielding the powder from the drizzle, and Ruaidri heard the silent, deadly click as he cocked the weapon and began to advance. Beneath the tricorne his eyes were black, burning with controlled rage, and Ruaidri had time only to credit his attacker with a modicum of self control in the face of such a deliberate taunt before Blackheath, the pistol gripped in both hands and extended to aim point-blank at Ruaidri's face, moved in.

"I've waited for this moment for the last two months," he seethed. "Nobody ... *nobody* harms my family. Ever."

The duke moved purposely, confidently, closer.

Ruaidri held his ground, his own hands coming up in a gesture of surrender, the broken branch gripped and ready in his right fist and his attention divided between the duke and the two figures watching in the darkness. *Now*, his senses screamed as Blackheath moved in. *Now!* In that last second he lunged forward, knocking the duke's arm high with his own weapon, grabbing his wrist and flinging him hard to the muddy street. The pistol went flying.

God help me, I don't want to hurt him. It would kill her ... she'd hate me forever.

Blackheath was getting up, his eyes murderous. Calculating.

"So it's to be like this, then," he murmured.

"You started it."

"*You* started it when you abducted my little sister."

"Let it go, Blackheath."

"I'll let it go when you're dead."

"She's happy. Whatever comes of this fight will destroy that happiness and break her heart."

Blackheath was advancing. Again, Ruaidri moved back, the splintered branch still in his hand, ready to repel another attack as the duke moved forward, unbeaten, unapologetic, furious in a way that might have made the blood of a lesser man run cold.

Furious in a way that would, Ruaidri hoped, make him careless. Prone to make a mistake that could let him end this with minimal bloodshed.

"You have no idea what makes her happy," Blackheath said coldly. "*None.*"

"Considering she chose to make her life with me here in America and not back in that ancient pit of snobbery and privilege ye call home, I think I've a damned good idea."

"You forced her, you cunning knave."

"No, I did not."

Ruaidri moved back, and out of the corner of his eye saw the two other men drawing their swords, ready to assist the duke should he need help. "Ye're used to having things yer way, Blackheath, but yer sphere of power and influence is in the halls of British government and society, not on a dark street in a little town in America. You and I are on that dark street in America, and ye've just met your match."

The duke was stripping off his muddy greatcoat now, tossing it aside.

"You want to fight like a common piece of scum now, do you?" he asked, also removing his hat.

"Given that's all ye think I am, 'twould seem to me I have no choice." He gripped his weapon. "Shear off, Blackheath. I'm warnin' ye."

Blackheath was unbuttoning his coat, pulling his arms out of the sleeves, tossing it atop his greatcoat until he was down to just waistcoat and shirt in the wet drizzle. "You abducted my baby sister and probably raped her. You abducted my little brother and for all I know might have killed him. You harmed members of my family ... *and you want me to let this go?*"

At that moment, the two other men moved in, one heading to Ruaidri's left, the other to his right. That one came in fast, tackling him around the neck with one arm and pummeling him hard with the other. One punch slammed into his jaw and lit his night up with stars, but as Blackheath's accomplice came in again Ruaidri twisted, clubbed him in the throat and dropped him, choking, to the mud. A second later the weight of the other thug hit him in the back. A flash of steel, a twist of his body and Ruaidri drove his elbow viciously back to catch the man in the ribs hard enough to crack bone and spin him around on his heel. A hard knee between the legs and he, too, dropped to the mud, there to lie moaning in agony.

"Impressive," the duke allowed.

Breathing hard and still brandishing his splintered club, Ruaidri eyed the duke as the two began to circle each other once more. "Three against one and ye still can't manage me. Got any more hired thugs in your employ, Blackheath? Odds too long for you against one Irish *parasite?*"

The duke, his flat, cold gaze never leaving Ruaidri's, sidestepped to the first fellow and extended a hand to help him up. The man rose, swaying, his eyes wide with grudging respect as he eyed Ruaidri and prepared to come in for more.

"That is enough, Cooper," Blackheath murmured. "I will handle this."

The second attacker was pulling himself up, grimacing with pain and dressed in the blue coat and breeches of the Royal Navy. A lieutenant, Ruaidri thought. The other looked like a common seaman. No matter, both had come from whatever damned ship had brought them here as protection for Blackheath. They'd be easy to deal with and so would the duke, who wouldn't know how to fight as anything other than a gentleman.

And in that moment Blackheath proved him wrong.

The duke's fragile veneer of control was gone. He snatched up the lieutenant's sword and with a guttural snarl, came in hard at Ruaidri, swinging viciously at his ribs. Ruaidri spun and kicked upward but the duke was onto him now, no longer allowing any surprises, no longer expecting a fair and gentlemanly fight and his boot hit only empty air. The sword slashed into his coat, parting the fabric, parting his skin, sending a sudden flow of blood down his side, damn, damn, *damn*. No time for that, he thought, no time to register the pain or what the blood loss would cost him because he knew that to give his attention to anything but his next move would only result in the death that Blackheath was intent on delivering him—and he was fighting for his life.

Blackheath came in again, feinting and lunging with the sword, his mouth tightening with resolve and his eyes going colder, blacker, deadlier with every parry that Ruaidri made with his chunk of tree-branch. Both men circled each other now, neither giving an inch, both of them looking for weaknesses in his opponent.

"For the record," Ruaidri said, "I never raped yer sister."

"Spare me the details, I don't want to know." Blackheath was circling him again, taking his measure, trying to find a way to end this.

"I married her."

"The marriage will be annulled."

"The marriage has been consummated for the past six weeks."

"*I do not recognize your marriage.*"

"Yer brother does," Ruaidri said, moving in a circle around Blackheath, the branch still gripped in his hand.

"In fact, he gave his permission for it. Told me if I didn't marry her he'd kill me."

Something flickered in Blackheath's nightshade-black stare, and out of the corner of his eye, Ruaidri saw the two seamen exchange glances.

"Andrew has no authority to be making such decisions. I am her guardian."

"She's past the age where she needs your consent."

Ruaidri felt the blood oozing out of the wound in his side and knew that time would soon be running out for him. His body, so recently compromised and so recently healed, was not infallible and he could see in Blackheath's thin smile that the duke knew it too, was now prolonging this dance of death in order to let Ruaidri's own body do him in. The matter decided him. Gripping the splintered branch in his hand, he lunged, Blackheath's shoulder the target for his makeshift spear, and as the duke pivoted neatly out of the way Ruaidri found himself tackled once more from behind, this time by the seaman with the lethal fists.

"Where's the lady?" he shouted, both arms locked around Ruaidri's throat and hauling him backward. "Damn you, tell us now or this ends right here!"

Home in bed, Ruaidri wanted to say, but the words would not come because the man had his arms locked around his throat, squeezing off his air. The stick fell from his hand as he clawed at the thug's wrist, finally hurling himself forward and the man with him until they both tumbled hard to the street, there to begin pounding each other until mud filled Ruaidri's mouth and the split in his side opened like a seam coming unthreaded and his knuckles came apart against his attacker's teeth. Someone grabbed the back of his shirt and hair and yanked him hard off his opponent and then Blackheath's white, gentlemanly knuckles collided with his jaw, sending shock waves through his brain and turning his knees to water. The duke hit him again and again and again until the blood was running in rivulets from his mouth and his world was a sea of stars. He went limp, grabbed up the broken stick as he fell and smashed it hard against Blackheath's ankle, hard enough to knock the leg out from under him. The duke went down, twisting and kicking out hard, his muddy boot grazing Ruaidri's skull; for a brief moment they both lay there, stunned—and then Blackheath lunged to his feet, hauled Ruaidri to his, yanked his head back by his queue and drew a knife.

"*Lucien!*"

A woman's voice, penetrating the soup that had replaced his brain, the cold blade against his throat—

"Lucien you stop it right now, do you hear me?! STOP IT!"

Ruaidri had a brief moment to wonder how and why Nerissa was out here in the darkness and then the duke, with a vicious curse, shoved him away, hard. Ruaidri went down, landing face-first in the mud, gamely pushing himself up and out of it once more to sway there on hands and knees, the first light of dawn showing all the little pebbles in the mud, a puddle edged with boot prints, someone's feet, all revolving in a slow, sickening circle a few inches from his blurry eyes.

"Stand back, Nerissa. This is none of your affair."

"It is too my affair! That is my husband you're killing and you will stop it this instant, do you hear me? Stop it!"

"Nobody ... *nobody* ... hurts my little sister!" Blackheath roared, his face twisted with rage, and as Ruaidri struggled to keep from falling on his face in the mud, the duke drew back his booted foot and prepared to deliver the fatal blow.

His wife's scream ... Blackheath's boot stopping before it could connect with his head ... and Nerissa, oh God, his sweet Sunshine sagging in a surprised Brendan Merrick's arms as he charged onto the scene with Andrew and the feisty little Mira, now shouting the house down around the mighty Duke of Blackheath.

"You blasted, bleedin', pond-sucking *idiot*, look what in hell ye've gone and done, you festering pile of bull manure!"

The duke stood there, blinking, the insane rage fading from his eyes as he beheld the shocking sight of his little sister lying unconscious in a stranger's arms while a tiny sprite of a Yankee woman gave him the dressing-down of his life.

"Well?" she raged, stamping her foot. "Are ye going to just stand there like an imbecile? Go help yer brother-in-law to his feet before he drowns in a puddle, you no-good sack of sh—"

"Mira, enough," said Brendan, still holding a limp Nerissa. "He's the Duke of—"

"I don't give a rat's ass who he is, he's more concerned with killing his brother-in-law than finding out what the tarnal hell's wrong with his own sister! You men, you're all thicker than a Maine fog, every damned one of ye! Fighting over the poor girl when she's in such a condition!"

Ruaidri struggled to his feet, staggered a few steps, reeled and fell once more. He tried to find and collect his thoughts, but they were nothing but a flock of sparrows flitting around the birdhouse that was his stunned brain, some going in, most alighting elsewhere, all of them elusive and unable to be caught.

"Condition?" he managed, but nobody heard him.

Brendan had handed Nerissa to Lord Andrew and was reaching a hand down to help him up. "*An bhfuil tú ceart go leor, mo chol ceathrair?*"

"I'm fine," He grasped his cousin's hand, grateful for the support as he found his feet. "Just ... catching ... my breath."

"What condition?" the duke demanded, his jaw hardening.

"You're as dumb as an ox in a blindfold if ye can't figure it out!" Mira went to Nerissa as she began pushing against Andrew's chest and her brother gently set her down.

"What condition?" Ruaidri echoed.

Mira turned on him. "The condition that *you* put her in!"

"What?!" thundered Blackheath, his face darkening with rage once more.

"What?" echoed Ruaidri, still trying to stuff the sparrows into their little birdhouse and now finding there were even more of them.

"She's going to have a baby, you numbskulls!"

Stunned, shocked silence. Blackheath's mouth opened in horror, and Andrew lunged forward to grab his arm before he could finish killing his equally stunned brother-in-law.

Nerissa, as shocked as the rest of them, leaned heavily against Andrew. "B-*ba*by?"

Mira shook her head, planted her forehead in her palm, and walked a little distance away.

And Lucien exploded.

"That's it, you're done for, O' Devir, you are bloody well done for, *this is the final insult*!"

He shook off his brother and lunged for Ruaidri. Nerissa, recovering both her wits and her composure, turned on him.

"If you so much as *touch* him I'll walk away from here and you will never see me again, Lucien! *Ever!*"

The duke froze.

She put a hand on her brother's chest and shoved him backward, away from her husband. "How *dare* you," Her eyes were hard and bright with furious unshed tears. She sloshed through the mud to the man she loved, making it clear where her loyalties lay. "*How dare you do this to us.*"

Ruaidri concentrated on curling and uncurling his

toes, trying to stay conscious as his head swam with confusion and the blood oozed from his side and the words *condition* and *baby* repeated themselves over and over again in his brain. The lass was giving her brother a drubbing that even he hadn't been able to deliver.

"Baby?" he asked, but she did not hear him.

She turned on the duke. "Ever since I was a child you've treated me like a doll, protected and sheltered me, manipulated the events of my life to suit your own wishes, told me what I could have, what I could do, where I could go, whom I should marry. *You wrecked my life* with what you did to Perry, you robbed me of my chance for happiness with a man I loved, you ruined him and you nearly ruined me and I will not, I repeat, I will *not*, let you do the same to Ruaidri, do you understand me?"

The duke brushed a bit of mud off his elbow. "He's a dirty, grasping, Irish maggot, my dear. You can do better."

The lieutenant rubbed at his jaw. "Sure knows how to fight," he lamented.

"Enough," Lucien said coldly. "You, Nerissa, are coming back to England with me. You, too," he added, with a hard look at Lord Andrew. "This marriage will be annulled."

Andrew stood unmoving. "How did you even find us?"

"Quite by chance, I can assure you. Our frigate recaptured a cutter taken off the coast of Nova Scotia by two American privateers only hours before. We were told that they and the brig *Tigershark* were on their way here. We landed a boat in darkness on some godforsaken beach a mile or two distant and an inquiry at the docks made it easy to determine your whereabouts." He turned back to his sister. "My patience, Nerissa, is nearing its end. Come with me, please."

"No."

"Nerissa, I will not ask again."

"Did you not hear a single word I just said?" she cried angrily. "I just told you to get out of my life, to leave me alone, to let me make my own choices, to respect them! I *chose* to marry Ruaidri, he didn't force me, I married him because I love him!"

"What?"

"*I said I love him*, damn you!"

Lucien just stood there blinking, his face a dreadful mask of shock, anger, and immeasurable pain.

"And furthermore," Nerissa said, her voice shaking with rage, "Don't think for one moment you can talk me out of this, make me see reason, manipulate events to bend them to your will or convince me to go back to England. I don't want to go back to England. I *can't* go back to England—"

"Yes, I know all about what you did, my dear, back on that ship. I can assure you, I can ... fix things, so that your name is cleared—"

"I don't *care* if my name is cleared, I'm not going back. My home is here with my husband and my ..." she put a hand on her still-flat belly, and the tears began to flow down her cheeks, "my baby."

"Christ," Lucien swore. He had turned white and looked as though he was going to be sick. He walked a little distance away and retrieved his pistol, his back turned to them all as he gazed at the glow in the eastern sky over the Merrimack. His hands, the knuckles raw and bleeding, were clasped in a death grip behind his back.

"If you will not annul this sham of a marriage, Nerissa, then I will find a way to make you a widow." He turned and looked at his sister. "Unless that's the fate you want for this man you think you love, let go of him and come with us. We're leaving this wretched hellhole and going home."

Brendan stepped forward. "Your Grace." His voice

was affable, but there was something in his kind amber eyes that was firm and unyielding, steel beneath a polite smile and easy-going manner. "'Tis my home you're talking about, and a lovely home it is, too. Faith, I do hope you were only speaking in the heat of the moment."

"Captain Merrick. Another turncoat, I see. Last I saw of you was back in '74 when you were in the Royal Navy and were about to take Charles over the seas to Boston. I've read about your exploits in our newspapers." His eyes hardened. "What is this place, a damned den of rebels?"

"We're Americans!" Mira shot back, "and proud of it!"

Brendan smiled tightly. "I will forgive the insult, Your Grace, as enough blood has been shed here today and there's no need for more. Now please, come with me. This den of rebels, as you call it, is waking up around us and will not show you, an Englishman and an aristocrat at that, the mercy my cousin has. In fact, I daresay you're not safe here at all. Come with me, all of you. You can stay with us until we figure this out."

"I am not staying with you or anyone else, I am taking my family and we are all going back to England."

"How?"

"The frigate that brought me here is cruising just offshore. Her captain is waiting for us."

Brendan shrugged. "I daresay his wait will be a long one, as there's no way he can get into that river with the piers sunken across its entrance, and no way that any ship here will allow him to. Oh, no, Your Grace. I'm afraid you're my guest until we get this sorted out, at which time either Ruaidri or I will bring you down to New York and deliver you into the hands of your countrymen, since that's the nearest city that they happen to still have a stronghold in. Until then, since you refuse my offer of hospitality in our home, you can make your quarters on my ship. I'm sure you'll find her quite comfortable."

Blackheath just stared at him. He was outnumbered, beaten, and he knew it. He glared at Ruaidri, his eyes murderous. "You'll die for this. I promise." And then, to Andrew, "You're coming with me."

"No, he's not." Ruaidri had managed to net his flitting thoughts and stuff them back into his pounding head enough to finally trust his own voice. "My mission as an officer in the Continental Navy was to bring that explosive back from England and hand it over to John Adams. I'm sure Lord Andrew will be free to make his own choices durin' both Adam's interview and whatever follows it."

"I will not permit you to hand my brother over to some rebel knave."

"Ye don't have a say in the matter."

Sensing the tension rising between the two once more, Brendan seized the duke's elbow. "Come, the town's waking up and you're not safe here," he said, his tone growing increasingly urgent. "Let me take you all out to *Kestrel*."

"I am not finished here, Merrick."

"Yes," Ruaidri said flatly, pulling Nerissa close. "You are."

Blackheath's eyes were beginning to glitter with cunning intelligence and deadly promise. He looked at Ruaidri and didn't say a word.

He didn't have to.

"I told you before," Ruaidri said. "You're no longer commanding the world around you from the House of Lords or that miserable pile of rock that's your ancestral home. You're standing on an American street, surrounded by Yankee sea captains, myself included, whose decision 'twill be as to whether ye ever make it back England."

Lucien stared coldly at him. "I should have killed you when I had the chance."

"You did have the chance and you didn't. Just as I had the chance, and didn't. And ye know why I didn't, Blackheath? Ye know why I held back during our fight? 'Twas because of yer sister and the fact I love her. Don't think for a moment I couldn't have ended yer life had I wanted to, but I wouldn't give her that grief. She's suffered enough."

"Big words from a beaten man," Lucien said coldly.

"Not so beaten. American jails are as capable of holding English dukes as they are British tars, soldiers and sea officers. Your gettin' out of this *hellhole* will depend on my charity, along with my cousin's. And the good people of this town, who don't have a whole lot of use for lofty English ideas and an aristocracy who think they rule the world. Those days are over. Done with." He offered his arm to Nerissa. "Good day, yer Grace. Perhaps when next we meet, yer way of announcin' yerself will be a bit more ... gentlemanly."

"You should have killed him when you had the chance," Cooper murmured beneath his breath.

"I tried."

Lucien watched them go. Beside him, Andrew stood sullenly, obviously torn between any misguided friendship he had with the Parasite and joining his brother. A little distance away, Merrick's gaze had moved to the waterfront, past the many masts silhouetted against the brightening eastern horizon to the river's mouth. It didn't take a genius to know what he was thinking—of the frigate waiting out there beyond it, a frigate that, O' Devir had made clear, was now about as accessible to him as a walk on the moon and was now fair game for any particularly enterprising Yankee sea captain—and Merrick, Lucien knew, was particularly enterprising.

He, Lucien de Montforte, was stranded here in this godforsaken hellhole.

And as the Parasite had reminded him, powerless.

He longed to smash something to vent his frustration, to forego the constraints of his breeding and heritage and finish this with either pistol or sword, and then he realized there was one sure way to finish it and it had nothing to do with sullying his hands with more physical violence.

"Nerissa," he called after the retreating pair.

She turned and looked at him, her eyes wounded, the tears still wet upon her face.

"It is bad enough that you would marry a man so far beneath you," he said. "It is bad enough that you would marry a man that your family does not accept, a man for whom you have thrown away your birthright, heritage and country, a man who will never be able to keep you in the comfort and luxury in which you've been raised and to which you've been accustomed." He waited for his words to sink in, and then he dropped the killing blow. "But for you to knowingly walk off with an accused killer, a man who murdered his very best friend...."

Bang. He saw the fatal shot hit home as the blood drained from the Parasite's face.

"I don't know what you're talking about," Nerissa said uncertainly, and tried to continue on.

"Don't you? Do you mean this vermin you've wed hasn't told you?" Lucien's smile was coldly triumphant. "Josiah Brown. A duel, 1776. You shot him, didn't you, O' Devir? Your very best friend in the world, and all over a woman you both purported to love." The blows he'd dealt the Irishman during the fight were nothing compared to the damage his words now caused, and Lucien felt a dark and savage satisfaction as he watched stunned denial and fear, yes fear, steal the color from that rascal's hated face. "Dolores Foley was the wench's name, wasn't it? And she's dead now, too."

The Irishman looked as though he'd been stabbed

through the heart with a knitting needle. "I didn't kill her."

"Of course you didn't," Lucien said loftily, and gave a dramatic sigh. "You didn't need to. But you did kill Brown, you were convicted and sentenced to hang, and it was only your friend John Adams's brilliance that got you out of the noose in an appeal that should never have been made."

O' Devir flushed with rage. "Ye know *nothin'* of what happened."

"Oh, I know all of it. Have you told my sister about this particular little ... tidbit of your past?"

By the dawning horror in Nerissa's face, he had not.

"I think we've all heard enough," Brendan said, nodding for his wife to join him as he took the duke by the elbow and tried to force him away. "Some things are over and done with, and that's one of them."

"Ah, well ... always best to know everything there is to know about a person before you marry them," Lucien murmured. His smile was pitiless and cold. "You're correct, Merrick. It is time to leave."

Chapter Thirty-One

The walk back to the house seemed to take forever. Nerissa was reeling from shock. A baby, which certainly explained her nausea these past few days and her sudden penchant for tears. Lucien showing up here in all his high-handed glory, Lucien who had once said he would never again meddle in another's life after his manipulations had nearly killed his wife and taken the life of his unborn child, Lucien who did not seem to have changed one iota, *not one damned bit*.

The tears clawed at the back of her nose, prickled her eyes and began to spill down her cheeks.

But Ruaidri....

He walked beside her, silent, bleeding, enigmatic.

"Is it true?" she asked, as they reached the anchor at the bottom of the drive where Brendan's family lived.

He would not meet her eyes. "I was going to tell you when the time was right."

"So it is true, then."

"Aye. All of it."

"You murdered your best friend? And killed a woman?"

"I didn't kill her. She's probably not even dead for all I know." He looked away, his face closed-up, his eyes dark with pain. "She was like that, ye know. Came and went. Attached herself to the hero of the moment, fell madly in love with him and the moment his star began to set she moved on to someone else."

"I ... I can't believe you didn't tell me any of this," she whispered, her world crashing down around her.

"I told ye, I was waitin' for the right time."

"To tell me you *murdered* someone?" her voice was high and thready. "People who love each other don't keep those kinds of secrets, Ruaidri!"

"Well, lass, ye weren't exactly forthcoming about things yerself."

"I have no idea what you're talking about."

"Ehm ... a baby?"

"I didn't know. It was Mira who put it all together, not me. Besides, if I'd known I would have told you. It's not like I deliberately kept something from you!'

His jaw tightened, and she saw him take a deep and steadying breath. "I don't want to talk about this right now."

"When were you planning on talking about it? Next year? Next decade? Next century?"

"Ye're makin' a scene."

"I can't believe this!"

"Believe it. It's true. Josiah Brown was my best friend, a former shipmate and eventually fellow captain. I killed him. Shot him dead. Your brother was wrong about a lot of things, but he got that one right."

"So you don't deny it, then?"

"There's nothin' to deny."

She walked the rest of the drive up to the house and sat down heavily on the steps. This man that she had married, this man whose past was as known to her as what lay beyond the moon, this man who had not quite lied to her but who had withheld a critical truth, moved to catch up. He reached down for her and tried to touch her cheek. She turned her head away.

"I can't believe you kept this from me," she said, dabbing at her eyes.

"I didn't murder him, Nerissa. Murder is intent. I never intended to kill him. It was an accident."

"An *accident*?"

Ruaidri sat down on the step beside her. She stiffened, angry with him and deservedly so. "An accident," he repeated. And then he drew a deep breath, put his bruised and aching head in his bleeding hands, and forced himself to go back through the years, to a tavern in Boston after he'd lost his ship, the people's acclaim, his pride following his humiliating capture as the Irish Pirate. A time when Dolores, who was little more than a courtesan but whose buxom beauty and bold eyes had been his undoing, still loved him. But Josiah's sun had risen as Ruaidri's had set, and Dolores had dropped him like an anchor in harbor, quickly hitching her wagon to the new hero instead. The pain at being betrayed by both his lover and his best friend had eviscerated what was left of his pride and happiness. Yes, he had loved her, yes, he'd been angry, yes, he'd accepted the challenge at daybreak thrown down by Josiah after Dolores, who was thrilled to have two of the most famous men in Boston fighting over her, drove them into a duel with a few well-placed taunts and lies in Josiah's ear.

"It was daybreak and there she was, standin' under a tree watchin' ... and she was smilin'," Ruaidri said. "We both turned and fired at the same time. Josiah was tryin' to kill me, because that's what love does to a man who thinks he's been insulted, who thinks the woman he loves has been wronged. His shot winged my arm. Mine was meant to miss him and didn't. I spun and fired just as he did and he lunged to the left as I pulled the trigger, tryin' to lessen the target he made. And I'd jerked the gun to the left to avoid hittin' him. He and the ball collided. He took it in the stomach." Ruaidri sat slumped and looking down at his boots, his bloodied knuckles thrust up through his hair and curling to grip it in hard fists. "He died in agony, cursin' me in his final breaths. And now ye know."

"And Dolores?"

"She left. Just turned around and walked away and I never saw her again. Probably ended up on a ship somewhere, tryin' to get her hooks into the next probable hero. She liked sailors. I don't know what happened to the manky bitch and I don't care."

A long moment went by, with neither of them looking at the other.

Blood ran steadily down Ruaidri's knuckles, seeping into his hair.

And Nerissa suddenly felt exhausted.

She looked over at him. "Why didn't you tell me, Ruaidri?"

He straightened up and looked off down the drive, toward the river. "Because I was scared, Nerissa. That's why."

"Scared of what?"

"Scared that ye'd leave me if ye knew the truth."

She looked down, tears filling her eyes, and fingered a knothole in the steps. "It hurts me that you didn't trust in my love enough to confess something so important."

"I'm sorry, Nerissa. I made a complete hash of it."

"Yes, you did. My brother hurt me terribly with his actions. And now you, by your failure to confide in me ... you have hurt me as well. At the moment, I don't think I can trust anyone anymore."

"I'm still the same man I was before ye learned any of this."

"You may be the same man, but I'm not the same woman. An hour ago, I believed in you. You were my hero, my knight in shining armor. Now I've been wounded by two of the people I love most in this world. Both of you treated me as though I was something fragile, breakable, unable to handle the truth or even make my own decisions. Both of you have let me down." She got to her feet. "I need to go rest."

"I'll come with you. We'll talk."

"No, Ruaidri. I wish to be alone. Go back to *Tigershark*. Get Jeffcote to stitch you up before you bleed to death all over again."

"Nerissa, please—"

"Better yet, go take Andrew down to Adams and get it over with so that he can move on with his own life and get back to the woman he loves. I need time to think, to make sense of all that I've learned today, and the last two people I want to see right now are you and Lucien."

She got up, opened the door, and without a backward glance, went inside.

The door shut with a hard, final thump and for Ruaidri, it was the most awful sound in the world.

❧

Nerissa trudged upstairs, head down to conceal her damp eyes as Mira's father Ephraim was coming down, frowning as he tried to set the watch he carried in his hand. He muttered a greeting and continued on, and she slid quietly into the room that she and Ruaidri had been given.

The bed where they had made love just an hour or so before lay as she'd left it when she'd thrown back the covers, gone to the window to watch her husband melt away into the darkness, and seen shadowy figures move out from behind the trees at the end of the drive and begin to follow him. It surprised her that anyone would be watching the house in the last hour before daybreak.

It didn't surprise her to find out that it had been her own brother.

Her blood running cold, she had charged from her room. She'd raced past Brendan as he'd been coming up the stairs with a breakfast tray, told him what she'd just seen and flown outside, trying to catch up to her husband and his pursuers before it was too late. And it almost had been. She saw again the vicious fight, both men so well matched, heard the brutal blows and seen again that awful moment as Lucien, insane with rage, had held a knife to her husband's throat. Nerissa knew her brother. She knew the depths to which he would go, the lengths to which he had gone for other members of his family to protect those he loved.

And she knew that he would have killed Ruaidri right then and there if she had not been there to intervene.

She sat down on the rumpled bed, her eyeballs aching from lack of sleep, exhaustion, and grief, and the still surreal claim on Mira's part that she was pregnant.

Pregnant.

Could she be? Well, why not. She and Ruaidri had consummated their marriage on the day they'd exchanged vows a month and a half ago. They had come together often on the voyage across the Atlantic. It was how babies were made. It was how babies had always been made.

Pregnant.

And it certainly explained the fact she her menses were late. Very late. It probably explained her unexpected and sudden tears, her jealousy and high emotions when Ruaidri had refused to discuss this Dolores-creature, and the fact that her nipples felt tender and raw, as well.

Again, the image of Lucien and the knife, Ruaidri half-conscious and about to die, rose up in her mind.

There was a knock on the door.

"Come in," Nerissa said woodenly, hastily wiping away her tears.

She'd half-expected it to be her husband. But it was Mira Merrick, her hair down around her shoulders and one hank of it tucked behind an ear. She came and sat on the bed next to Nerissa.

"Life ain't always easy," she said quietly. "And sometimes it gives us surprises we aren't quite ready for." She reached out and took Nerissa's hand. "You didn't know you were breedin', did ye?"

Nerissa shook her head, feeling the tears squeezing past her eyes despite her best efforts. Mira's gentle compassion and empathy were about to open the floodgates on her emotions. She didn't trust herself to speak.

"I wasn't quite sure myself, but the bloom in your cheeks, the way you weren't eating, and that bullcrap about land-sickness ... I put it all together and made a wild stab in the dark. Didn't know if I was right or not, but at least it got those two men of yours to quit killing each other by knocking them both over the head with it."

Nerissa knuckled another tear.

Mira squeezed her hand. "Can I say something?"

Nerissa nodded.

"I think ye're bein' too hard on yer man."

Nerissa choked back the sudden lump in her throat. "I can't believe he didn't tell me."

"He didn't tell ye because he was afraid he'd lose ye."

"I've never seen my husband afraid of anything. Not even Lucien when he was about to kill him. The word 'afraid' is not part of his vocabulary, Mira."

"It is when it comes to you. He loves you."

She sniffed and with unladylike despair, wiped the back of her hand across her nose.

"We were talking about settling here," Nerissa said plaintively. "There's you and Brendan, and the connection we both have with Amy makes me feel that you're already family. We talked about building a home. And now ... now, I just feel sick at heart."

"Still think ye're being too hard on him."

Nerissa sniffled again, and felt the tears coming again.

"That man loves you to the end of the earth," Mira added. "I know a fair bit about fighting, and I can tell you right now that he was holding back when he and your brother were going at each other. Brendan told me all about your husband, how scrappy a lad he was, how tough and cunning he is. They grew up together in Connemara. Do ye think he didn't have a reason for letting your brother beat up on him like a dusty rug? He could have killed him and didn't, because he knew what that would've done to you."

"He was no match for Lucien."

Mira made a noise that was half-guffaw, half snort. "Well, family loyalty is all well and good, but you ought to open your eyes once in a while and try lookin' at the truth that's standing right in front of you. Anyhow, doesn't matter, does it? You're sitting in here crying with a baby brewin' in yer belly, that good-looking man ye married is off buying provisions to sail out of here with Andrew, and *my* husband, who's recovering from a fall that nearly killed him not three months back, is getting *Kestrel* ready to take your other brother down to New York to deliver him safely into the hands of the damned British." She chewed at a hangnail. "Kind of a mess, don't ye think?"

Nerissa raised her head. Guilt filled her heart. "Oh, Mira...."

"Don't 'oh Mira' me. You've got some hurt feelings to fix, some soothing to do. Now stop feeling sorry for yerself, get off that pampered, well-bred butt of yours and go find and forgive your husband. And while you're at it, might as well make peace with that high-minded brother of yers, too."

Nerissa shook her head. "I can forgive Ruaidri," she said, her mouth tightening, "but I cannot forgive Lucien."

"Gonna just let him sail out of here and back home to England, then?"

The tears welled back up in Nerissa's throat, filled her sinuses and burned like fire as she fought to keep them from spilling once more. She couldn't trust herself to speak, instead just nodding jerkily and looking away —and missing Mira's calculating stare.

"Have it your way, then," she muttered, getting to her feet. "But I'm a-telling ye right now, you don't fix this, ye might never again get the chance and it's gonna eat at your gut worse than if ye'd swallowed a bucketful of seaworms."

The other woman stood up, and with a meaningful glance over her shoulder as she went to the door, walked out.

Nerissa just sat there, looking miserably out the window.

Soon enough, Lucien and her brother would be gone from this little town and on their way home to England. How stricken Lucien had looked when she'd told him to get out of her life. It felt good at the time to deliver such a blow to her brother after all he'd done to ruin her life, but now ... now, as the dust was settling around Mira's words and her own confusion and heartache caught up with her, the idea of him sailing away and truly out of her life, brought her indescribable pain.

I can't forgive him. I just can't.

She was still sitting on the bed staring miserably at the floor when her bruised and battered husband came quietly in an hour later.

She looked up at him, saw the uncertainty in his eyes, and with a sob, stretched out her arms to him in forgiveness.

He didn't stop to ask if she was certain she even wanted to give it.

They made love for a second time that morning. By the time the tide had turned late that afternoon, Lord Andrew was aboard *Tigershark* and Captain Ruaidri O' Devir was on his way to Boston to complete the mission on which John Adams had sent him. In his wake was Brendan's schooner *Kestrel*, bound for New York to bring the Duke of Blackheath back to the British.

And Nerissa, standing silently at the window and watching the two vessels grow small with distance, was all alone.

Chapter Thirty-Two

John Adams was all smiles and gratitude upon being presented with Lord Andrew de Montforte and what he assumed would be the substance that would end this war in the Americans' favor. He and his wife Abigail plied the young nobleman and their favorite captain with food and drink, caught Ruaidri up on what had been going on here at home, and invited him to stay the night. But the Irishman, thinking of his wife back in Newburyport, politely declined. Adams saw him to the door, still smiling—and leaving Ruaidri to wonder how long his high spirits would last once confronted with Andrew's stubborn defiance. He was glad that his part in this undertaking was over. He didn't envy Adams one bit.

As he and his brother-in-law parted company, Andrew left him with explicit instructions.

"I was nicknamed the Defiant One for a reason," he said, holding out his hand in friendship. "I'm as stubborn as they come, but I've got nothing on either Lucien or my sister. You're a good man, Ruaidri O' Devir, and I've seen the best of you. It might not be today and it might not be tomorrow, but when Lucien gets over being a pig-headed arse, he'll realize you're the best thing that ever happened to our sister."

Ruaidri nodded. "And what about you?"

"Oh, don't worry about me. Adams seems like a fine fellow, but he'll get nothing out of me and neither will anyone else, including the Royal Navy. I've had a lot to think about this past month and a half, seen things I never want to see again. That explosive should never have been invented. Some day I'll die, and the formula on how to make it will die with me. You have my word."

"I wish you godspeed, Lord Andrew."

"And I wish you luck in making my stubborn siblings see reason. Farewell, my new brother. Stay in touch...."

No animosity, no hard feelings, just a young man who understood that another man was only doing his duty and took nothing personal from it. Even so, Ruaidri sailed home with a heavy heart.

He'd only been gone for a day, and yet he found Nerissa much as he'd left her, morose, distant, and sad.

He knew about pride and the toll it took on a person. He knew about regrets and how hard it was to acknowledge them. And he knew about heartache when he saw it.

If ye don't have family, he thought, *ye don't have anythin'*.

He wondered if Brendan had reached New York. He'd carried a flag of truce, his ticket for sailing that singularly unique and justifiably famous schooner into New York without getting blasted to Kingdom Come. But having a duke on board was rather good insurance against such things, Ruaidri thought.

He rather wished *he* had a duke on board to guarantee him that same safety as, unable to get so much as a smile from his wife, the dullness in her red-rimmed eyes hurting him in places he hadn't realized were capable of feeling pain, he pulled together his crew once more and set a course south.

Toward New York.

Where, he hoped, he'd have it out with Lucien de Montforte once and for all. Before he found some mighty English warship to bring him back to England. Before he boarded it and sailed away.

Before it was too late.

❧

The shadows were long outside the inn, autumn's dead leaves skating down the cobbled street outside on a wind off the mighty Hudson.

He could have dined with General Clinton tonight, been feted and fed, bowed and scraped to and toasts drunk to his health. It wasn't every day that a famous and powerful duke all the way from England visited a place like New York, especially in the middle of a war. Lucien might otherwise have embraced such expected treatment, but he was in no mood for it tonight, and even less for company. Sycophants. Posturers and fools. People begging favors, people seeking audiences. This was only his second night in this colonial hell-hole, and his impatience with those around him had reached its end.

He wanted nothing more than anonymity.

And to be alone.

One of the benefits of being in a place where nobody knew you, of course, was that you could put on your hat, throw your greatcoat over your fine clothes and go find a rough-and-tumble tavern where it was all the more certain that nobody would know you, nobody would want something from you, and you could spend the evening drowning your sorrows in a pint of ale.

Or maybe two.

It was as he was lifting the second heavy tankard to

his mouth that his senses all prickled with alert, and he paused and looked around him. People milled about, eating, laughing, drinking, playing backgammon, but Lucien de Montforte knew that he was not alone.

Someone slid into the chair across from him and he raised a surprised brow.

"O' Devir," he murmured, and took another sip of his ale. "Back for more, are you?"

"Aye, well, ye know me. Just a dumb Irishman. I'll always come back for more."

Lucien eyed him flatly. "What do you want?"

"Well now, what I want is to be back home with my wife, talkin' about buildin' a life together and preparin' for a little one. Know what my pet name was for her, Your Grace? I called her Sunshine. Called her that because she was bright and warm. Because she was full of sunlight and cheer and she lit up everythin' around her, includin' me heart." He raised his hand to summon the tavern wench, who was quick to set him up with a cold, foaming tankard of his own. "But she's not full of sunlight and cheer any longer, and the reason for that is us. Or more specifically, *you*."

Blackheath, his nostrils flaring with contempt, looked away, but not before Ruaidri saw the flash of pain in the dark eyes, eyes that were sunken and exhausted, eyes that looked haunted.

"What do you want?" the duke asked again, not deigning to even look at him.

"You to come back to Newburyport with me."

"You're mad."

"Not mad. Desperate."

"I would sooner spend time in the company of a street sweeper than I would yours, you para—"

"Aye, yes, I know, we've been all through the whole parasite-thing and what ye think of me, and I don't really give a fuck what ye think of me so let's just get that over with and out of the way, now. What I *do* give a fuck about is yer sister's happiness."

"You are crude, O' Devir."

"Guilty as charged."

"You tire me."

"Ah, well, the feelin's mutual."

"I don't know what the devil our Navy's coming to if they'd just let a blackguard like you into New York. The enemy, for God's sake. How did you find me?"

"It's common knowledge that ye're a guest of the general. I waited outside his quarters and then followed ye."

"Where's your ship? How were you not apprehended?"

"'Twas easy enough to drop anchor in Connecticut and hire a local fisherman to bring me the rest o' the way."

"This is ... unacceptable."

"Not to me it isn't. Worked out quite well, actually."

Ruaidri sat back in his chair, sipping his ale and studying the duke until the Englishman finally turned his head and deigned to fully look at him. When he did, Ruaidri was taken aback, and not by the very visible evidence of their brutal fight apparent in the duke's bruised and cut cheekbone that was suddenly presented to him. He expected sullen fury, disgust, even hatred in his brother-in-law's face but no, the black eyes were flat and dead, like a stone that had lost its polish.

"You came all the way down here to get me? At risk to your own life in a bastion of English strength and power?"

Ruaidri grinned and raised his tankard in a mocking little salute. "Guess I'm just a dumb Irishman."

The two sat together, the duke staring down into his ale, Ruaidri giving him time to digest both the fact that he'd sought him out and the reason for it. Neither said a word for a long moment. Horses and carts clattered past the window just outside and nearby, a group of British officers laughed and swore good-naturedly as someone lost in a game of cards.

At last, Blackheath shoved his nearly-empty tankard aside and wearily rubbed at his brow. "How is she?"

"Hurtin'."

Blackheath said nothing, but the skin tightened perceptibly around his mouth.

"Hurtin' because she misses her family. Hurtin' because she said things to you in the heat of the moment she wishes she could take back or say differently, hurtin' because she wants yer forgiveness as much as you want hers but she's got the same stubborn pride as you do so there she sits, mopin'." Ruaidri took a sip of his ale. "Just like ye're doin'."

"She asked me to leave, to get out of her life, and so I did."

"We all say things when we're angry. Doesn't mean we actually mean them."

"Does she know you're here?"

"'Course not."

The duke took off his tricorne, which he'd had pulled down low over his forehead, and Ruaidri saw more reminders of their brutal fight. The cut on his cheekbone went all the way into his hairline, his lip was swollen, and there was a puffiness above one eye.

"You look a damned wreck, Brit," Ruaidri said, and took another sip of his ale.

"Yes, well, you wouldn't win any beauty contests yourself." Blackheath stared hopelessly down into his ale. "Should've killed you when I had the chance."

"You had the chance and didn't."

"As did you, and you didn't take it, either."

Ruaidri rubbed at the bruise on his own temple. "So where does that leave us?"

"Alive, for a start."

"And you down here and her up there, and both of ye so full of hurt that ye can't think of anything else."

Lucien said nothing.

Ruaidri crossed his arms on the table and leaned close. "A long time ago, Blackheath, back when I was just a young lad, the press-gang came to my village in Connacht. I was taken away from home and forced to serve the Royal Navy, and when they dragged me away from my little sister I had no idea that it would be thirteen years before I'd see her again, thirteen years before I'd know that my mam had died, thirteen years before I could begin the business of healin' and forgiveness. In all that time there wasn't a day went by that I didn't wish I could get back home and see my loved ones, to take care of them as a brother and son should. My da had died years before and the women in my family, well ... they were my responsibility." He leaned back and took a sip of his ale. "But the Royal Navy ... it's a jail sentence for a pressed man, and those opportunities to take care of my own were denied me. When I finally got away from the English and started fightin' for this side, I was so full of righteous, pig-headed pride that I let my need for revenge, my quest to prove myself after years of 'aye, sir' to people who'd as soon spit on me than acknowledge I was as human as they were, get in the way of goin' back home. I nearly lost my sister because of that pride, and I see you sittin' here doing the same damned thing as I did."

Blackheath said nothing, only staring down into his drink once more.

"I may not be the man ye'd have chosen for yer little sister any more than I'd have chosen Christian to be the man for mine. I know how it feels to see one's little sister fallin' in love with someone that ye'd just love to hate. And I know how hard it is to let go, to give that permission to your sister to find a life with a fellow of her own choosin', to set her free to find her own happiness." Ruaidri leaned close once more, his gaze intent as he stared into the duke's eyes. "You owe her that, Blackheath."

The duke remained silent, a little quiver at the corner of his mouth the only sign that Ruaidri's words were hitting home.

"I'm no blue-blooded Englishman, I'll never be able to give her London balls and appearances at Court like that piece of shite Perry or any other nob ye might've picked for her could do. But I can give her happiness, I can give her the freedom she's craved all her life to spread her wings and be Nerissa de Montforte O' Devir, not Lady Nerissa, not a pretty little bird in a cage watchin' the world go by and resentin' the bars that keep her from joinin' it. What do ye think will make her more happy, Blackheath? Balls and Court appearances and wealth and status, or the wings to fly high and free?"

"What are you, a damned poet?"

Ruaidri shrugged. "No, just an Irishman."

"She will be poor here, dressed in rags, living the life of an American bumpkin."

"She will be my wife, Blackheath, and I think ye know enough about me by now to know that I'm nothin' if not ambitious. I'll go far in this new country, I'll attain things here that I, a lowly Irishman, could never aspire to, let alone reach back in yers. Yer way is the old way, Blackheath, and everythin' about ye represents it—the privileges and expectations of class, birth and breedin'. This is the new world, and 'tis proud I am to call myself an American. Like it or not, I represent the new way of things, hope, liberty, opportunity, and I can give your sister all of that and let her be free to find them herself, without being constrained by name and title and class expectations. She has a chance to fly here, Blackheath. But she can't do it unless you set her free to try her wings and the two of ye make peace with each other."

"I'm not going back there."

"You're a bigger fool than I am if ye don't."

"She hates me."

"She loves you. Ye're her damned brother, for God's sake."

The duke looked up and out the window, unwilling to meet Ruaidri's eyes, and the lines around his mouth grew deeper, the skin almost white.

"Family is all we've got, Blackheath, all any of us got. What else is there? Who else is there? There's nothin' on God's green earth more important than our families. You know that; 'tis why ye're here, why ye chased yer sister and me across the Atlantic, why ye were willin' to go to an American jail for killin' me the other night. It's also why ye *didn't* kill me. Ye didn't do it because of any mercy toward me or fear of incarceration or even death should ye've managed to cleave my skull in that first strike. Ye did it for *her*."

The duke looked down, but not before Ruaidri saw a sudden gleam of moisture in the corner of his eye.

"I know I'm not the family ye wanted or would've chosen for her, but I'm the family ye've got, and ye're the family I've got, and you and I need to make the best of that, if only for her sake."

A muscle worked in Blackheath's throat and he stared rigidly out the window. "Always heard the Irish were stupid, not wise."

"Aye, stupid. I'm an American naval officer who risked everythin' comin' into a British stronghold to come get ye. Can't get more stupid than that, eh?"

"Why did you do it?"

"Because of her. *Because I love her.*" Ruaidri picked up his tankard and drained it. "Because if I let ye sail off across that ocean and somethin' happens to ye, 'twill kill her. Because if I leave here empty-handed, her guilt and grief over how ye two left things is going to gnaw a hole in her heart that will never heal." He directed a hard stare at his brother-in-law. "'Twill leave one in yours, too."

The duke remained looking away. "It took courage to enter this place and to face me."

"It doesn't take courage to face ye, Blackheath. Just desperation." He stood up. "Come back with me."

The duke finally looked up at him, something unreadable in his black, fathomless eyes. Defeat. An acceptance. Despair. "You really do love her," he said tonelessly.

"If ye have any doubt, then the man standin' across from you is a figment of yer imagination and this entire conversation is a product of that ale ye've been starin' into for the past hour." He picked his hat up from the table and reaching into his pocket, left a generous amount of coin in its place. "Are ye comin' with me or not?"

Blackheath looked back down into his drink, and Ruaidri waited.

Blackheath didn't move.

"The hell with ye, then," Ruaidri muttered. His own heart twisting with anger, he donned his hat, turned, and stalked away. Toward the door. Back into the lion's den and what he hoped wouldn't be detainment, capture, or imprisonment if anyone recognized him or the man he just left decided to turn him in. But before he could reach out and grasp the latch to let himself back out into the cold November afternoon, another hand was there on the door, pushing it open for him. An elegant hand, strong and well-bred, the back of it draped in expensive lace that peeped out from under the cuff of his coat.

Ruaidri paused, and the duke waited.

Held the door open for him with a faintly perceptible bow.

"You are quite right, O' Devir," he murmured, meeting Ruaidri's gaze with a resolute one of his own. "Family is all we've got."

Chapter Thirty-Three

"Family is all we've got," Andrew was saying, making himself comfortable in the library in a chair near the fire. "You've got to forgive him, Nerissa. He only did it because he loves you."

Andrew had returned from Boston the day before, his explosive's secret still his own, both the Americans and the English the poorer for not having the formula and the world itself, Andrew thought, all the richer for it. Offers of monetary compensation, arguments about the nobleness of the American cause ... none of it had swayed the young English inventor and Adams was not one to stoop to threats or torture. Andrew had left the frustrated but quietly resigned American leader to lament British stubbornness and had made his way back to Newburyport.

"He hates me," Nerissa said. "Oh, God, why can't I stop crying?"

"It's the baby talking,'" Mira Merrick said, passing through on her way out the door.

"Oh, I need Ruaidri," Nerissa said, and put her head in her hands. "Why, Andrew, did he send you home in some random vessel instead of bringing you back from Boston himself? Where is he? I need him so badly...."

Above her, Andrew and Mira exchanged glances; then Mira shook her head, opened the door, and slammed out into the frosty morning.

"Told me he had business to discuss with Adams. He'll be back, only takes a few hours to sail home from Boston."

And a few more to sail home from New York, Andrew thought privately. *Providing one doesn't get caught.*

"I don't think I can bear it once you leave," Nerissa said plaintively. "You're the only family I have left. And you'll be going home soon."

"Yes, I am." He got up and came to sit next to his sister, troubled by the gauntness of her beautiful face, the hollowed look in her quietly suffering eyes. He took her hands. "I have someone to get back to, Nerissa."

"Celsie," she whispered, and dug at a loose thread on her cuff. "I'll probably never see her again."

"Never's a long time, Nerissa. This war won't go on indefinitely. It can't. We'll come visit."

She nodded in a quick, jerky little motion.

"And Lucien, you and I both know he'll pull strings to get your name cleared. Move mountains, if he has to. He's good at that. If anyone can do it, he—oh, damnation," Andrew said, and moving closer to his sister, pulled her into his embrace as the mention of their eldest brother's name caused the tears to flow once more.

"I wish I could take back what I said to him," she said brokenly. "I can't live like this."

"Stop beating yourself up over it. You had good reason to be angry with him." Andrew cleared a long fall of blonde hair from her face. "He did, after all, try to kill your husband."

At the memory of that horrific fight, the knowledge she'd come so close to losing either or both of them, the tears came harder, so hard, in fact, that she never heard the quiet click and whoosh of the front door being opened, never heard the footfalls of two men coming into the entrance hall, didn't feel the cold draft of air that preceded them.

Beside her, Andrew had gone still.

Even the tabby cat sleeping in Nerissa's lap suddenly raised its head.

"Dear me. Gone only a few days and the world just falls apart," said a smooth, urbane voice. A familiar voice.

A beloved voice.

Nerissa's head jerked up, and through her tears she saw her brother, that adored and infuriating face, not-quite-as-self-assured as he was trying to appear, standing just within the door. Ruaidri was just behind him, smiling.

"L-Lucien?"

He stretched out his arms in invitation, his eyes begging forgiveness, and before the cat could even flee her lap, Nerissa was running across the room and throwing herself into his embrace.

"You came back," she sobbed, burying her face against his coat, feeling his arms going around her. "I'm so sorry for what I said, I didn't mean any of it, I was angry and scared and upset—"

"I know." He hugged her close. "And you had good reason to be. I'm sorry, too. I was a beast."

"Why did you come back?"

"I couldn't leave America without saying goodbye," he said. "And, begging your forgiveness."

"It's me who should be begging yours," she said brokenly, and pulling back, looked up into his face. "Why did you come back, Lucien? Truly?"

"Ah, well, seems a certain Irishman with more sense than you and I put together decided to take matters into his own hands," Lucien murmured, with a grateful glance over his shoulder.

"Ruaidri?" She stared at him. "But I thought you were with John Adams ... you mean, you went down to New York and brought Lucien back?"

"Wasn't easy, lass. I don't know who's more stubborn, you or him."

Ruaidri crossed his arms and leaned against the door jamb. Over Nerissa's shoulder, past the duke's tall, imposing form, he caught the eye of Lord Andrew sitting on the settee, the cat that had been in Nerissa's lap just moments before, now nestled happily in his.

The young inventor grinned.

And Ruaidri, gazing in satisfaction as the oldest and youngest de Montforte siblings embraced and forgave, grinned back.

❧

It was a cold and biting wind that twisted the hem of her heavy petticoats and clawed at her hair as Nerissa, her body sheltered by her husband's big, protective one, stood on the Ashton pier and watched two of Brendan's sailors make fast the little boat that would take Andrew and Lucien out to *Kestrel*. The turning tide had swung the schooner's bows to face them, and soon her long, jaunty jib-boom would pivot around all the more until she faced the distant mouth of the river and the short journey down to New York that awaited her.

Her captain stood a little distance away, his blue coat edged with red and a heavy woolen scarf around his neck to try and beat the cold. His wife, her hair in a long braid down her back and covered by a knit cap, insinuated herself under his arm and watched as the farewells were said.

"We should probably get a move on, Brendan, if we

want to get them down to New York. The way this parting's going, they'll be saying goodbye to each other well into next week."

"Let's give them another minute, *Stóirín*...."

"Now you make sure you write," Nerissa was saying, gripping Andrew's hands in her own and looking up into his eyes. "I want to know all about the next invention you take it upon yourself to create. No flying machines. No explosives."

"I will, Nerissa."

"And please make sure Celsie feeds you. You've grown thin, and I'm worried about you."

"I'm sure I'll survive just fine."

Nerissa hugged him fiercely, and managed to hold her tears in check as he walked down the ramp and into the waiting boat, now bumping impatiently against the pier. She took a deep and steadying breath, and then turned, wondering if this would be the last time she would ever see her brothers.

"Lucien," she said. "I won't say goodbye."

"It's not goodbye," he returned. "It's farewell for now. Farewell for a while."

"Yes," she said, the lump rising in her throat as she saw Brendan Merrick discreetly consulting his watch a little distance away. It was time to go.

"You'll write to me when the baby's born," Lucien said to her, but his gaze went to Ruaidri, enacting a silent promise.

"We'll write," he said, knowing his wife was choking up. "Her time will be here before ye know it."

Lucien de Montforte wrapped his arms around his little sister and hugged her deeply for a long, loving moment. Maybe he'd find a way to get back here when the time came. Maybe he'd find a way to bring his whole family. The future held both hope and surprises. At last, he pulled himself up, discreetly knuckled his eye, and turned a gaze full of black menace on his new brother-in-law. "I'm counting on you to take care of her," he said solemnly. "Because if you don't, I'm going to come back here and kick the living daylights out of you."

Ruaidri laughed and stuck out his hand as Lucien set himself away from his sister. The duke took it in his own and the two men, both so different and yet both so alike, shook warmly.

"Take care of yourself, Ruaidri O' Devir."

"May the saints and the good Lord himself bless and keep ye, Blackheath."

"I think you've earned the right to call me Lucien." The duke smiled, and it was a long moment before he released Ruaidri's hand. "I'll be back. You can depend on it."

He turned and nodded his readiness to Captain Merrick, and a moment later, had joined Andrew in the little boat.

I'll be back. You can depend on it.

Nerissa pushed closer to her husband, and felt his arm go around her to pull her close, steadying her as Brendan and Mira, both of them already planning their next cruise against British shipping off the coast of New York after they delivered their aristocratic passengers back into the hands of the English, joined them in the boat. A moment later, a sailor was loosening the ropes that tied it to the pier and the little craft was cutting through the cold, swirling waters of the Merrimack.

I'll be back. You can depend on it.

"You all right, Sunshine?"

She looked up and into the beautiful, long-lashed eyes that she held so dear, the strong Celtic face with the bold black brows and wild, unruly hair that had enchanted her from the moment she'd first met him.

"I'm all right," she said. "But it's time to go."

"Aye, lass. 'Twill only hurt all the more, standin' here watchin' 'til ye can't see them any longer." He bent his head and dropped a kiss against her hair. "Besides, I've got somethin' to show ye."

"Show me?"

He turned her gently, and began to walk her off the pier and back toward the street.

"Show you."

"What is it?"

He waited until they reached the street, and then he pointed off to their left, to a gentle, wooded rise a half mile away.

"I see trees," she said, her mind still on her brothers in that little boat behind them, and *Kestrel* beyond, waiting to take them home.

"Ye see land," he said quietly. "Land that's for sale. Land that I thought might look nice with a fine brick house on it overlookin' the river and the sea beyond. Land where we'll build our home and raise our family, Nerissa." He smiled as she gave a little exclamation of surprise and delight. "Should we walk there and have a look at it, together?"

"Oh, Ruaidri ... I would love that."

"Let's go, then."

He offered her elbow and she linked her arm in his, and together, they walked away from the waterfront.

And just before they turned the corner from Fish Street onto High, Nerissa paused and looked over her shoulder, back toward the river....

At the beautiful *Kestrel*, the jib now blooming on her nose and her tall, raked masts already beginning to move as she carried her new family, and her old, toward the next chapters in their lives.

Another day for Brendan and Mira.

A new day for her brothers.

The rest of her life, for her and Ruaidri.

I'll be back. You can depend on it.

❧

Turn the page to keep reading and start the journey over with Book 1 in the bestselling De Montforte Brothers series, The Wild One.

A Heartfelt Thank You!

Thank you from the bottom of my heart for reading my book. If you enjoyed it, please consider posting a review. Reviews don't just help the author, they help other readers discover our books and, no matter how long or short, I sincerely appreciate every review.

Would you like to know when my next book is available? Sign up for my newsletter:

Also, please follow me on BookBub to be notified of deals and new releases.

Thank you again for reading and for your support.

More in This Series

The DeMontforte Series

"The bluest of blood; the boldest of hearts;

the de Montforte brothers will take your breath away."

The Wild One

The Beloved One

The Defiant One

The Wicked One

The Wayward One

The Admiral's Heart

The Fox & the Angel

My First Noel

The Heroes of the Sea

Love the characters in the DeMontforte Series? Continue on with the Heroes of the Sea to revisit shared characters.

Master of My Dreams

Captain of My Heart

My Lady Pirate

Taken by Storm

Wicked at Heart

Lord of the Sea

Heir to the Sea

Never Too Late for Love

Scandal at Christmas

My Saving Grace

PREVIEW WILD ONE

Book 1 of the De Montforte Brothers Series

BY DANELLE HARMON

Prologue

Newman House, 18 April, 1775

My dear brother, Lucien,

It has just gone dark and as I pen these words to you, an air of rising tension hangs above this troubled town. Tonight, several regiments — including mine, the King's Own — have been ordered by General Gage, commander in chief of our forces here in Boston, out to Concord to seize and destroy a significant store of arms and munitions that the rebels have secreted there. Due to the clandestine nature of this assignment, I have ordered my batman, Billingshurst, to withhold the posting of this letter until the morrow, when the mission will have been completed and secrecy will no longer be of concern.

Although it is my most ardent hope that no blood will be shed on either side during this endeavour, I find that my heart, in these final moments before I must leave, is restless and uneasy. It is not for myself that I am afraid, but another. As you know from my previous letters home, I have met a young woman here with whom I have become attached in a warm friendship. I suspect you do not approve of my becoming so enamoured of a storekeeper's daughter, but things are different in this place, and when a fellow is three thousand miles away from home, love makes a far more desirable companion than loneliness. My dear Miss Paige has made me happy, Lucien, and earlier tonight, she accepted my plea for her hand in marriage; I beg you to understand, and forgive, for I know that someday when you meet her, you will love her as I do.

My brother, I have but one thing to ask of you, and knowing that you will see to my wishes is the only thing that calms my troubled soul during these last few moments before we depart. If anything should happen to me — tonight, tomorrow, or at any time whilst I am here in Boston — I beg of you to find it in your heart to show charity and kindness to my angel, my Juliet, for she means the world to me. I know you will take care of her if ever I cannot. Do this for me and I shall be happy, Lucien.

I must close now, as the others are gathered downstairs in the parlour, and we are all ready to move. May God bless and keep you, my dear brother, and Gareth, Andrew, and sweet Nerissa, too.

Charles

SOMETIME DURING THE LAST HOUR, it had begun to grow dark.

Lucien de Montforte turned the letter over in his hands, his gaze shuttered, his mind far away as he stared out the window over the downs that stood like sentinels against the fading twilight. A breath of pink still glowed in the western sky, but it would soon be gone. He hated this time of night, this still and lonely hour just after sunset when old ghosts were near, and distant memories welled up in the heart with the poignant nearness of yesterday, close enough to see yet always too elusive to touch.

But the letter was real. Too real.

He ran a thumb over the heavy vellum, the bold, elegant script that had been so distinctive of Charles's style — both on paper, in thought, and on the field —

still looking as fresh as if it had been written yesterday, not last April. His own name was there on the front: *To His Grace the Duke of Blackheath, Blackheath Castle, nr. Ravenscombe, Berkshire, England.*

They were probably the last words Charles had ever written.

Carefully, he folded the letter along creases that had become fragile and well-worn. The blob of red wax with which his brother had sealed the letter came together at the edges like a wound that had never healed, and try as he might to avoid seeing them, his gaze caught the words that someone, probably Billingshurst, had written on the back....

Found on the desk of Captain Lord Charles Adair de Montforte on the 19th of April 1775, the day on which his lordship was killed in the fighting at Concord. Please deliver to addressee.

A pang went through him. Dead, gone, and all but forgotten, just like that.

The Duke of Blackheath carefully laid the letter inside the drawer, which he shut and locked. He gazed once more out the window, lord of all he surveyed but unable to master his own bitter emptiness. A mile away, at the foot of the downs, he could just see the twinkling lights of Ravenscombe village, could envision its ancient church with its Norman tower and tombs of de Montforte dead. And there, inside, high on the stone wall of the chancel, was the simple bronze plaque that was all they had to tell posterity that his brother had ever even lived.

Charles, the second son.

God help them all if anything happened to him, Lucien, and the dukedom passed to the third.

No. God would not be so cruel.

He snuffed the single candle and with the darkness enclosing him, the sky still glowing beyond the window, moved from the room.

Chapter One

BERKSHIRE, ENGLAND, 1776

The Flying White was bound for Oxford, and it was running late. Now, trying to make up time lost to a broken axle, the driver had whipped up the team, and the coach careered through the night in a cacophony of shouts, thundering hooves, and cries from the passengers who were clinging for their lives on the roof above.

Strong lanterns cut through the rainy darkness, picking out ditches, trees, and hedgerows as the vehicle hurtled through the Lambourn Downs at a pace that had Juliet Paige's heart in her throat. Because of Charlotte, her six-month-old daughter, Juliet had been lucky enough to get a seat inside the coach, but even so, her head banged against the leather squabs on the right, her shoulder against an elderly gent on her left, and her neck ached with the constant side to side movement. On the seat across from her, another young mother clung to her two frightened children, one huddled under each arm. It had been a dreadful run up from Southampton indeed, and Juliet was feeling almost as ill as she had during the long sea voyage over from Boston.

The coach hit a bump, became airborne for a split second, and landed hard, snapping her neck, throwing her violently against the man on her left, and causing the passengers clinging to the roof above to cry out in terror. Someone's trunk went flying off the coach, but the driver never slowed the galloping team.

"God help us!" murmured the young mother across from Juliet as her children cringed fearfully against her.

Juliet grasped the strap and hung her head, fighting nausea as she hugged her own child. Her lips touched the baby's downy gold curls. "Almost there," she whispered, for Charlotte's ears alone. "Almost there—to your papa's home."

Suddenly without warning, there were shouts, a horse's frightened whinny, and violent curses from the driver. Someone on the roof screamed. The coach careened madly, the inhabitants both inside and out shrieking in terror as the vehicle hurtled along on two wheels for another forty or fifty feet before finally crashing heavily down on its axles with another neck-snapping jolt, shattering a window with the impact and spilling the elderly gent to the floor. Outside, someone was sobbing in fear and pain.

And inside, the atmosphere of the coach went as still as death.

"We're being robbed!" cried the old man, getting to his knees to peer out the rain-spattered window.

Shots rang out. There was a heavy thud from above, then movement just beyond the ominous black pane. And then suddenly, without warning it imploded, showering the inside passengers in a hail of glass.

Gasping, they looked up to see a heavy pistol—and a masked face just beyond it.

"Yer money or yer life. *Now!*"

❧

IT WAS the very devil of a night. No moon, no stars, and a light rain stinging his face as Lord Gareth Francis de Montforte sent his horse, Crusader, flying down the Wantage road at a speed approaching suicide. Stands of beech and oak shot past, there then gone. Pounding hooves splashed through puddles and echoed against the hedgerows that bracketed the road. Gareth glanced over his shoulder, saw nothing but a long empty stretch of road behind him, and shouted with glee. Another race won—Perry, Chilcot, and the rest of the Den of Debauchery would never catch him now!

Laughing, he patted Crusader's neck as the hunter pounded through the night. "Well done, good fellow! Well done—"

And pulled him up sharply at he passed Wether Down.

It took him only a moment to assess the situation.

Highwaymen. And by the looks of it, they were helping themselves to the pickings—and passengers—of the Flying White from Southampton.

The Flying White? The young gentleman reached inside his coat pocket and pulled out his watch, squinting to see its face in the darkness. Damned late for the Flying White . . .

He dropped the timepiece back into his pocket, steadied Crusader, and considered what to do. No gentlemen of the road, this lot, but a trio of desperate, hardened killers. The driver and guard lay on the ground beside the coach, both presumably dead. Somewhere a child was crying, and now one of the bandits, with a face that made a hatchet look kind, smashed in the windows of the coach with the butt end of his gun. Gareth reached for his pistol. The thought of quietly turning around and going back the way he'd come never occurred to him. The thought of waiting for his friends, probably a mile behind thanks to Crusader's blistering speed, didn't occur to him, either. Especially when he saw one of the bandits yank open the door of the coach and haul out a struggling young woman.

He had just the briefest glimpse of her face—scared, pale, beautiful—before one of the highwaymen shot out the lanterns of the coach and darkness fell over the entire scene. Someone screamed. Another shot rang out, silencing the frightened cry abruptly.

His face grim, the young gentleman knotted his horse's reins and removed his gloves, pulling each one carefully off by the fingertips. With a watchful eye on the highwaymen, he slipped his feet from the irons and vaulted lightly down from the thoroughbred's tall back, his glossy top boots of Spanish leather landing in chalk mud up to his ankles. The horse never moved. He doffed his fine new surtout and laid it over the saddle along with his tricorn and gloves. He tucked the lace at his wrist safely inside his sleeve to protect it from any soot or sparks his pistol might emit. Then he crept through the knee-high weeds and nettles that grew thick at the side of the road, priming and loading the pistol as he moved stealthily toward the stricken coach. He would have time to squeeze off only one shot before they were upon him, and that one shot had to count.

❧

"EVERYBO'Y OUT. *NOW!*"

Holding Charlotte tightly against her, Juliet managed to remain calm as the robber snared her wrist and jerked her violently from the vehicle. She landed awkwardly in the sticky white mud and would have gone down if not for the huge, bearlike hand that yanked her to her feet. Perhaps, she thought numbly, it was the very fact that it *was* bearlike that she was able to keep her head—and her wits—about her, for Juliet had been born and raised in the woods of Maine, and she was no stranger to bears, Indians, and a host of other threats that made these English highwaymen look benign by comparison.

But they were certainly not benign. The slain driver lay face-down in the mud. The bodies of one of the guards and a passenger were sprawled in the weeds nearby. A shudder went through her. She was glad of the darkness. Glad that the poor little children still inside the coach were spared the horrors that daylight would have revealed.

Cuddling Charlotte, she stood beside the other passengers as the robbers yanked people down from the roof and lined them up in front of the coach. A woman was sobbing. A girl clung pitifully to the old man, perhaps her grandfather. One fellow, finely dressed and obviously a gentleman, angrily protested the treatment of the women and without a word, one of the highwayman stuck his pistol into his belly and shot him dead. As he fell, the wretched group gasped in dismay and horror. Then the last passengers were dragged from the coach, the two children clinging to their mother's skirts and crying piteously.

They all huddled together in the rainy darkness, too terrified to speak as, one by one, they were relieved of their money, their jewels, their watches, and their pride.

And then the bandits came to Juliet.

"Gimme yer money, girl, all of it. Now!"

Juliet complied. Without a sound, she handed over her reticule.

"The necklace, too."

Her hand went to her throat. Hesitated. The robber cuffed it away in impatience, ripping the thin gold chain from her neck and dropping the miniature of Charlotte's dead father into his leather bag.

"Any jewels?"

She was still staring at the bag. "No."

"Any rings?"

"No."

But he grabbed her hand, held it up, and saw it: a promise made but broken by death. It was Charles's signet ring—her engagement ring—the last thing her beloved fiancé had given her before he had died in the fighting at Concord.

"Filthy lyin' bitch, give it to me!"

Juliet stood her ground. She looked him straight in the eye and firmly, quietly, repeated the single word.

"*No.*"

Without warning he backhanded her across the cheek, and she fell to her knees in the mud, cutting her palm on a stone as she tried to prevent injury to the baby. Her hair tumbled down around her face. Charlotte began screaming. And Juliet looked up, only to see the black hole of a pistol's mouth two inches away, the robber behind it snarling with rage.

Her life passed before her eyes.

And at that moment a shot rang out from somewhere off to her right, a dark rose exploded on the highwayman's chest, and with a look of surprise, he pitched forward, dead.

❧

ONLY ONE SHOT, but by God, I made it count.

The other two highwaymen jerked around at the bark of Gareth's pistol. Their faces mirrored disbelief as they took in his fine shirt and lace at throat and sleeve, his silk waistcoat, expensive boots, expensive breeches, expensive everything. They saw him as a plum ripe for the picking, and Gareth knew it. He went for his sword.

"Get on your horses and go, and neither of you shall be hurt."

For a moment, neither the highwaymen nor the passengers moved. Then, slowly, one of the highwayman began to smile. The other, to sneer.

"*Now!*" Gareth commanded, still moving forward and trying to bluff them with his display of cool authority.

And then all hell broke loose.

Tongues of flame cracked from the highwaymen's pistols and Gareth heard the low whine of a ball passing at close range. Passengers screamed and dived for cover. The coach horses reared, whinnying in fear. Gareth, his sword raised, charged through the tangle of nettle that grew dense at the side of the road, trying to get to the robbers before they could reload and fire. His foot hit a patch of mud and he went down, his cheek slamming into the stinging nettles. One of the highwayman came racing toward him, spewing a torrent of foul language and intent only on finishing him off. Gareth lay gasping, then flung himself hard to the left as the bandit's pistol coughed another spear of flame. Where his shoulder had been, a plume of mud shot several inches into the air.

The brigand was still coming, roaring at the top of his lungs, already bringing up a second pistol.

Gamely, Gareth tried to get to his feet and reach his sword. He slipped in the wet weeds, his cheek on fire as though he'd been stung by a hundred bees. He was outnumbered, his pistol spent, his sword just out of reach. But he wasn't done for. Not yet. Not by any stretch of the imagination. He lunged for his sword, rolled onto his back, and sitting up, flung the weapon at the oncoming highwayman with all his strength.

The blade caught the robber just beneath the jaw and nearly took his head off. He went over backward, clawing at his throat, his dying breath a terrible, rasping gurgle.

And then Gareth saw one of the two children running toward him, obviously thinking he was the only safety left in this world gone mad.

"Billy!" the mother was screaming. "Billy, no, *get back!*"

The last highwayman spun around. Wild-eyed and desperate, he saw the fleeing child, saw that his two friends were dead, and, as though to avenge a night gone wrong, brought his pistol up, training it on the little boy's back.

"Billeeeeeeee!"

Gareth lunged to his feet, threw himself at the child, and tumbled him to the ground, shielding him with his body. The pistol exploded at close range, deafening him, a white-hot lance of fire ripping through his ribs as he rolled over and over through grass and weeds and nettles, the child still in his arms.

He came to rest upon his back, the wet weeds beneath him, blood gushing hotly from his side. He lay still, blinking up at the trees, the rain falling gently upon his throbbing cheek.

His fading mind echoed his earlier words. *Well done, good fellow! Well done . . .*

The child sprang up and ran, sobbing, back to his mother.

And for Lord Gareth de Montforte, all went dark . . .

❧

If you enjoyed this excerpt, keep reading The Wild One!

Also by Danelle Harmon

Introducing

The Bestselling, Award-Winning, Critically Acclaimed

DE MONTFORTE BROTHERS SERIES

"The bluest of blood; the boldest of hearts;
the de Montforte brothers will take your breath away."

 # 1 Kindle Store bestseller: The Wild One

The Wild One

The Beloved One

The Defiant One

The Wicked One

The Wayward One

The Admiral's Heart

The Fox & the Angel

My First Noel

HEROES OF THE SEA SERIES

Master of My Dreams

Captain of My Heart

My Lady Pirate

Taken by Storm

Wicked at Heart

Lord of the Sea

Heir to the Sea

Never Too Late for Love

Scandal at Christmas

Pirate in My Arms

About the Author

New York Times and *USA Today* bestselling author Danelle Harmon has written many critically acclaimed and award-winning books. A Massachusetts native, she has lived in Great Britain, though these days she and her English husband make their home in New England with their daughter Emma and numerous animals including three dogs, an Egyptian Arabian horse, and a flock of pet chickens. Danelle welcomes email from her readers and can be reached at Danelle@danelleharmon.com or through any of the means listed below:

CONNECT WITH ME ONLINE!
Danelle Harmon's Website
Danelle Harmon's Blog

Want to know when the next new title from Danelle is released? Click here!

Even more ways to connect:

CPSIA information can be obtained
at www.ICGtesting.com
Printed in the USA
LVHW041431131221
706069LV00017B/1044